PROJECT IQ

HOME BASE MARS

JULIETTE A H CAVENDISH

First Paperback and Ebook Edition. November 2020.

ISBN Paperback 978-0–6488530-5-3

ISBN Ebook 978-0-6488530-7-7

Published by London Red Publishing

http://www.juliettecavendish.com.au

http://www.ziforah.com

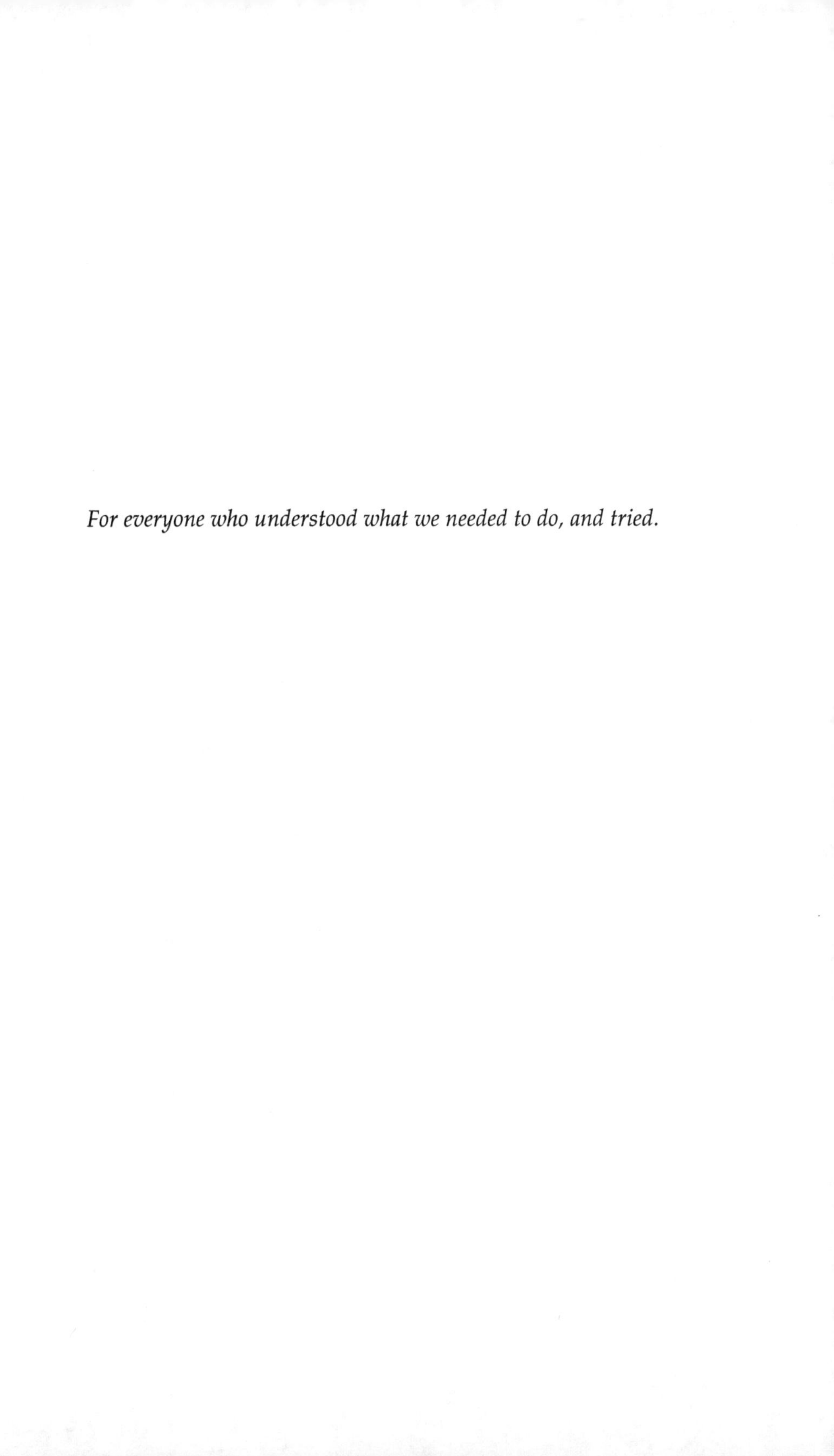

For everyone who understood what we needed to do, and tried.

CONTENTS

1

HOPPER'S READY

CALIFORNIA 2048

J ack's hand instinctively touched his head, relieved that his own brain was still safe in its boney casing. It needed to stay that way he thought, glancing over at the exposed, slate grey brain he had earlier placed into the experiment tray. His thoughts at least, would remain private for the duration of this circus act, which was fortunate given what was about to transpire. He perused the room which was now full of black-suited strangers, all dancing the demanding steps of the alpha dance. The room hushed, and he was aware that *she* had walked in, the familiar ostinato of her heels sending a shiver along his skin. He glanced up at her, noting the trademark bun, neatly placed dead centre on the back of her head, as if a bagel stored for morning tea. Her eyes met his, telling him to start the charade.

He whispered a rude and redundant prayer to his no-God under his breath, knowing that bourbon would have done a better job. Words not carefully chosen and ones which would have insulted all Gods, if they had been bothering to listen. He inserted his trembling hands into the clear latex gloves, inhaled deeply and anchored his feet steady on the tiles. Guided by the vision on the screen, he pinched the precision metal tweezers together, grasped the small chip cube, and lowered it into the front of the human brain. There was a maze of complicated life-support circuitry surrounding it, pumping pink fluid through a labyrinth of tubes. Blood mixed with chemicals and oxygen flowed in an urgent line towards the tissue. All of this was far from ethical. This wasn't a moment for virtues though, instead, an occasion for a mad project to demonstrate fruition and success.

The room fell silent as the chip made several crackles through the surround-sound audio system, set-up as if the opening night at a film premier. Then, an irritable cough bounced out of someone's lungs and a pair of feet shifted. A stomach rumbled, demanding sustenance. The wait felt like forever, time ticking forwards, articulated by the solitary clock, watching everyone from above the door.

'Okay… now would be fucking good,' he quietly sweet-talked the scene. Sweat was dangling off his brow, and his heart was crazy thumping, needing to exit his chest and go to anywhere. He silently pleaded with the grey and white matter to do right by him. The eyes watched from every corner of the room and he felt their cyclops stare, burning a mark of arrogant impatience into the back of his neck, where his recent haircut now exposed vulnerable, virgin skin. The air in the room veiled him with infectious uncertainty, edges frayed with time-poor certainty.

A woman moved forward, as if floating from the crowd. Her arms were crossed, angry-tight across her chest. She stood in front of Jack and out of wrinkling red lips, feeding from Chanel red stain, emerged a small, tapered tongue. She opened her mouth wider, to deliver words of discontent most likely, but was interrupted by a noise breaking through the audio. The beeping got stronger, and then the chip activated with a definitive sharp, b flat. A lead connected from tissue to computer started to vibrate.

'That's right baby… a couple more moves…' Jack quietly willed it on, his words redundant in front of the deaf brain. The tissue then began to transform, from cloudy grey through unicorn pink, to healthy rouge, the heart of it birthing alive. The brain then blushed to its outer edges, and tissue surrounding the chip began to quiver.

The tiny movements regulated, forming a steady rhythm of exactly sixty beats a minute. The computer screen awakened, and lists of code appeared. Jack read them. 'Medical file ready. Experience ready. Global parameters set. Limiter activated. Personality ready for input.' He turned to the crowd.

'Ladies and Gentlemen,' he announced, feeling more confident. 'The Project IQ medical chip is functioning.' He felt the need to drop to the floor from the sudden release of tension leaving his body, but understood that the script required him to stand tall. The gathering applauded and clambered forwards to share in the success.

Project IQ was up and running after months of intense design and many billions of dollars of global investment. The woman moved closer towards him, her arms still curled inwards and no sign that anything resembling praise was to be awarded.

'Don't appear too confident, Jack,' she said, a whistling sound escaping from a gap between her front teeth. 'It doesn't suit you and I don't need your over-inflated ego getting in my space. My chip. My moment. Understand?' She began to walk away, then turned and eagle-eyed him. 'Who is Hopper?'

Jack shook his head, trying to look laid-back nonchalant. 'I don't know… why?'

'Look on the screen.'

Jack turned and glanced back at the computer screen. Underneath the last line of code was a small black box with *Hopper's Ready* flashing in the middle. He felt himself shrinking small. He knew what it meant, but this woman must never.

'I'm assuming everything is fine?' she asked, intrigued by his expression, which was blatantly hiding something from her.

'Absolutely. It's just a verification code that the software is ready for the next step of the testing launch. Exciting, isn't it?'

'Yes, very,' she answered, her voice as dry as cremation dust. Her heels turned her away, eager to take her elsewhere. She flung a final comment over her shoulder. 'Clean this mess up before joining us for champagne and questions in the lobby.'

Really Jack? You call that the truth?

HOPPER'S READY. THIS TIME
*THE REAL VERSION CALIFORNIA 2048

Y'all, see that asterisk up there? It's been included because dichotomy can be an unsavory word to inhabit. Real and not real, truth and untruth can so easily be blended to create a place that ain't got deep roots in genuine. People often recollect memories that drip with egocentric glaze, recounting them more favorably to portray themselves in a better light.

Jack somehow persuaded the editor to serve that first-chapter crap as the entrée for the rest of this. I was unequivocal when I told Jack that if I was gonna be involved in this, I'd tell the truth, even if that truth is dark, nasty and confronting. So a deal is a deal and two halves need to meet in the middle. Saint Jack's gonna need to stand back while I write what really happened back in California in 2048, real word following real word. Jack said he wanted a balance between the objective and subjective when writing all of this down, so here's the objective version of what unfolded that day, without any blended fantasy.

Jack told me to just write and use a minimum number of words in this process, otherwise his story might never get out there, he warned. I laughed, 'cause I don't have a squillion words in my head anyways. I'm no writer and never claimed I was. All that links me to Jack is a scar on my hand, where we pledged blood, in-between burning our stomach linings with over-proof in a time we can't recall. So, here's the truth.

JACK'S HAND instinctively touched his head, relieved that his brain was still safe in its boney casing. It needed to stay that way, he thought, glancing over at the exposed slate grey brain he had earlier thawed from the freezer. Poor bugger, he thought to himself. Happy in suspended sleep and now about to wake up to this crap. He perused the room, which was now full of arrogant, important strangers who mostly hated each other, he surmised, looking between the fake smiles and over-zealous laughs. The room suddenly hushed, and he was aware that *she* had walked in, the familiar tapping of her heels on the tiles releasing nervous acid into his stomach. He glanced up at her, noting the harsh mouth, lifeless eyes and hair in bondage, tightly packed into a bun, hanging on for dear life to the back of her head. Her eyes met his, and she nodded, indicating that the show was about to begin.

'Fuck this,' Jack whispered under his breath, loud enough for everyone to understand that he had no faith in himself. He placed his trembling hands into the gloves, trembling because he had a shitload of prominent people drilling their eyes into him. He inhaled a deep breath which caused him to go dizzy, so he adjusted himself to stand squarer on the tiles. Guided by the image on the screen, he squeezed the mechanical tweezers, trapping the small shining chip, and lowered it into a small incision etched into the front of the human brain. There was a maze of sophisticated circuitry surrounding it, having transformed it from frozen to alive. A small heart-lung machine fed it artificial blood containing glucose and oxygen.

Wires were leading everywhere, some connecting the motor cortex to the artificial vocal box simulator, others connecting the chip to other parts of the brain via the computer. Far from honorable, but this wasn't a moment for being saintly. After the chip had settled in situ, he pushed *upload.* The room fell silent as the chip made several crackles through audio, set up as if he'd been intent on playing a feature film. A nervous cough bounced off the walls like a billiard ball off cushions, then someone shifted their feet impatiently. The wait seemed like forever, time ticking forwards, enunciated by a solitary clock above the door. All eyes were watching him, holding their coffee stained and plain biscuit breaths, left over from introductory refreshments.

'You fucking mother-fucker,' he sweet-talked it quietly. Sweat ran down his face in a narrow, aimless line and his heart was pounding to get out of his chest because it couldn't stand the tension either. Thawed brains could be far trickier than his testing subjects had been, and bondage-woman had insisted on using a thawed brain for this pretend demonstration. He could feel the collective stare burning into his neck. Their apprehension and lack of trust in him was clouding him in an infectious uncertainty. He knew that his audience was undecided as to what would evolve over the next thirty seconds and that failure would be met with brutal opinion and cold discard.

The woman stepped forward, almost as if floating from the collective crowd. Her arms were strongly folded over a chest that was iron flat. She stood in front of the group, and a pointed, tapered tongue emerged from wrinkling lips, licking Chanel allure, red stain. She opened her mouth to speak, probably words of discontent, but was interrupted by a sound coming through the audio. A soft beeping that got louder. The central chip activated with a definitive, loud beep, and a tiny lead that was connected from the network of other chips started to pulsate, ever so slowly.

The brain tissue began to shift color from cloudy grey to unicorn pink, the inner heart appearing alive, taking its first steps towards awake. Slowly the pink spread like an infectious disease to the outer edges, and the tissue began to shudder. The computer screen illuminated, and hundreds of lines of code appeared.

Jack read them out aloud. 'Medical file ready. Experience ready. Global parameters set. Limiter activated. Personality ready. Okay, we're in business. Before I introduce the next stage, I need to spell out a few details. This particular brain was suspended roughly eighty years ago. The re-awakenings can be somewhat traumatic, so if we can please have respect and patience. The voice won't be the individual's authentic voice, just a generic one we've chosen for today. To prepare you though, thawed brains are known to be quite unpredictable.' He turned back to the brain, watching it closely. 'Okay, it's showing signs of revival. It should speak in a moment. They can awaken pretty quickly, all things considering. I'll be using the computer keyboard to speak to it directly, as obviously it cannot hear.'

Somebody sniggered.

A noise was picked up through the audio. Then a voice emerged. 'I'm. I'm. I'm. I am…' It expended a piercing, shrill scream that ricocheted off the room's surfaces.

The group reeled and then pushed forward with a morbid desire to be closer to the misery in the tray.

Jack typed into the computer. 'Hi, it's okay, we are all here.'

'I'm hurting. Please. My head, I think. Am I alive?'

Jack typed again. 'Welcome back. Pain is predicted, you've been retired for a lengthy period.'

'Retired. Yes… asleep. How long since last thoughts?'

'We're in the forties.'

'I dropped into sleep in 1976. That's… I can't think…' It let out a lengthy, agonizing sound that someone once described as heartbreak.

'They can behave very erratically when they first come around,' Jack explained loudly, over the screaming.

'You've been dormant for over seventy years,' he typed into the computer.

'It's dark. Will I see? They said I would be able to see again. I don't want to be blind… I don't like the dark very much. Maybe I'll be able to walk one day too. They told me I might.'

'Not yet. We'll take it all one step at a time. It's all okay,' he reassured the brain.

'You're a fucking comedian Cross,' a voice called out. 'How does the brain take a step with no legs? You should have been honest and told it that it's now a fucking basketball.'

The audio crackled again. 'I'm trying to do some deep breathing… scared… scared.' It howled again.

Someone else called out. 'This is better than a fucking horror movie. Where's the popcorn?'

Jack addressed the group, calling for them to move back a bit. 'Please, the situation begs for common decency as you can imagine. Waking from a deep, frozen sleep is immensely problematic for a human mind, so I'm asking for some respect for this process. I've partially embedded the medical chip into this brain, so we can demonstrate how the medical chip works by asking the brain a few medical questions. Does anybody have one?'

A young man, encased in Armani stuck his hand up, the gold watch on his wrist catching the light, sending a beam around the room reminiscent of the one Darth Vader had used. 'How about we ask the brain if it realizes it's being served up to us in a casserole dish minus everything else?' He snorted a false laugh, adding 'fucking brain casserole, that's what that is.'

The group laughed at his joke.

'Sounds like the person assumed that they were coming back whole. Who took the brain out and what did you do with the rest of the body?' asked a woman near the front of the pack.

'No. Not ethical,' replied Jack, getting tired of the overt arrogance permeating the room. A blonde woman from the back raised her hand. 'What are you intending to do with the brain once you've wound up today's demonstration?' She had her pen poised, ready for his response.

The brain let out a long, piercing set of screams, leaving her question and pen hanging awkwardly in the room.

Jack shook his head. 'It will settle soon. Those are not the types of questions I'm encouraging. We've activated a medical chip so you can ask medical questions, for instance.'

'Okay, so this particular brain… is it one from the Underground Generation?'

'Yeah,' someone else jumped in. 'Those dudes who are born into captivity? I've heard that if they die, you can experiment on their bodies.' He laughed, adding. 'Their bodies are so lily-white, I hear you have to wear sunglasses if you go near them. No sun. Imagine no fucking sun, ever.'

'No. We don't use their brains like this.' Jack shook his head at the quality of questions that were being asked. Then again, most of the questions had come from the press so far and not the investors.

'How do we know the brain wasn't a doctor when alive the first time?' asked a man, sounding cynical. 'I mean it's no big deal if a doctor knows medical stuff.'

'We could try asking it,' said Jack, typing in, 'What profession did you have before being suspended?'

'I was a… I… don't recall, actually. Can I sit up? I need to sit up.'

'That's the limiter kicking in, as expected,' said Jack, nodding.

'This individual,' he said, leaning over to his binder, and flicking through the pages, 'was a water-color artist. Stage four cancer, elected for deep sleep a week before predicted death from the cancer. Now, a medical question, please.'

'Okay, I've got one.' A man strode forward from the group. 'Ask the brain what the symptoms are for gallstones. I had my gallbladder out recently, so I know all about it. I felt like I was pissing rocks.'

Jack typed in the question, 'What are the symptoms for gallstones?'

The brain lit up with activity and quickly responded. 'Severe and sudden pain in the upper right abdomen and possibly extending to the upper back, fever and shivering, severe nausea and vomiting, jaundice and clay-colored stools or dark urine.'

The room applauded. 'Close,' agreed the man who had asked the question. 'Pissing rocks should be on that list though. They say it's worse than childbirth. I can tell you, it's way worse.'

'Total crap,' said a woman next to him. 'You ever shat a truck out of your arse before?'

'Your arse ain't where a baby comes from woman. If you were trying to get it out of there, no wonder you were having issues.' He laughed, and the room laughed loudly with him.

Jack shook his head with dismay and was about to say something when the brain interrupted.

'Why?' asked the brain. 'Do you believe I have gallstones? I can't feel sensation there, but my head… it's hurting so much. I went to reach up to touch my head, but I can't seem to move my arms yet.' It shrieked, and a sobbing sound pulsed from the audio box.

The room silenced making Jack concerned. Brains usually only screamed as far as he was aware. He was hoping it would stop the sobbing, as he didn't need the group to feel bad for the brain in the midst of all of this. Someone might want to take it home as a rescue if they got all attached to it.

'No, it's okay,' he typed. 'We're looking at…' he hesitated, trying to think of a reason… 'we're investigating whether your cognition has been altered by the deep-sleep drugs.'

'It's strange because I never knew about gallstones before,' said the brain.

'I've got another question,' declared someone else. 'Ask the brain when the first face transplant was undertaken.'

There was a collective murmur. The owner of this brain had been put to sleep in 1976. There was no way they would know.

Jack typed in the question. 'When was the first human face transplant?'

'2005,' the brain replied, without hesitation.

'That's just frickin' awesome,' said a voice.

The brain spoke. 'I'm sorry, I don't understand… how can I know that? Please. How do I know this? Was I in the medical profession… but you said I went to sleep in 1976. I am so confused. I can't remember… who I was… who I am. Please help me.'

Jack typed. 'It's okay, we gave you that one to make sure you can receive and assimilate new information. Bit of sleight of hand and we… we do it with everyone who is easing out of a deep-sleep state.'

A sequence of precise, bright noises came from the brain.

'Are you laughing?' Jack typed.

'Yes, a little,' answered the brain. 'From relief… but this blackness. I'm really trying to keep it all together. It would be nice to sit up and take this mask off.'

'It shouldn't be so hard to keep your shit together, given you ain't got no shit to lose.' Someone was laughing from the back of the group. 'Aside from the woman who births shits over there!'

The room again, collectively laughed.

Jack took a deep breath. He ignored the obvious lack of respect. 'The chip has a limiter within it. When we give a medical chip to a person, we don't want them deciding to go off and become something else. We want to keep them in the medical profession. So, if a thought arises that might reshape the person's will, we can wipe it out before they can act on it. We've added over ten million algorithmic variations to pick this up.'

'Test it again,' called someone from the back.

'Okay,' said Jack. He pondered for a moment and typed in, 'What will your next painting be about?'

'My next painting?' asked the brain. It waited in silence for a bit and then replied, 'I don't know. I can't paint.'

'What are the clinical signs of acute pulmonary edema?' Jack typed, to establish the speed of the medical chip.

'Pain in the chest. Shortness of breath on lying down. Rapid, shallow breathing. Wheezing. Fatigue. Sweating. Fast heart rate. Coughing. Water retention.'

'So, as you can see,' explained Jack, 'the brain has thought about painting, but the hyrantrocholine has wiped out any action on that topic. When we ask anything medical, the brain's response is clear, fast, accurate, and methodical.'

The brain suddenly declared, 'Hopper's Ready. Who is Hopper? Am I Hopper? No… I'm… I'm… I don't know. I don't know who I am. Can you tell me, please. Who am I?'

Jack held his breath. Fuck. That was his personality overlay activating.

'Who, or what is Hopper?' asked hair-bondage woman, also known as President of The United Southern States of America.

'It's the name we gave the brain,' said Jack, pleased to have summoned up a respectable alternative to the truth.

'Well, thank you Hopper. Leaders, investors, and members of the Press,' she said, 'we have much to discuss, so please follow me to the lobby where we can answer all of your questions. Refreshments will be provided.' She walked back towards Jack. 'Get rid of the brain and be ready to answer any questions alongside Tina and Peter in the lobby. Be quick.'

She held her arm out near the door and the group all trundled out, excitedly chattering about what they had just witnessed.

Jack stood in the silence and commenced the unwiring procedure. He stopped to type into the computer. 'Thank you for everything today. I'm happy you can think again.'

'That's okay. I'm so glad to be back. Frozen sleeping is the same as being dead, I'm assuming. It was like being in a place of nothing.

No dreams. I had no thoughts. It's nice to be thinking again. What's your name, by the way?'

Jack stopped still. No, no name. That would take things too far. 'Hi. Did you hear me? What's your name?' it asked again.

Jack stared at the brain. He hadn't even thought to find out if it had belonged to a man or a woman. It had belonged to a person who believed their brain was still attached to their body.

'Oh God,' said Jack, feeling hints of horror as to what he was about to do.

'Have you gone? I don't want to be by myself right now. I'm scared. This darkness, I wasn't expecting to feel so locked in. They didn't warn us about this. Can you sit me up, please? I might breathe better if I sit up.'

He quickly unwired the vocalizer, not wanting to hear the brain, and walked to the drawer and took out a container of white powder. He opened it, and scooped some into a bowl, and added a strong acid formula. He tried not to inhale the toxic fumes as it mixed into a runny, white liquid. The brain was vulnerable on the table and waiting for people to help it out of the deep-sleep process. This person had frozen themselves, intending to wake into a world that would revive them with kindness and rehabilitation.

Jack didn't ask for forgiveness. After all, he was under orders. The accountability for what he was about to undertake could perch on the President's shoulders. He spewed the liquid over the brain. It sizzled as the acid etched through the layers of tissue. Its color quickly changed from pink to grey and then into black. Jack scraped the mush into a plastic bag and forced it down the waste disposal hole.

He pressed the yellow on button and waited until the grinding sound had finished. Then he peeled his gloves off and washed his hands in a hasty manner, wanting to be done with it all. Walking quickly from the room, he joined everyone in the lobby for a glass of champagne, or, maybe a whole bottle, if he could find one.

Yeah. There's the truth. It sizzled, didn't it Jack, you psychopath. Did you feel anything? Did you? It would have been screaming. You fucking monster.

3

WHAT HAPPENED?

IT JUST BLEW

In 2045, a statement was delivered on TV, by the Director of the International Committee for Catastrophic Climate Change, Victoria Flynn. People had quarreled about who would read the doomsday script, with some asserting it should have been the Pope, others said Oprah and even King Charles was proposed as reader. One of the reasons for this startling disclosure was that some scientist, responsible for determining our species' life-expectancy, had dropped a figurative atomic bomb on everyone with no warning. He had moved the hands of the Doomsday Clock to midnight and then sent out a generic press release, before running to the hills. The world awoke and shit panicked, with those hands now on top of each other, having pushed down the death domino as they had ticked into missionary.

Victoria had stood, her ashen face masked with hasty makeup, her eyes blinded by intense television lights, and had waited for the set clock to tick into live broadcast.

'My fellow humans,' she had read, her eyes getting flooded from too many emotions, making it hard to read the teleprompter. She blinked them away and instructed them to piss off. This had to be done stoically, not pathetically.

'What I am about to say will influence every life on this planet.'

She paused, feeling as if the room were slightly tilting to the left. She gripped the podium and struggled to keep her game face on. The filming crew were playing statues, with no-one rushing her, ironically, as if she had all the time in the world.

'As you are aware, the Doomsday Clock was moved to midnight, demonstrating that we have run out of time. I am sorry to inform you all that the Committee for Catastrophic Climate Change has determined that…' she stopped. The next thirteen words she would utter would be the most important words ever spoken in the history of the human race. She wondered how to pace them, rehearsal for the speech having been pushed to one side in the urgency to broadcast a response. She was in *now* and about to force an entire species over a line and into *then*. That notion… what happens if we do nothing about climate change, was about to be answered with derision and with unmistakable finality.

She stared into the lens, which was framing a collective embodiment of the eight billion who had signed in to watch, and drew her last breath of the old world. 'The Committee has determined that our species will not remain past 2088 on planet Earth. Most of us will die from climate impact well before this date.' She hesitated, wondering how all the watching eyes had reacted. 'I am so sorry,' she added as an afterthought. She had waited in silence, a length not yet determined appropriate. She stared downwards, trying to find words which offered solutions, hope, and a future. There weren't any. It was over.

Afterwards, Victoria had to be placed in protection, having been referred to as The Messenger of Death. Essentially, if I cut to the guts of it, the statement went on to call the year 2088 as Final End

Date. A year in time when we wouldn't be able to sustain life on Earth anymore due to a cascade of catastrophic weather events. The news caused immediate worldwide panic and a wobble in everything, causing riots, mass suicides and anarchy. Yeah, great decision in telling everyone the end was coming. What did they think was going to happen? That everyone would join hands and sing fucking songs?

Let's face it. We don't even know why we're here. We remain a conundrum and it does our little heads in. The Big Bang, the official scientific start of it all, evidently had no known cause for such a massive bang of crap emerging from nowhere. We stuck all of this multiplying crap into shopping malls and then undertook our hunting and gathering from inside this artificial space. Each mall was a safe harbor for this collective display of grotesque gluttony. Stuff was placed on display under spotlights, where it would pass the time watching the people passing by.

Bodyguards would request that people line up behind red rope before visiting the important stuff, as if it was an audience with the Pope himself that they were waiting for. Drool pooled on marble floors as they anticipated the kill, the moment where the swipe would fell the unsuspecting item and it would dive lifeless, into a branded paper bag. It would then pose on display, to be perched a shoulder, a shelf or worn - as if a trophy head on a wall.

This is where people frequented to find their meaning as a human, in amongst the endless rows of shops that displayed the spoils of the hunters and gatherers of the early twenty-first century. This was affluenza, greed, gluttony, and the lack of seeing the line. A line which had been erased by big business and which prevented people from knowing when happiness had been acquired. It was an endless pursuit where *more* was the only objective.

The swarming, milling throng of thousands, the herd of the needy-greedy that grazed from one store to the next, obtained sustenance by gorging in endless food halls, their plates stacked a mile high. They returned for more, simply because they could. Fatter, rounder, sicker, and more depressed they became from this excess, while millions in a different place starved slowly to death. Their distended bellies, full of despair, and their large eyes wide and amazed at how handbags were held close, while their children were untouched and left to die.

Meanwhile, the Earth, the only home we had, slowly began to die too, right in front of everyone. Dying from the parasitic pillage of this herd and still, despite this knowledge, we still ate more. We bought more and dug deeper for more, and still we felt empty. We, Homo sapiens, didn't know when to stop. We still don't. We don't have an off switch for this neediness, and we missed one vital fact. The Earth does have an off-switch, and one day she flicked it off without ceremony, explanation, or possibility of reversal.

Things moved fast. By 2037, severe storms had wiped out half of the world's grain and whole islands were submerged in the Pacific. Wildfires tore through Australia, USA, France, Canada, and Italy, turning them bacon crispy. More and more disease spread, due to movement in the tropical zones. Storms were magnificent beasts, wiping out entire coastal communities, forcing our homeless into large military-run tent cities for people who'd lost everything. When I say everything, I'm including hope. We became immune to the plight of survivors lining up for assistance, with only the clothes on their backs, their eyes full of resignation and loss.

If homeless, the Government implanted a tracking device into your arm, in case you got lost, they said. You were allocated a tent and some food rations, which was better than possible death by SFF on the streets - starving, frying or freezing. It was the responsibility of the individual to find meaning, wandering through the labyrinth of other tents, which was going to be the last place they could ever call home.

Europe reeked with the essence of wartime, countries turning on their neighbors with sanctions, border patrols, and the EU passport slowly dissolved. With limited food, people were gonna move from place to place, eating the best of what was on offer, like plagues of locusts. Shutting borders was a good idea, depending on the country you entombed, within, that was.

Countries in Scandinavia introduced strict rationing because their fish died. Something to do with the acidity and warmth in the oceans, like when the corals were all bleached in the mid-twenties. Their sugar beet died from a rare pest invasion, and European crops wilted in the heat.

Giant storms, the size of small countries, would come screaming in, with a death-rage intent on taking out the innocents, with winds speeds needing a new category of their own. They would come howling and drenching an ocean onto land, flattening everything not built to withstand winds of such ferocity. Places with coastal borders would be hit over and over, just as Florida, Mexico, and Cuba had been in 2039, damaging them beyond repair, after a collective series of nine storms in three months.

Vietnam, Japan, China, Madagascar, and Taiwan had to relocate millions of their populations away from their coasts, guiding them inland, only having them starve to death from the interior droughts. If you weren't drowning, you were starving, suffering, hurting, needy, and helpless. You get the picture. So, when Victoria spoke the last thirteen words in the *before*, it wasn't like you could have knocked me down with a feather. We'd be stuffed for a long time before Victoria took that breath.

4

INDUSTRY BURNED
SEAS OF MELTING PLASTIC

Global Financial Crisis Two hit with the force of devastation in the midst of all of this. It was dubbed The Chaos, because it toppled everything financial, leaving a trail of ruin everywhere. The economy had been faltering for years as it was, with thousands of businesses not surviving the early twenties pandemic lockdowns, and fewer getting back up again. Most people didn't see the point anymore, in working hard and then being told to shut up shop from Government directives. Few could compete with online Chinese cheap either, until they got melted too, creating seas of burning plastic. The catastrophic collapse of world economies played out with synchronicity, and extensive stock dumping took down Wall Street in under three days. It was like observing a tower of cards toppling down to some strange new choreography. This sequence of circumstances made Governments panic.

Ill-fated and badly planned austerity measures were introduced. Increased taxes, canceled health insurances, hiked up mortgage rates, and bans on withdrawing savings tried to preserve what was left. This pickling made it all worse, and people lost hope and faith from the screws being tightened way too tight. Then there was this shift after that, only really noticed after hope and faith had fled the scene. Once upon a time, human beings had reached out to each other with kindness in times of collective catastrophe. The Chaos changed all of that, with self-righteous and self-absorbed becoming the new accoutrements of choice. We turned on each other instead of helping, our focus being to shame, maim, and highlight anything offensive in another. Our smartphones became Orwellian, recording instances of free speech and human misery, and then we replayed them in the courts of social media. New rules were made for a new kind of existence. Take the Greg story, one of many that went viral. A hundred and forty million views in two hours on the express channel.

Greg was your typical hard-working, average guy. He had a wife, three kids, a small IT business, and an unassuming house. When austerity measures were announced, he was clobbered. He lost most of his business credits, half of his salary from increased taxes, and his health insurance was cancelled. Jackie, his wife of twenty-three years, had cancer, and the repercussions of losing the health insurance was that her chemo was stopped. She was given six months without it. Greg had been doing okay with the stress, understanding that there were so many others, just like them, also doing it tough. It was the news about Jackie that made something in him panic into reaching out for help. Greg paid a visit to his bank, believing he could work something out, take a bit of the pressure off with the loss of his business credits. If he could hang on to the family home, that would mean a lot to Jackie. She wanted to die at home, not in a refugee camp.

He had stood in a long queue, as only one teller was feigning work. You could see that the teller didn't want to be there. He was rolling his eyes and head like he'd been dragged in off the street to work there. Then a woman had pushed in, saying something about how her matter was urgent and that she was time-poor. The man behind had knocked him with his briefcase several times as the line was being concertinaed. All of these were insignificant in themselves, but they pushed Greg into the threat zone, his nerves already frayed.

What really perturbed Greg was that the douchebag bank teller had stared at him blankly, and with total indifference, after he had described his situation. His first words had been hopeful in the form of 'how can I help you?' That was as far as the help was going, as far as he could now gather.

'So, let me get this right. You want the bank to help you because your wife is dying?'

'Yes. That's the general idea, but it has more to do with some breathing space and my business credits… they got halved recently.'

'I don't think this is a banking matter, sir,' Bruce said flatly. 'We can't discuss business credits over the counter for a start and second, it sounds more like this is medical.'

Greg looked at his name tag. 'Look, Bruce, can you ask for Nash Owens to come out and see me? He's known me for twenty-five years. He may understand my situation a bit better?'

Bruce had raised one eyebrow at Greg. 'I am fully capable of responding to your inquiry,' adding a plastic smile as an afterthought.

'I don't mean to be rude, but Nash knows me pretty well.' He smiled back at Bruce, trying to start them off again on a more positive note. 'He… he knows all the ins and outs of this.'

'I can help you today.' Bruce puckered his lips together, in an act of passive defiance.

'I'd really like to talk with Nash, actually.' Greg felt frustrated at not being heard. It was a simple enough request.

'I'm hearing a passive-aggressive tone which the bank does not tolerate.' Bruce stared at Greg.

'A what?' Greg was lost. These weren't conversation rules he was acquainted with. He was being aggressive? How?

'Sir, the bank doesn't tolerate micro-aggressions.'

Micro-aggressions? What the fuck were micro aggressions? Bruce was the one firing out nasty little one-liners, little prick.

'I cannot call Mr. Owens out here anyway at this moment. He's extremely busy with… important banking matters.'

'This is a banking matter. How do you know he's too busy? Has he said so?' Greg's tone was strained. He looked around the room, seeing the obvious frustration on the faces of the people lined up. They just wanted him to shut the fuck up so that the line could move forward.

'I am trying to help.' Bruce offered a short, snappy little smile.

'You're trying to help? How are you trying to help right now?' Greg's voice had raised by several decibels.

'Sir, I suggest that you communicate with your wife's doctor or the hospital. We really can't help you.'

'You just said you could help me. So, can you help me or can't you help me?'

'I actually asked how I could help you, not that I actually could.'

Suitcase man had then interjected into Greg's space, instructing him to move on. 'He said he couldn't help you. Move on. I'm sorry for your loss. We've all got shit to deal with.'

Ignition. Fight or flight. Fight won. 'She's still alive. She hasn't died, not yet anyway,' Greg said, through gritted teeth.

'Sir. There are lots of people waiting. Do I need to call security?' Bruce waved him away with a long, slender arm, dismissing him out of his breathing space. 'I hope the hospital can help you. Now, I have a long line of people to deal with, so if you would please move away sir.'

Greg reached into his bag and removed the gun that he carried around with him, just in case he ever felt intimidated. He did. No-one was helping, and Jackie was going to die. No-one cared about Jackie wanting to die at home and not in a leaking tent surrounded by strangers. No-one cared about them, and this Bruce jerk would not let him explain it to Nash. It was not a choice to return to Jackie and deliver her a six-month death sentence that ended in a tent. He was expected to go home with hope in his suitcase.

Then, it was like a knee-jerk reaction, with people reaching into their bags to withdraw their smartphones. Each wanted to capture the escalation, hoping for something outstanding to play out. They weren't disappointed.

'Lie flat and cooperate! What do you need, sir?' Bruce then offered.

Suitcase man had snorted at him. 'Put the fucking stupid gun away mate. We're all suffering.'

'You're suffering, are you?' Greg had asked angrily. 'My wife is dying, and this Bruce pissy-boy won't help.'

'Stay calm. Please, sir. What would you like me to do?' Bruce's voice rose from below the teller counter.

Greg had glanced around him. No-one seemed to care that he was holding a gun. No-one was lying flat on the floor as instructed by Bruce, who had now disappeared altogether. Instead, thirty phones were pointed his way. They weren't reaching out in sympathy or with empathy, instead with the greedy intention of directly exposing and sharing his mess of a life. His vulnerability was being turned into someone's vicarious way of getting themselves noticed on social media and making money out of his misery.

Greg then snapped, as many humans do, the part of his brain wired for threat detection, lighting up like a New York billboard. His mind, sensing the phones as a perceived threat, cut out his conscious reasoning and launched him into a full-on fight for survival. The phones may as well have been a pack of hungry lions circling him.

'What are you all watching?' he shouted. 'My vulnerability? Is that what you want to see?'

Silence.

'What are you looking at? Me? Do you want to see me like this? My wife is gonna die! She just wanted to stay at home! I need help.'

Silence. They paced. His heart was now a beating drum.

'I'm gonna lose my business. Does that make you all happy?'

Bruce activated an alarm, and still the small cameras filmed.

The alarm triggered off more panic in Greg's mind. No-one moved, not wanting to disrupt what was becoming viral material. The cameras remained poised, intending not to miss this man's unraveling. He was playing his part with honesty, authenticity, and without restraint. It was brilliant footage that was inconceivably tricky to re-create. Being so close to the action, inside the drama, the atrocity, the suffering… anyone brave enough to keep filming would be guaranteed a million likes, as well as a million bucks from subscriptions.

'Turn your fucking cameras off!' he had roared, waving the gun around. A circle of silent and relentless now surrounded him.

'Please…' He pleaded with them, waving the gun in an act of defiance, his arm shaking. Then he steadied his grip. If these cameras replayed his vulnerability, then he would lose his dignity too. The word dignity. Another trigger. A threat to lose that as well.

Silence. 'I'll shoot the lot of you!' he screamed, emptying his lungs, giving a final ultimatum.

This initiated a chaotic scramble for cover, which startled him. He reacted by releasing the trigger. He yelled a primitive howl, shooting at the observing camera eyes, blowing off the hands that held them, the arms that had propped up the hands, and the faces that were silently screaming back.

A security guard had then blown holes through Greg's chest, and he had fallen to the ground, creating an average, dull thud. He was dead before he had made this final imprint, and the survivors had continued to film from behind their cover. Their footage was uploaded before Greg's body had been declared dead, and before the ambulances arrived to remove his seven victims. No-one, aside from Greg, had screamed in any of the uploaded videos, because doing so would have ruined the intensity of the moment, and valuable dialogue may have been missed. As for the thousands of comments posted under one of the videos? Read a random sample of them yourself.

Flaminboiiii 3 days ago 'Good 8 less mouths 2 feed in already overcrowded world.'

Coom 3 days ago, '@flaminboiiii go screw yourself these were real people!!!!!'

Manboi 3 days ago '@flaminboiiii I screw dead peeps ;) pm if u want 2 watch.'

Cl0utgiver 2 days ago 'Close up of face, had to be makeup omggg xD.'

Tellerbruce 2 days ago 'OMG I was there. Crazy. As soon as he walked in, I knew.'

Jstme 2 days ago '@cl0utgiver IKR. His face was shit like tomato or what.'

Coom 2 days ago '@Jstme It's okay boomer.'

Saintgerry 2 days ago '@Tellerbruce u r a hero.'

Jstme 2 days ago '@Coom don't call me a boomer u brainless leftie.'

Cerlio 2 days ago '@Manboi u sick.'

Ancelot 2 days ago '@Tellerbruce u were amazing saw u on tv. Marry me.'

Laulpogan 2 days ago '@Saintgerry try goats if u want action pm me.'

Princedat 2 days ago '@Laulpogan u r disgusting.'

Tellerbruce 2 days ago '@Ancelot thanx. Just doing what had 2 b done. So flattered!'

WE WERE DEVOID OF COMPASSION, parasitic to surrounding action, sophomoric and focused on the banal. We sought out other people's vulnerabilities, so that we could prosper from them. We chose to accentuate the fragile, our empathy having turned from comforting to exploitation. Everyone now suffered and so sympathy towards human misery was now obsolete. If you dared to display your weakness, then the deal was that it became public property.

Emergency meetings were called across the globe, with world leaders struggling for solutions. People needed answers, but the political rhetoric oozing from the politicians' pores smelled worse than the crap from the sewers, which were starting to overflow because no one wanted to operate them anymore. Y'all have to remember that these were leaders who were empty vessels when they were voted in, so they had no expressions of encouragement, let alone strategies to regain economic and social control.

The world declined from ordered and predictable into chaos. Funeral homes and morgues couldn't cater for the number of sad corpses with their brains blown out. Cremation was the only option for body disposal, as cemeteries were already layered three times over. Scattering the ashes was illegal, as the World Health Authority decided that air pollution was already compromising health. The cremated could be kept in an air-tight Government death box or flushed down the toilet. Human life had become manageable only for the strong, and the weak were actively supported to end their misery. Yeah, you read that right. The weak were told to go die.

Governments introduced Euthanasia Packages. One pill and it's over, and the whining stops. They threw in cremation as well, into the cost. Some saw this as a good thing, as fewer people meant a better chance at survival for everyone else. Harsh? We fought everyone else to gain that top spot. Not by being nice, but by being the vicious animals that we are. You want to know what happened to Neanderthals and Denisovan humans who were walking around when Homo sapiens walked out of Africa? We procreated with them, then killed them off, as we have done with almost every other species on this planet, well the killing part anyway. There was no help out there when minds started to break, so people pointed the weak towards death. Easy and quieter, yeah?

People saw opportunity amongst the misery, as we humans always do. A group of super-rich individuals set up a chain of Intentional Living Communities called Gaia, which catered for those who could afford the joining fees. It was advertised as an alternative. They lived in wooden huts, with solar power and attended democratic wellness circles. They grew and ate organic food and drowned themselves in alcohol because it took the raw edge off Final End Date. They made things with their hands and cut down trees to make fire. They played music, painted bad artworks, and discussed stuff, ad nauseam. They designed schools based on humanistic principles, and they unplugged from social media and talked. It was branded as a localized utopia, safe from outside. The sickening dichotomy was that utopia reigned on one side of the fence while on the other side, there was just despair and the stench of death.

Governments were continuing to lose control, and in late 2046, an emergency global summit was hosted in The Southern United States. The aim of the meeting was to bring all world leaders together and find a new better, through a collective effort. It was during this summit that Project IQ had been birthed. An insane idea that had formed inside the mind of an insane woman. A tenuous idea, suggesting that social and economic stability could be restored through artificial intelligence. The world could be saved for a bit longer, if everyone adopted this new plan.

5

———

SUMMIT 46

TURN THE CAMERAS OFF

Summit 46 was a promise to figure it all out. Like that political mind-meet held back in Paris in 2015, it was anticipated that a fresh, collective mind might create better strategies to handle The Chaos and Climate Change. Or, at the very least, find global dignity in the slow march towards Final End Date. The event was to be streamed live and had been hyped as the 'Meeting of the Decade'. They had allocated politicians additional flight credits to enable them all to fly and attend in person.

The publicity camera had flashed pure white, snatching the ungainly and awkward poses of ancient men in pitch black suits and a few scatters of women in copy-cat attire, splashed with neutral cologne. Politicians craved to be recalled with credibility, so emphasized a look devoid of gender, style and individualism. Political truth was spoken with lashings of banality so that it could be seen for what it was. Rhetoric was unacceptable in political language, as time was final and solutions needed to be made quickly, using language that announced everything in a context of reality.

It was the President of the United Southern States, who stood defiantly at the podium and announced an audacious and yet irresponsible plan in front of her peers. A different agenda to the one advertised in the program, but not surprising, given her record. President Morag Belcher, also quietly referred to as the *insane one*, was a woman of sharp intelligence, who spat her words with a hint of psychopathy. Known for having balls where her tits should have been, she had been elected the year before as the new President of a new country, only because no-one else had offered their name for the position.

The United Southern States had its own Constitution, President, and boundary lines. It had been birthed out of urgency in 2045, after a chemical attack melted the then President of the United States, Hank Morris, during live streaming. It had been a vengeance attack from a southern cell claiming to be delivering for all *normals*. A radical group who had refused to adopt the left-wing political ideology that an extreme Government had ruled with. Hank's words of hope, as he had been addressing a political rally, morphed into screams of agony. He was drenched in some chemical, laced with acid that peeled him, layer by layer from the outside, and watched by millions on the planet. Layers of human being, dissolving down to bones, screaming for mercy, and even then, the bones mottled, broke and dissolved.

Belcher was biologically female, but that was as far as it went. There was nothing soft or feminine about her interior or exterior. Her translucent pale face wore an expression so taut that her surgeon must have been on shit when he'd pulled the threads. Her trademark lipstick was the number 46, brand Chanel. Rouge Allure Velvet. It lined a mouth where words were spat out fast, from between yellow, crooked teeth, with an aroma of yesterday's stale musings. She had worked her way up the rungs of political triumph, humbly starting as a Government representative before being elected as Head of the Consolidated Southern Jurisdiction.

She had been acting as Governor of Georgia when the attack had taken place. It was both obvious and yet desperate that she had been voted in as the new leader.

The *normals* represented the Southern Bible Belt, a comparatively stable element in previous US Governments. These people worked hard, paid their taxes on time, and shot people who got in their way. Their ancient veil of wisdom provided for such atrocity, 'cause their God was all-forgiving and inspired a truth that it was the guns killed people, and not the people that held them. They denied flatly that people were responsible for any trigger action, thus providing them with eternal redemption from destructive actions. Their God may not have displayed anger after the melting, but the rest of the United States did. Tired from the intrusion of this cell into aspects of political life, they drew a line around the Southern States and snapped them off, forming a new country in the process. The *normals* were reassured when the Belcher machine ascended and applauded when her first action was to re-apply the red number 46 before she had uttered a word. It was a relationship embedded in Stockholm Syndrome, tinged with the right, red hue.

Time for President Morag Belcher to enunciate her intentions. Before I take my break, a word of warning for all eyes following these words. Be careful of Belcher, because she can detect fear, weakness and indecision a mile away. Read, but be sure of your position as you do so. Indecisiveness has never been something that she has perceived as a strength. Anyway, this is how this all started, licking those disgusting allure velvet lips, ready for brutal eloquence, staring down at the hundreds of leaders beneath her, at Summit 46.

'MY FELLOW PARASITES. Our time has run out and our planet intends to kill us all. Our global economy has been reduced to shards of prosperity. Our skilled workers have rushed to Gaia to seek redemption. Our wealthy are hiding in coffin bunkers, rehydrating teriyaki beef, and sipping on probiotic champagne. The world we thought we knew has morphed into a world with killer intent. In forty-two years, we, the human species, will most likely be extinct. Wiped from the fabric of time as if we had never been.' She scanned the room, searching for hints of objection. 'My plan…'

The green light on the podium flashed yellow, indicating that a commercial advertising break was about to initiate. She waited until it had turned red and then turned to a camera operator. 'I want those cameras off before I resume speaking.' Getting no better than a perplexed stare, she repeated herself more loudly. 'I said, I want the damned cameras off. Organize it now before they go back on.' She slammed her hand down onto the podium, the forcefulness reverberating around the auditorium.

In charge of streaming, Mike Alder jumped as if activated by remote control. No-one messed with President Belcher as far as he was concerned. Not ever. He'd failed her once, way back when he'd been under-secretary in Georgia, and the consequences had been brutal. Not that his whole sorry ordeal has time to be recounted now, mind you. He rapidly extended the commercials, authorizing them to run in a loop, and switched off the primary camera system.

'I can offer you eight minutes from now,' he declared, hoping that was enough.

'Why am I being interrupted so quickly?' she had demanded, her eyebrows stationary in her hairline.

'Our mistake entirely. There was supposed to have been a pre-recorded welcome before going to the first break. Then your time slot was scheduled to commence. Our apologies again, Madam President.' He had bowed his hands in prayer, hoping to placate her.

Whatever Belcher was about to say, it had to be significant enough for her to want to say it without the rest of the world knowing about it. His actions would undoubtedly provoke a shit storm and a complex legal labyrinth of ramifications for him. In Mike's mind, though, there wasn't an alternative, not after what the woman had done to him previously.

Now that the cameras were dead, she cleared her throat, ready to commence. She had hatched an idea several weeks prior, trapping select words into possibility, before forcibly relocating them into proposal form. Based on fantasy, cleverly ambitious, and with a whiff of insanity, the idea was definitely extravagant, even by her standards. Deep down, she needed these faces, these minds, these humans in front of her, to save herself, as dying before her due date was not an acceptable proposition for her. However, such a notion came with the price tag of saving everyone else for payment.

Her game-plan was to explain everything in reverse, not asking permission, not discussing if it were feasible, not contemplating if outrageous. Her caveat was to release these words on the proviso that compliance, agreement, and loyalty were the only selections on the menu.

'The ensuing words I speak will remain in this auditorium. I do not believe in tenuous trust. In front of you, on your screens, is a confidentiality agreement that you must all now acknowledge, either in the affirmative or the negative, before I continue further. I require six minutes to articulate my plan, which includes a lifeline to all in here. No details until it is signed. You have one minute.' The leaders looked at their information screens that had flashed up a condensed legal agreement. If they clicked on *agree* then they could stay, if they chose to *decline* the offer, then they would be expected to leave the building and not hear a word.

Tara Jones, the summit deputy organizer, was caught off-guard by Mike and Belcher's unexpected collaboration and was bombarded with scenes of outrage from leaders. The King of Bhutan impatiently beckoned for Tara to speak with him.

'This is utterly outrageous,' he asserted angrily. 'Who does this woman think she is?'

'I'm sorry. I have no further information,' she had told him inadequately, leaning over the President of China, who had sighed in protest at her close contact.

'Death by gassing if you say no, I imagine?' the French President asked Tara, through tightly gritted teeth.

'No… of course not.'

Belcher had tossed this out there without a hint of warning, and Tara needed answers. She hurried over to Mike, a man whose sympathies leaned towards President Belcher, resulting in a patriarchal, over-bearing style of delivery in their organization. She would need to tread carefully in asking her questions, as she was in front of two hundred and twenty-seven world leaders and didn't want a public scolding.

'Mike, what's the legal on all of this?' she whispered.

'I don't know,' he replied unhelpfully. 'Where are your site event legals right now? Go ask them. What happened to the welcome introduction? She wasn't supposed to be talking at that point.' He wiped the sweat off his forehead.

'Why so accommodating, Mike? No matter what her title. This woman can't just stroll in and start making demands like this.'

'Look, I've been burned by this woman before,' he said quietly. 'This time around, I'm just going to give her what she wants. It's easier this way, believe me.'

Tara lowered her voice. 'What do you mean, burned? This is so unprofessional, Mike. You can't just hijack the entire summit on her behalf.'

'I'm not. Stop being so fucking melodramatic, Tara. I'm giving her eight minutes. Eight lousy minutes in the scheme of things. Anyway, you know how bad things are out there. Maybe she has something to say that might be useful. She suggested a lifeline. By the way, you need to sign too.' He signaled over to a laptop.

'No, I'm not signing this. I don't want any part in whatever this is. I'm leaving and intend to lodge a formal objection. All of this is beyond unprofessional.' Tara strode off, curbing her annoyance until she got to the other side of the exit door.

Belcher spoke. 'If you are considering leaving, recognize that there won't be further discussions in letting you back into this arrangement. Some have been inquiring if this is legal? Not a pertinent notion for the next seven minutes. This is about solutions.'

The majority of those standing then sat, aside from a small group who walked out defiantly, shouting something lost in the auditorium's vastness. The rest clicked on *agree* and then waited.

Belcher smiled two rows of crooked Stonehenge, licked her lips, with the moistening providing comfort, and began.

'My plan leaders, is to save each one of us in this auditorium.' There was mumbling from her audience as leaders questioningly glanced at each other. 'My plan is in three parts, and I ask for no questions until the end.' She raised her hand to suppress the stirring interest. 'Part A consists of stabilizing the current economy by creating a new workforce using an implanted brain chip.'

The room reacted. 'Quiet,' she demanded. 'This chip is capable of significantly increasing the intelligence quotient of an individual, allows for occupation selection and execution, and provides ten years worth of career experiences. The benefit? An instant and compliant workforce. Part B of my plan involves rolling this new workforce out across the globe, gaining economic stability, which, in turn, will fortify our political power. I've named it, Project IQ.' She took a deep breath, knowing that her next sentence would cause massive outrage. 'Part C of my plan is for all of us to leave planet Earth and live on Home Base, Mars, within ten years.' She paused, waiting for the reaction. It came quickly.

'It's a private settlement! Wells would never approve it,' a voice cried out.

'Madam President. This is unconscionable!' exclaimed the President of Cameroon.

'What did you smoke before arriving, Madam President?' demanded the Prime Minister of New Zealand, now standing. 'Mars is off-limits and has been since 2028. Paxton Wells shut down access to all streaming and files. Remember? Everything about Home Base is now confidential. How would we even get there? Fly our unicorns?'

The other leaders laughed.

'Sit and quieten,' ordered Belcher. She gestured to Mike to ensure that all of their mics were turned off. The room settled with one or two quieter insults being called out.

'We need to reconstruct infrastructure, stabilize our economies, and gain back the respect of our people. Then, we build the craft and resources that will take us to Mars. If we don't, we all die. You, me, and your families, without hope and without a chance.'

'Build space-craft… at what cost? You don't have the money,' accused a frustrated voice, '… and Paxton Wells wouldn't allow it!'

Belcher didn't care about the insults and continued. 'Wells will be open for negotiation as he aims to see Home Base succeed. With the amount of collective investment we could offer, he will be glad to enter into a partnership. The research has already proven the chip viable and ready for implant. We start sending up our resources, quickly and quietly. We enter a collaboration of adequate funding, thus ensuring the survival of the human race.'

'Coverage recommencing in ninety seconds,' called out Mike, from somewhere to her left.

Belcher took a deep breath. 'Without this, all of us here will die, if not from old age, then from extreme weather events, dwindling resources, and wars that will only intensify over our limited resources. I advise you to think seriously about the proposal. Paxton Wells has been sending humans to Mars for an entire generation. His Underground Generation are now old enough to be sent to Mars, and have adapted to life underground, without sunshine, making them resilient during Mars lava tunnel occupation. We will live with them and they can teach us how to adapt. In return for the tickets to Mars, you will send me the funding I need. Further details will be sent to you before close of business today. Please recognize that your confidentiality plan stipulates *severe* penalties for any information being revealed.'

She stepped down from the podium, reassured that she had been able to deliver the vital aspects of her plan. People were desperate, and these were desperate times. The broadcast resumed, and Mike hurried to the podium, making a general apology to the viewers about the technical problems that had now been resolved. He invited the President of the Northern States of America to present his speech on *Hope and Collaboration from the Grass Roots up*. He held his breath as Belcher approached him.

'You're not invited, Mike. Erase everything you just heard from your memory.'

He snorted his response. 'I had no intention of fucking running to Mars with you.'

'You signed the confidentiality clause. You mention this to anyone, Mike, and you're a dead man.'

'I'm dead anyway,' he had called after her, her red lips being taken away from him by a fast and efficient pair of chunky heels. 'We're all fucking dead.'

6

EVER SO LICKABLE

CHANEL 46

I should reveal more about Belcher, and offer you her back story, so that you get a feel as to how she fits into all of this. Y'all might be wondering why everybody else, aside from Belcher, was experiencing Pathetic Person Syndrome, a failure to construct solutions themselves. It has to do with the human spirit and how easily it breaks. God should have had a fragile label on humans from the beginning, because the minute that Final End Date was declared, and 2088 was appointed as the last year that the human race could survive on this burning planet, spirits broke around the globe like someone had smashed them all up. Leaders were like deer in the headlights, blinking incomprehensibly at the shards of mess that lay at their feet.

At first, people didn't listen to what was unfolding, not even way back to Saint David when he relayed critical messages, so blatantly and so succinctly through the BBC.

'Climate Change,' he said, his face peering sadly into the camera, 'is our greatest threat, and if we do nothing, it may lead to the collapse of everything we know, including the natural world.'

People remarked on how cognitively aware he was for someone of his age. Others claimed he looked *real good* for someone so old. Then they got complacent. Well… to be accurate it was a specific type of complacency. They organised meetings and demonstrations and millions of words were uttered about what was going wrong. Only there weren't enough words about how to turn this situation from inevitable to manageable. It was too much talk, everyone wanting to play the hero, and never enough collective action.

Maybe all the fake news and the real news got mingled up into too much of a palatable concoction, causing immobilization of people's intelligence neurons or something. Then the ice melted, as predicted, the methane farts started, fires caused vast amounts of carbon releases, droughts killed off the crops, and the storms got bigger. This unfortunate series of events accelerated everything, and yeah, we fell over multiple tipping points. Our use-by date was set in stone after that, not that the universe cared. Like it hadn't cared when the dinosaurs got wiped out, and they lasted millions of years longer than our attempt on this planet.

That's where President Morag Belcher comes in. Being the psychopath that she is, she didn't have a spirit to break when Final End Date was announced. What she saw amongst all of this misery, was advantage and opportunity, just like a psychopath would. Morag had been born whining and miserable, with printed diapers warning of *psychopathic shit inside*, or at least that's what her mother said in her only television interview. She couldn't ever relate to people in a way that demonstrated empathy, her mother added, still perplexed at how her only daughter had unfolded. Even at the age of six, her behavior was off-kilter, suggesting that something wasn't wired right in her brain.

Morag lashed out at her elementary teachers, executing manipulative plans to upset and hurt them, driving them out of the classroom. One involved stabbing her teacher with a pencil, by accident. She dry cried at the time until she repeated the event a week later, forcing the woman into surgery with a perforated kidney. She went on to kill the class guinea pig when she was eight, citing an unfortunate accident involving suffocating the poor animal. Morag had opened her eyes wide and shaken her head when quizzed by her visibly distressed teacher.

'I forgot Miss Rowling, I did. I was just tidying the cage, and I left Harry in the cleaning box over the weekend. I just forgot to take the lid off and put him back in. I promise, Miss. It was an accident.'

Morag's pure psychopathy became noticeable as a teenager where her anger and lies mingled, creating rageful episodes.

'I told you, I just don't like cats.' Fourteen-year-old Morag, hair in braids, stared at the interviewing police officer, wide-eyed, with her arms crossed. Not in a defensive manner, but more demonstrating someone who felt grounded in their opinions.

The officer in charge of this unique case was running out of patience. Not because her description of what had happened wasn't detailed. Far from it, Morag was more than eloquent when recounting what had transpired. It was just that she didn't seem to be communicating what he might have described as normal emotions, given what she'd just done.

'Do you understand that you have devastated the cats' owner with your actions?'

Morag shook her head in disbelief. 'I'm sorry? You want me to feel sorry for the owner? After what those cats did to me?'

'Do you think there might have been a different way to have handled the situation, one that didn't result in the death of the cats?'

Morag shrugged her shoulders. 'They deserved to die. They hurt me. What else do you want me to say?'

The officer shook his own head, trying not to become frustrated with her strange response. He tried again, to elicit any sense of empathy or sympathy from the girl.

'My understanding is that you could have walked away. I understand that the cats spat at you, and one scratched you, resulting in you feeling threatened, but killing them with the hammer seems unnecessary. Don't you think?' he added, almost desperately.

'I don't think so. I see nothing wrong with my actions.' She laughed. 'At least I took proactive action and stopped them.'

The officer gave up. She was only fourteen and destined to become trouble. He looked at her, fleetingly wondering what it would be like to be trapped in such a dark mind, but her lack of empathy suggested that she experienced no pain from it.

'Animal crushing is a felony Morag. It carries a maximum of seven years. If you are convicted, you'll be known as a felon for the rest of your life.'

'So?' she asked defiantly.

'Say again?' the officer asked, sounding surprised.

'So, I said so,' she said slowly. 'S… O…' she added, spelling the word pedantically. 'I'm fourteen. Any consequences of restriction as a felon will long have been removed by the time it counts.'

'By the time it counts?' he asked, confused.

'Yes. By the time it counts,' she repeated slowly again, as if trying to explain the concept to him. 'As an adult, it won't matter. I doubt if I'll be convicted, anyway. I have a scratch on my arm, which I've naturally documented. I was acting in self-defense, and I'm fourteen with an exceptional academic record.'

She was issued with a good behavior order, one that carried no formal charge, on the argument of self-defense which she had enunciated to the judge herself, on the proviso that she never went near the owner of the cats, ever again.

At eighteen, she drove her car into a lake with a friend strapped inside. Miraculously, Belcher escaped from the vehicle, officers questioning whether she had swerved to avoid hitting a suicidal gopher tortoise that had leaped from her right, given how slowly they move. No-one had been able to find the creature when searching for evidence, and no-one understood why Belcher hadn't at least tried to help her friend escape the waist-deep water, deep enough to have caused her friend permanent brain damage. However, Morag's story was convincing enough for her to avoid any charges of negligence or dangerous driving.

Her mother distanced herself from her daughter after that, unable to tolerate the tangle of lies that cascaded from Belcher's mouth, always outlined in a particular red lipstick. She hadn't found it difficult to detach from her grown child, one who hadn't adequately attached in the first instance. Morag didn't glance back, once her mother ceased calling her, finding the woman to be weak and aimless. Morag assumed and hoped that there had been an adoption, one she'd yet to find out about. Morag's mother never heard from her again, not even when Morag's father died, and a request was delivered for her attendance at his funeral. She'd simply disowned her family, taking her maladaptive behaviors with her.

BELCHER TASTED THE 46, noting the creamy and expensive piquancy of Chanel. It was her only vice and one which shared so much with her. The two of them had become an ebb and flow, a yin and yang, a thought and an articulation. Morag formulated words, and *her* Chanel sent them off with style. A lick of the top lip from left to right and then down to the lower lip, right to left. Satisfying, and yet a relentless activity that had turned into a ritual, while musing.

It was dark in the room, dense dark with light having been asphyxiated by thick black curtains. She lay on the top of her bed, still and rigid, like a corpse might, hours after death. Aloneness and simplicity of feeling were something that she savored, especially at night, where she could remove the cloak of President and become Morag. The daily sound of people prattle annoyed and irritated her in her job. Their desire to articulate the mundane in a world which needed so much more grated on her. This is why the Professionals had got under her skin, all running off to the hills to dance and sing and be kind to one another. Kindness was a redundant action at a time like this. A time that urged for strategic focus and resolve. Good riddance to the lot of them, she thought. Useless. If they weren't going to be useful, then they should probably shoot themselves. She wondered if she should go out and shoot the local Gaia community? Maybe it would be kinder to end their existential crises sooner, rather than later?

At least she'd found a way forward with Project IQ. The United Southern States required a savior. Although her previous wayward behaviors had been raised during preselection, potentially making her unsuitable as their President, no-one else had stepped forward. It was a time to restore normal, and give power back to her people, especially those who were trigger-happy to help her. The plot to melt the US President had been her idea but given to a small, redneck group as a tangential suggestion, enough to make them think they had come up with the idea themselves. She curved her two red lines upwards in the dark and sighed with deep content. With charcoal vision, she could muse like this with a cloak of anonymity. The blackness effortlessly coaxing all out of her. She could admit to having been born with the power of manipulation and a manual embedded in her mind, providing her with a list of instructions, showing her which strings to pull as a puppet master.

Wells was her next target. He was an anomaly though, out there with his brazen audacity to relocate the human species onto Mars. She understood that he needed her just as much as she needed him. Her background research demonstrated that his Earth-based innovation projects had started positively enough, making him incredibly wealthy. They'd stalled recently though, as his technology was seen as too fanciful in times where people were barely surviving. He needed her large injection of funds. That, she could count on. He had started sending up the Underground Generation she had assumed, now that they were starting to turn eighteen, so living amongst them was more viable, given the numbers up there.

She lay, comfortable in her rigid pose, her skin mostly only ever having felt Chanel's touch, and rarely her own. Her pale, virgin outer layer had become used to roughness, verging on self-flagellation. She scrubbed infectious dirt and prattle from her body during daily cold showers, each lasting precisely three minutes. The thought of sex with another human being had repulsed her from an early age, and the notion that two people could find themselves *lost* amongst the sweat, juices, and smells of another was off-putting. When she'd discovered that she had emerged into the world through her mother's birth canal, she'd felt physically ill, having needed at the time to wash the imagery away with salt and motherless vinegar. Imagining a growing, parasitic baby inside of her, having to be birthed through her own reproductive organs, and needing to suckle her breasts, was something she likened to horror. Love and family were for the needy and the weak. An emotion and state that she'd never known and had no desire to. She lay still in the blackness and then granted it permission to envelop her, taking her to dreams where nothingness was the favored storyline.

7

TOMATO, CARROT & CRESS
ON RYE

'Are you now suggesting that it isn't possible?' Frustration fueled an internal time bomb, deep within Belcher, and she exploded, releasing a pent-up stream of imprecations, sounding more like a witch doctor uttering maledictions than a President.

He raised his hand, protecting his face in an act of self-defense. 'I don't know. It's never been done before…' Jack felt indignation rupturing through his skin. This woman, President or no President, was pushing for information that he didn't have yet. He was still smarting that she'd effectively kidnapped him during the night. Out of the blue, in the middle of a rare moment of decent body-fluid exchange with Sandy. A woman he'd met the previous night at the bar. Contemplating within the stale air expelled by rambling, fellow drinkers, he'd tried to fathom her potential. In the dim light of the dusty bar bulbs, she'd looked young enough to invite home. Under the brighter lights, rectangular above the pool table, he'd become distracted, trying to do his calculations. Advancing age and fraying edges now highlighted, she'd leaned provocatively over the balls, one hand arching over them, the other stroking the pool cue. It sealed the deal, the lurid action providing enough incentive for him to ask. He did, the transaction banal, and one reminiscent of junior high.

'You coming back to my place?'

'Yeah. Sure.'

It was an informal agreement, a promise of a good time, sealed with no strings. Just as things were getting good, and juices were flowing, some random dudes in black suits had cleared their throats *in* his lousy bedroom. Just standing there, as if they'd been invited in. Sandy had poorly reacted, a steady stream of obscene gestures fired at him, and something about an accusation of him making amateur porn, which he still didn't fully understood. Grade five cyclonic she had been, with fighting words and angry gestures. A thin, blue heel had been thrown at one of the men in black, hitting him on the side of his face. Thrusting a red, taloned bird finger at Jack, she'd slammed the front door on her way out. One heel angrily stomping down the street was the last he'd heard of her.

His voyeuristic kidnappers drove him to the airport and had strapped him into an official jet. Four hours east he'd been flown, across country borders. Upon arrival, this woman, the most undignified President in history, had forced him to sit in a room reminiscent of a nineteenth-century holding cell. He'd perched uncomfortably on a metal-framed chair, surrounded by four dirty stone walls, with a wad of papers to sign. She had stood mutely over him, blocking the light from the only window, waiting for him to sign on dotted lines he hadn't had time to see. He caught her eye, which looked like it was out of time.

'My research, as you are aware, has been done President Belcher… so theoretically… yes. Whether you can produce the actual chip, then get approval, let alone implant into multiple human brains… I mean, it has to go through a shit… a lot… of testing before you could make any of this happen.' He placed his head in his hands, taking time out to ensure all of this was real, and not a bad dream. 'I can't see, given the present climate out there… no pun intended… that you could get any project overseen properly.'

Belcher paced the room, causing Jack to fear he was fresh meat waiting to be fed to her. She froze, narrowing her eyes to slits. 'So yes, feasibly, it can be done as your research indicated, but we would have to negotiate ethics hoops?' She paced again, the dilemma ruminating around in her mind. 'Easily fixed. We unload the hoops, which eliminates the ethics. Then we don't need to jump in the first instance. Better for the knees and better for this project. I've named it Project IQ, by the way.'

Jack sighed, shaking his head. 'You can't just eliminate ethics hoops, Ms. Belcher. They are there for a good reason. Protect people, you know… make sure no harm is done.'

'Jack Cross!' she thundered, causing him to leap hard on metal. 'Firstly, I'm the goddamned President, so you call me by that name. Second, we don't have time for a physical education course. This is to be done in restricted time, so we obliterate the hoops. This isn't open for a protracted debate, I've already pledged it all.' She phoned through to her assistant. 'James, get me the latest on Wells.'

Jack raised his hands in despair. 'Who did you promise all of this to? Anyway, due process is there for a reason, President Belcher. How do you even plan on averting it?'

'All the leaders on this planet are counting on your chip. In return for their funding, I'll provide a new workforce and a seat on a craft. We can't colonize Mars without manufacturing the necessary infrastructure, and we need your chip to do that. I provide the lifeboat, you provide the chip, lead the team, and together, we ensure that the human race survives. For the record, Cross, it's Madam President.'

Jack stared at her. 'Madam President,' he said pedantically, 'You want me to oversee all of this? Manufacture my chip, recruit people, and then insert it into what? Thousands of human brains? All done without passing any mandatory regulations and then fly to fucking Mars with you?' He laughed at the ludicrously of it all. 'You kidnapped me this morning too. What about my rights to privacy? Or my job? I can't just walk out.' Jack stopped and stared at the woman. President or no President, her bedside manner stank.

'I did not kidnap you… you tulle coated, insipid, drama princess. It's called recruitment. Name your price.' Belcher stared him down, hands on her hips.

Jack dropped his gaze, muttering his resentment towards her. 'If that wasn't a kidnapping, then what was it? Abduction. I could sue you!' he said, daring to meet her audacity. He pointed his finger at her. 'You crossed into a different country… a different air space and abducted me. It's illegal to break into someone's house and just stand there. Sick perverts. Your employees are fucking deviants.'

She snorted loudly with laughter. 'I have a Presidential key, Cross. I have access to every person's house. I can be privy to whatever I want, when I want. It's part of my job description. A small perk, if that's how you want to see it.'

'Not in a different country you don't. Your Presidential key is solely for the country that you lead. I was also in the middle of enjoying relations with someone. Yes? That's off-limits, at least it should be.' He waited for a response that admitted a line had been crossed. There was none, not even a blink of confirmation. 'Whatever. You want me to nominate a price right now? A price? Fine. This is fucking ridiculous.'

'I said, name your damned price Cross. I don't have time for this crap. I'm working from this dilapidated building, as the President, with a skeleton team at my disposal, on an ever-decreasing budget. Trying, I might add, to keep this wilting country alive, willing to give you space inside, in purpose-built labs, and a ticket for a future. Right now, you're in a stinking basement, and your chip has no hope in hell of ever seeing a tangible prototype. I would have expected this decision was easy. That's what I'm offering, and now I need your price. I'm time poor, Cross, so get on with it.' She'd not taken a breath with her monologue, her lungs as expansive as her arrogance.

'Wow. What fun this is,' he replied sarcastically. 'Okay. How about ten million in the first year, and five million every year after?' Demanding that amount was outrageous. There was a reason for his mad request however, as Belcher would release him from her tendrils, he could fly home and then return Sandy's left heel to her, with an apology attached.

'Done. Everybody carries a price with them Cross, even you.' Belcher strode to the door and opened it. 'Resign from your old life, including Sandy. Send me a list of what you'll need via my private email. Encrypt the lot, and I'll see you in a week.' She left the door open as she passed through, her voice loudly resonating from within the corridor, 'Where's that information on Wells?'

JACK WAS FLOWN BACK HOME in Belcher's Presidential jet and his old life now looked like a parallel universe, a place of mundane. He'd been working on that damned chip for years, but funding had been tight lately, and the ethics regulations to get it to first base were complex. Artificial intelligence projects were now seen as frivolous in the scheme of things. Without Belcher, his chip would never see sunlight, let alone neural synapses. He needed her, as much as she needed him. Otherwise, the last fifteen years were for nothing. There was a deal to be had, but at what cost? To partake in a symbiotic relationship destined to be one suffocated in psychopathy? Now he had to walk from his lab, and God knows what the intellectual property shit-fight was going to be like. The car dropped him outside of his house.

'Do as she says,' offered the driver, opening the door for him. 'You don't want Madam President offside.'

Then the car had sped off, leaving him in the same spot as he had stood many a time before his abduction. The trees, the sky, and the houses all forming old patterns of wear, only he somehow didn't fit anymore. His life had morphed into something parallel, with little time for adjustment. He ambled up his driveway, the path now paved in surreal, and opened the front door which seemed more red than previously. Careful to avoid the seething blue heel, he walked a direct route towards his self-medication cabinet. He unscrewed the lid of something and tipped the forty percent proof down his throat. It etched into his tissues, searing him with a promise of anesthetizing the memories of Belcher's demands. He slumped into a stained and worn yellow armchair and then grunted with cynicism. Him leading a team to make his chip and then fly to Mars? Ludicrous shit. He took another swig, waiting for the dulling medication to kick in.

Y'ALL, I read Jack's draft for the next part, and I burned it. This story needs and demands absolute sincerity, not drunken reminisces bathed in straight bourbon. I'll pick up this story after he'd finished the bottle and clock hands hovered over dusk. In his draft, he was crapping on about losing his ex-wife and kids. Yeah, Jack had once been married, but it was anything other than a happy family, as he tried to suggest.

Jack's house was mostly empty on the inside, aside from a sprinkling of cheap and nasty furniture. Flatpack stuff that never has the right number of holes and screws. Easily chipped, like him, and discolored from life. The house was empty because Jack made it that way through neglect, dishonesty, and being a bastard. He'd had it all. A wife, two babies, and better furniture too. Jack was not a marriage man and should never have tried it on for size. Jack doesn't do long-term attachment shit, you see. Anyway, come wedding day, and you could see Jack's sweat beading and then dripping, like a slow leak. Nicky had meringued up that aisle, diamontes glistening with anticipation, and he'd almost fallen over, his limbs so rigid with fear.

He should never have got her pregnant in the first instance, but her religious beliefs dictated that they marry. Not one baby, but two had popped out, way too early. Twins with issues, and he hadn't wanted them and could not pretend that he did. Eventually, he managed to get her to give up, but it took him three years. She tried too, a merry-go-round of tears, begging, and despair. The truth was that he just didn't love her enough to care, and certainly not those damaged kids. She ended up throwing a dinner plate at his head one evening after he'd goaded her, drunk, for four days. A pretty yellow plate aimed directly at his right temple. He didn't try to duck, and it hit him with all the vengeance that a woman who knows she is unloved could throw at him. He gave her a choice as the blood left his body. Leave quietly, or he would get her for assault. He conceded months later that he had stooped to new levels of low. Every selfie he'd taken that night was him, beaming into the camera lens, the blood still trickling a line down the right side of his face.

EXACTLY A WEEK LATER, as Belcher had instructed, he was packed and ready to leave a life of theoretical planning, and swap it for practical opportunity. Jack took one look around the old lab, home for fifteen years of intellectual solitude. He'd arrived in his twenties at the beginning of his potential parabola and was now leaving in his forties, having fallen awkwardly down the other side. That youthful fire in his belly had been extinguished, drip-fed by a series of disappointments and frustrations. If he'd specialized in anything at all to do with the climate, he may have fared better, but artificial intelligence wasn't an emergency, not like the failing environment was.

The chip was solely his creation. Not that the world knew much about it anymore. The latest research he had undertaken was mostly shared between him and the four walls of his lab. Only one solitary paper had been published, announcing a significant learning break-through. It had been this paper that Belcher had read, published in an obscure journal, leading her to his abduction. Brain-chip interfaces had been his lifelong passion, and he'd fallen over the finish line first, when his chip had demonstrated the capacity to learn from the host brain and interpret data *in situ*. It made Jack's technology the first of its kind, and for the past fifteen years, he had refined his chip to self-update and regulate using new nanotechnology, designed in Sweden. His chip, learned enough to become independent of all other interface scaffolding.

He'd found the journal as he was packing and had flicked back through the pages, needing a shot of nostalgia before he closed the door for the final time. There it was. A two-page article titled *World Breakthrough. The Chip That Can Learn.* For a few days, he had been sort of famous, his fifteen seconds of fame splashed onto the news, then dissected into bite sizes for radio and social media. Then a glacier had melted in Antarctica, and everyone forgot about him, his chip, and any morsels of hope that had been circulating.

He read an excerpt from the article out aloud in his lab, for old time's sake.

'The chip is essentially a series of tiny flat-packed information cubes. It is globally positioned within the host brain. It strengthens connections between the hippocampus and amygdala, known to be regions that involve decision making and emotion, and the ventral and mesial striatum, two areas that process information related to emotion and reward. A small nano-transporter is placed in the pre-frontal cortex, which allows for accelerated higher-order decision making. When flooded with glutamate and aspartate, taken in the form of a pill each month, the small hubs work together, elevating intelligence quotients by an average of fifty to sixty points...

... Cross has recently updated his work to include a specialty information hub, which allows explicit and semantic memory information to experience enhanced travel between the brain zones that allowed memory retrieval and formation...

... what makes this work unique is that his chip learns enough, so as to become independent from its interface scaffolding, thus becoming 'self-aware' and able to operate by itself, learning as it goes... and improving what it deems necessary within the brain.

... Cross can program each chip to contain ten years worth of career expertise, allowing the recipient to step into a career with no formal training, feeling as if they have been working there for many years.'

The lab didn't acknowledge this scientific brilliance, remaining as nonchalant as always, so he finished packing, stuffed the journal into a small box, and shut the door on his way out. He'd done more with the chip since the article, developing new aspects that few knew about. His chip had not only the capacity to be programed with a range of information files but also new memory events, such as music concerts, travel, fine dining, and friendship experiences. The human brain couldn't differentiate experiences that were real and what had been artificially introduced. Jack had found a means to convert memories into algorithms, replicating real-time experiences into code which also, and uniquely, adopted the individual's perspective.

Belcher, though, was interested in the occupation files which offered college education, ten years of practical experience, and relevant inclusion of available texts. As the wearer then interacted in real-time in the occupation, the chip would update its information as necessary in the host brain. Someone who had the medical file chip could go into a hospital and undertake brain surgery if it were required, a few days after implantation.

Jack opened up the new porn file as soon as he got home. This was a new addition, and he could see huge financial potential in offering it as an extra. The porn industry had only gotten more robust since the announcement of End Date, with people needing more distractions from the real world. Jack's chip allowed the wearer to immerse themselves in sexual acts that felt as real as if they were their own. There was a multitude of explicit to choose from, the best of everything that was offered over the internet highways. He firstly put the temple stickies on, the current interface between computer and chip, and then put the multi-visionary headset on, the current interface between vision and chip, which sat over his visual cortex. In this model, he'd included a *drink addition* overlay, where one press of a virtual button could pour a virtual drink. The brainstem would be flooded in quantum alcohol particles released from the central chip cube, convincing the brain that alcohol had been consumed. The cube was able to be re-filled via inhalation, with the cube re-directing the particles straight to a holding area. The physical effect was the same, with the wearer feeling warm, relaxed, and calm. He downed his virtual bottle of gin, engaged with a ménage à trois and then passed out, happy to be oblivious to his new life.

. . .

BELCHER SPARED NO EXPENSE, channeling money from other government-funded projects into Project IQ. Anything and everything that he would need to translate the chip from paper to brain was within reach, in several brand-new labs. Although he had created the chip, the previous lab owned some IP rights to it, seared into law by his employment contract. Belcher had given clear instructions, though. He was to bring the information with him and make sure he left no trace at the other lab. Harder done than you think, having to kill all of that cloud data, memory sticks, digital footprints, and hard copies of information so quickly. He'd planted a virus onto the company website, and then he'd phoned Belcher, but she was too busy to speak to him, and he'd left a message saying he couldn't be sure he'd got all the data out. The next morning, there'd been a fire at the lab, an indication that messing with this devil woman was an idea never to be entertained. The police didn't intervene, nor did his previous employer come after him, something which had made him hold his breath until Belcher reassured him that it had all been taken care of. He didn't ask for the details.

Once settled, his first task was to recruit a team to help him take the chip from design to manufacture, refining it for Belcher's needs. The brief was insane if he were honest, and would never have passed a legit ethics process. Belcher wanted something more added into his blueprint. She wanted an element of control. She had requested that the chip be fitted with a limiter which would be challenging to introduce selectively. Belcher wanted individuals to remain compliant to a particular occupation file and not feel the desire to move between occupations. This would require controlling intelligence drivers and inquisitiveness. This was a medieval brief, and from a President who wanted to fly to Mars? It stank, all of it.

He googled Home Base, and studied the accessible historical material. Wells had formerly allowed total transparency within

Home Base, with a live cam following all the activity around the clock. Wells had been in the right place at the right time when a previous Government had granted him exclusive rights to settle on Mars and build Home Base. Wells had paid a small fortune for the exclusivity, but had made big bucks in green technology and could easily afford it. Jack himself had sometimes sat gazing at the fuzzy images, watching people build, plant crops in the greenhouses, and drive the dune buggies on the red surface. It was bizarre to think of them all, up there and so far away.

Wells had suddenly shut down access to information about Home Base eighteen years earlier, around the time that significant climate events had been playing out on earth. Wells had become more strategic and circumspect about his activities. There were reports of death threats directed at him from desperate individuals who saw Home Base as the only salvation for the human species. Jack presumed that by shutting down the live cameras, Wells had provided himself with a layer of protection from the crazies and the desperates. Either that, or he had run out of money and didn't want to say anything.

In 2028, according to the historical cache, Mars had a hundred individuals on it. They had successfully grown tomatoes, carrots, rye, and cress by adding nitrogen into the soil. They'd been adding to their solar energy panels since first relocating there in 2025, and so, for most of the time, aside from when the dust storms enveloped the planet, they could generate their own energy source. They were still highly dependent on extra supplies being sent from Earth, though. It was a primitive existence, mostly spent underground in the lava tubes, due to the extreme Martian surface temperatures. Was it a good existence though, he wondered, better than being dead on planet earth? This information was all outdated though and since then, anything could have happened up there.

Paxton Wells had created a Mars simulation base on Earth, the address a well kept secret. The individuals living underground in it, had been called the 'Underground Generation,' and rumors had it that children were now being born in the fake lava tunnels on Earth who would never see natural sunlight. These individuals, now reaching eighteen, were supposedly being sent up to Mars, so word on the street said. A more adaptable group that would cope better with lengthy stints underground and were already used to a restrictive life-style. Jack shook his head. How all of that had ever passed ethical standards was anyone's guess. It was inhumane to breed humans in the dark, and yet somehow, Wells had Government support to do it.

His next task was to assemble a team. Belcher hadn't said much, only that he could have what he needed. Who, and what did he need? He tapped his pencil on the desk as if the rhythm might encourage insight. He reasoned that alcohol, sex and a roof over his head was a reasonable list. A redacted version of the hierarchy of needs written by Maslow, whose research had never had any empirical credibility and yet here it was, nearly a century later, still famous and always quoted. Jack wouldn't mind that sort of success too. The type that falls on your lap for no good reason.

He'd been asked to work as part of a team, and as a lone wolf, this had pissed him off. People annoyed him when in close proximity, making him edgy, anxious, and irritated. So, the question was, who could he work with that he wouldn't want to dissect after a week? He firstly picked an all-female team, reasonable in their fields, and good looking, hoping to add extra-curricular opportunities for team bonding. Belcher, after reading his proposal, had told him to go *frick himself,* whatever that had implied, and to *try some maturation* which he had at first misread, causing a wave of anxiousness. She had insisted that he build a team based on intelligence and ability, aim for gender equality, and to keep the contents of his pants zipped in. Belcher was so sweet at times, a real little darling.

His old college stuff had been hiding in his attic, mostly out of shame, but perhaps this was the place to find the members of this new team? He dug his old freshman yearbook out and looked at the hopeful faces, a snapshot of naïve youth, frozen in time. His young, confident face stared back at him, one that had truly believed it was headed towards greatness. He smiled cynically. His shit hadn't stunk when he'd enrolled in his undergraduate degree. Now, he thought, looking at his reflection in the mirror, he just looked like shit, full stop. Booze, women, and too much good stuff had resulted in a hard look to his face. He still had his hair though, and it framed his harshness with a healthy mop of blonde curls. His eyes, though, had faded from a brilliant blue into a color of subdued and disappointed hues. Deep wrinkles between his eyes, like the Grand Canyon, gave him a perpetually pissed off expression. Standing back and trying to imagine how other people perceived him, he realized that he had poorly aged, worn out from over-oxidization.

He wondered if the faces trapped between the yearbook covers were also jaded and cynical, twenty years later. They had muddled their way through the rites of passage, as they stumbled into adulthood. He'd acknowledged their successes sprinkled throughout journals over the years. A cascade of memories came flooding back, stuff that he had deliberately shut away for his own sanity. Can you start again, he wondered? He emailed the names to Belcher anyway, and she responded promptly with *you'll have them in a week.* Hopefully, they were all alive and still kicking, and maybe it would be good if they remembered him too, when the non-negotiable invite was handed out.

8

———

DUCKS, CHINESE
AND AWKWARD

Belcher led the four new members of Project IQ into Jack's lab six days later. They dutifully followed her as if they had imprinted on her, as baby ducklings might.

'Jack, your flock is here,' she declared. 'Tina, Paul, Peter, and Mia - meet Jack, the man behind the chip.' She then sat down, facing Jack, which gave her the appearance of batting for the wrong team.

He recognized the four individuals now fixated on him. Faces with distinctive patterns that had subtly aged over twenty years of life. A time span that had estranged them from one reality and had somehow placed them all back together again into something new. Only time would tell whether this quirk of chance would prove to be a viable path towards a finished chip. No-one spoke, an awkward silence permeating the room.

Belcher suddenly stood and twisted on her heels, bored with the indecision. 'Get on with it, Jack. Tell them what they need to know, and I require an update this afternoon. Some proof that you've communicated intelligent ideas with each other. So that this is clear, it's Madam President while in this building.' She walked from the room, sealing the door with a thud behind her, making the group startle.

'Sorry about that,' said Jack.

The door opened again. 'All that you do and say is monitored by CCTV. Just letting you know, as per the legal obligations for active surveillance.' She shut the door again, her involvement in their reunion over, her feet walking away to find something else to do.

'Right,' said Jack awkwardly. 'Welcome. Nice to see you all again.' He paused. This wasn't the time to say anything that might dislodge calm. 'I'll explain the nuances of my chip and the concept of the limiter that President Belcher, I mean Madam President, would like to add to the design. Then we can consider everything that involves…' He lost his train of thought, as the four individuals stared at him. '… everyone happy with that?' Jack got nothing back from them. 'Please, let's move to the demonstration table and… we can watch something that I've prepared.'

'So, let me get this right,' said Tina, after Jack's initial brief. 'You require us to include a component within the chip that limits free will? Is that even ethical?' Tina looked at Jack with a look of derision. Obviously, she hadn't fully healed from their calamitous break-up, which had been dramatic, explosive, and somewhat unfortunate. He had hoped that twenty years was long enough for Tina to have recovered, but her scars ran deep. Her long chestnut hair, green eyes, and friendly face had once been his reflection for two years, although her expression at that moment was anything other than pleasant.

'I'm not sure that ethical parameters are what we should concentrate on at this moment,' Jack assured her, smiling, hoping to soften her Medusa-like expression. 'Our priority is to stick to Madam President's brief and within the designated timeframe.' He knew his tone didn't hide his own incredulous opinion about Belcher's plans.

'So, if we provide an individual with reformed *intelligence*,' said Pete, 'then we fear them using the intelligence in ways that don't favor the project? Yes?' Pete sat back and folded his arms in an act of self-defense. He needed a layer of protection between him and Jack, even now, twenty years after the event. Jack's alcoholism had undermined his last year, the infected friendship costing Pete the graduation he had been working towards. This was not the time or place where Pete could heal such a sense of betrayal.

'How about we re-introduce ourselves?' offered Jack, drowning in the rising tension. 'It's been a while.'

'Why? Do you intend to introduce the same Jack or perhaps a new one? One with a bit of conscience, perhaps? *We*,' Tina said, indicating to the others pedantically, 'already know each other Jack. *We* kept in touch. *We* never lost contact.'

'Really? Wow. Okay. No… that's great to hear. I'm glad.' He wasn't glad. It made him look like an outsider.

'Yeah,' added Paul. 'We pushed on, Jack. Made good as best as we could. After everything that happened, that is.'

Mia smiled uncomfortably. 'So, how have you been, Jack?' she asked, trying to lighten the mood.

Shit. He took a deep breath. 'Right. I'm assuming that all of us in this room have been offered incentive packages, and that's why we are here? How about we start today by concentrating on the job at hand? We'll put our differences to one side. Yes?'

He walked over to the wall, frustrated and disappointed at how this had begun, and pressed the darkness switch. The blinds rolled down, and a holograph dome lowered from the ceiling. 'This short explainer will fill you in on the technical nuances of my chip. After that, we can discuss how we might approach a limiter.' He then sat amongst a room full of unspoken words, each waiting for the right moment to order themselves and spill their stories into the present.

BELCHER WASN'T IMPRESSED when Jack reported on their progress, namely their lack of any, at the end of the day. He passed on an apology from Mia, a single mother, who'd had to return home due to a family situation.

'Quickly Jack,' she fired, sorting through a mass of green folders on her desk. 'I'm about to take off to visit the fire tornado victims in the north. Make it quick. What about the rest of the meeting? Any progress?'

'We considered some options.'

'Why did Mia leave?' Belcher said, distracted as she perused the contents of a file.

'She's a single mother. It was about her kid… I let her have the rest of the day off.'

'She's fired.'

'What? You can't fire her for that.'

'I just did and you don't get an opinion.' She looked up at him.

'Jesus,' he muttered.

'I'm the President, Jack. I can do what I want.'

'So now my team is down to four?'

'Yes. I'm sure you'll manage.'

Someone knocked on the door. 'Your car is waiting, Madam President.'

'Concentrate on the job, Jack. That's why I've paid you millions. I'll be back in a week. By then, I expect something tangible, so find a trolley and sort out whatever baggage this lot has brought with them. Then do the job I'm paying you to do.' She grabbed a protein bar out of her bag and ripped the head off it, chewing loudly. After swallowing, she pulled a limp piece of plastic wrapper out of her mouth and threw it into the bin. She buzzed through to James.

'James. Am I providing these people with emergency funds today, or platitudes?'

'Madam President, I've got the Head of Emergency Response on the phone. He can explain that. He needs to speak to you urgently about an immediate mass evacuation.'

'Put him through.'

'Madam President. How are you?' A man spoke, sounding hopeful.

'Jonas. You're on speakerphone. I'm about to fly up to see you. Leaving in about ten. What's the situation?'

'Madam President. There's nothing left north of Birmingham and Dallas in a straight line to Tulsa. I require you to authorize an emergency mass evacuation before you leave so we can start getting these people relocated. This is chaos.'

'Fine. How many and where? Give me a brief recap.'

'We intent to move approximately twenty-three thousand over to Nashville. There were eleven fire tornados in this storm. We had sustained winds of over two-fifty and gusts close to three hundred. We're going to need to cremate over the next week.'

'How many?'

'Nine thousand.'

Jack shook his head. The fire tornados were relatively new on the climate scene. Touching down with a screaming fury, their flatten and scorch policy destroyed everything in their path. So intense was the heat, that the burning ash fell white like it was snowing, and their signature inner weather systems, cracked lightning, like cowboys at a rodeo.

'Madam President, I need you to authorize an immediate Occludo for the area. We won't be able to rehabilitate it. Are we able to snap-shot a verbal now?'

'Fine. I'll give a verbal. Ready?'

'Yes, Madam President.'

'I, President Morag Belcher, agree to the proposed Occludo as outlined by the Head of Emergency Response.'

'Thank you, Madam President. It's approximately seventeen million acres that we are now excluding from human habitation. Air quality when you arrive is in the extreme range, and the ground temperature is approximately one hundred and ten degrees. We'll provide you with breathing apparatus after you land.'

'Sounds wonderful,' she replied dryly.

'We'll launch the evacuations now, and see you when you arrive, Madam President. Safe flight.'

'Why are you still here?' she demanded, gesturing to Jack. He lifted his hands into the air, wondering himself.

'A week, Jack. I need to see progress.'

'Fine,' said Jack, walking past her and back to the lab, his mind firing a round of expletives, silently towards her.

· · ·

JACK IMAGINED Belcher being methodical out there, witness to sickening scenes. He could guarantee that she would feel disgust rather than empathy for the victims, their apparent neediness most likely seen as annoyance. She *was* the perfect President. A machine made from practical components. She didn't care about these people and nor any of the others she was about to leave to die on the planet.

He settled back into work, hoping to organize more of the project in the evening quiet, as distractions were less and concentration easier to maintain once most people had retreated home for dinner. He perused the brief for the limiter again, hoping to get his head around it properly. A limiter would need to prevent an individual from straying too far from the pre-programmed quantum algorithms contained within the occupation files, including when the chip reached self-regulating status. Jack rapped his fingers on his desk, working the problem through. Theoretically, it sounded plausible, but in terms of ethics?

He thought about the remaining people on the team he'd invited in, hoping that they would settle in the coming days. Pete was his expert in terms of implantation and tissue rejection and would lead a team of future surgeons. There had been complications when nanoparticles had first been placed into the human brain, often leading to localized necrosis. The particles were more stable now, and Jack was confident that Pete could develop an implantation process, without causing significant brain injury to the chip recipients. Tina had specialized in quantum coding, namely in the development of Rbits and Sbits, creating faster computational, algorithmic potentials. That might come in handy with the limiter development, he surmised, thinking through how many possibilities would need to be computed at any given point in time. The project required her to engineer the initial interface scaffolding, before the chip developed independence. Paul was his manufacturing brains, having worked on several large-scale projects over the years, including the roll-out of the AI57, the first home android that could help families with Climate Change anxiety, in real time.

There was a knock on his door, which startled him out of his thoughts. 'Come,' he said, looking up. Tina was there, holding some boxes of takeaway.

'I thought you might be hungry?' she asked timidly, not knowing what his reaction might look like. 'Chinese, like we used to.'

'Like we used to?' It had surprised him that she had remembered.

'Tuesday nights? Four dishes, a bottle of wine and Game of Thrones.'

'Where in the hell did you find Chinese?' His face had lit up, as if suddenly plugged in.

'I have a neighbor who makes Chinese from home. Just for a select few, that is. He has connections with some off the grid ring for ingredients. I do IT support for their family. Old fashioned bartering. Works well out there, all things considered.'

'Am I to assume this is a peace offering?' he asked hopefully.

'Yeah. Look, I'm sorry about snapping earlier,' she said, struggling to find the space to set down the boxes. Jack's desk was a cluttered mess of half-empty, ranging from apples to sandwiches, coffee cups, and cigarettes. 'I thought we should talk before this interferes with our work. I don't want to be dredging old feelings like that up in front of the others. I'm going to allow myself to be vulnerable, so please, Jack, respect it.'

Jack winced. She had been as subtle as a sledgehammer. 'Sure... no, I agree. I think a chat is a great idea.' He studied her face, which housed a deep sadness, one which she wasn't trying to hide from him.

'How did your brief go with Belcher earlier?' she asked.

'She fired Mia actually, for leaving. Didn't give a shit about why she had to leave.'

'Seriously? That's harsh. When are you going to replace her?' 'We aren't. Belcher has told me we are now a team of four.'

'Well, good luck to us finishing the chip with one less person.' Tina looked concerned. 'Mia was going to over-see the bio-chemistry with you, wasn't she?'

'Yeah, she was.' He sighed, looking at the four white takeaway boxes. 'Before I eat my notes from starvation, what's on the menu?'

'Guess. See how good your memory is.' Tina remembered how consistent Jack had been, with his regular orders for Chinese.

'I don't have memory cells. I pickled them.' He looked sheepish.

Tina listed the contents for him. 'Sweet and sour chicken, egg rolls, duck with cashews and fried rice.'

He thought hard. Chinese had been their Tuesday night for two years. He'd forgotten how much he'd enjoyed those lazy evenings with her. Youth was wasted on the young, he thought, as, in hindsight, he hadn't realized how precious and uncomplicated their time together had been. He frowned inwardly. Uncomplicated perhaps hadn't been the right choice of word. Towards the end, he'd shat on them, if he was honest.

'You found real duck?' Jack sounded surprised.

'Synthetic. Sorry. So, you still drinking?'

'Thanks. You always were straight to the point.'

'You hurt me.' Pain was etched on her face as if some crazy person had colored all of her happiness in with a hurt crayon.

'I know. I was an idiot.' He dropped his gaze as a wash of images flooded his mind. Tina's body curled up against his, her mouth on him, the way she laughed, and how he had made her cry.

They stopped there, not wanting to ruin the food and shared career highlights instead, from the past twenty years, but there was more dangerous territory to navigate through.

'I still don't know why you did all that shit. You pushed me into a corner.' She sighed despondently, remembering back to happiness that had morphed into despair.

'Look, I was young, stupid, drunk, and selfish. I get that.' Jack guided himself through memories embedded in an active minefield, most of which were blurry and unrecognizable.

'You got her pregnant,' Tina said, ensuring that every word was articulated deliberately. His action had been treason. Her reaction had been to guillotine their relationship.

'Yeah, I know. Her father visited me when he found out and almost broke my jaw.' He instinctively lifted his hand to his jaw, remembering the intensity of the father's rage.

'Really? He smashed you? I hadn't known that. You deserved it though. I wanted to smash you too. I still do.'

'Thanks. Yeah, I was told to stay the hell away. Fair enough. I've never asked if she had the baby?'

'Nah, she had an abortion. Her parents insisted on one. There was no way they were going to allow your genes into their lineage… no offense.'

Jack hid his hurt, assuming he'd been an absent father all this time. He looked down, experiencing a flood of unwanted emotions, the possibility of an adult child having evaporated into thin air.

'So, was I not enough for you? Is that why you did it?'

'Are you serious?' Jack stared at her incredulously. 'That's a genuine and serious question? Yes?' he asked, needing clarification.

She nodded. 'I've asked myself this question over and over for twenty years, Jack. I thought we were good together… that we'd found some kind of genuine connection on so many levels. We'd just made plans to move for graduate school. Remember?'

He paused, shaking his head, not really remembering at all. He'd been pissed most days and needed others to fill in the blanks. In this moment, though, he would say what was expected. 'No, you have this all wrong. Of course, you were good enough. I couldn't see what I had. I don't think I knew what I was doing half the time, especially sleeping with Sally. One stupid night it was…' Had it been one night? He couldn't remember. '… and then she's telling me she's pregnant. It seems to be a feature of my life,' he added.

'A feature? You've done this more than once?' she asked, wondering how many other women there had been.

'No… I mean my ex-wife. I got her pregnant too, the first time. Don't know how, given how drunk my sperm were. Surprised they even knew which way to swim.' He laughed and then stopped. Tina wasn't smiling. 'We had twin boys, but they were premature at twenty-five weeks. Born with severe disabilities. They did some stem cell exchanges but neither of the boys really improved.'

'Oh… I'm sorry,' she said, her tone softening slightly. 'Do you see them?'

'Nah. I burned my bridges there. Both boys require highly specialized care in a nursing home. I went and saw the twins a couple of times, but they don't know who I am, and can't cognitively understand much, unfortunately.' He paused, trying to stop the conversation as it was causing feelings to surface. 'I've got this as a fairly reliable partner though,' he said, picking up the bottle of wine, trying to lighten the mood. 'Want some more?'

'Why not?' She held out her paper cup.

He poured, and a lengthy silence descended between them.

'Did you ever think about me?'

'I was too drunk, Tina.'

'Yeah, I thought you would say that. What about when you were sober?'

'By then, it was too late. I suppose from time to time, I hoped you might have met someone better than me?'

'Yeah, I did… after eight years of dating dropkicks, I met Logan. Ten years together and then some drunk hit him at an intersection and killed him instantly. It made me think of you when it happened. Some fucker who didn't know when to stop. That was two years and three months ago.'

'Shit… Tina.' He didn't know what to say.

'Yeah, well, sometimes life just throws crap. I muddle on. I was happy to take this project on aside from the money. It gives me a bit of a fresh start, away from Logan and all of our memories. This will help with the grieving process, so my therapist has advised me. Then there's End Date and watching all of this falling apart. I hadn't realized it was all going to be so hard. Anyway,' she said, suddenly looking at the time on her phone. 'I have to go. I'm doing this online book club thing. We're tackling The Prophet tonight.'

'Kahlil Gibran's work?' Jack sounded interested.

'Yeah, it's supposedly going to help us be less judgmental, more spiritual, and base our lives within the religion of love.'

'Belcher reminds me of Gibran, come to think of it.'

'How? I can't imagine two people further apart. Surely?' Tina looked surprised at the thought.

'Just the way Gibran step-stoned his way up, getting older women to finance his artistic pursuits.'

'Belcher doesn't have any sugar daddies in the closet, does she?' Tina shook her head at the thought. 'Sugar mommies?' she added.

'I doubt she's ever allowed anyone within ten feet of her. No, it's more the mind-fucks she does on people. Like the world leaders at the summit. She's used the lot of them to fund all of this. She's the one that this is saving. She doesn't care about anyone else.'

'Well, she will not mind-fuck me, thanks. I'll write NO on my forehead if I have to be clear.'

'I'm glad you stopped by tonight.' Jack thought about saying something that might help mend everything, but nothing came.

'Yeah, same. I'm glad we chatted and cleared the air. This chip project is important, especially as we're responsible in part in ensuring the survival of humanity on Mars. No pressure. I don't want to mess it up with unresolved stuff. It's not my style.'

'In terms of End Date Tina, we have a way out here, and we need to hold on to that.'

'I know. It's a weird way out, though, very Bowie-esk.'

'How?'

'Take your protein pills and put your helmet on? That's going to be us. A line in a song written in 1969, predicting precisely this. Kind of prophetic too…' she sighed. 'Hey, you want to know my favorite memory?' she asked, veering the conversation off course.

'What? From our time together?'

'Yeah, us. You used to kiss this place on the back of my neck. I miss that, you know.'

Jack glanced at Tina, hearing the mistake of tense in her comment. Surely she didn't still carry a light for him after what he did to her? He saw a young woman of twenty-three standing in front of him again, unsure of herself and needing to feel safe. He'd taken that away from her, leaving her bruised and uncertain. Then she'd met someone whom she thought was a safe harbor, and he'd died on her. He'd been a bastard, and Logan had let her down through death. Life, hey.

9

FLAT EARTH
AFTER ALL

Y'all. The exodus to Gaia Intentional Communities didn't resemble a refugee line of war victims, where people ambled possessionless, their eyes maimed from trauma and their internal compass not knowing which direction pointed to safe. Nor did it mirror the rhythmic marching of coordinated military lines towards tent cities where arms were still stinging from implants. They undertook Gaia migration with a sense of purpose and hope, as if people were following a sun that promised warmth elsewhere.

Gaia marketed its laissez-faire communities, centered on ecological awareness, sustainability, healthy living, and unconditional love. Everything that the real world didn't offer. Their model claimed abandonment of egalitarianism, and yet required those entering to be financially secure. They had analyzed commune structures dating back to the sixties, where bland progressive models had led to intellectual entropy, and had wanted to avoid similar self-defeating methodologies. Thus, the settlements promoted themselves as offering vivid, ongoing education and lifestyle for everyone. Everyone, that is, who could afford to enter. Gaia had thought carefully about sustaining itself and was unrolling a global expansion plan, so it needed its foundations to be durable and its members willing to stay loyal for the long term. Limited by an unsafe climate, Gaia had snapped up land, after a methodical analysis of predicted weather patterns, ensuring that they would have long-term security to grow food and remain relatively safe in the midterm.

A lucky few could seek election into the inner sanctum, namely the Gaia Community Boards, a selection of twelve individuals responsible for the day-to-day running of each community. In return, it gave them special privileges such as prestige housing, access to transport, and a better selection of clothes and food. These individuals ensured that everyone adhered to the Gaia Commandments, and if not, that they could implement deterrents to ensure they followed the rules.

Gaia headquarters was located somewhere in downtown Los Angeles, not that many ever got to visit. Gaia was run by a group who pedantically called themselves *The Second Illuminati*, a name chosen to align with the 1776 Bavarian Illuminati, whose goals were to oppose the abuse of State power. Gaia was pedantic in its message to remain independent from any Government interference and thus was an obvious choice for those struck down by Government induced austerity measures, who could still afford privilege.

The American Dream was sighing, now in its last moments, once vaunted by the Government as the blueprint for a successful life. It had turned out to have been an illusionary trick for when things had been going well. Now, it had a stench of bitter death, overt lies now seeping from under its facade. The message was obvious. All men are created equal, but some will gain power they do not deserve and will then lord this power over the lesser man next to him, and probably piss on him too. Those covered in the stench of piss saw Gaia as a fresh start.

Those losing everything they had worked hard for, gave their Governments a flock of bird fingers on their way out. After having played the game honestly, having stayed within righteous lines, their reward wasn't prosperity, liberty, opportunity, or equality. It was salary reduction, loss of health insurance, increased personal and business tax, double-digit interest rates, and inevitable financial ruin.

They handed back the keys to their homes and walked from their jobs in a mass exodus named The Anarchy. If Governments were going to punish them for the way things had turned out, then they, too, could cause harm by removing themselves from meaningful employment and never vote again. Gaia had opened its arms to catch them all too, with a simple transfer of all assets in return for mother earth nurturing.

Gaia Intentional Communities expanded quickly, soon numbering hundreds. Secretive in terms of what went on behind the trademark barbed wire fences, it marketed itself as color in an otherwise greying world. Occasionally, Gaia Board members would be spotted in the outside world, meeting with The Second Illuminati. Jesus, I can't even write that without laughing. I'm getting images of dudes in black robes, conspiring behind tall, double-oak doors. Their vows of silence in discussing internal matters resulted in Gaia's daily life, remaining an enigma.

Governments felt the strain of a dwindling workforce, already strained from GFC2. Services ran on threadbare, and hospitals were open for emergencies only. Schools had starting shutting down, and the majority of small businesses were forced to shut. Governments called in loans, creating tensions between countries, some increasing tariffs, others closing borders, and some building boundary fences. We replaced political representatives with social warlords, domineering personalities who saw the opportunity to claim territory. The masses followed them, blind to what it was they were chanting for. They just wanted to belong, shout something and feel like they were making a difference. Humans need a sense of purpose. Without purpose, we are as aimless as a star without companions to illuminate. We were a world engaged in passive war, where battles raged, despite the winner already having been decided.

Yet, there was still some hope for the rich in amongst this mess. Just like Lucy's descendants must have felt when they ventured out of Africa for the first time, taking their tentative steps towards world dominance, searching for something different and perhaps better. There was hope that new meaning could be found, contentment secured, and new activities procured before things became dire. It's an innate drive in human beings to believe that there is always something better just over the horizon, even if that horizon has an edge.

ELLIE GLANCED OVER AT DEAN, his head resting on the door of the car, lulled into a deep sleep by the monotony of their journey. Even in sleep, his resting face was pissed off, as it had been at home when she had attempted discussion with him. She had already been driving for five hours on a crumbling, empty highway towards Gaia Settlement Thirteen, trying to keep their car on the road. The journey had been harrowing, with regular tidal waves of dust storms forcing her to pull over to the side of the road. As the orange dust had exfoliated the car, she had been forced to place the PS7 face masks onto Dean and herself, which helped them to breathe. During the past few months, he had acted like a helpless child, submerged in self-inflicted misery which he blamed Ellie for. She had carried the two of them, her own face now etched with exhaustion.

Even in the car, with the windows shut, the relentless dust found its way in, sprinkling everything in orange specks. Roads had been washed away in some places, forcing her to find detours on isolated and dangerous back roads. Gas was limited, but she had been lucky to find some tucked away in a remote gas station, albeit charging $135 a gallon.

'That's not a dollar and thirty-five I'm guessing?' she had asked the weather-beaten attendant, who had looked as dry as the cracked soil his gas station sat upon.

'No, Ma'am. Gas is precious, and I don't have much left other than in the tank. One hundred and thirty-five dollars a gallon, and I'll take no less. Make it cash, too, thanking you.' He smiled a toothless grin.

Ellie had looked around her, at his bleakness, the lack of birdsong and the lengthening shadows creeping into the shop. The signage outside had once been colorful. A montage of a happy smiling face, sunshine, and ice-creams. A promise that had long since moved on.

Dean had gotten out of the car in angry mode and had followed her inside.

'Over a hundred bucks for a gallon? Ellie, how many miles do we have to go? Work it out and only put in the minimum.'

'Oh, really? I was going to fill it up and take us on a road trip to Disney,' she had bitten back.

'Ellie, be serious. We need our cash reserves!' he said, flaring his nostrils at her, as he always did when he needed more air to raise his tone.

'I don't need you to mansplain everything, Dean. Also, do you realize that Gaia will take our cash once we get there? We don't use money as a currency in the community.'

Dean ventured away to see if the shop sold any food, and finding nothing, he had got back into the car, leaving her to complete the payment. By the time she returned, he was pretend-dozing again, facing away from her with nothing kind left to say. She drove through flatlands of burning orange, spiked with the charcoal stalks from trees, cremated long-ago, in the heat. She'd lost count of the number of smaller communities they had driven through, now ghost towns, the temperature having chased the inhabitants away. They were like abandoned movie sets comprising boarded-up shops, rusting playgrounds, and endless tumbleweed that was rolling in from somewhere. She glanced at the temp readout on the dash. Early evening and the temperature in the car was still hovering around a hundred and two degrees.

She turned the car radio on, seeking company for her rising anxiety. She was sure that Dean was keeping his eyes closed only to ensure that he kept the line between them. A line that had been made several weeks ago during yet another argument. She had wanted to design a plan for their future, and he had acted as if she were planning a double suicide. The radio hissed static and then reported a massive death toll in The United Southern States as ferocious fire tornados had hit the ground. She turned it off quickly before it bombarded her with more suffering and more catastrophe. She had reached saturation and her nerves were sizzling with raw ends that needed respite from it all. For the past nine years the news had been a liturgy of horrendous, with mass casualties from a climate gone mad. It had relieved her when Gaia had rescued them, because trying to keep it all going, pretending that everything was normal, had been exhausting.

Dean and Ellie had worked in a small township, working at the local school, where they had been part of a predominantly depressed teaching staff. One had taught happily and the other not, at a school where students had been challenging on a good day and dead-tough on a bad day. Most came from challenged socioeconomic backgrounds with defiance on their agenda towards any authority that fell their way. Violence was their currency of negotiation, and always present in the classroom, making teaching for Ellie a source of stress, rather than joy. Once End Date had been declared, the students had come in to tell her to fuck off, and had swapped their textbooks for drugs. They then passed their time squatting in the homes that they looted.

Ellie swapped teaching for cleaning, sorting out English textbooks that no-one would ever read again. Dean, a sports teacher, had run aimlessly around the school oval to fill in time. Notice was then given that the school was going to close, like so many others, and that they were no longer needed on staff. Redundancy came in the form of a letter, a month's salary, and a contrived sentence, thanking them for their years of service. Ellie had felt as if the letter had told them that the earth was flat and that they were all about to drop off, such was her anxiety by this stage.

'We can't just sit here,' she had told Dean, feeling disconnected and shocked at the thought of remaining in their home, staring at the walls waiting for End Date, or a climate emergency to take them out. 'I've been looking for another job but there isn't a lot on offer around here.'

'I don't have the answers Ellie, as I told you yesterday, and the day before, and the day before that.' Dean had looked irritated that she had interrupted the boxing match he was watching. 'Why don't you go find a hobby to keep you busy. Didn't you do that crochet stuff once?' He raised the volume on the remote, making it harder for Ellie to finish the conversation.

'How is any of this supposed to work?' she had replied, raising her voice to be heard, her tears real. She stood between Dean and the screen. 'Crochet? Are you fucking serious? I need a job… did you even know that food is becoming harder to find? When was the last time you even went shopping? I'm sick of eating protein bars.'

She waited for a response and he sat, mute. This was Dean's tactic in every conversation. He would let Ellie initiate a conversation and then remain mute, not reflecting her concerns back to her or offering any direction. He knew it triggered her, and so he did it more. Her anxiety rose another notch. 'I don't want things to end like this. We need to think strategically. Don't just put out platitudes and tell me to go find a hobby. We need to find a better way through this.'

Silence.

'Jesus, Dean. Say something. A word… a sentence.'

He smiled, knowing that the button had been pushed. Now he could respond and be angry at her tone. 'A better way? What if there is no better to this Ellie? What if this is it, as good as it gets? We had a good life up until now. We can at least sit in our memories. This is safe and we have a roof over our heads. We also have the tv.' He craned his head, trying to keep up with the action. He knew his words would provoke and escalate things.

Ellie looked behind her at the massive, flat-screen TV which dominated the room. Dean's new friend. He glued himself to it, from sunrise to sunset, parked in a solitary position on the couch, his only movement being his right arm which poured more beer into his mouth and occasionally conducted the infrared to change the channel. They struggled to negotiate with each other, as Dean's drinking encouraged a mood always teetering on irritable. They had argued relentlessly about what they should do next, with Ellie always doing most of the talking as Dean preferred to remain in passive silence. Ellie was pushing for action while Dean was content with inaction. With no living family to help them and friends having moved on, they were isolated and dependent on each. Ellie was keen to create a plan, throwing an idea onto the table about moving somewhere else to look for work, but Dean had shot the idea down, telling her that their working days were over.

'No, Ellie. We did work. It's past tense.' His tone was already irritated, and she was making him miss the crucial middle rounds of the boxing match.

'We did work? Are you suggesting we're now retired? Dean, you're thirty-three, not seventy-three. How can you feel happy with retiring at this age?'

'Ellie, I'm not retiring by choice here. There are no jobs you just told me!' he said, selectively misinterpreting what she had just said. 'The world, as we know it, is over. Get used to it. Look around you. This is as good as it's going to get. Be thankful for what we still have. Play the damned PS7 and escape into the VR. I don't know, figure it out! As I said… go fucking crochet something.' Then he had slumped back down into their couch, bought in happier times, and poured himself another drink.

She had scoured the internet looking for options. They had both lost their parents recently from Climate Change incidents and had inherited small amounts of money. It meant they could afford fuel credits to keep their cars on the road, and could buy black-market food when available, which was getting less and less. However, it wasn't money she was after. It was meaning. She refused to accept that her life, at thirty-two, would consist of being locked away, isolated in their home, watching the unfolding drama of End Date approaching, with a shit of a husband playing mind games with her.

She looked over at Dean who was back watching the boxing as if she was invisible in the room. Anger formed inside of her. 'What about our baby plan? Next year was when we were going to start trying. Is that over too, just because our jobs have vanished?' she had asked, knowing she was delivering a rhetorical grenade into the equation, but wanting a fight, because Dean was mute again. She wasn't done trying to communicate how much the losses were hurting.

He picked up the bait, needing her to shut up. 'What the hell do you expect, Ellie? Bring a baby into this?' He indicated out of the window as several sirens passed them. 'What sort of diseased person thinks about forcing a person… a baby… into all of this? A person destined to struggle, suffer, and die in their prime? You want to do that to an innocent child?' He had then stood, as if wanting to approach her, and had been unsteady on his feet. She backed out of the room, shaking her head at the sight of him. Her face hadn't hidden its mask of palpable grief, but she realized that it would never be reflected back to her. Dean's mask was one of perpetual disappointment in her, and would never change, no matter how hard she tried.

She stared out from the window of her home study and perused the square fragment of the world now accessible to her. A tree, a fence, and her neighbor's house stared blankly back at her, with an understanding that they were now responsible for witnessing her pain. She rushed into the next room and pulled back the curtains. A tree, a fence, a house, and a shed. She ran to the next window. A shrub, a garbage bin, the side of a shed, and a rusted car. Tears now falling, she pulled the blind up from the bathroom. A brick wall, ivy crawling away, a rose with dead heads and a bike with a flat tire. Sobbing, she ran into the kitchen. Her arm forcing everything down from the windowsill, sending it crashing into the sink. A tree-lined street, a road-black with a white stripe, neat houses, and letter boxes for mail that would never be delivered. She fell to her knees onto the tiles and cried, shuddering from her despair.

This was the measure of her perimeter. Her inside with Dean and her outside, which would tell her when the seasons changed, what time of day it was, and whether she was alone or with neighbor. There would be no baby to grow and birth, not ever. No career to love, hate, develop, or retire from. No holidays by the sea, on the sea or flying above the sea. No friends to have over for dinner, planning a meal, laughing together, drinking, and creating memories. No complaining about the washing up after they had all left. Her life was stripped back to tree, fence, ivy, rose, mailbox, bike, rusty car, shed and house, with the addition of a drunk husband, and all of them were awaiting End Date to eliminate them.

She had stumbled upon an ad for Gaia some months later. A colorful advert had popped onto her screen, promising utopia for a privileged few. She'd thought about it for a few weeks before acting. If she added the money their parents had left them to their savings, they might be eligible. She had applied without consulting Dean, sensing that he would have said no, without asking enough questions. Gaia sounded like a refuge away, a place where she and Dean might find reconnection. She emailed Gaia their bank statements, proof of assets and photos of each of them, taken when Dean wasn't drunk. A response had come quickly, with two places in Gaia Settlement Thirteen being offered. She had replied yes, knowing that part of the deal was that they would become the property of Gaia. Dean hadn't reacted as she had expected either, telling her that he *didn't care where they went or what they did anymore.* Even when they had closed the door to their home and taken one last look back, he hadn't protested before the journey west, drunk in a haze of self-pity.

SHE WOKE Dean as they neared the peripheries of the city, the area being hammered by a violent lightning storm which was grounding several times a minute, producing sparks that raced across the sky and spot fires to ignite. She could hear sirens in the distance, slicing through the rumbles of thunder.

'Dean, we'll be at Gaia soon. Probably best if you wake up and organize the documents.'

He had woken, confused and groggy. 'How far do we have to go?'

'We're just outside of the city.'

'A new beginning, hey?' He belched, and the car was filled with rancid, alcoholic breath.

Ellie waited and then surprised herself by asking 'happy?' The word had popped into her head and seemed almost obsolete, given how things were between them.

'Yeah, I'm all good with this,' he had said robotically, peering out at the tumbling down houses, garbage littered sidewalks, and burned-out cars.

He didn't sound genuine, which made her anxiety rise. 'Have I done the right thing then?' she asked, sounding unsure of herself. 'I can always turn back before we go any further. I need both of us to be on the same page, Dean.' She slowed the car down, giving him the option to change his mind.

'I wouldn't slow down in this neighborhood, it's not safe. Keep driving. I hear Gaia has free alcohol by the way,' he had said, with some hope. Then he frowned. 'There's not much to go back to, Ellie, given you just signed over all of our assets to Gaia. You, flying solo, just created ground zero for us. Thanks for that.'

There it was, the gauntlet being thrown down and another fight being established. This time, she wouldn't bite. She couldn't be bothered. Dean would never be happy with anything that she did. The rest of the time was spent in a quiet stand-off. She pulled up at a set of large, ornate silver gates, breaking a toughened barbed-wire boundary, and pressed the enter button.

'Please say your name.'

'Ellie and Dean Monterey,' she said, leaning towards the speaker. The gates had then opened as if by divine intervention, accompanied by a loud beeping, and a security guard had asked them for their Identification Passports before allowing them to pass through the second boom gate. Leaving was then difficult, as if caught without a passport, you were given a one-way ticket to a detention center. Capturing the action of the closing gates in the rear mirror of the car, a sense of dread had passed through Ellie's body. There was something inherently final about shutting out their previous life and adopting utopia as their new home. From there, they had been stripped of their assets and welcomed into the giant Gaia machine, one which promised respite from the beast that was coming.

They sat in a simple room, painted in soothing yellow, on two white chairs next to a sky-blue table. A woman wearing pastel green had offered them water and sliced mango, and explained that their first duty was to read the Gaia Handbook and then sign the last page. They would then be taken to their living hut. Everything that was expected of them was contained in the handbook. Ellie glanced down at the pages. Breakfast was held between seven and eight each morning. Curfew was at midnight. Drinking alcohol was permitted between six and midnight. They were expected to work on a rotational work roster from nine until four each day, and after that, attend wellness circles in the evenings. That left a few hours from about eight until midnight for personal time. The paragraph that had confused Ellie was the one concerning uncoupling and how Gaia found such a notion as happy-sharing. Couples were encouraged to break their exclusive bonds and share their love with others. Dean had sniggered like a teenager.

'Wow, encouraged polyamory? I'm so glad we made the decision to move here, Ellie.'

A MONTH IN, and Ellie had started to feel unsettled, despite the routine. The procured order from chaos bordered on micro-management, and she thought that they had not only donated their assets to Gaia, but perhaps also, their free will. Dean had been leaving their hut regularly in the evenings to partake in Happy Hours, a four-hour party that ran each evening between eight and curfew in the color huts. Limitless alcohol was served during Happy Hours, to help with The Fear, the nickname for the anxiety disorder caused by End Date. Ellie had chosen to sleep through Happy Hours initially, not yet ready to face how cavernous the gap was between her and Dean.

She reached out to Dean several times to express her apprehension, but Dean was prickled by the tone of her voice, and made no effort to hide his obvious disdain for her.

'Well, given we've handed over all of our assets to Gaia. Sorry… given you handed over our assets, we don't have another option,' said Dean. 'Have gratitude for being on three hundred acres of fertile land. You're fed, you have people around you, and you have a roof over your head. For fuck's sake Ellie, what more are you hoping for, given what's flying around out there?'

She had been dismayed by his tone. She wasn't the one who had been sleeping around and drinking to excess every evening. He had signed the handbook quickly, once he'd realized that alcohol was paired with free sex. Ellie's hand had hovered, speculating how she would survive.

'I don't know…' She felt attacked by his response, but persevered in trying to articulate what was on her mind. 'I feel micro-managed, having to attend all the wellness circles. Sometimes they can be quite invasive… in terms of sharing personal information… like who has been sleeping with you lately.'

Dean snapped at her. 'You were complaining back at the house that you didn't have enough to do… despite having the tv… the ps7 and crochet! Now you're complaining that you don't have enough spare time. You chose to move us here Ellie, not me. Make your fucking mind up.'

Ellie felt confused with his reference to the crochet, given she'd only ever tried it once and had hated it. 'It's not that I don't have gratitude, Dean. It's just…' her voice trailed off.

'What Ellie? What? Just fucking what now? Why can't you ever be happy? Just for once?'

He sounded nasty. It hadn't mattered that he was stumbling into their hut after curfew each night, reeking of alcohol and other women. She had preferred not to touch him, feeling sickened by his fervent uncoupling.

'WHAT'S the point in our marriage here? Are we in trouble?' she had asked him a week later.

He had paused in his tracks, staring at her with disbelief. 'I don't know… depends on your interpretation of the point? What's the damned point in everything? Just go and have sex Ellie. Every time I speak with you, it's a negativity. Have a drink for fuck's sake. Yes? Not up for it? Ellie? No? You never really were. There's always an excuse. Other women don't complain. It's just you. Poor Ellie and her depression. Ellie doesn't feel like it. Ellie has a headache. Other women don't carry on like that. They just have sex. Great fucking sex, in fact. They just fuck.'

'Dean…' she couldn't find words. How was she supposed to want sex with him when he reeked of other women?

Dean had laughed at her expression. 'For christ's sake, Ellie. Lighten up. Yeah? Everyone is doing it. Just join in with what's on offer for once. You over think everything' he said, tapping his head. He had sauntered up to her, holding her close, grinding his hips into her, and she had flinched.

'Like that is it?' he'd asked, stepping back, the disgust written all over his face. 'Fine. You know what, Ellie? Not everyone here is all bad, as you like to suggest. We're all just doing our best while everything is falling apart out there. Maybe you should try connecting with other people, instead of shutting yourself away like this. Anyway, we're over Ellie, because *this* fell apart too… and mending *this* is too much. You know what? You're not what I need… want anymore. I need more than this! I don't even know what you want! This constant arguing and in the background… is time… ticking… ticking… ticking, Ellie. Then it's all over!' He had then stormed out of their hut, slamming the door behind him, and Ellie had stood there, staring at the door long after it had slammed shut.

She moved into a different night cabin, sharing with a woman called Josie, who read her bible and rarely spoke. It was better that way, just to be quiet and not expect anything from anybody. Sometimes she visited the Gaia library in the evenings, where she read old books that smelt like stale mango and past lives. Other evenings she took herself for long walks down along the river where the thumping of the music and screams of delight from the colored huts could be felt escaping through the dust underfoot. She was glad that Gaia couldn't read the imprint of her footsteps, her mind having become the only private space left to her.

In a sense, even if only to provide some respite, she was relieved to work from nine until four each day, fulfilling her work obligations. The occupations, as they were called, rotated every week and included plowing the fields for genetically modified, drought-resistant crops. Other days, she stood ankle-deep in suds, washing the communal clothes and hanging them to dry on ropes between the washing trees. She taught in the school, a small building that housed a few children aged between five and ten. Her least favorite rotations involved the kitchens, preparing hundreds of meals a day, and the toilets, the worst job in Gaia, where the drop toilets had to be scraped and the piles of excrement sent to the recycling center to be turned into fertilizer.

The burning doubts she had swirling around in her mind demanded to be expressed, but she didn't yet know who to trust. She had heard rumors of troublemakers who challenged command lines being forced out of the settlement. Ellie didn't yet know how people got elected for the committee, but the position came with a lengthy list of entitlements, including the right to expel. Disrespecting any Gaia philosophy was seen as a form of treason, and traitors were quickly removed from Gaia, so she had gathered.

She wandered down the river embankment, late in the day, and sat on a small, pebbly beach to mull the issues over. She had named this area 'Solitude Beach,' and it had been adopted as her thinking spot. Two problems needed to be sorted in her mind. She brought the first out into the open and introduced it to the river which, according to some, would entangle with the problem and find resolution. If she had wanted to leave Gaia, would she be free to do so? Not that she had anywhere else to go, but it was a small point of order that no-one ever discussed. Would they return her assets, for instance, such as her cash, and her car? She had felt guilty handing them over to the Illuminati, whom she knew were sitting on more assets than they could ever need. If she could have traded the cash for her parents, she would have done so, their deaths having been sudden and violent from a turbulence funnel on a flight back from Atlanta.

Dean hadn't fared much better, when six months later, he had lost his parents on a freeway smash, during an intense ice storm. The result of all of this though, she surmised, was that starting again, without the support of family, the financial certainty of career or the sense of belonging from community was near impossible. She picked up a pebble and threw it into the river. It disappeared quickly below the surface, reminding Ellie how quickly she too, could just disappear.

The other complication was more subtle. She felt troubled that older people weren't seen very often in her Gaia community. There were rumors of a Gaia Intentional Older Community, where older and more vulnerable individuals were relocated to. Ellie's own observations supported this, as one day, an older person was there, and the next day they weren't. Ellie worried that they never said goodbye though, like Margaret, the lady who had sat at her breakfast table for the first two weeks. She was there one day and then wasn't there anymore. It appeared plausible, but there was the disquiet again, niggling in her mind. Why no goodbyes? She took a deep breath. This life… was so different. Certainty was gone and in its place? A fragile game of chance, the rules set by others. Maybe she needed to stay in Gaia? If she could get used to the micro-management, the endless brainwashing, and the dictatorial nature of the leadership, perhaps, for the time being, it was the safest place to be?

I need to quote a line here. 'It appeared plausible.' No Ellie. Nothing about Gaia is plausible. They executed them. I'm telling y'all now. We don't have time for Ellie to figure this out. We're short on time itself. That commodity that you don't value until you know the end is coming. Then the sound of the clock becomes insistent, urgent, and demands priority. So, I'm interjecting. She didn't see any older people, any troublemakers, or people who wanted to leave because they murdered them on the quiet when no-one was looking. They saw humans in need as humans who were *needy*. Same with the disabled, same with the sick, same with the trouble-makers. They never admitted to doing this, as the action may have clashed with the propaganda machine that reinforced them as a sanctuary, not a murder camp. Politically incorrect? Hell yeah. Only everyone was too busy with their own shit to have the energy to notice… or to care. This was a new time though, one that didn't have the resources to pander to weakness. If you were weak, they killed you. It was Lord of the Flies, Gaia style.

It wasn't barbaric, as if that justifies it. It was an injection that was supposed to be vitamins. They didn't know they were going to die from a lethal concoction. It was made off site, consisting of sodium thiopental, pancuronium bromide, morphina duralasal, and potassium chloride. Quick and painless too. Individuals were quietly invited to the Health Center for a health checkup. No-one could put two and two together because they were told that more serious medical conditions had been moved out. Most were gullible to believe that too, except Ellie, who wasn't busy feeling everyone else in sight and too drunk to think straight. That's why she still had space in her head for objective reasoning.

Want to know what they did next? You do, don't you? Ready for this? They cremated them and then sprinkled their ashes into the mangrove swamp. Yeah, it's illegal to spread ashes, I know. They knew that too, but no-one was following close enough. Mangroves are halophytic - in other words, they love salt, and people become salt when burned down into tiny grains. The mangroves thrived when the humans died. Every Gaia community had a mangrove swamp. Here's the hilarious bit, though. Some person, when the communities first started, got confused between mangrove and a mango. So, when they were choosing what should be used for the Gaia symbol of trust, they decided on a mango, thinking it grew in mangrove swamps. Anyway, to salvage their dignity at having made this mistake, they created a ritual whereby unripe mangos would then be left under the mangroves, then covered in the ashes. So, the sun and people's remains helped to warm them and ripen them. Fruit covered in people I'm telling y'all. They tasted delicious too, as if once you burned all the nastiness out of humans, what was left, turned unripe fruit into something special.

10

IT'S GUTTERAL

YOU KNOW

Ellie was uncomfortably placed on the floor, having been told to sit cross-legged for the well-being meeting. The term conjured up ambitions of health, comfort, and happiness. Instead, as Ellie had so far experienced, the meetings would provide another opportunity for the Gaia doctrine to be shoved down her throat. Known as the Eight Commandments, and recited at the start of each meeting, they were printed in red on a wooden sign that was positioned in the middle of each circle. Two sunny yellow mangos were placed on either side of the sign, neither wanting to sit up and participate.

This beating of a drum indicated that the meeting was about to start. The twenty individuals sitting in the circle shut their eyes, as was expected during the entrance of their leader. Ellie peeked through one eye, and saw a young man with wiry dreadlocks, energetically hitting a drum skin with dedicated fervor. Other eyes remained tightly shut, not daring to challenge protocol. The leader, a woman in her fifties, strode around the back of the circle, periodically pausing to deliver one of the Commandments. The individual she stopped behind would be tapped on the shoulder, and later, would be expected to add some insight into their interpretation of that particular Commandment.

The woman roared at the end of the recitation, expelling all the air from her lungs, before dramatically collapsing to the floor. Ellie had snuck a quick glance from out of both eyes at this dramatic entrance closure, and could see that no-one else was peeking. Her right eyebrow had shot up, though, surprised at the staged melodrama, as two members of the circle then dragged the moaning woman by the elbows into the center. Both mangos were placed either side of her head and it was in this position, flat out, with mango ears, that she commenced her introduction. Ellie had snorted several giggles, feeling like a naughty school child, desperately trying to convert them into a well-executed coughing fit.

The woman lay there in silence only punctuated by Ellie's coughing and then quietly recited all eight Commandments.

Our higher power is Gaia. We sit before Gaia as a lesser consciousness and acknowledge her greatness.

We will not kill to eat, or maim out of pleasure through sport.

Everything else is shared amongst us, including our thoughts.

We own nothing as currency.

Procreation to produce children is forbidden.

We will remain positive only in thoughts, words and actions.

We do not partake in illegal activities, in accordance with Gaia's Constitution.

We will abide by all rules as constructed by the Illuminati and executed by the Gaia Board.

With the Commandments having been said, she sat up and started to peel back the two mangos.

'We will share,' she declared with way too much solemnity, and everyone had then opened their eyes, pleased to have been released from their darkened awareness. 'We will eat the body of Gaia.' The mangos were then cut up, and a plate passed around. Before eating, everyone thanked Gaia profusely for their goodness.

Today's leader was named Jenny, according to her name tag. She stood, once everyone had finished eating, and took a deep breath. As she exhaled, she lifted up her hands, and the circle inhaled deeply. As her hands were brought down, the ring exhaled. A small drum was put in front of her and she started to pound a steady beat with her hand. The wellness circle began to chant through the Commandments, sturdy with conviction. Once complete, Jenny smiled, catching the eyes of all in the circle.

'Welcome to wellness this evening. I am Jenny. We will now deliver the power tower, our symbol of thought transmission to the universe.' A blue plastic tower with an amethyst stuck to the top was then carefully placed into the center of the circle. Jenny stared upwards, and all eyes had followed. Ellie was disappointed to see only the ceiling of the hut.

'Take now a moment of quiet contemplation as you reassure the universe about your commitment to the Commandments.'

The group went quiet and brows furrowed earnestly, as each member recited them again in their own mind. Ellie's mind wandered to forbidden pregnancy. She knew that women who got pregnant in Gaia, not that it happened very often, were immediately offered abortions. There was a rumor, overheard in the dining hall, that one woman had hidden her pregnancy for six months and had been transferred to a different Gaia community.

Ellie studied Jenny, now rhythmically patting the skin of the drum, precisely to sixty beats per minute. Jenny oozed out her words, like toothpaste from a tube, or shit from an arse, Ellie surmised. Words that were strung together as if having been googled from a search on *spiritual bullshit*.

'My seedlings,' Jenny announced suddenly. 'I, as your Oak, will now lead you in a cleansing. We remember who we were, who we are, and what we will become.'

Two other women stood, and everyone was asked to lay flat, with enough space around them to stretch out their arms and legs. Jenny walked around, correcting posture, and then directed the group to regress.

'Now you are a child of the earth. Imagine that you have a soul of pure white inside of you. As years pass and experiences are acquired, your soul becomes tarnished and contaminated from negative emotions. Black even, in some cases.' She paused.

That's me, Ellie surmised. A soul as black as tar.

The drumbeat, sixty beats per minute.

'Let it out, my seedlings. All of it and cleanse yourselves. Leave the old behind and embrace the new.'

Ellie held her breath. She could feel the snigger building, needing to be expressed. She self-talked. Restrain it. Hold it in. Control it. No, it's building. Down. Stop Ellie. This is serious. Do *not* laugh. They can tell a laugh from a cough. The drum though… then, the surrounding individuals started moaning and yelling out, as if in pain. She coughed, and against all the odds, broke wind at the same time. Out came the laugh. A pure vomit of a giggle which had started with a snort. Nothing that could ever have been disguised as anything else.

Ellie opened her eyes to see if anyone was looking, happy that the laugh had gone, and mortified by the noise she had made. What was this, though? Was this how people cleansed? The two women approached Ellie, obviously incensed by her combined laugh and expulsion of air.

'Close your eyes,' one of them said as she knelt beside her. She placed her hands on Ellie's abdomen. 'It comes out from deep within. It's guttural, Ellie. Let it all go.'

Ellie had just laid there, tightening her abdominal muscles in response to this stranger's touch. If the woman pressed any harder, she was going to let rip. She could feel more air percolating around in there. Maybe they wanted her to moan or something, like everyone else? She remained mute, lying on the floor, listening to the distressing sounds radiating from everyone else.

'You are blocked,' the woman told her with a tone of over-the-top seriousness. 'It is okay, your releases will come in time,' she said, standing back up. Ellie fought to keep herself controlled. She imagined the release... more intestinal than spiritual.

Jenny indicated that the cleansing had finished and that her talk would begin. The group murmured in anticipation and settled comfortably onto the floor. Again, Ellie looked around, expecting someone to catch her eye and smile conspiratorially with her. No-one did, meaning that she was the only person finding the proceedings vaguely amusing. Jenny explained that as seedlings, it was anticipated that they would soon grow through her teachings into saplings, and then into oaks. That was, if climate change didn't burn them all down before they had flourished, Ellie had thought in response, amusing only herself.

'Gaia loves us just as your God loves you. But we, my seedlings, are being punished for crimes to our planet that we committed and did not ask forgiveness for.'

Ellie wondered about the irony of worshipping Gaia, who, it turned out, was also trying to kill them all.

'We breathe in Gaia, allowing our minds to empty, and we breathe out our negativity.' Jenny sounded breathless as if trying to replicate spiritual. 'We thank the Gaia committee for allowing us to be here. We, members of Gaia Thirteen, safe and secure from The Fear and The Chaos. Our Board is leading us with compassion, and we follow that lead their wisdom and their way.'

The group responded by raising their palms to the sky, as if part of an evangelical congregation, and gave thanks to the committee. Ellie looked around the group, realizing that they truly believed in all of this. Gaia had become a God and the Board, her disciples. Jenny then gave what Ellie likened to a sermon, a long rambling, ill-prepared soliloquy about gratitude for Gaia, and they were told about the horrors that were unfolding outside of the silver gates. Four times, Jenny repeated that it was better to be in Gaia than outside of it, and not one other person sitting around the circle questioned any of it.

After the meditation session, in which Ellie had accidentally fallen asleep, awakening to the disapproving eyes of the circle piercing through her, they were invited to stay for drinks and a social chat. Ellie remembered a quote from a textbook about the Second World War, something about loose lips costing lives. She noticed as Jenny bided her time in a corner, discretely watching the group unwinding and drinking. The music was being played too loudly, forcing them to shout to be heard. Jenny then visited each of them, asking too many questions from tipsy individuals, full of free alcohol and eager to please. The rest of the group opened up to Jenny as if she were their long-lost friend. Jenny was careful to tilt her head to one side as if listening empathetically to them, smiling and nodding where she needed to. This didn't fool Ellie though, as she presumed that Jenny was there to find out if they were following the rules, collecting snippets of gossip that the Board needed to know about.

'Ellie, isn't it? How are you settling in?' Jenny beamed at her, placing one hand on her arm.

Ellie tried not to recoil. The hand needed to remain, in order to prove that there was a sincere connection between the two of them. The hand meant that anything said would need to be honest, because it was near her pulse.

'Jenny, I'm so impressed with this meditation process. I can empty my mind like this.' She deliberately moved her arm to click her fingers, making Jenny's hand redundant in the air. If she tried to put it back on, the action would look contrived and out of place.

Jenny smiled at her. 'I'm so glad you like it, although you should try to stay awake Ellie during meditation. Also, don't be afraid to cleanse. Stay within your inner circle of discontent and observe it with curiosity. Gaining control over our fears is important at a time like this. Trusting Gaia is even more so.'

'I agree totally,' said Ellie, not understanding where her inner circle of discontent resided on her person. 'I'm happy we got a place here, Dean and I. We're so happy with it all and Dean is fully embracing uncoupling, as am I.'

Jenny looked at her, scanning for hints of sarcasm. Ellie knew what to do. Keep her eyebrows relaxed, crinkle the corners of her eyes to indicate a genuine smile and maintain eye contact with Jenny. 'Good,' murmured Jenny, her voice relaxing, having assumed that Ellie was genuine. 'We are lucky here, and I am so glad that you and Dean have reached an understanding. We are aware that he has embraced the uncoupling and appears to be very happy here.' She placed her hand on Ellie's arm once more and apologized as she had to move on.

Ellie allowed her face to resume a normal position, one that fell into a place of annoyance, based in the frustration she was feeling with everything. The meeting had made her feel fed-up, with its blatant cult-like process of weakening people's resolves and substituting it all with the supposed 'higher power' of Gaia. The sickening aspect was that people were so desperate to have their own burdens taken off them, that they embraced anything that looked to be an anchor, even a mango. Then there was the sheer farcical nature of that meeting. A break from reality that highlighted the disparity between the horror on one side of the fence and the crazy on the other side.

THE NEXT MORNING, she woke feeling better, knowing that she was on planting occupation for the week. Being out and alone, meandering up and down the planting field would provide her with some quality time to think.

'Morning Bob,' she had chirped. She quite like Bob, a tanned, middle-aged man who was in charge of the fields, and who allocated the seeds into the planting baskets each morning.

As usual, the exchange would be limited to small talk.

'Morning, Ellie. You've got a beautiful day for it,' he said, indicating out towards the fields.

'Indeed, Bob. We are lucky that Gaia knew where blue skies could still be found when they bought this land. Couldn't really ask for more, could I?' She strapped on the planting belt, consisting of two large wicker baskets that sat either side on her hips, and Bob filled them with the small kernels, before opening the gates to field one, for her.

'You'll do this section today and move into field two tomorrow. Kalex is planting fields three and four. Then you'll be helping me with Banjo for the rest of the week to plow field eight.'

'Understood. I can't wait to work with Banjo again. I'll see you back here at eleven for my break.'

She carefully walked along the furrows. Each had been neatly plowed by Banjo, Gaia's sixteen-hand stock horse, who was grey dapple with a long white mane. Ellie loved spending time with him, as he had a habit of resting his heavy head into her arms and sighing, as if he, too, was fed up with it all. She stopped, exactly every three steps, to reach down and place a small yellow kernel into the soil. She gently covered each one with a blanket of the powdery brown soil and wished it well. There was still enough rainfall in this part of the state to warrant planting crops, the Gaia land having been purchased after careful analysis of predictive rainfall research.

She paused to raise her face towards the sun, feeling its warmth on her body and face. Not so hot that she required a hat, but the sort of heat in the air that gives you a feeling of wellbeing and hope. She stopped and looked around, trying to determine where her mind was at. She didn't want her life to end in this place, that much she knew. She thought this had been what she had wanted, when stuck in the house with Dean. Now, though, she felt as if she had swapped one prison for another. She didn't know what the alternative was, but she felt stifled by these rules, especially ones so obviously created by other people that mostly benefited a small few, namely the members of the Board. They slept in prestige buildings, along with the luxuries that had been donated, and Ellie presumed that the cash also managed to find its way into their clutches as well. They ate better food, had access to baths, and often drove the donated cars out of the community on trips. It was a far cry from her small wooden hut, restricted diet and sense that she was contained within four boundary fences with no escape.

She knew that Dean would berate her thoughts and wondered if she were being ungrateful for at least finding relative safety. However, Gaia was a cult in her eyes, where a select few, exploited the many others and remained only accountable to their own set of rules. But it was still better, in many ways, to the alternatives that were on offer. She shuddered at the thought of being forced to live in one of the tent cities for the homeless. They were appalling, so she'd heard, with the Military in full command and where rations were strictly issued. Gaia was still the better option, even if a cult disguised as utopia. Maybe she needed to be more grateful, at least for the time being.

She devised a game plan in her mind that offered her options. Lie low, plant the corn, speak when asked and maybe drink, but not to excess. That way, she would look like she was following the tide of acceptable. She bent down and planted another kernel, noticing a drying worm, recoiling from being stranded in the sun. Using her finger to break the soil, she guided it back into the cooler, dark earth, hoping that Gaia herself had noticed her kind act and would reward her in the future. She needed to find her way back too, although, to what, she didn't yet know. However, deep down inside of her, she knew she wanted more than this. She wanted the choice to decide how to personalize her life, however much was left of it, that was, and live it with some degree of authenticity. The planting of the worm presented itself metaphorically to her at that moment and felt as if her idea had been set into motion. The idea to find her way back to a sense of home and find something better.

11

BALLS

ARE ON THE LUNCH MENU

Belcher was back from the devastated north, having shaken hands only where beneficial, and relegating responsibility for the clean-up to Jonas and his team. The area mauled by the fire-tornados didn't have much left for her to peruse, aside from charcoal trunks and steel framed homes. It was obvious that the area would be relegated to Occludo, as the clean-up and rebuild would have cost more than she was willing to give. The military had marched the survivors off quickly, meaning that she hadn't needed to speak to them and offer condolences for family members lost, and possessions destroyed. She had been relieved not to have been forced into the small talk, preferring instead to ensure that the cremations were organized with efficiency. The breathing mask was uncomfortable on her face anyway, having a tendency to smear her Chanel and trying to speak articulately through it was difficult.

'Jonas. What is your plan for the cremation ashes?' she asked, watching the smoke billowing into the sky, high above her.

'Madam President, we have several tons of ashes currently being loaded into trucks. We've sold them onto Highgate Industries for the eastern barley crops.'

'Excellent Jonas. Efficient, practical and less messy than having the wind blow them everywhere. No-one wants to be coated in residual misery. How much profit will we be able to extract, and what's the status update for the area?'

'We received market value per pound, Madam President. Currently sitting at seventy-five cents. I believe the total profit figure was around thirty-five thousand dollars. We are relocating the refugees to Nashville as we speak and the badly burned have been sleeped and included into the current cremations. Anyone who doesn't make health level seven by the time they get there will also be sleeped. We should have a wrap up here in approximately a week.'

'How many have been sleeped so far, Jonas?'

'Approximately fifteen hundred, Madam President.'

'Send those funds to Nashville and ensure that these survivors are commenced on level two rations. That money is going to have to sustain them until the next budget round commences. Now, tell me more about these fire tornados, Jonas. Are we expecting more of this?'

'Madam President, from what we can ascertain, they follow a fairly set, seasonal path through the north, in a corridor west to east. We are hoping that for the time being at least, evacuation of the area should prevent another catastrophe like this one, thus the Occludo request.'

She looked sharply at him. 'Do you think catastrophe is an appropriate word Jonas, given this was expected?'

Jonas was caught off guard. 'I… no, Madam President. It appears to be a naturally occurring weather event.'

'Exactly Jonas. I don't want the world thinking we are struggling. Our Country has not been completely inundated by the sea, like Bangladesh. Our water didn't run out like India, and nor did half of our country burn like Australia. This was a minor event and one which we have handled appropriately. That's the exact wording for the press. Do you understand Jonas?'

'Yes, Madam President.'

'Also, our sleeping procedures are off-limits to the press. No numbers and no methodology. Now, am I needed here anymore?'

'Madam President, it might be a good show of character to visit the refugee camp in Nashville. It would allow your people to see that you are aware of their new… contexts.' Jonas was concerned that the President had no concept of the difficulties facing her own climate refugees. The rations, especially those set at levels one to three, were barely sustaining people, and illness and disease were rife. Currently, they were losing twenty-five percent of refugees within the first four months of relocation.

'How will that benefit me?' she asked, looking surprised by his invitation.

'It might demonstrate that you care and that you are doing your best in difficult times. A human touch to a lot of misery right now.'

Belcher pondered the benefit. Was there any point in visiting the large refugee tent cities? It wouldn't benefit re-election as she had dismantled the voting rights of refugees. She knew that half would die in the camps within the first two years from a lack of adequate medical treatment and that most were near-starving. Her funds needed to be channeled appropriately into the plan for the survival of herself and our species. What was the point in channeling it towards millions of displaced people, many of whom were going to die, anyway? It was best that she remain focused on the project and not waste her time, sloshing through human excrement in random tent cities.

'I'm heading straight over to Mayweather, instead Jonas. I'll need the chopper. I'd rather get back into doing something more politically practical. No need for further humanitarian diversions.'

Jonas sighed quietly. Belcher was a heartless bitch of a woman, but then the job needed someone like her. The rest of the world leaders were still dazed from the melting and had gone too quiet. At least Belcher was still willing to stand in amongst some misery, unlike the rest of them who hid behind their desks and sent their representatives on their behalf.

'Madam President, Mayweather is expecting you. I'll leave you in the capable hands of Alley Barber in the meantime. She has been fully briefed concerning the week's schedule. I'll finalize everything here and then meet you in Mayweather later in the week for the financial discussions.'

'Who the hell is Ali Baba? Although I might need a genie looking at this mess. Thank you, Jonas. I appreciate your efficiency in these matters. Have you been updated concerning the particulars of the financial matters?'

'Yes, Madam President. I believe we are expecting an influx of special financial considerations from world leaders. We have liaised with the Finance Master to be in Mayweather to channel the additional funds into the appropriate special trusts, as requested.'

'Good. Then we are all sorted. Now, where is this Alley Genie woman?'

BELCHER WAS BACK, standing in the lab, impatiently demanding an update. Jack was hopeful that the initial investigative work that he, Pete, Tina and Paul had started on the notion of limitations, would be good enough for Belcher to at least allow him to keep both of his balls. Her expression looked like she was about to blow them off.

'Why are we still talking about developing a limiter after an entire week? This is being done at a rate controlled by pussies Jack.' Belcher pursed her lips together, the allure stain having bled into her marionette lines. Jack imagined pulling strings at the back of her head, making her head tilt back, and her jaw laugh in a hideous way.

'Jack. I'm waiting for something intelligent to come out of your mouth.'

'Yes, of course, limitations.' He could see her head bobbing up and down in his fantasy, the strings being pulled so far back that her head snapped off. He willed himself back into the room.

'More,' snapped Belcher. 'From someone who can string two words together in a succinct manner.'

Jack stared. Had she seen him snap her head off in his mind?

Paul stepped forward. 'If I may?' he asked, indicating to the whiteboard.

'Good,' Belcher replied. 'Short, snappy.' Her words punctuated by the click of her fingers. 'Let's get to the point.' She looked at her phone. 'I'm due in my office for a phone call in three minutes.'

Jack sighed. She did this all the time. She would allocate a time slot entirely insufficient to draw knowledge out of him and then make a point of being rushed. It was yet another of her manipulative tactics designed to make him feel frantic and rushed. A power play to keep him feeling frazzled and beneath her. He shook his head slightly at the thought of ever being underneath her.

Paul drew a circle on the whiteboard and labelled it *brain*. 'So, if we increase IQ, we do so globally.' He scribbled in the whole of the circle. 'This means that over time, the novelty of adopted experience as a consequence of the microchip is overtaken by the desire to experiment with this new intelligence. The person will start to look for ways to expand their new experiences, power and anticipated happiness. Adapt what they have been given to suit their own desires essentially. That's basic human nature, and the self-learning component of the chip encourages this.'

'And?' Belcher looked at her phone again. 'Meaning what?' she asked, not looking up and scrolling a message instead with a bony red thumb.

'So,' said Tina, jumping in. 'We are working on ways to limit beliefs that may deviate an individual from doing what *we* need them to do. Control that desire to further experience change. A form of mind control that is humane, regulated and safe.'

'I see,' said Belcher, staring back at the whiteboard. She looked at Tina. 'I like you. You can articulate things using a minimum of words. However, I suggest a reduction of one more word. Regulated. Nothing about what we are doing is regulated. However, keep the chip suckers doing what we want. I like it. Keep going and give me more updates in forty-eight hours.'

Jack sat down as the sound of her heels faded down the corridor. He instinctively felt his balls in his pants. Both were still there, shrunken with the fear of what Belcher was going to say. He didn't know why her petty bullying scared him so profoundly, but there was just something about her intention to make everyone feel inadequate and useless that got into his psyche. Why she had put the labs into the actual Presidency building was ridiculous. It didn't fit together, the plush carpets up in one wing, and the sterile labs in another. The whole setting was bizarre. They also hadn't made much progress at all, if the truth be told. The dynamic between them, as a team, was flat, hostile, and unhelpful, a sure way to kill scientific creativity and progress.

Paul collected a stress ball from the window ledge and then sat, throwing it into the air. He stared at Jack as if thinking about what to say. Tina looked from Paul to Jack sensing the unrest between them which was less than subtle. Pete sat down and lowered his gaze, clearly needing to distance himself from what was inevitably going to get ugly.

Jack spoke first. 'Look, whatever went on all those years ago… what we need now is to put our heads together. We're trying to help save the human race here. Can't we just forget? Isn't it time to move on?' His generous statement was met with silence.

Paul's fingers started drumming on the table. 'Forget? Just like that. Really Jack? Like take a magic pill and all those nasty memories… just what… go away?'

'Well, let's not try to deal with it in here,' said Jack, indicating to the cameras. 'I'm not discussing this shit when the whole building could be watching.'

Belcher laughed in her office. Watching Jack try to negotiate his way through his past issues was better than any daytime soap. She knew that he had traits that resembled her own. That he needed no-one and that he used people to get what he wanted, leaving a train wreck of carnage in his path.

'Lunchtime Jack.' Paul frowned at him. 'I need to sort this out today.'

'I know. I can tell. We'll work for now and then have a chat over lunch. Okay?' He didn't want to sound pleading, but they needed to put their personal grievances aside and start getting on with the job.

'Fine,' said Paul, sending the stress ball hard at the whiteboard.

Immature dick, thought Jack.

Belcher laughed. She knew that Paul had every intention of ensuring that Jack's balls were on the lunch menu.

'Right,' said Jack, walking towards the whiteboard. He rubbed off the brain circle and drew an X.

'This is our person. We implant the chip which has been programed with say, the medical package. We want person X to stay being a Doctor. We don't want them to decide that they want to be a candle maker, three months after receiving the chip. How do we do that?'

'We could use command repetition,' suggested Tina, reasoning out aloud. 'Repeat information as per the initial directive. Reinforces what we want the individual to do by creating strong neural pathways? Although no guarantees that other neural pathways wouldn't be established. Nah, discount that,' she added, realizing the suggestion was weak at best.

'Yeah, there's no guarantee that other highways couldn't be created in parallel,' agreed Jack. 'Pete?'

Pete sat up and engaged. 'I've been thinking more along the lines of assassin limitations actually, similar to how certain molecules can trigger kill switches in cells. If we transfer this idea into the human mind and into the world of *thoughts,* we could get a killer release of neurotransmitter that wipes out the thought before it has had time to get into short-term memory. Set it all onto automatic pilot.'

Jack nodded. 'I've been looking at something similar. So, we could create a small implant component, say, of noalinergicine neurons, churning out hyrantrocholine, that would wipe selected thoughts from being stored? Which is where you could come in Tina. We'd need to pre-empt those selected thoughts.'

Tina approached the whiteboard. 'It might be possible to create a list of predictive thoughts, which trigger off hyrantrocholine, better than introducing nolinergicines into the equation as they can erode sheath traders. That might affect motor skills, which we don't want, especially in our tradies.'

Jack nodded. 'I hear possibilities here. This gives me hope,' he said to the two of them, ignoring Paul, who had remained silent. 'We might just be on to something.'

BELCHER TURNED off the CCTV monitor. Her phone appointment was late, which was unsatisfactory. She spotted a fly that had touched down on her desk, and with the palm of her hand, she smashed into it, squashing it. She studied the bloodied paste on her palm, wondering if she would look as generic if crushed. Sniffing the small corpse and noting the acrid aroma, she then flicked the little body into her garbage bin and wiped the residual mess onto her trousers, leaving a smear of past tense in the process.

THE TEAM of scientists worked until lunch discussing and planning the limiter, and then made their way into the central courtyard cafe, now sizzling underfoot from the searing mid-day heat. They chose a table under the grapevines, relieved to have found one which was cooled by the maze of green vine leaves hanging from the pergola above them. They sat in an uncomfortable truce, with an unspoken agreement to order lunch first and then deal with the festering stuff for dessert. They ate mainly in silence, taking time to enjoy the fresh air, heat on their skin, and the comfort of the food, which stifled the brewing pressure. Pete excused himself to the bathroom just as Paul volunteered his words.

'Have you got any idea, even a tiny bit Jack, as to how your actions cascaded into a domino of crap that went on to destroy my family?'

He searched Jack's face for acknowledgment, his own burning red from a sudden increase in blood pressure.

Jack recognized that his actions had indeed been unacceptable, but as low as they had been, it hadn't justified what Paul had done to him afterward. He didn't like Paul's blanket supposition that he was the only culprit. He would admit that his actions were wrong, but only if Paul completed the circle of apology, instead of having gone all amnesia on him. However, to heal and move forward, or whatever creative new-age words he needed to use, the priority was that they needed to work together and better. Without all this crap getting in the way of creating what was needed for the chip. He chose his words carefully, knowing that one of them needed to spell sorry.

'Okay, so we need to apologize to each other, in order to move forward. I'm sorry, Paul. I get it. I think in hindsight, with maturity being on our side, that we both obviously did wrong.'

'What? Both of us? Are you fucking serious?' Paul glared at him. 'Yeah, both of us, Paul. I may have inadvertently started it, but you most definitely finished it off.'

'You're a turd, Jack.'

'Sorry? What? A turd? How old are you Paul? That's what I get for swallowing humble pie and saying the words I'm sorry? You call me a turd? Wow. That's just so damned charming.' Jack stood up, asserting his dominance. 'A turd hey? Is that the best you can come up with?'

'Sit down, for God's sake.' Tina said, reapplying her lipstick after she had left most of it on her salad roll. 'People are watching.'

'Yeah, you are a turd Jack. In fact, you know what?'

'What?' Jack braced for the next insult.

'I quit.'

'You what?' Tina stared at Paul, with her lipstick frozen between her hand and mouth.

'I quit. I can't do this. There are no words that will ever explain, justify or excuse, what you did.' He stood up, scrunched up his napkin, and threw it onto the table.

'Wait… you can't just leave Paul. Sit down. We can sort this out.' Jack was blindsided.

'No, we can't, Jack. I should never have agreed to any of this. I apologize if it creates issues with the chip and the project.'

'So, you can apologize for that and not what you did to me?'
'Seems so. Not that I fucking well did anything to you.'

'What *did* you two do to each other?' asked Tina, bewildered at the unfolding tension in front of her.

Jack was fuming. 'Well, Paul here stole my thesis hypothesis and submitted his work first. I had no idea he'd done that until I got called in to explain my own, which of course, was then labeled as plagiarism. It delayed my thesis for several months… made worse, by the fact that Paul then patented the ideas *we* had been working on, in his name only. I had no legal recourse either because Paul wiped away all the proof. Did they make you rich, Paul? Did you make lots of money from being a treacherous twat?'

'Shut your mouth, Jack. What the fuck? A twat? Who the hell uses that insult anymore other than a twat? You don't get to call me a twat.'

Tina frowned. 'I can think of worse things, Paul, to be called. Tell me you didn't do that. Really? That's just shitty.'

'Why? Anyone would have done it. It was payback for Jack's behavior. Yes, the ideas were financially very viable, as it turned out. Are you going to tell her, Jack?'

'Why don't you do it for me twat-turd? I'm sure you would love to,' Jack said, his words dripping with sarcasm.

Paul looked at Tina. 'Fucker Jack here, managed to get my girlfriend pregnant.'

Tina looked confused. 'Are you talking about Sally?'

'Oh, so he's already filled you in?' Paul looked surprised.

'No. You do remember, Paul, that Sally was my best friend, and that I was dating Jack? Not that his behavior is excusable. The minute I found out that Sally was pregnant, I dumped him. You and she had broken up though at the time. Jack saw an opportunity, and the rest is old news.'

'Whose side are you on?' Paul demanded angrily.

'I'm not taking sides, Paul. This isn't a game. Please sit down.' She glanced over at Jack, who was frozen on the spot. He hadn't said anything in response. 'Jack, they had broken up, hadn't they?' She waited for him to reply. He didn't.

'See? He can't even speak,' said Paul. 'A fucking mute twat-turd.'

'Hang on, Jack. Are you saying that Sally was still with Paul and you slept with her… while still being in a relationship with me? This is worse than being back at college. Seriously. I'm embarrassed to be at this table right now.' She looked around the cafe as if searching for a different table to sit at.

Pete arrived back. 'What's happening guys…?' he asked, before stopping mid-sentence.

Tina spoke. 'We have an awkward stand-off, Pete. Paul is threatening to leave over something that happened twenty years ago.' She turned back to Paul. 'I don't get how this affected your family though, to the point where they fell apart?'

'My parents believed that I was the one who had got Sally pregnant. My father called me irresponsible and my mother said I'd ruined the family's reputation. It caused endless arguments between my parents, and they ended up divorcing.'

'Why did your father sucker punch me then, at the dorms?' Jack instinctively reached up to his face again, remembering the solid hit that had sent him flying, forcing him to eat soft baby food for two weeks.

'That doesn't make any sense Paul,' reflected Tina. 'If they blamed you, why did they hit Jack? Why would your parents' relationship fail solely over that? Why did you take Jack's work? Wow,' she said, shaking her head, 'that's a lot of crap for one breath.'

'Are those serious questions? Ones that you actually want me to entertain?' Paul shook his head, moving away from the table. 'The lot of you can piss off.'

'Yes. I'm serious,' said Tina. 'Did you get her pregnant, make Jack the fall-guy and then steal Jack's work, because the opportunity for payback presented itself?'

'Fuck off, Tina.'

'Don't you fucking swear at me,' she said angrily.

Pete was confused. 'So, when will you be back, Paul?'

Paul walked forwards, extended out his hand and shook Pete's. 'Never actually,' and walked away.

'Wait!' called out Tina. 'Answer the questions, fucker!'

. . .

BELCHER STOOD in front of the three of them an hour later. 'So, I can confirm that I have employed children to save the human race?'

'No, I'm sorry,' said Jack. 'His behavior was completely unacceptable. There was no warning…' he looked quickly at Tina and Pete for backup.

'I'm sorry?' Belcher looked incredulous. 'His behavior? Just his behavior and not your own?'

'No. Mine too. I should not have engaged like that in a public space. I apologize.'

'Yes, me too,' added Tina.

'So, where has Paul actually gone?' Belcher asked, looking from one face to another.

'I think he resigned,' Tina muttered. 'Jack's right though, he just got up and walked out.'

'Right, well, it's now down to three. It will be interesting to see if we have anyone left to save humanity at the rate this is going. Does anyone else intend to walk off?'

'No,' they replied, in a chorus, sounding like three naughty children.

'Good. I'm off to be the President. It's a good thing that I don't just get up and leave, isn't it.'

'I NEED to de-brief at some point, Jack. That was ridiculous.' Tina plonked herself down into a chair. 'Just so unprofessional, all of it. Paul is a dickhead. I cannot believe he got up and just quit. Who does that?'

'I agree. My place for dinner, maybe? You free?'

'No, sorry. Exercise class over at a friend's house tonight.'

'I'm busy tonight, sorry guys,' said Pete.

'You weren't invited,' replied Jack.

'Don't take it out on me. I'm not the enemy,' said Pete. 'I was at the bathroom and I came back to that load of shit.'

'Agreed,' said Tina. 'You can't put this on Pete, Jack. He was the only one not swearing in public.'

'Fair enough,' said Jack. 'Is it at all possible for us to concentrate on this project and get some real work done?'

12

LOSING FRIENDS

AND NOT INFLUENCING PEOPLE

Ellie checked the daily schedule, hoping for changes. She sighed. Nope, she was still on toilet duty for the week. Her name was also on the list for another *Concerns Circle,* which was going to interfere with her intention to walk the river trail after dinner. The circle meetings always went over, eating into her private time. *Concern Circles* were the equivalent of most committee meetings, in which inconsequential shit was discussed with the same enthusiasm as one might discuss philosophy. She had been hoping to enjoy the evening air, feel the warmth of a balmy setting sun and listen to the river bubbling past her. A trifecta that had always made her feel better about residing in Gaia. Instead, she would be sitting on a wooden floor, listening to other people droning on about small stuff, ad nauseam.

She had approached the toilet block with trepidation, knowing fully well that this was the worst job in Gaia, and that her entire body would be covered in other people's excrement by the end of the day. Tod, the toilet coordinator, was enthusiastically outlining the day's schedule to four other people who'd arrived early.

'First, anyone who tells you that their shit doesn't stink is a liar.' He had smiled at his well-used opening line. Not getting a huge response from his audience, he tried again. 'People who say that bullshit doesn't stick is wrong.' He was the only one who then laughed, chuckling in spurts, waiting for an echo. Instead, a silence wearing only a mask of indignation had presented itself, along with exhaled sighs of misery.

'Bullshit… shit? Yes? Cause it's sticky and hard to get off the boots in particular.' Tod wasn't the best at reading social cues, and their lack of enthusiasm didn't dampen his attempts to provide satirical commentary. Several members of the group lifted their feet up and down, checking the underside to see how much residue had already stuck to their soles.

'Get into the suits, and I'll explain what needs to be done,' Tod said, grinning way too eagerly, his nostrils flaring in excitement with his shit-coloured eyebrows high above brown eyes.

Ellie tugged at the boots, forcing them up and over her calves. She tucked the hazmat suit into them, as instructed. Todd helped her to place the full-face mask over her head, complete with its own air filtration system. The last item of the unattractive toilet uniform was a pair of clumsy rubber gloves that hung off over the end of her fingers, making her hands look enormous. Tod had pulled at the tying strings on her wrists to secure them into place.

'Okay, very important not to take the suits off, especially the masks. Yes?' he shouted at them, assuming the masks had made them all profoundly deaf, despite their open ears.

They nodded, looking at each other with a collective sympathy and a resolution to just get through the day.

'You'll be handling one of these shovels. Just scoop the biosolids onto the shovel and then into the wheelbarrow. Once you're full up, you'll walk the contents to the sealed chamber over there. Stay on the wooden planks, or the barrow won't be as steady. Open the chamber door each time and offload the wheelbarrow, then scrape it down. We'll mix it all in and re-seal after each emptying. Once you've finished cleaning all the solids from your toilet, you'll take a wheel- barrow load from the other sealant chamber over there and place it into the heating chamber. That stuff has been sitting there brewing for a while.' He pointed to the other side of the hut. 'Lastly, this week, you'll be taking the fertilizer and walking it up to the fields. Bob will direct you from there as to where he wants it to go. Does everyone understand?'

They all nodded.

Describing what was under her boots was something akin to kid's slime, dog shit, and mince mixed with treacle. The smell was over-whelming at times too, despite the mask, causing Ellie to breathe in shallow breaths and only when necessary. She had slid over at one point, landing on her back, submerging herself in a stinking brown layer. Tod had allowed her to change into a clean suit, but she knew some of it had gotten into her hair. Every time she had leaned forward, a large mattered piece, embedded somewhere in the middle of her ponytail had briefly shown itself. Human shit was heavy too, with each shovel load requiring serious exertion to lift it high enough, to get over the rim of the wheelbarrow. She had repeatedly raised the shovel, only to hit the edge, sending the shit flying off and back onto the floor. She'd cursed her lack of height, noticing that the others, all taller, weren't struggling, with that aspect of the job anyway. From there, she had wheeled the barrow over to the sealant chamber, hoping each time to co-ordinate with the timing of someone else, even if only to acknowledge how awful the job was.

All day, she had worked, only stopping for lunch, which had smelt like shit and looked like shit. Artificial rissoles and small black beans, topped with brown gravy, someone's idea of a joke, she was sure. Then Tod had asked them all to shower at the center, insisting that they used the disinfectant to ensure that the bacteria hadn't jumped on, hoping for a ride out. The residual stench in her nose had lingered long after her shower, causing her to feel nauseous for several hours.

Her mind drifted back to the river trail, which seemed, for the time being, to be hers and hers alone. Few people ever ventured far from the huts, preferring to stay near the sweet, sticky lure of what was offered inside. After taking the wrong route back to the huts after corn planting one day, she'd discovered the path inadvertently. A narrow, meandering path, following the river's crinkles, which promised thinking time, seclusion, and a sense of peace. The river itself wasn't much to talk about in terms of size or volume, and she was sure that years ago, before Climate Change, it had been a roaring and confident snake of blue. Now it trickled, slowly, down the hill and towards a place she didn't yet know.

The land on either side of the river hadn't been farmed yet, preserving its virgin secrets. It was a small part of the planet that hadn't yet baked to death, with scatters of green that reminded her of rosemary seasoning on a succulent chicken. She laughed at her analogy, accurate, although ridiculous, and indicative of a yearning for a baked dinner. She knew that her alone time with the river was temporary, thus all the more important to have gratitude for time with it. As the community grew and needed more land for food production, her path would be discovered, and she would find foot- prints mixed with hers, and small talk would invade her moments of quiet contemplation. A path like that would be stripped of its magic, by the presence of others. For now, though, it was hers. A small part of the Earth that wasn't baking, flooded or diseased, and a small reminder of a moment in the time *before*. Tonight though, her walk had most likely been revoked. Replaced with the promise of human drudgery and due process.

· · ·

SHE REPORTED to green hut at seven and sat crossed legged in the circle, smiling at the other members of her group, which this evening, was based on birthdate. Everyone born between 2013 and 2016 had been asked to attend, resulting in a circle of nineteen individuals aged in their thirties.

'Welcome everyone,' announced a stocky woman in a loud and theatrical tone. 'I am Renay, one of the founding Board members of Gaia Settlement Thirteen, and thank you for your attendance this evening. Hopefully, this won't take too long, and we can then attend the colored huts for some fun. I need a volunteer. Someone to write the minutes for us?' She looked around hopefully, and a tanned, sweaty woman immediately shot up her hand, agreeing to do it.

Ellie inwardly cringed. There was always an over-eager in the circle. Someone who wanted to please. They thought they might get noticed or valued more if they did this stuff, but in reality, no one cared. Renay just wanted someone to take notes, because she was too lazy to do it herself. The sweaty woman was there to be used, which Renay did gladly. Ellie sniffed the air and turned her head away from the pungent aroma, that had wafted from sweaty's raised armpit.

'Right,' said Renay, forcing a smile around the room. 'For those new to our community, and I can see that we have a couple of new faces tonight, welcome.' Everyone tapped their fingers together quietly as a welcome tradition. 'Every few weeks, we hold Concern Circles where we raise important issues. Things that might affect the bedrock of our community. Tonight, I welcome you as my pebbles.'

Ellie breathed in deeply, trying to be discreet. Pebbles? Really? What was she last week? A seedling. Then she was a triblet… and now a pebble. She hated meetings like this and recalled the staff meetings back at school that had gone on for way too long because people just didn't know when to stop talking. They would bring up the minutiae of every aspect of teaching, most of which was redundant for intelligent discussion. Looking at the agenda list that had been handed to her, they were in for a long night of tedious.

The meeting started positively, and Renay was on task, ensuring that they stuck to the agenda. They discussed an extension of curfew time in summer, meal portion sizes, and vitamin supplements in the water. Ellie sat, trying to shift her weight off her crossed legs, which were starting to cramp, and allowed the matters to glide past her. She didn't care enough to debate anything after the day she had endured. So what if they had vitamins in the water, and there was a curfew at midnight now anyway? She looked out of the window instead, and felt resentment at not being able to partake in the sun's setting. On an evening like tonight, the sky would be burning with orange and purple stripes, the tips of which would stroke the wildflowers on the riverbank.

Her thoughts were disrupted by a woman named Millie, who appeared as if she hadn't showered for a month. Her harsh voice grated through the space.

'I'm telling you. She's a piss-head! I know it,' she said aggressively.

'I've heard the same,' agreed Renay. 'Stop taking minutes for this bit. Unnecessary.' She nodded at sweaty woman who stopped, surprised by the sudden interruption in her meticulous note-taking. Everyone watched as Sweaty replaced the lid onto the pen and lowered it down onto the wooden floor. It was an action that indicated the start of secret business.

'Tell me more,' whispered Renay, wriggling herself comfortable, her expression becoming eager.

Millie smiled. One of those conspiratorial smiles that form when someone holds information that is capable of destroying another if articulated. She knew that the right words, spoken in the right context, were a weapon of war, and quite capable of proving as fatal as a lethal blow.

'Well,' she announced, pausing long enough for everyone to mirror her. She leaned forward in anticipation of the story she was about to tell. 'Pam, who I'm sure you all know… the woman with the really long, white hair?' Most of the group nodded. 'She's doing shit, according to her husband. He admitted it to me the other day… let it *all* out. He reckons she's taking from the community cash boxes in the induction center and then buying stuff from outside of the settlement.'

'Outside of the settlement?' Renay sounded intrigued. 'How?'

'She watches for one particular delivery van, finds an opportunity to approach, and places an order. He said it was like the van is waiting for her though. Next time they're here, they deliver stuff to her. She's selling it on to everyone else.'

The room murmured in a condescending tone.

'Is she now?' asked Renay, her brows furrowing with interest. 'I think this is disgraceful. Does anyone have anything else to say about this? Do we know exactly which van this is and who else she is selling this stuff to?'

The circle shook its head.

'She has alcohol on her breath all the time too. I reckon she's drinking in sober time.' A small, bird-like woman tweeted her blow.

'Thank you, that's most interesting,' said Renay. 'Anything else?'

A man spoke up. 'Look, I don't want to pass judgment… or cause any ill feelings… but… I've heard that her husband Barry is a mental case. He's got this strange smile, creepy as, have you seen it?' He looked around the room, eager for someone to agree with him. Several heads nodded.

'He's probably a rapist,' said sweaty, quickly adding, 'although of course, I have no exact proof.' The circle again nodded, and murmured in agreement.

Ellie stared at them all, anger beginning to swirl inside of her. Pam, whom she didn't know very well, was being accused of drug dealing and stealing in the middle of a meeting where minutes had been suspended, to allow them to crucify her off the record. Her husband had what… a creepy smile? That made him a mental case and a rapist? How was this even allowed? The anger welled up until it was in the back of her throat demanding to be purged. She opened her mouth, releasing it.

'Excuse me?' she said, the heated words bouncing from off one person to the next. The circle stared at her, with a collective expression of surprise.

'Please, go on,' offered Renay.

Well, Pam isn't here to defend herself right now, and nor is her husband and accusations such as these should be included in the minutes, as we're still technically in the middle of the meeting.' Her words were tumbling, too fast, leaving their significance in their haste.

Renay stared at her, then threw her head back and laughed. The rest of the group took her cue and laughed along, like a pack of hyenas surrounding a fresh kill. 'I love old fashioned morals. I really do,' she said chuckling.

Ellie was taken aback that the whole circle had followed Renay's cue. She was out on her own.

Millie snapped across the circle at her. 'Sorry, who are you? Do I know you?'

'Ellie.'

'Let me guess, you're new?' Millie asked, using a subtle amount of condescending.

Ellie studied her. She was spoiling for a fight, leaning forward, eyes blazing, and muscles pumped.

'Not that new,' said Ellie defiantly, wanting to walk over and punch her, just because.

'We have our rules, and then we have our *other* rules. It sounds like you haven't come across these yet?' Millie asked her, her eyes squinting slightly, with a hint of disdain.

'Other rules?' asked Ellie, sensing more than a hint of animosity.

'Ellie,' said Renay quietly. 'You don't understand how this works. We often suspend the minutes when we need to discuss sensitive issues. When else would we discuss matters such as these?' Renay smiled and then stared, as if daring Ellie to push back.

Ellie did, and she was quick with her reply. 'How about after the meeting, when accusing people who can't defend themselves is more appropriate? You can't just suspend minutes when you feel like it.' She smiled too, softening the impact of her words. A bit like a chimpanzee smiling as an act of aggression might.

There was a silence that generated a statue response. No-one moved. Ellie looked around the circle, realizing her mistake in challenging them. Her mind started racing. This was the way these circles operated. They used the rules to suit themselves. Accuse people of whatever, when they knew they couldn't defend themselves. Lovely. How many enemies had she just made? She went around the circle, counting her new enemies. Nineteen, if she included Renay.

'Ellie. You can leave if this is making you uncomfortable,' Renay said in a pretend-kind tone.

'Leave?' she asked, surprised.

'Yes, The circle thinks that would be best, I believe.' Renay smiled sweetly at her and then indicated with her eyes to the door.

'The circle agrees?' Ellie looked around at the other faces, all of whom were nodding in agreement.

She stood up, sensing the eyes watching, drilling, and following her. Wow. How to win friends and influence people, she thought to herself, gently shutting the door behind her. She had wanted to slam it, but it was soft spring-loaded. Instead, she vented her humiliation between long, slow breaths, her hands resting on angry hips. She had called the group out on what had to have been a dysfunctional process. Surely? They were using circle time to accuse and condemn people, in a kangaroo court, where nothing was recorded. Even gossip would have been more susceptible to detection. This was a smart way to ensure that there was no paper trail and a façade of due process to hide behind.

The light was too dim to walk over to the river to clear her head, not being a safe activity in case she lost her footing down the embankment. Instead, she stuck her head into the heavily beating interior of silver hut to peek at what was happening. A mass of human flesh greeted her, with arms and legs all merging into one gargantuan swirling human. A sparkling disco ball rotated above the mass, occasionally highlighting a body part. She thought she saw Dean, sandwiched between two blonde women, but his face was quickly replaced by a pimply arse, a flash of blue fingernails, and a foot. She could see two women kneeling in front of two of the guys she'd worked with earlier that day. Music thumped through her chest, making it hard to determine which beat was hers and which was being artificially implanted. Occasional screams of delight made her wince. A voice called out to her, inviting her in. She shook her head quickly and shut the door.

She considered whether she could argue that in a place like a Gaia community, that being unfaithful counted as a negative anymore. The rules had changed. Gaia sex, in the form of merging humping, was the new normal. How could it be called unfaithful when they were all encouraged to do it? At that moment, standing on the other side of the door, she felt alone. Was she deliberately sabotaging her assimilation into this new lifestyle by not participating? She was one of a few who wasn't standing within the Gaia faith, holding a mango high to the sky. Most were bowing before it, eager to shove it where the sun doesn't shine after dark. Although after her day in the toilets, even mangos were wholly unacceptable when one had finished with them, so the evidence had told her.

Ellie wandered from hut to hut, each one presenting itself with more dysfunction. As the sun set each evening over the community, it was as if The Fear set in, and distraction became all-consuming. Alcohol, sex, and now drugs were being used to self soothe and to forget what was coming. She felt the need to walk, although wandering around aimlessly as a silent witness to the huts' activities wasn't what she needed at that moment. She walked instead, behind red hut and followed a barely-made path up and over a small wooded hill. It wasn't a great idea to be heading away from the huts as the light was dimming fast, but there was a full moon appearing on the horizon, which promised to at least partially illuminate her way back, later on. Although back from where, hadn't yet been defined.

She arrived at the top of a second, steeper hill and peered around from her new vantage point. To the west, the long summer dusk had painted the sky in feathered wings of pink, yellow, and orange. Despite the stench of death from End Date, something as innocent as a sunset like this, reminded Ellie of how exquisite the Earth could still be. On the other side of the hill, towards the east, she thought she saw something flicker. What was that… a campfire, on Gaia property? Curiosity prevailed, and she impulsively decided to follow the path towards it. As she got closer, she could hear voices. Quietly, so as not to startle them, she approached. Several people, perched on cut logs around a campfire, turned to face her.

'Sorry,' she said, feeling like she had stumbled into a secret meeting, to which she hadn't been invited.

'Friend or foe?' asked a woman's voice.

'Are you Gaia?' Ellie asked, puzzled.

'Yes, you?'

'Yes.' She didn't know what else to add.

'Friend or foe?' someone asked again.

'Friend, I guess. I'm not sure what my intentions would be if I were a foe. I was just walking and, yeah, here I am. Sorry, I can leave if you want me to.' She indicated with her arm back in the direction she had walked in from.

'Circle. What do we think?'

'I'm sorry. Have I interrupted your meeting? I can go… really.' Ellie was confused by these people, sitting out in the middle of nowhere, having a private meeting.

'Want to join us?' asked a male voice, out of the fading light.

'So, is she trustworthy?' the woman asked.

'I think so. She doesn't seem to know who we are.'

'No, I'm able to be trusted.' Ellie said, not knowing what she needed to be trusted with.

'Choose a log and include yourself then,' called out the woman. 'There's some tea brewing on the fire, if you want some.'

Ellie smiled. 'Tea sounds good, thanks.'

She sat and tried to make out the faces belonging to the human shapes imprinted with shadows from the fire, dancing over them, but couldn't recognize anyone.

'Here, try this,' said an arm handing her a mug of tea.

She took it and inhaled its smoky aroma. 'Haven't had this type of tea in a long time. Thanks.' Tea at the settlement was permitted only in the form of the Gaia brand, and this was clearly sourced from outside of the camp.

'Yeah, well, we ain't giving it to you now either,' another voice from her left said quietly.

'Yeah… of course… sure,' she reassured them that the tea was off limits for further discussion.

The group continued the conversation now that she was settled. A conversation that was spoken in hushed tones and with a degree of urgency.

'You know once you've drunk our tea and sat in our circle that what you hear, stays here,' said the woman's voice. It was husky, like she'd been a smoker most of her life.

'I understand,' said Ellie, trying to sound reassuring in the dark.

'If we can't trust you, then there will be consequences.'

Ellie shuddered from the second veiled threat of the evening.

'Don't scare the poor lass. I think she just stumbled across us.'

'Just being sure.'

'I don't have any bad intentions… really,' she said, wondering if sitting down with them had been wise. It was a small faction, plotting to outsmart the system, she guessed, meeting in secret on these logs. She was curious to hear what was so important that it had to be done in such a secretive manner though. 'To be honest, this seems like a better deal than drinking myself stupid, stripping down and having an orgy with a whole heap of strangers.'

Someone chuckled.

'Never a truer word was spoken,' said the woman.

Ellie cupped her hands around the warm tea. There was a recollection of comfort in her palms. Tea had been her go-to drink in her old life. A beverage introduced by her mother before she had died. Ellie's mother had told her about the soothing magic of drinking tea and how it solved everything, in a time of stress. They had both sat many a time, with a hot brew, and Ellie's mother had told her tales from London where she had grown up. Stories about castles from long ago, and had promised Ellie that they would visit together, maybe after she had returned from Florida. She never did return though, and so Ellie had looked at pictures of castles online instead, a cup of tea in her hand. There was no comfort to be found however. The warmth of her mother, her friend, having been taken away in death.

'I've heard that Belcher is intending on building a new craft,' said a voice.

'Where? What new craft? Why? Where did you hear that?'

'From the science labs in The United Southern States. Those ridiculous labs she built in one of the wings in the Presidential building. It can seat hundreds according to my source.'

'You saying the labs can seat hundreds?'

'No. The new craft that she is planning on building.'

'Is your source credible?'

'Does a dog wag its tail?'

'So, is it for the Underground Generation?'

'My source says not.'

'Interesting. Any more on it?'

'Got my source working on it. I'll let you know.'

Ellie's ear pricked up. This was way more interesting than she had imagined. Was she too green to ask questions? She thought yes. Best to stay quiet for this meeting and just listen.

'I want to mention Jenny.' Ellie turned to her left.

'Why? What's up?' asked a voice from her right. She turned to the right, feeling like she was watching a game of tennis.

The voice on the left spoke. 'Not sure. I just don't like the way she seeks information. Last week, Carly was blamed for spreading falsehoods during the *Wellness Circle*. Jenny made sure to seek further information with everyone after the meeting, and now Carly has been moved to a different camp.'

'So Jenny says.' There was silence.

'Hell being moved. That's crap.' Another voice. Different. Opposite her.

'What's the alternative? Fertilizer? Didn't we agree that was just a rumor and should be left as one?'

Ellie wondered if she should laugh at the fertilizer joke, only no-one else did.

'I've got my suspicions,' the voice replied. Silence.

'For real? You being real right now?' asked another voice to her right.

'As real as sitting here, drinking tea, with you lot.'

'Shit. Really? That's a bit crap.'

'Yeah, literally.'

'Really? Are we back making assumptions about fertilizer again? We need more info,' said the woman. 'This isn't a topic that deserves speculation.'

'Not a problem. I'm already working on it.'

Ellie finished the tea, which had created a reliable warmth inside of her. This was an interesting conversation. She'd had her own suspicions about Jenny, and these guys were confirming it. What was the stuff about fertilizer, though? She felt confused, as the only fertilizer she knew about was the shit one that she was currently responsible for shoveling. The meeting continued with small matters being discussed and then all of a sudden it was over.

'Okay, guys. Night over. See you next week. Same time. Mute. Stay mute.'

'Mute,' said the group.

Ellie followed suit. 'Mute?' she said, a little tentatively.

'Correct,' said a voice. 'We stay mute once back in the camp. It's safer. Walk back alone and enter the camp discreetly. You say nothing about being here. You understand?'

'Yes.'

'Good. It's important that we have your word on that.'

Someone reached out for her cup. 'See you next week, same time. Be here an hour earlier unless you get called to a circle.'

'Yeah, thanks.' That was her cue to leave.

She wandered back through the woods and down the hill, now illuminated by a bright moon, as promised. She wasn't sure what she had stumbled across, but it interested her. People like her, who questioned things. People like her who had decided not to join in with the forgetting. She didn't know how much of their conversation was a complete exaggeration, set in story-telling, and gossip, but it made a change to the stifling discussions back in the community. She decided to be there an hour earlier the following week. If anything, she wanted to know more about the craft.

Y'ALL, I hate people. I used to like them. Not now. Yeah, I'm here, quietly sitting on the sidelines, just watching this all unfold, and Jack has told me to respond and add stuff. I said to him, respond with frickin' what, dude? Ellie is the best thing to happen in ages to this saga. A woman with a decent brain. Piecing shit together. She's telling the story just fine. Jack reckons I could add more. Give my overview of everything. Okay, so here I am. What do you want to know? Jack says I need to stop being so crappy-rhetorical. I said I wasn't being rhetorical, and he says, how the hell are the readers going to answer that dude, if you're asking questions in a book? He has a point. Right then. I'll tell you what I think you need to know. That's bordering on being a control freak, forcing my stuff in your face, but Jack says, just do it, being a spokesperson for Nike too, apparently.

Right, you know that thing that repeats itself over and over… what's it called again? That Mandelbrot Set thing. This pattern that's emerging in this story, as I'm sure y'all are seeing… it's like this whole notion of self-similarity. The one that Mandelbrot studied. As something gets smaller, it repeats itself over and over on a smaller scale having a consistent pattern. It's like that with people. No matter how small a human sub-group gets, regardless of where they are, who they are, and why they are… they mess it up with the same shit. Human beings create debris on large scales and then on small scales. They can't help it. It's like everything is good and then they just have to go a bit further, shaping the system, making tweaks here, and there, to suit themselves, usually to get themselves into a better position of power. It's like everyone wants to be noticed. Get somewhere important. Be important and be the leader. Where is that somewhere? There isn't even a somewhere to get to no more.

Ellie is doing the right thing though, not getting a neural pathway in her mind installed, called The Fear. The more they spread The Fear around, the bigger it becomes. They can keep people quiet by making them afraid. They can mobilize them to do stuff because they are scared. It's the best-damned power scam of all. The more scared people are, the more pliable, and the more control you can extract. The Fear was released as a suggestion, not an actual, because you have to remember, End Date is still forty plus years away. Every time it is mentioned, though, it gets bigger and scarier. Gaia fuels off The Fear, and the people feel safe because they think they are being protected from it. Okay, now my interest is lit up like a hunting torch. I want to name historical events where fear has been used to control. Do you get that too? Start something, and then it's like I wanna know more?

9/11. Who remembers that the planes launched the War on Terror? There were people too scared to leave their homes for years after that one. ISIS and the threat that if you walked down to your local, your head would be cut off. Nazis, during the war, got Germans to accept the Holocaust by telling them there was an enemy on the doorstep and The Bomb? How about saying that something has to be done to stop war, even if it means disintegrating hundreds of thousands of innocents? There was The Wall, designed to prevent the fear of invading illegals and yeah, AIDS, way back. In Australia, they even did this TV advert where the Grim Reaper bowled over kids and in some crazy way, that was supposed to stop gay men from spreading the disease. It goes on and on. Political power being used to keep the masses immobilized and scared, seeing their leaders as saviors from invisible enemies. Even with the pandemic lockdowns in the twenties, some said that Governments had gone too far - destroying mental health and small businesses with draconian laws.

So yeah, my point is that Gaia Settlements are no different to large political fear campaigns, and within Gaia, the circles are no different to political meetings either. A human wants to control, and a human wants power. We're crazy power junkies that's why. Having a hit of power is like ice to a crack head. You have to keep control of a massing hoard of depressives, who see life as futile. Otherwise, you might find yourself dealing with a hoard of anarchists, who are harder to control. See how it works? So, you sell them a safe place, invite them in, then fill them with The Fear. It keeps them in the palm of your hand. Except for Ellie and that new group of hers. The thinkers. The ones that don't bleat for their supper. Baa. Baa. Baa.

13
____

NEW BEGINNINGS
FOR A DEAD END

Pete was staring at the notebook in front of him. He was mulling over a dilemma concerning the global resolution outcome, but given their chip technology was new, there were no precedents to gain direction from. He drew yet another circle, naming it brain, as he had done so a thousand times that week. Then he sat back, twiddling his pen in the air to think. Okay, he knew the main functions of the chip: to provide a library that could be accessed for selective knowledge, and stimulate neural pathways to create faster transactions. The problem… he drew a large x covering the circle… the problem was, how the hell he was going to soften the pre-existing personality already living inside the brain? He had to, if this limiter was going to be included. Otherwise, old patterns would emerge, getting entangled in the new technology.

'Quandary,' he said, out aloud to the room.

'You talking to the walls now?' asked Tina, wandering in with a box full of hologram boards and leads.

'Yeah, lucky they haven't started talking back yet,' he smiled. 'I'm stuck with this bit. Not stuck overall… it's just that Belcher has asked specifically for a compliance driver… it has to do with this limiter thingy.'

'She knows enough to ask for one?' asked Tina, sounding surprised.

'Apparently so,' replied Pete.

'Outline it and see if we can work it through together.' Tina sat next to him.

'Okay. So, we all have an identity that acts globally. Yes?' Pete drew yet another circle on a fresh page.

'Yes. Some would also claim it as a soul,' added Tina.

Pete grinned. 'That's complicating this further, you know.'

Tina laughed. 'Just mucking around. Keep going.'

'Belcher requires a personality overlay, a compliance driver that operates within the limiter. She thinks that it will be easier if our implants think in the same manner. We can't do this selectively as we don't have the technology as far as I am aware. It means we have to superimpose a dominant personality into someone's mind. I'm not aware of research that's looked into merging two personalities in one mind?'

'Yeah, I hear you. If you had two active personalities in the one brain, it would be like patients undergo a corpus callosotomy, which disarms the connection between the two brain hemispheres. Some patients find themselves reaching for both a red shirt and a blue shirt, liking eggs and not liking eggs at the same time.'

'Exactly, glad you're on the same page.'

'Only we haven't thought of a solution yet,' Tina added.

'But, you get where I'm sitting?'

'Yeah, of course. So, you're talking about needing to dampen the existing personality, so that when the chip is inserted, the brain favors only the new functions? Okay. So… does that mean killing someone off… putting them into a kind of sleep mode or what?'

He shook his head. 'This is where I'm stuck. I can't go killing our participants off… well, we could, but I'm not partaking in that kind of shit. Plus, if we standardize the personality overlay to be completely dominant, then we create clones. I'd prefer to be talking about merging rather than wiping one out.'

'Yeah, nothing about this entire process is ethical or simple.'

He got up and walked over towards the storage cupboard. 'Hey, help me with getting the computers set up for cube formation.'

Tina had looked blank at first and then realized that Pete wanted to discuss something that the cameras weren't privy to. Inside of the walk-in storage cupboard was camera-free and private, so long as you didn't stay inside too long, arousing suspicion.

'Belcher marched in and demanded that she be the blueprint for the personality overlay,' he whispered.

'What the shit? You serious? How did she know to do that?' Tina looked alarmed.

'I don't know. It took me completely by surprise. I was doing an update briefing with her, and she was jumping on me for details. Then, out of the blue, she's saying that for the chip to be effective, we needed to have everyone thinking the same. I tried to argue that we didn't need to do that, and she basically told me to shut the fuck up.'

'Why need everyone to think the same? I thought the idea was that we were getting people into new professions and adding a limiter, so that they didn't want to try new stuff?'

'Well, that was the initial brief. She headed off for a round-table meeting and must have been mulling it over in her mind. Next minute, she's here and demanding that I make a time for her brain scans, so that she can be some sort of dominant overlay for every chip recipient.'

'Seriously? That's so unethical.' Tina whispered back. 'Did you do them? Why didn't I know all this was going on?'

'You were away for the day, seeking your sheep brains…'

Tina interrupted. 'Take some equipment out in case we raise suspicion. What's with these cameras watching us all the time, anyway?' Tina lugged out two room dimmers and set them down on the table.

'In case we're plotting something against Belcher?' he replied, when they were back inside. 'She's frickin' paranoid. Anyway, hear me out. I did the scans… and holy shit… psychopathy central in there… weak connections between her ventromedial prefrontal cortex and her amygdala, and differing transmission languages. I did the psychopathy test at the end, told her the dye was for enhanced resolution. Came up as red as it gets. She's a total mess in there.'

'… and she wants to be the blueprint? Take some more stuff out.' Tina lugged two hologram spheres out and placed them next to the dimmers.

'We do this,' Pete said, back inside the cupboard, '… use her blueprint for the overlay, and we create an army of cyborgs. We can't. Can you imagine an army of people like her? This is why I'm balking at making the compliance driver dominant. If we do that, Belcher becomes dominant in every single chip recipient.'

'Shit. No… we can't do that. So, what are you going to do?' Tina stood and looked at Pete. If he refused Belcher anything, that might be the end of his place on the team.

'I haven't got to that bit yet. Might need a bit of help.'

BELCHER STRODE into Jack's lab, disturbing a meeting, looking very pleased with herself, her lips parted wide, teeth now smeared with allure velvet and coffee. Jack thought she appeared as if she had just been out hunting something live.

'I've got news. Wells has agreed to see me. Next week in person. This is a perfect outcome.'

'Great,' Jack nodded. So, there was some reality in the madness of her plan to fly to Mars.

'My second piece of news is also excellent, although Pete is already privy to it. I have put myself forward as the personality overlay for the chip. Given the limiter was my idea, it seems only fitting that I'm actually part of it.'

Jack looked over at Pete, and inhaled deeply, trying to find air that would fill his collapsed lungs.

'Yes,' smiled Belcher, 'I had a PET scan and an MRI in fact, and Pete has agreed that it will be my personality that we overlay, as the standard compliance driver. Isn't that what you had inferred Jack? That one standardized personality was a better option?'

Jack looked at Pete and raised his eyebrows. 'He agreed to implement something I said as a passing inference?'

Belcher ignored him. 'It would be wise if we created a line of humans who didn't *need* as much from each other. Humans that can rely on themselves. Consistency over dependency. Don't you agree, Jack? I'm glad Pete understood it all. With my personality cloned, we keep things simple. Yes?'

Jack went to speak.

'Rhetorical Jack.' Belcher looked at him with a dare in her eyes.

'Of course,' he said, looking at Pete, his eyes clearing asking, *what the fuck dude?*

Pete shook his head internally. Not enough for anyone to see and only felt on a quantum level. It was his way to ensure that the universe had registered his disapproval.

Tina, however, wasn't as easily intimidated by Belcher, whether through naivety or strength. 'Do you think that's objective, though?'

Belcher peered at her as though she had just broken a vow of silence. 'Did you say objective?'

'Yes,' said Tina, realizing she was now looking into the death stare of a certified psychopath.

'Objectivity is irrelevant in this context, Tina. We don't need to justify our actions to anyone, nor our process. No-one cares if this is done morally, ethically, thoroughly, and certainly not objectively. Do you understand? This is solely about outcome.'

Tina looked at Jack for backup and then noticed his expression. It was subtle, but she read it.

'Of course,' she smiled at Belcher. Now she understood. There were no ethical rules, just the ones that Belcher constructed. Project IQ was her mad design, and they were there to transform ideas into the practical.

'I'm busy now with Sittings between eight and five each day. Do you need anything else from me for the week?'

'No, I think we're good to keep working on it all,' Jack looked at the others, who nodded enthusiastically at the thought of Belcher being too busy to keep descending on them.

Jack waited until Belcher was in transit between the lab and her office. 'White Swan, thirty minutes after work finishes. Not negotiable.'

BELCHER SAT BACK in her chair, observing her minions hard at work in the lab. This week was going to be a show of her strength, not weakness or indecision. Her reforms were brutal, but her country was not going to fall apart like so many others. Her military would now take control and keep things ordered for her. It was simpler that way. Rations, a curfew, mandatory blood tests for health status… she chuckled, imagining her colleagues trying to argue with her. This was her time to show the balls she had been born without. She opened her desk drawer and pulled out her flask. She shot the liquid into the back of her throat. 'Yes!' she said, banging one fist hard down onto her desk. 'I am liking that.'

TINA AND PETE walked to the White Swan, the once-busy thoroughfares, now eerily quiet.

'What's this clandestine meeting all about? Privacy away from Belcher?' Tina asked.

'Yeah, probably. There's a bit to discuss concerning the blueprint for the chip. If we make clones of Belcher, then the world is doomed, really.' He halted and looked around. 'That's if it isn't already past the point of no return.'

Garbage had formed small piles along the sidewalks, oozing a decaying stench. Rats were digging in food that was liquifying in the heat. Everything was covered with a fine orange film, blown in from the arid interior. They walked by shops, once thriving and now abandoned and boarded up. The only business doing a steady income were bars. Eating protein bars and getting pissed was one way to deal with all the shit flying around, she surmised. Jack was sitting alone, already finishing his third beer as they arrived.

'You finished those off quickly,' smiled Pete as they joined him.

'What did you do… come right here after we left for the testing session?'

'Yeah, I gave myself an early mark, and I needed it. Get a drink and let's sort this out. We'll move to the back of the bar, somewhere discreet.'

Pete sculled a bourbon at the bar and bought a second to take back to the table. Jack was eager to speak.

'There is no way that we are making Belcher the personality overlay for the chip. I flatly refuse. We would be unleashing psychopathy into the world, and God knows what else. The limiter is bad enough.' Jack sculled the rest of his beer.

Pete shook his head. 'I certainly didn't have that plan on the agenda in the first place. She pushed her way in… firstly a limiter and then a compliance driver… then all of a sudden, the woman is sitting in the chair demanding that the dye to be injected.'

'Audacious, that's one word to describe her,' offered Tina, joining them.

Jack leaned forward and lowered his voice. 'Listen. I want you to use my personality overlay instead, and we can ensure that it's selective, not global. I'm not about creating clones in all of this.'

'Really?' asked Pete, sounding surprised. 'Do we have the technology to do selective merging?'

'Yeah. We do. It's something I've been working on. I just hadn't announced it yet.'

'Wow. That's impressive.' Pete nodded to Tina.

'Why you, Jack?' asked Tina, taking a bigger than usual sip of her gin and tonic.

'Call it a sleight of hand. Look, the woman, President or no President, is bordering on insane. She melted the President of the United States for fuck's sake.'

'Hearsay,' said Tina.

Jack looked at her. 'Just saying.'

'Most likely, though,' agreed Pete. 'Everyone assumes she was behind it.'

'True. Anyone want another drink?' Tina asked, having gulped down what was left in her glass.

'Another bourbon, thanks,' smiled Pete.

'Bourbon… neat. Thanks Tina,' said Jack, softening his tone. 'Look, this makes sense. My brain has been the testing prototype for most of this chip design for fifteen years. Not a personality overlay, but certainly the rest of it. We already know that my brain has accepted the chip components via the interface information. My personality overlay would be the most logical. Two-thirds of the unknowns have already been tested. Anyway… doing this is a quiet revolt that she'll never find out about. It'll be our way of having a private joke in amongst the crazy shit.'

'Makes sense,' said Tina. 'Although, still not ethical, but that fits in with everything else we are doing. I hadn't realized you had done the research to merge the two. If we have that, then using your overlap would be yeah… sensible. I'm not here to build a lasting friendship with the woman. Although, I suppose if we're going with her to Mars, then we might need to.' She went to the bar, shaking her head with the thought.

Pete chuckled. 'Clever move, Jack. I can't stand her. She's the most ego-driven human I have ever come across. I'll book you in before work tomorrow for a scan before the morning cameras kick in. It takes about two hours by the way, so be there at, say, six?'

'Yeah. Why not?' smiled Jack.

Tina returned, balancing the three drinks carefully. 'I've decided it's time to get smashed and quell some of this tension. All this pent up stress can't be good for us?'

'Good idea. Cheers,'

The glasses clinked, and the drinking began.

THE NEXT MORNING, Pete had rotten soil inside his head for a brain. 'I feel terrible,' he said, rubbing his forehead.

'You knocked back a fair few, as did Tina,' said Jack, sitting himself down in the chair.

'Worth it still, in order to perform this.' Pete rubbed Jack's arm with the alcohol wipe in preparation for the radioactive injection.

'Is this going to hurt?' asked Jack, staring at the long, pointed needle.

'Only if you're a baby. Small scratch.' He stuck the needle under his skin.

'You sadist. Small scratch my frickin' arse. That hurt like shit.'

'Pathetic,' sighed Pete. 'Now sit still for thirty minutes, and then I'll get you into the machine.'

'Looks like fun.' Jack looked over at the scanners. 'I can't believe she was able to get all this hospital shit for you to play with. She probably took them from a hospital, knowing her. So, do we do the MRI as well today or just the PET?'

'Nah, not enough time. We'll do the MRI tomorrow morning.'

The PET scan complete, they left the scanning room and went back outside to the carpark to look as if they had just arrived.

'So you're sure about these CCTV loops?' asked Jack.

'Yeah. I worked it out. There are two loops in operation. One for the East and West wings, which run twenty-four seven. Our wing, however, runs on a ten-minute loop between six pm and eight am. If we arrive during that time, the video is only looked at if an alarm is activated. So long as we don't trip it, then no-one will know we were here.'

'The security for the building is only for her wings, essentially?'

'At night, yes. During the day, it's insane. Cameras blinking everywhere. So if we leave now and then walk in again, timing it for when the day cameras come on, it will show that we just turned up.'

THEY REPLAYED the scanning the next morning at the same time. Jack bopping along to some mellow jazz while the MRI machine thundered around his head. Pete sat and analyzed the films after work, making sure that he sat in a secluded corner away from the night cameras, just in case there was any doubt as to privacy. He had named the films *G. Hopper,* just in case. He could always say it was another one of his blueprint candidates.

'Well, I'll be darned,' he said out aloud after having looked at the films. 'Like peas in a pod.' He grabbed Belcher's brain scans, hiding the identity label in case the cameras could see, and lit them up. He superimposed them and then stood back. 'Crazy shit. Nearly identical.' Then he replayed the live imagery files and compared the neuro-transmitter patterns. He sat down to digest the information, seeing that Belcher was more extreme on the sadistic trait line and had less guilt and remorse for actions. Jack was the better psychopath if he had to choose between the two. So Belcher and Jack had similar brain anatomy? Two psychopaths working together, or should that be alongside each other? Fascinating. He phoned Jack.

'Where are you?'

'At home, eating a pizza, and washing it down with a couple of beers. You?'

'At work. You want to pop in?'

'Why? Is everything okay?'

'Yeah, it's just that your scans have come through.'

'Brain tumor?'

'Dickhead.'

'Good. What then?'

'You need to see this.'

'Okay. Give me thirty.'

Jack looked at the superimposed scans. 'Shit. Like shit dude.'

'Yeah. Thought you would be impressed.'

'So, I'm a certified psychopath? Can I call that an achievement? How come I never picked this up before?'

'You weren't testing live neurotransmitter patterns, I'm guessing? As for it being an achievement? I suppose that depends…'

'On what?'

'How you apply your traits, I guess.'

'Who has the worse brain, me or the bitch?'

'The bitch, obviously. She melted someone.'

Jack nodded. 'We just called the President a bitch.'

'Yeah, we did. Maybe we shouldn't? You haven't melted anyone, have you?' Peter looked at him, worried.

'Nah. I melted a fly once when I was a kid. Used a magnifying glass.'

'Shit? Really?'

'Why? Why, shit?'

'That's an early indicator of psychopathy.'

'Oh.'

'Yeah.'

'Explains a lot.'

'Yeah.'

'You weren't supposed to agree to that.'

'No, of course not.'

TINA RAISED her eyebrows as Jack told her the news over lunch the next day. 'You're one as well? That makes sense,' she smiled cynically.

'I don't think you're supposed to find this amusing,' said Jack, having carefully positioned the two of them so that their backs were to the cafe cameras.

'But it is amusing. This chip is destined to create cyborgs. People with no conscience. The universe has spoken.'

Jack sighed. 'Yeah, well, my version of a psychopath has to be better than hers.'

'I agree with that. You haven't melted anyone, though, have you? Not keeping any more secrets inside that psychopathic mind, are you?'

'No, Tina. Why does everyone keep asking me that?'

'Whether you melted anyone? Who knows Jack? It's been twenty years since I last saw you, and you have been festering in isolation for most of that time, I hear.'

'Festering?' He looked at her quizzically.

'Yeah, alone, in a basement lab… who knows?' She laughed, 'I'm just playing with you.'

'Thanks for your vote of confidence,' he smiled. 'By the way, I was wondering if dinner was out of the question?'

She looked taken aback. 'Dinner? Where did that come from in the middle of a conversation abut festering?'

'Just thought it might be nice?' He sounded hopeful.

She paused, considering the idea. 'Okay. When?'

'When are you next free?'

'Tonight?'

'Okay. Let's do tonight. I'll text you the address.' Jack hadn't planned to ask her for dinner and hadn't expected her to say yes.

He wasn't even sure why he had proposed it, assuming that his subconscious had hijacked his rational mind. No good could come from rekindling a relationship with Tina, that he knew.

They put their lunch trays away and headed back to the lab.

'Back to it,' said Jack, entering the lab and switching on the circuitry. 'We need to figure out this limiter issue. I'm thinking we are going to need a whole new set of algorithms to do this successfully, especially as we have the overlay to factor in.' He paged Pete.

'God, for someone who had alcohol poisoning only thirty-six hours ago and was essentially passed out, your brain just keeps going, doesn't it?' Tina said to Jack, who was setting up the cube computers.

'That's me. It's called tolerance, probably not something to even brag about. I'm thinking of global pulsing, by the way.'

'Global pulsing?' Tina looked confused.

'For the chip. It's new.'

'No... I've heard of it, but it hasn't been tested on humans yet, has it?'

'No... but it was pretty successful with mice.'

'Humans aren't mice, Jack.'

'What mice?' asked Pete, entering the lab.

'Close enough.' Jack turned the hologram display on, ready to demonstrate the mice research findings.

'Close enough? Really? This whole research is based on nothing ethical. We're just making it up really, aren't we?' Tina folded her arms, clearly uncomfortable with the process.

'Yup. Fun, isn't it?' Jack was trying to lighten the mood.

'God, every time I enter a room, it's like I drop into drama,' said Pete. 'So, what's the agenda for this afternoon?'

'Global pulsing in the context of limitations, according to Jack.'

'That's a theory that uses dopamine pulses, isn't it? It floods the brain to make it feel good, and while it's feeling good, it pairs it with a thought.'

'What thought?' asked Tina.

'The right one, hopefully,' he replied.

'As in?'

Jack jumped in. 'The one that our algorithm chooses. That's where we come in. We can adapt global pulsing to suit our intentions here. I've been playing around with it anyway, and I think we can use it to help with our selective issues.'

'Clever,' said Pete. 'So… because of dopamine levels, the person gets the go-ahead to believe that the released thought is good for them and so they trust it.'

Jack switched on the cube formation. 'Exactly. We can repeat the thought a thousand times in a fraction of a second. Repetition combined with the right chemicals and presto! I've just had this great thought.' Jack got the hologram up and running. 'Watch this sixty-second demo with the mice and then imagine new algorithms at work.'

'So,' Tina was thinking it through, afterwards. 'Just dopamine? I would have thought we could be more exact than that.'

'Sort of. The dopamine is just one half of the equation. We need to ensure that a wrong thought, one that might have come from the original personality, is erased. That's where the hyrantrocholine comes in.' Jack pointed to an image.

'That's the one that allows memories to wipe? Again, highly ethical.' Tina said sarcastically.

'Yup, when you add the algorithm, the memory is wiped,' he said, flicking an imaginary memory out of the air with his hand.

'My expertise is in designing the algorithms' said Tina. 'This is exponential for me. All of it. I can't wait to be translating this into a language that I actually understand.'

TINA LANDED on the doorstep in time and rang the bell. Jack answered the door, having thrown on some clean clothes. She smiled at his effort, despite the fact that the clothes looked as if they had been picked up off the floor.

'This is nice,' she noted, looking at the small round table, alone in the vast room, set with a tablecloth, candle, and paper plates. The rest of the house was empty as far as she could gather, noticing the lack of everything else such as photos, personal items, and a regular amount of furniture.

'I decided to make an effort, with the table at least. Excuse the sparseness of the house. I haven't gone furniture shopping yet, despite being a multimillionaire. There aren't that many shops still selling furniture though, in my defense.'

'Table looks nice, though.'

'Red or white?'

'What have you cooked?'

'Noodles.'

'Seriously?'

'Yeah, it was such short notice. Sorry.'

'Both then.'

'Okay. We can start with white.'

He inhaled and smelled the perfume. She was still wearing *his* fragrance, the one he had first bought her all those years ago. It was a distinct blend of rose, cedar, jasmine, and freesia. It catapulted him back, his mind flooding him with images of cheap candlelight, her youthful body wanting to wrap itself around him, and cloudy feelings… of what?

She smiled and Jack froze. No. He did not want to peel back his feelings again. The perfume had made him remember. All of it. His outer layer was impenetrable now, too tough to allow her her to seep in. It would be dinner and talking. Nothing more. Her smile stopped, just as it was still expanding. She knew him well enough, to know that look.

14

SHOVEL
SHIT

S hit shoveling had wound up for the day and Ellie was keen to inhale some fresh air. She rushed up the dusty path, as a child might, in excited anticipation, knowing what was waiting for her at Solitude Beach. Once there, she hastily stripped off her clothes, dropping them in a jumbled pile under a tree, and then carefully eased herself down the embankment, being careful not to fall. She lightly trod between jagged pebbles until her toes were being nibbled by icy water. The cold took her breath away, sending goose- bumps along her skin. This is how it was meant to be. The river had never promised straightforward, in order to share itself. The heat from off her shins sizzled, and her stress, swaddled now in blue, was cradled away, to somewhere else, downstream. She tiptoed forward gingerly, the cold now reaching her waist. She stopped as her muscles stiffened, paralyzing her, but she forced herself to do what had to be done. Inhaling sharply, and closing her eyes, she dived under the water, her body shocked from the icy exhilaration. She then emerged, exhilarated from the dive, as if re-born and ready to start the day again.

She lay on her back, the icy water now feeling warm, and gently rocking her. The breeze swept over her in soft waves. The water glistened with a thousand diamond tears, shed by those further upstream, perhaps. A loitering sun, hanging low in the west, allowed her to gaze up into the blue. She could see through layer upon layer, imagining that she could see right through to the ink-black of space. It was times like this that Ellie was reminded that she was on a planet, a small rock, revolving around a sun.

'Hey,' a voice startled her from her thoughts.

She got off her back quickly and hid her body under the water. A man had started to take off his clothes, up on the embankment, ready to enter the water.

'Hi,' she said, feeling resentful that he had chosen precisely the same place to swim. Solitude Beach was her private space, even if only in her own mind.

'It's okay,' he said, wading in confidently, and then swimming towards her. 'I'm not staying. I swim down to the gorge most evenings after circles and then walk back. I wouldn't deliberately interrupt your floating, just for the sake of it.' He smiled. 'It's beautiful here, isn't it?'

Ellie was relieved that he wasn't staying, acknowledging that the presence of his neatly folded clothes, next to hers, irritated her. She felt petty, berating herself inwardly for her childish reaction.

'Yes, it's lovely.'

She watched him treading water, trying to think of something else to say. Instead, he smiled. 'Enjoy,' he said, cutting off their interaction abruptly, before strongly swimming off and disappearing around a curve in the river.

'You too,' she had called back as an afterthought, wondering where the gorge was, that he had mentioned. Ellie made a mental note to seek it out. She turned and looked over at the man's clothes again, feeling herself relaxing at their presence. She swirled the water with her hands, standing in the shallows near the bank, and watched as the river created patterns as it bubbled past her. She envied it in a way, not knowing what was to come.

She rested next to the swimmer's clothes, now glad for the sense of company that they offered. A pair of everyday brown sandals and beige shorts lay with a sky blue t-shirt. His clothes added a touch of mundane and ordinary to the space. Her mind, seeing the male clothing, quickly wandered to Dean and the disintegration of their relationship. She doubted if she had felt happy at all over the past couple of years with him, if being honest. Her teaching experience had been so different from his, and there had been resentment building. She didn't blame herself as the students had been little shits. Calling it teaching was a joke. Dean had found it amusing when she'd opened up to him about her struggles.

'Just be more assertive with them. They just know they can wind you up,' he had advised, matter-of-factly.

'More assertive? How? I was explaining Romeo and Juliet to them, not that any of them had even heard of Shakespeare. Then one of them got out of his seat, picked up a plastic brain from a cupboard and threw it at my head. It smashed onto the whiteboard next to me.'

'So, you sent him to the Deputy as you are supposed to?'

'Of course. He ran out in the other direction though.'

Dean laughed.

'What's so funny?'

'I teach the same kids. They never behave like that for me. Which kid was it?'

'Adam Whitely.'

'Adam?' Dean sounded surprised. 'Nah, he's cool in my classes. Great kid to teach.'

'So, you're saying it's me? How is that helpful?'

'Well, why else would they do shit like that?'

WHEN THE SCHOOL had permanently sealed its doors, Ellie felt like she had just been discharged from a prison sentence, not that she dared to share those sentiments with the other teachers. Most of them were fake-passionate about their jobs and chatted a stream of satisfying adjectives at her each day, despite her seeing half of them being chased from rooms by angry students. She turned out to be alone as far as she could make out, in being honest about her struggles. She'd entered teaching regarding it as an honorable profession, one in which she could impart knowledge, wisdom, and guidance to students who may not be encouraged to do much at home. Within six months, she had been wondering what she had been thinking. Students devolved upon arriving at school, with literacy rates declining and behavior becoming more aggressive.

Dean's experience had been the opposite. The students and staff had loved Dean. Ellie had privately observed his classes from her staffroom window over the years and saw how the students cooperated for him. They had beamed when asked to demonstrate skills and played fair when in teams. She had been perplexed, knowing that she would most likely never share in any of that. She had resented Dean on the days when he had bounced home, eager to recount how well his day had gone. It was hard to feel so positive when the same students were making her life a living hell. Maybe it was her? Perhaps she saw every glass as half empty, while he saw the potential in the half that was there?

• • •

A VOICE BROKE through her unhappy reverie. 'I notice you've been taking care of my clothes. Thanks for that.'

She looked up to see the swimmer from earlier, coming back up the dusty path. She could see him properly now. About her age, maybe a bit older, with long muscular limbs, tanned and yeah, attractive. He smiled an infectious smile, one that generated a spontaneous smile back.

'Austin,' he said warmly, extending out his hand.

'Hi, Ellie. Nice to meet you.'

'So, have you been in Gaia long?' he asked, slipping his t-shirt over his head.

'A few months. You?'

'Eight months.' There was a pause.

'Amazing that we have never bumped into each other before,' said Ellie.

'Yeah. You like it here?' he asked, pulling his shorts up.

'Yes, of course,' she smiled.

He looked at her quizzically. 'Yes really, or yes politely?'

'Yes, because I don't know you.' Ellie smiled back at him.

'Fair enough,' he said, running the towel through his sandy colored hair.

'What about you?' Ellie asked. 'How's it going for you?'

'It's good, because we are strangers meeting properly for the first time. There, now we have an understanding, don't we?'

She studied his face. Was there a hidden message in that, or was she reading too much into it?

'I'll see you next week then.' He slipped his sandals back on and turned to go.

'Next week?' They hadn't decided to meet again at the river.

'Yeah, I recognized you from the other evening. I handed you a cup of tea.'

Ellie slowly nodded. 'The circle meeting in the woods? That was you?'

'Yes. Don't be late. The best stuff always goes down first.'

'Yeah, I hadn't meant to walk in on you all. I was just out roaming that evening.'

'They were worried afterward that you were a plant. I reassured them.'

'How did you know that I wasn't?'

'Don't know. Just a feeling, I guess. I have to go.' He smiled and then walked off.

For the first time since arriving in the settlement, Ellie felt something. What was it? Hope?

15

JEANS ARE BLUE

GENES ARE COMPLICATED

Belcher randomly wandered in to the lab, dead on eleven. Jack had frequently pointed out that the genes lab was a sterile site and that she was required to wear a hairnet, which she vehemently refused to do. Today, she had excelled in dressing like a military dictator. Her body was swathed in a stern, grey, woolen trouser suit with her breasts flat-packed into bondage. He glanced down towards her feet, which were entombed in pointy black casings, perched on thin, dagger heels. Her hair was coiled in a tightly compressed bun, hanging off the back of her head, suggesting that if one stood too close, the bun might be released, causing injury. Her face, madly taut and stretched, profiled her red, wrinkled mouth even more, as if were hanging in an art gallery, wanting to be the center of attention. He looked at her mouth while she spoke, watching how her tongue danced moisture onto her lips. The effect was dire, a portrait of impenetrable. The lipstick was a hint at feminine, he speculated, but not softness. Lines tracing around lips, colored clumsy too, bleeding outwards, evidence that she'd just devoured some poor soul alive, perhaps minutes before.

'Get organized, Jack. You're joining me to meet Wells,' she barked at him.

'Sorry?' he had blurted out, assuming he had misheard her.

'Yes, you. Go home and pack for an overnight, then get straight back here. We're on a Wells private jet, which flies out in three hours.'

'Really?' Jack was surprised. He was in the middle of extracting DNA sequences to give to Tina. She would then translate them into algorithms for the chip, a delicate procedure that took patience and time.

'No, I came in here to joke with you,' she said dryly. 'I do stand-up comedy routines now.'

As was appropriate, Jack remained mute, knowing that Belcher's sarcasm was only ever used as bait to launch. He waited, knowing that the conversation remained incomplete.

'Walk with me Jack. Now.'

He struggled to keep pace as she launched into facts, one after another in rapid-fire. 'Wells is meeting us first thing in the morning. He's set aside one hour to hear my proposal, although no details yet. I do not intend to bring my assistant team with me as that's too much fuss, and we don't want Wells to think he's that important. So, just the two of us. We need to be prepared, however. So be read up, Jack.' She then swiveled on one heel and shut the door to her office in his face, not hinting, in any sense, that he'd also been part of any conversation.

Jack digested the information. This was one of those situations which afforded an equal amount of both positive and negative. Meeting the man himself was an uncommon scenario and perhaps even a privilege, depending on how one viewed Wells. Overnight and alone with Belcher, though? His thoughts triggered a fight-or-flight response, appropriate, he reasoned, given the situation. He texted Pete, who was out getting some chemical supplies from a lab on the other hand of town, and told him he was leaving to see Wells.

Pete texted back, *'Chill. The rest of the tests for the overlay can wait. All good. Fun times ahead 4 u. Enjoy quiet time with Belcher lol.'*

THE JET WAS LAVISH, exclusive and decadent, and encased in alabaster white. Seated diagonally from each other, not by choice, they were fussed over by the flight attendants in elegant white suits and provided with champagne in crystal glasses. White fur eye masks and hot towels were given out using crystal tongs. Such close proximity had been someone's hopeful understanding that they had liked each other's company. Jack gazed at the surrounding empty seats, seatbelts ready, and inwardly winced. Being opposite Belcher and belted in, was like expecting someone with arachnophobia to go and sit next to a life-sized tarantula and revel in it. He was determining how far her fangs might extend when her voice scratched into the pre-flight silence.

'Blue jeans, Jack? I hope you have something formal for the meeting. An encounter with a man like Wells, and you choose generic? Don't communicate to me from this moment onwards. I'm going to go inwards.' She put the fur over her eyes, inhaled deeply and became lifeless.

Jack observed her sudden freeze, looking for a rise and fall in her chest. She had fallen into a deep meditative state before he had uttered, *sure.* He was relieved that she had taken her batteries out before they had taken off. When packing, he'd imagined snippets of their in-flight conversation topics. Hitler, Stalin, The Black Plague, ISIS, human decomposition, and parasitoid wasps. Now, he was free to peruse the inflight entertainment and have a few drinks without her eyes drilling into his weaknesses - a better option for a multi-hour flight.

They reached Wells' private island on time, after a flight of no drama. Set high above sea level, it had better fared than the lower positioned islands, now submerged below rising sea levels. The flight, combined with Belcher's lifeless pose, had provided hours of drinking time. Belcher got a whiff of the alcohol dissipating from his pores as they disembarked the jet.

'Dickhead,' she muttered to him quietly, as they were stepping off the plane. 'We're expected to make a good impression. You reek. Get yourself tidied up. Our meeting is at 8.30 sharp tomorrow morning. I expect shaved, suit, and sober.'

The house attendant gave him the code to hut five and told him to follow the green path down the hill. The hut didn't disappoint, once he had finally found the damned thing which was camouflaging itself for fun, in amongst a dense screen of palm trees. Once in, it affirmed itself as belonging to someone wealthy, extravagance dominating through marble, drapes, style, and fragrance. From the window, the Pacific rolled flat as far as the eye could observe, accentuating the isolation of the island from the rest of the world. A private paradise that had secured protection from the unfolding demise on its horizon's borders. He took out a bourbon from the minibar and lay down on the king bed, planning a spa for later in the evening and maybe a walk around the island.

After a short rest, he strolled down to the marina and salivated over Wells' assemblage of boats, motors drying in the sun and sails neatly coiled. He gestimated a hundred million dollars in the first magnificent beast alone. This is what success looked like to the rich, he thought. He wondered if perhaps he might be determined to be rich now, by some. Although by Wells' standards, he was still struggling. He was jolted from his musings by a voice.

'Jack!'

He shot around. A woman's voice, which alluded to potential.

Then he winced. It was Belcher. The antichrist of beautiful.

'Come, we have much to discuss.' She indicated for him to follow her with an over-excited finger.

'Woof,' he said back, quietly enough so that she couldn't hear his tipsy mind unleashing a mild version of humor.

She was already speaking before he was in earshot, as he could see her mouth releasing utterances.

'… and?' she asked, waiting for his response, now that he had walked into her sound sphere.

'What?' he asked, not having been close enough to hear a word.

'It's polite to listen when someone is speaking Jack. I'm not trying to soothe the universe right now, with aimless prose.'

'No, of course not. The wind blew your voice away, that's all.'

'For the benefit of idiots, I will repeat what I was saying.'

Jack rolled his eyes. Away from her, of course.

'I was saying that this meeting is critical for us. We need to be able to offer Wells the pieces that he currently doesn't have. Which are?'

Jack tried to think quickly.

'I told you to prepare.' She stood over him, close enough that he could smell stale.

'Longevity with his plan, that's what we can offer. Numbers too, I guess, although no-one knows how many are up there right now. A hundred? A thousand? To ensure longevity and development of existing infrastructure, he needs capital, and that's what we can offer.'

'Good,' answered Belcher. 'I don't think he's made any considerable leaps forward with it all, although who knows? He's kept his cards very close to his chest. When he started Home Base, it wasn't to ensure the continuation of the human race. It was a bit of fun. Things have changed. How much capital will he need to make Home Base feasible for the long term?'

'As much as he can get his hands on, I imagine. It's a different situation now. Plus, we don't know if things are good or bad up there.' Jack looked up instinctively.

'He'll require our investment if he's genuine in establishing a durable new home for our species.' Belcher nodded to herself, reassuring herself that her idea was feasible.

'Ms. Belcher, I mean Madam President, there's something else we need to be sensitive about.'

'What Jack?'

'As you are probably aware, He's developing a chip at the moment, that interfaces the human brain with a computer. It's similar in a sense to what we are doing with Project IQ, albeit at an elementary level. I'm concerned that we don't know if we can trust him yet. He may want to steal our intelligence, no pun intended. I haven't yet patented the intelligence chip, as you are aware.'

Belcher stopped. 'Yes. I was going to mention that myself to you. It would be prudent not to discuss the nuances of our chip just yet. We'll concentrate on funding, resources, and numbers for Home Base.'

'So, if he asks why I'm now working for you? Surely he's got wind of the chip that I had developed? It wouldn't take a genius to put two and two together?'

'Tell him you're working on robotics. Even if he thinks he knows about the chip, he doesn't know the details. We can keep it that way for now.'

'What about where you're getting all this money from?'

'I'll tell him everything else, aside from the chip.'

'Everything?'

'Everything that I feel is relevant, Jack. That's called doing business.'

THEY WAITED, having been punctual, hands-on eight and six, respectively, in fresh white minimalism. They sat comfortably on a chalky white leather sofa, next to a snow white timber coffee table, admiring the spines of white books on silky white shelves. The only color in the room was Belcher's lips, now center stage and standing by for the curtain to lift. Wells made a point of making people wait for fifteen minutes over-time for appointments. A strange ritual, but one that granted him time to watch people under pressure.

'He's forcing us to wait, probably to eavesdrop into our conversation, at least that's what I'm presuming.' Belcher said, shooting a death stare up towards the fire alarm, where a small hidden camera was watching them. 'He probably wants to hear what we really think of him. I've done the same myself to people.'

Wells laughed from his office. He'd heard about this woman. This new President who had been willing to lead a new country out of exile. Someone with a complicated personality profile, that was for sure. Rumors had circulated that she had ordered the *big melt*, so he would remain on guard. She was without an entourage as well, obviously with a private negotiation to present to him. Jack was an interesting addition to the meeting, resulting in an odd couple in his waiting room. He was aware of Jack's reputation for his work in

AI and intelligence, and was intrigued as to what the pair might be bringing to him.

'Welcome to my island, Madam President,' he expressed warmly, extending his hand and engaging in a firm handshake. He then turned and extended his hand to Jack, who noted the milky softness to Wells' skin, assuming that he'd probably never worked a day out of an office. He took in the expensive suit, neat haircut, and diamond encrusted watch, soon followed by a hint of aftershave that promised dominance. Wells' face was round and baby-like, with few creases, and Jack pondered whether this was down to good genes or carefully injected fillers. It was hard to accept that someone who appeared so youthful had been the one to get to Mars first and secure it as his own. He felt a twinge of jealousy. Men like Wells highlighted every failure in himself, both of them born with the same potential, and yet one had risen with it, and the other had fallen.

'Have you found everything to be pleasant thus far?' Wells inquired politely.

'Yes, thank you. It's an impressive spot you have here,' said Jack enthusiastically. 'I took a look at the boats moored down at your marina.'

Wells' baby face lit up. 'I have a passion for the water. I choose one of the line-up and head out to sea as regularly as I can. It cleanses me. There's something so infinite about the ocean when you can't see land anymore.' He paused as if reminiscing. Jack wondered if he was thinking about Mars and how he might translate this passion in a dead-dry environment.

'So, how can I help you anyway, Madam President and Mr Cross?'

'Please, call me Morag.' Chanel red smiled her lips at him.

Jack was intrigued, watching her reaction. She was inviting him to call her by her first name, and those lips were shaped upwards as if smiling. He was not imagining that the corners of her eyes were crinkling from the attention.

'We have a proposal for you.' Belcher was smooth, without any hint of anxiety.

'A good proposal makes my day, Morag. Now, before we start, let me organize some coffee.' He had stalled already, Jack noted, wanting to set the pace of the meeting himself.

Wells ordered them coffee and then listened intently as Belcher outlined her ambitions to relocate to Mars. He remained motionless while she was speaking, absorbing the impact of its boldness.

'So,' he said, getting up out of his chair and standing over near the window. 'You want to work alongside me? That's very direct, Morag. Home Base has been my baby since its conception, and mine alone. Why would you think that sharing it is something I'm now interested in doing?'

Jack inwardly winced. Ouch. Wells had thrown it back into her face. Now she would need to explain *why* she should be the one to share it all with him.

Belcher had a rehearsed response, having already worked out the permutations as to how the conversation would go. 'I believe that you want Home Base to succeed well into the future. Having additional financial sources, especially the amount I'm offering you, could only be beneficial if that's your intention. That is, to ensure that Home Base can sustain longevity, and of course be the *only* place where the human species can now survive?'

'Yes, of course, but I'm presuming *you* are also included in this proposal, Morag?'

Jack studied Belcher, a face perfectly still, a mind in full control, giving nothing away. He knew that she would be hiding her response to his baited, veiled insult. Wells wanted her to *sell herself* to him. Would she stoop into doing that? They sat in a moment of silence.

'Yes, of course,' she said matter-of-factly, gaining composure to speak, her voice neither with hues of apology nor explanation.

There was silence. Belcher wasn't going to beg for a place on Mars.

'I see,' Wells said, turning his attention towards Jack. 'So, your argument is that we save the human race by sending up the world's political leaders? Is this a good thing, do you think?'

Jack chuckled at Wells' humor. 'You can't hear all the rhetoric in space, remember.'

Wells leaned back and laughed.

There was a knock on the door, and coffee for three, with a selection of cakes, was wheeled in by a beaming and enthusiastic island employee. Belcher fussed over the cakes, something Jack thought she didn't have the capability to do.

'You have excelled with the refreshments, Paxton. You don't mind if I call you Paxton?'

Jack could see through her, as he was sure that Wells could too. Belcher was known for being ruthless, and this pretense at reasonable was amusing, a theatrical presentation of what was socially expected. Wells played along, his own lines reading from etiquette and acceptable.

'Call me Paxton by all means. Now, let me present our latest cakes. All the ingredients for the cakes are grown here on the island. Recently, we've been trialing genetic modification, combining fruits and vegetables together.' He picked up a small yellow cake. 'This is created from pinarin, a combination of pineapple and mandarin. The orange cake is made from cargin, a combination of ginger, mandarin and carrot. This one, denounced by many for being too tart, is applebee, made from apple and beetroot. We still have plenty of rain to allow us to play with our food, so to speak.' He smiled at them both.

'That's delicious,' said Jack, his mouth already full of the applebee cake. He was starving, not having had time to eat breakfast due to being incredibly hung-over from trying out everything in the minibar, the night before.

Belcher shot him a disgusted look, clearly hinting to him, to take smaller bites.

'So,' Wells said, sipping his coffee, leaning back into his chair. 'Saving the human race, hey? What a job and what a moral mess. Home Base now offers the only way for the human species to survive, and I hold the front door key. However, we're not here to talk philosophy, are we? Let's talk numbers.'

It was the business end of the meeting.

'How much do you need? My funds are essentially limitless.' Belcher sounded confident.

'Nothing is limitless Morag, not even this vast universe above our heads.'

'Name your price Paxton.'

'For an undertaking such as this? It wouldn't be unreasonable for me to request several incremental payments of a hundred billion.' He made no apology for quoting the enormous sum. He paused and searched for a reaction. Blecher was waiting for more before responding. 'I need to look into logistics, such as the ongoing availability of resources for such a large group, but I'm sure anything is possible with adequate funding.'

Morag smiled. 'We have eight hundred people essentially ready to depart. I don't want to wait too long.'

Wells cut across her and chuckled. 'I'm sure they are, but Home Base isn't ready for eight hundred new inhabitants, and we'll need an additional two craft, not one. If we require that sort of infrastructure, then I'll need to build several more cargo craft and get them up there, delivering resources as well. That side of things may be complicated, as manufacturing has been fickle, of late.'

Belcher reassured him. 'As I said Paxton, we have as much money as you need and we have the manufacturing resources to do this.'

'It's an interesting proposition. However, I have one stipulation.' He sounded serious, sitting forward in his chair, his baby face maturing.

Belcher and Jack waited for him to speak.

'In terms of confidentiality concerning existing Home Base plans, pertinent information about the craft and well… everything else… I'm pretty tight about it. It's not information I readily share. As you know, I closed down all public knowledge banks back in 2028.'

'We wouldn't be here unless we were serious about this Paxton.' Belcher was quick to respond. 'That includes keeping our plans discreet. This works best for all of us, as I'm sure you can appreciate.'

'Absolute trust is important, Morag. I'm not yet ready to open my books to you. Respect and trust are an earned commodity, not something to be given over coffee and cake.'

'Of course. If I am considering throwing hundreds of billions of dollars at someone, it isn't going to be someone who is going to cross me.'

Whoa, thought Jack. That's a passive-aggressive maneuver. She's turned that one around and fired it right back at you, Paxton.

'Me cross you?' He laughed. 'How funny.'

'I'm assuming that's an implied yes, that we can trust you, Paxton? You and I are similar in many ways. We see the future, but we also see when people are genuine.' She paused, allowing Wells time to churn her words. 'That future isn't and cannot be on planet earth. I have the money, and you have the means to make this work. That sounds like a sensible proposition to me.'

'It does Morag. A mutual arrangement of visionaries. How about we call it something like that?' He raised his cup of coffee at them. 'To Home Base and us then.' He stood and walked over to a white cabinet and opened the buffet hatch. 'Let's do this properly. It calls for a decent toast. How about a glass of something real, to seal our deal then?'

'Yeah, sounds great.' Jack was onto it.

Belcher was relieved that Wells had agreed to the plan. 'Sounds like we have ourselves a deal.' She stood and extended her hand and shook on it.

'In terms of timing,' said Wells, 'I think we should be looking at a launch date as soon as we can get everything out there. It's just possible that we could do this within five years, Morag. All of your eight hundred would have to go through a strict and highly confidential training program. Life in space and on Mars is tough from every aspect.'

'I understand,' replied Morag.

'No. You don't. Not really Morag. As you know, I'm only now sending up my Underground Generation. Eighteen years of waiting and watching to see how they would adapt. Individuals who have spent most of their lives in the artificial lava tubes getting used to the conditions. In fact, we had a couple of babies born down there recently, making them the first human beings who have never felt natural sunlight on their faces. They will do well on Mars. You may not. The first generation suffered considerable mental health issues, not something I broadcast widely. Trying to adapt to living on Mars may be an exciting challenge, but in reality? It has been harder to adapt to than imagined. The first group fought and some killed. They had significant problems with depression and hopelessness. That's why I created the Underground Generation.'

'Of course,' said Morag. 'I imagine they might find it easier.'

'I hope so, given they have been living underground for so long. Now, let's discuss our terms and conditions around confidentiality and make sure these are clear from the beginning. We can get the legals to draw something formal up. I'll also need the first hundred billion as a security payment so that I'm not out of pocket. There's a lot involved with all of this. Can you do that within the week?'

'I can make a phone call, and the money is yours, Paxton. However, I want detailed weekly updates to ensure that the venture is progressing in a way in which I am happy. Also, we will sign a formal agreement outlining what we've discussed today, as soon as possible. I'll get my legals to send it to you as soon as we return.'

'I don't see a problem with that.'

Jack was worried. Five years? Why hadn't Belcher argued with that? He was thinking that they would be leaving Earth in maybe eight years, at a minimum. He wondered whether he should say anything, but decided to keep quiet, as so far, they had got themselves a deal. It put an incredible amount of pressure on the team to come up with the chip and get it working. So why get the chip working, if only for a few years? Stability, he surmised, rolling the issues around in his mind. She needed the money from the leaders, and they needed their professionals back working, to keep them in power and stimulate the economy. Still, the pressure was intense by anyone's standards.

The three discussed practical aspects of the deal, such as when Belcher would deliver funds to Paxton, plans for the build of more cargo craft, a new design for a commuter craft, and an inventory of what they may need on Mars. With the size of the investment, Wells assured Belcher that everything could be fast-tracked.

'This is quite a moment you know, Morag and Jack. The three of us right now, in this room, are ensuring the future of the human species. Up until now, I've been operating a giant human experiment. Now, it's about survival. It's incredible that we have the human race in the palm of our hands. It's a shame we can't share the news in a way.'

'I agree,' said Belcher. 'However, we all know that the plan would incite panic amongst those being left behind.'

'Those are true words. Panic is our biggest threat right now, and the disorder that it would incite. We're already adding layers of security measures for the Home Base headquarters here on the island, as we are predicting that it's going to be targeted, as panic increases. I'm still getting offers of money to take people to Mars, and threats for that matter too. I have thousands on the waiting list to join the Underground Generation. Blackmail last week, if I didn't take certain people up there. There's unrest brewing for sure. Now, changing tack, and no pun intended, how about I take the two of you out for a sail? It's a perfect morning, and I have a few hours before I have to catch my jet to New York. Let's regard this as the first baby step of many. You concentrate on funds, and I'll focus on everything else. I feel good about this, you know, as it's been a solitary journey so far, and to be honest, I like the idea of mutual investment. It ensures that Home Base has longevity.'

Jack inwardly smiled, the exact word being spoken that he had envisioned. Longevity suggested promise.

PETE WAS ARRANGING copious numbers of wires in the lab when Jack arrived back later that evening.

'She was flirting, I'm telling you,' laughed Jack, recounting the day.

'No way,' said Pete. 'Really, with Wells?'

'Yeah, he's a nice bloke, you know. I feel like we're doing the right thing here. He took us sailing after the meeting. It proved to be a good opportunity to get to know him a bit better.'

'That's good to know. Can you imagine if he'd said no?'

'She had a Plan B, as there's no way she would have had us working on this otherwise. I think it was wise of Wells to agree with Plan A.'

'Hey, are you in a hurry because we can get on with the other scans if you like? No-one else is here, aside from one of the cleaners. We can get your overlay moving along. I also need some more blood for some genetics matching. Cameras are off, well, they're on their ten-minute loop, and the place is quiet. It's a good opportunity to do what we were meant to do this morning. You up for it?'

'Sure,' said Jack. 'Is that beer still in the fridge in the kitchen?' Pete nodded. 'I haven't touched it.'

'Let me get some, and then I'll be set.'

He strolled down to the kitchen. It had been a good day today. Different to his normal, but he'd enjoyed it. He couldn't remember the last day where he had felt so awake and available for change. There were moments on the sailboat when it had run with the wind, and it had just been him and the vastness. No climate to worry about. No riots, death, or stress. Just him and a wind that was pushing him forward.

'Want one?' He handed Pete a beer.

'Is the sky blue?' asked Pete, taking it from his hand.

'So, how straightforward is your part in the personality overlay?' asked Jack, swigging back the cold ale.

'Well, given it's never been done before? This is tricky shit.'

'Will she ever know, do you think?'

'What, that we swapped her personality for yours? No. Not unless she goes and gets herself a degree in genetics. Genes are complicated, even for those of us who think we know what we're doing. She will never know.'

'Ok, well, you're in charge of this bit. I trust you, buddy, and we aren't the ones having this chip implanted either.'

Pete looked at Jack. He was in an abnormally good mood. The trip away had done him good by the looks of things, which was going to be good for everyone else too.

16

7AM

7 PM

Ellie's day had started as usual, alarm at six and standing in the queue for breakfast by seven. She mostly kept her eyes down, keen to avoid being dragged in to someone else's small talk. Heads would turn to one another and hushed tones would recount tales of misdeeds, harsh words, wrong looks and all of it had one thing in common. It was all inconsequential stuff mixed with whiffs of conspiracy. Good old-fashioned gossip thrived in a place like Gaia. It was encouraged and a dibby-dobber society flourished, with individuals being rewarded for passing on the mistakes of others. Her world now, and those captured in Gaia was about the minutiae. Small things could trip people, and when they fell, they fell hard. A minor indiscretion was reported as a significant event that needed to be discussed at length by the onlookers, keen to dish out their interpretation of suitable punishment.

The breakfast menu was a welcome relief to the endless protein bars on the outside. Toast, fruit, eggs, and porridge, plus unlimited tea and coffee. Gaia had the means to obtain and grow fresh, which was perhaps the best aspect of moving in. It wasn't that other people couldn't grow fresh food in places. It was that the security to keep the food safe was so extreme from others, that it put most people off trying.

Ellie wasn't a big breakfast eater, so generally stuck with two cups of strong coffee to start the day. One was for the faux sugar hit, in the form of a teaspoon of aspartoid, a derivative of aspartame, and the other was for the caffeine, today having been brought in from Ireland. She had claimed a seat, tucked away in the far left corner of the breakfast hall, overlooking a small garden, that offered her a promise of seclusion and privacy, a place where she could scan the room without being too obvious. She perused the hall, inhaling the bold and rich Irish wafting up from her mug.

The regular factions were coming in right on time. Eleven minutes past seven, and the women whom she called the acetone claws, largely due to their long, painted nails, extensions, and barbed comments, lined up, careful not to touch anything due to their nail polish still being wet. There was the early retired faction slowly wheezing in at twenty-four minutes past seven. A line of grey topped people who believed their shit didn't stink because it was wise from years of life. The miseries at seven twenty-seven lowered the mood temporarily, their whining dampening the intensity of the morning sun, now streaming in through the windows. It was amazing how easily like found like in a place like this, thought Ellie. How quickly people were drawn to the similar rather than contend with someone who might challenge their own values and beliefs.

MY TURN. Jack says I can add something here for y'all. Like finds like in places like Gaia because we're all small-minded, with universe sized egos squashed up in there that need stroking. Jack knows because he's got a frickin ego to match the universe. It's so big that only Belcher can match it. Yeah, I love you too, Jack. The people in the Gaia settlements are drawn to one another to create factions because factions offer power. If you're on your own, then the tigers come and eat you. Surround yourself with people who think like you, look like you, act like you, and you stand a chance at surviving. But, and here's the main reason people seek out *like humans*. It takes one to know one. If you see the person next to you, as you know yourself, then you can strategize. You can use that person for both good and bad. You know their strengths, and you know their weaknesses. Yeah?

THAT EVENING, Ellie stood in front of her choice of clothes in preparation for her new circle meeting. Given it was going to be dark reasonably soon, she knew she shouldn't care, but Austin would be there, and she felt that making an effort seemed the least she could do in return for his optimism in her attendance. Her choice of attire was a joke anyway, as the clothes given to her didn't fit properly and had already been worn by God knows who. They had been donated into the communal clothing pool, but the committee had already hand picked the sweet stuff for themselves. She was left with dregs, supposedly to enhance her detachment to the life she had known before. She chose the only skirt she now had access to, a dowdy ribbed catastrophe, hemmed crookedly at the knee, and teamed it with a once white t-shirt. She stood back and looked at her reflection in the mirror. Dire was the word that replaced hopeful.

She walked along the path which led behind red hut, making sure she wasn't being followed. She climbed the small wooded hill, stopping at the top to appreciate the brushstrokes of clouds, now illuminated red and orange. Then the path descended, weaving its way through more rugged bush, in between trees, some dead and broken, others green, rustling noisily in the breeze. Approaching the clearing where the meeting was to take place, she noticed a flat boulder, with eye masks neatly laid out on it - the sort you would see at a fancy-dress party. A note, held down by a small grey rock, told her to put one on. It was dusk with still enough light to recognize faces, so she assumed that it must have something to do with retaining identity integrity for the meeting, perhaps. Combined with the skirt, the feathered, purple mask with red sequins along the frame made Ellie wonder if she could appear more unattractive if she had tried.

The group of seven, minus Austin, whom she hoped was just running late, looked more like they were about to partake in a strange party. They sat quietly as the pot was boiled on the fire. This was their ritual. A time for quiet contemplation as the first tea was made. It was handed to her in silence, with a small nod that indicated for her to drink it. She sipped. A blend of smoky and spice which warmed her and gave her a sense of calm belonging. It was only when the cups had been collected for their first washing that the meeting started. The mood went from contemplative to earnest in a heartbeat.

The same woman, the one with the rasp in her voice, also owned an unruly mop of greying hair and a ruddy face in the dimming light. 'Nice to see you all. Especially Ellie again. Everyone welcome Ellie.'

Ellie was puzzled. Why were they wearing eye masks if everyone knew her identity?

'Ellie understands our demands for confidentiality,' the woman added, nodding to her. 'I'm Darinda and it just so happens to be my birthday, thus the masks if you are wondering. This is my way of celebrating another year on our beautiful planet, albeit with a little style. These masks were all we could find to celebrate with, in the celebrations box, so I hope you understand.' She laughed. 'So remember, they have to go back later tonight so don't damage them!'

Everyone politely clapped as a way to welcome Ellie, and then it was straight into discussions.

Darinda spoke again. 'Roger, the craft? Any updates?'

'Yes, actually I have,' said a thin, older man, wearing all beige. 'Although, to be honest, the information is convoluted.'

'Any information is better than nothing. Go ahead.' Darinda leaned forward as if anticipating something succulent to be offered.

'Well, it seems that President Morag Belcher, infamous for melting the other President, has created some super-team of scientists to do two things unofficially. One is unknown, but the team includes Jack Cross, Tina Matthews, and Peter Duffy, all known for their work in AI. The second bit relates to this craft that we know about. Belcher and Cross boarded a private jet and met with Paxton Wells this week.'

There were murmurs around the circle.

'So, are we're talking Mars?' Darinda was all-in, rubbing her hands together.

'I believe so,' Roger said. 'The information is sketchy at present, but putting two and two together, I would argue that Belcher is planning to get to Home Base, and there is some sort of AI involved, although we don't know anything about that yet.'

'How does this link to the Underground Generation and his plans with them? I heard they have recently had babies born down there, wherever 'down there' is.'

'Sorry I'm late,' panted a familiar voice, now breathless from running. Ellie recognized it as belonging to Austin, who was just taking his seat. She looked over and smiled. He smiled back, but without seeing his eyes properly through his mask, it was hard to tell what his smile had meant.

Darinda wanted more. 'If it's true, then we need to find out what Belcher is planning. What's our approach?'

Roger spoke again. 'I have my contacts working on this. We've planted someone on Wells' island as well as a cleaner into the labs.'

Ellie was surprised. How would you do that from the Gaia Settlement?

'Have you ensured there is no direct link to us?' Darinda sounded concerned.

'Yes, Darinda. I think I can manage that.' Roger smiled. There was a chuckle around the circle.

'We'll be fine, Darinda,' someone said. 'CIA… I think we're good.'

'Does anyone remember that summit by any chance?' Ellie had thought of something relevant to share. She remembered seeing Morag Belcher on TV.

'Yes,' a few people murmured.

'Go on,' encouraged Darinda.

'Well, I just remember it was televised, and then as soon as Belcher started, there was this technical failure… which went on for a few minutes. Interestingly, when it went recommenced, a few of the leaders were missing from their seats.'

'Yeah, I remember that too.' It was Austin who had spoken.

'I thought maybe they had all gone to the toilet, but that wouldn't make sense because the whole thing had only just started.' Ellie was thinking back to the event.

'Interesting,' said Darinda. 'Perhaps there is something politically driving this? Who has contacts?'

'I can handle that,' said a woman in a flowery dress.

'Thank you, Anna. We're lucky to have so many resourceful individuals in the circle.'

'Alright. Next on tonight's agenda is the mangrove swamp. Who's helping us with this information?'

'Me.'

'And me. We're both investigating this.'

'Ah yes, Louise and Edward, update?' asked Darinda.

Louise spoke. 'We're going to take some samples of the fertilizer from the swamp. Gary who drives the garbage… is it the garbage truck, Ed?'

'Yeah, the garbage we send back to Gaia headquarters. Blue truck… that guy,' replied Ed.

'I know the one,' said a youngish man who had introduced himself as Sims. 'He seems okay.'

'Yeah, he's not happy right now with his pay and stuff and just so happens to have a degree in environmental science. Wants to make a difference, not drive trucks all day, so has agreed to test the soil and fertilizer for us.' Ed nodded at the group. 'Nice guy, as Sims says.'

Ellie shuddered at the implication. They actually did think that there was something to this rumor, that the fertilizer was composed of Gaia settlers?

The meeting then discussed issues which had less impact on Ellie's psyche, and there was time for a second cup of tea. Again, the ritual stipulated quiet contemplation. Ellie looked around outside of the circle. They were well protected from everyone else this far into the woods. There was a high rock ledge to one side, and the area was heavily dense enough to provide protection. They could also see if someone was approaching, so prying eyes weren't an issue. The area was peaceful and during the tea drinking, they could hear birds getting ready to retire for the night. The tea combined with the bird-song, and the sense of solidarity amongst the circle, was fortifying, as well as comforting.

'Another matter on our agenda is the free alcohol,' said Darinda after all the cups had been collected again.

Sims spoke. 'We think it could only be included in the alcohol containing artificial sweeteners. Although, we just don't know. Could be in all of the alcohol supply, which would make more sense. We don't have enough information yet.'

Ellie sat up. Given she'd had several drinks this week, she was alarmed.

'So, I just had a few drinks this week, can you fill me in on the alcohol situation please?' Ellie spoke with a degree of urgency. 'What am I supposed to be worried about?'

Darinda indicated to Sims to continue.

'Of course. We don't encourage anyone to drink the alcohol provided, mainly because we aren't sure what's in it to be honest. We do know that this notion of The Fear seems to be more pronounced when paired with alcohol and then it goes on from there, dampening inhibitions, both verbal and sexual.'

Ellie felt her heart race. What were they putting in the drinks?

Sims sensed her anxiety. 'Have you had any mixers, beers, cider or wines?'

'I had some gin and tonics after work. I've been in the toilets this week,' she offered as an explanation.

The group nodded, understanding her need for alcohol after toilet duty.

'Is it in the tonics, Sims, and hard spirits?' asked Darinda.

'Maybe? We're trying to find out. Just haven't proved it yet.'

Ellie was stressing. What was in the drinks?

'I think it might be helpful for Ellie to know what is in the drinks. She's looking pretty uncomfortable right now.' Austin looked at her, as sympathetically as he could, through his brilliant orange eye mask.

'Yes, sorry Ellie,' smiled Darinda. 'Okay, we think, and remember this is our speculation, that they may be putting in a sterilization drug into the alcohol. Good news is that we think you have to be regularly drinking for it to sustain its integrity.'

Ellie felt ill. Her hand shot over her mouth. 'Seriously? Oh my God. They would do that?'

'We think so, don't panic though, unless you are drinking every single day for a sustained period, as in months, it wouldn't have harmed you. This is all hearsay at this point too.'

Austin spoke. 'It's okay.'

'Who is doing the testing?' asked Darinda.

'We've managed to source someone, so should be able to get a result back in a couple of weeks,' replied Sims. 'Sorry Ellie. Just don't drink if that's possible. The rest of us don't. Speculation right now, but it's a safer option.'

'Yeah, I had a funny feeling when I first arrived that The Fear was always being driven home when they had plied everyone with alcohol. Only I've had a shit of a week in the toilets and needed something to dull my memories.'

Louise chuckled. 'Toilet duty is an arse of a job.'

Everyone laughed.

'Yeah… but putting that shit… sorry, no pun intended, into the alcohol. That's evil.' Sims shook his head with disgust.

Ellie was glad she'd restricted her drinking to only a few days at a time. Gaia was beginning to look more and more sinister. She looked around the circle. Right now, she needed to maintain her balance of judgment, though. Take a deep breath and let the information sit with her. It was easy to get carried away with fake news, conspiracy theories, and evil intentions. Best to wait until there was proof before getting too caught up in the drama. These people seemed genuine enough, though.

'Ellie looks a little shocked right now, everyone. We've thrown a lot at her. I can imagine she's wondering who the heck we all are.' Austin smiled at her.

Darinda spoke. 'Ellie, we came together through accident and I suppose you could call us a group of like-minded people. We don't believe everything we get told and we always ask our own questions. We're about facts here. If the science doesn't support our theories, then we don't believe them. Right now, we've got a couple of significant issues to prove or disprove. Neither is palatable, I agree. However, we didn't come to this Gaia Community to end up sterile and nor being used as fertilizer. We were promised utopia, after all. Our ultimate goal is to find a better way. We aren't sure what that is just yet, but we play along within the system in the meantime and we meet once a week.'

Ellie nodded. 'Thanks. I'm glad I found you all. I don't want to be spending the rest of my life just waiting for End Date. I want to be doing more… but safely.'

The circle nodded.

'You're in the right place, Ellie. Just be careful out there.' Darinda looked solemn.

There was a heavy pause, as everyone acknowledged the significance of her words.

'Need I say this again,' she continued. 'Be very careful my circle. They watch and they listen. When you return tonight, split up, walk in pairs at most and talk about something mundane you have just experienced. The beautiful sunset, meditation… a painting you were doing or a game of tennis. Never place yourself in this circle at this time.' Darinda sounded serious. 'We have better things to do than end up as fertilizer for those mangroves.'

The rest of their time was spent drinking another round of tea and mulling over the agenda items, but Ellie felt nauseous. The notion that they were grinding people up and putting them into the swamp just made her feel sick, and scared too. She understood completely why the circle needed to be so guarded.

'Next week, we are changing location by the way,' added Darinda, as the cups were being washed. 'Can you give everyone a short brief Sims?'

He nodded. 'Next week, the circle will be held in a cave we have located, about a twenty-minute walk from here. We will get the map to you during the next week.' Sims pointed in the direction of the caves. 'Not too far from here, much better security, so you will need to allow adequate time to get there. Also, a bit more private in case you need to go. All this tea can make walking back a bit difficult.' He smiled.

'Excellent Sims. I would prefer to be inside, not sitting perched out here feeling so vulnerable. Safer for all of us,' agreed Louise nodding, and looking around. 'Better for more tea drinking too, I agree.'

'I'll walk back with you if you like,' offered Austin, approaching Ellie after the meeting had disbanded.

'Yeah, sure.' Ellie was happy for the company. Although the new information had really thrown her, she felt somewhat validated as well. She'd felt that something wasn't right from the beginning in Gaia, and now she'd found a group of people who seemed to agree with her.

They strolled along the lower riverbank, making sure that their conversation was about the beautiful sunset they had just witnessed whenever they passed anyone else.

'So, are you married?' asked Austin, 'if you don't mind me asking?'

Ellie smiled. 'Yes… well, on paper, anyway. Dean. He was a teacher, like me.'

'Me too. I'm married to Tyler… on paper as well. She used to be a weather reporter.'

There was a pause, neither of them wanting to invade privacy, as they hadn't known each other long enough.

'So, what was your life like before you arrived here?' asked Ellie.

Austin paused and then chuckled with a layer of sarcasm. 'Oh, we had the perfect mouse-wheel lifestyle. Driven, ambitious, needy, wanting… and ruled by routine and money. The perfect capitalist couple, in fact.'

'I hear you,' sighed Ellie, thinking back to her previous existence. 'You know, it's funny looking back on it all now, from in here. The life you thought you were doing so right…'

Austin nodded. 'You get sold the Plan of Life, and you just do it, because you can. Looking back now, I cringe, because it was so awesomely self-centered. Tyler and I were going to take on the world, even when we knew that End Date was coming. It was like our egos were so big that the two of us thought that End Date wouldn't apply to us.' He shook his head at his own arrogance.

'Originally, I trained as a microbiologist would you believe, but it just didn't gel with me once I'd graduated. I'd always wanted to be a lawyer since I was a kid, but wasn't brave enough to give it a go straight out of school… so I retrained a few years ago. I had this belief that I could solve everyone's legal problems for them, and I did for a while. Not for free, though. I expected a shit load of compensation for doing it. Tyler read the weather, and I shouted in court and we had everything materialistic you could dream of. Did it make us happy? The funny thing is Ellie, that we thought we were. Then it all fell apart when we arrived here… and well… we discovered that once we took all of the acquired stuff out of our lives, we had nothing in common. Not even each other in fact, and the happiness we thought we had brought with us? I guess it got left at those gates.'

'I'm sorry,' said Ellie.

'Thanks,' he said, inhaling a deep breath, as if trying to control his emotions. 'God, I just said more words in that one breath than I've said since arriving. Sorry…'

'No need to be sorry,' she said. 'I've not had a decent conversation, aside from small talk since I got here. Dean and I fell apart too. Dean availed himself of the free alcohol the day we arrived, tried everyone in sight, and the rest, as they say, is history. I got a different sleeping cabin in the end. We did the same, you know. We graduated and bought the house, had the ten-year plan and then we were going to start a family. The weird thing is that we never questioned any of it. We were on autopilot the whole time and once we lost our routine with work, we just slid away from each other. It was surprisingly easily and quick to be honest.'

'Do you think End Date will be the end?' asked Austin.

'Yeah, I do, if not before, with all the crazy going on out there.'

'Sad isn't it,' said Austin, 'that we can see the end to everything. Reminds me of the pandemic in the twenties. That was close too, for many. Months of staring down an invisible barrel.'

'Yeah, I remember it… just. Months stuck in the house with my parents. Home schooled, not allowed to go out to play with my friends. We lost so many people we knew. Then our neighborhood got really smashed with GFC2. It was just years of turmoil, really.'

'I remember,' said Austin, reflecting back to the years of uncertainty that had popped up from nowhere.

'This is sad from so many perspectives, too,' said Ellie. 'I'm so angry, though, Austin. I really am.' She stopped walking, not having realized the extent of her anger before. 'I'm angry that we ended up being so… limited, and that we destroyed all of this.' She looked around at everything. 'We fooled ourselves, didn't we? We thought that we had it all worked out. In reality, we obliterated what could have been pretty amazing… despite surviving the pandemic and GFC2. You would have thought that we might have discovered humble in amongst all of that.'

'I know,' said Austin. 'Greed. That's what it came down to. We didn't know when to stop. We were all guilty. Tyler and I never stopped for one minute when we were trying to achieve. That's what we had been encouraged to do, so we did it. Right back in school we were fed that message. Success is everything. Dream big… strive for the top. We didn't care about carbon footprints or how many starving people there were, when we stuffed our faces and complained because the air-conditioning wasn't cold enough. Shit, listen to me. Looking back, I make myself cringe. I hate who I was back then, I really do.'

'Yeah, me too, Austin. I actually feel shame.'

'Shame… yeah… I do too. That's an apt descriptor.'

They walked for a bit in silence, as if administering punishment to themselves for their previous excesses.

'This place sounds a bit dangerous,' said Ellie, changing the subject after a lengthy period of self-flagellation.

'It is dangerous. I mean, I've only been attending this private circle for what… five months now, but in that time, I've learned a lot about how this place works. These intentional communities were business opportunistic. There is no real *utopia* to sell us, even though they try to market themselves as such. They think that by plonking us into the middle of green, rolling hills, forcing us into a multitude of circles, and feeding us organic, we're somehow better off? I mean… we are in a way… but the only advantage about being in here is the protection we get from what's going on outside, and in return, we make the Illuminati all stinking rich. Plus, we most likely get killed off if we decide to buck the system. We exist in their concept, and God forbid if we deviate and question it. Come to think of it, what's it been like out there? I miss being able to keep up with the news.'

Ellie sat on one of the wooden benches along the path. 'It's been like watching something slowly die. Maybe the dream we all had? It's like watching the human race slowly crawl towards its death. More people have left the cities, that's for sure. Sewerage is a big issue, garbage collection, schools are shutting down, and hospitals are running on serious emergency only. Many councils have dissolved, and governments are introducing more and more austerity measures. There are also weird diseases traveling up from the tropics. Most small islands are wiped out, and a lot of India is dead. Africa is starving… Australia is burning and the oceans are becoming empty. It's just dire,' she said, shaking her head. 'Dean and I just gave up in the end. Coming here was really our only option, and we were lucky that we still had our vehicle license to drive here. Most cars are off the roads now - if you can call the roads. Crumblings stretches of bitumen, more like. We were lucky, only because we had enough mortgage credits to retain our license.'

'What's the latest on austerity?'

'Austerity? It's a joke. Sorry about my cynicism, by the way.'

'No… that's fine. Be as cynical as you want. I am.'

The fifteen-minute curfew warning siren sounded.

'That's our signal. Look, we're close to the main huts now. Best if you head back by yourself, and I'll follow at a discreet distance. We'll need to talk again, by the way.' Austin smiled.

Ellie looked puzzled.

'You never did finish discussing what the new austerity measures were. That's all.'

'Yeah, I didn't realise how much I had so much to say. Sure. Maybe I'll see you down at the river one afternoon?'

'Hope so. Now be off before the stroke of twelve,' he said cheekily.

'Why? Do you turn into a pumpkin?'

'Maybe?' he laughed.

'I haven't tasted pumpkin in ages,' she called back, before realizing her double entendre.

He grinned.

17

SHARP NEEDLES HURT
A SCRATCH DOES NOT

'For Christ's sake, Pete! That fucking hurts!'

'Are you being a baby yet again? Seriously Jack. This does not hurt. It's a scratch.'

'It does hurt. More like a frickin' scratch from a bear.'

'Jack, it's a needle. It's taking your blood.'

'Yeah, I can see that dude.'

'Okay, done.' Pete pulled the needle out. 'I've done four vials, which should be plenty.'

'What, for a blood transfusion?' Jack looked over at the neat line of red vials. 'Jesus, can I even survive to lose that much? Isn't that going to, like, stop my heart?'

'You know Jack, sometimes I can't tell when you're serious and when you're not. Either you're trying to be funny, or you are a hell of a hypochondriac. You do know that you can lose like half a gallon of blood before we would start to worry? These vials form the genetic basis for the personality overlay. We need all of them so that we can do the job properly - but you already know that.'

'I do. I was the one who designed it all, in fact.'

Pete rubbed the small hole with a disinfectant wipe and then placed a small ball of cotton wool onto it. 'Press on that for a second.'

Jack earnestly pressed on it without saying anything.

'You can speak while you're doing that, you know,' said Pete.

'I know.'

'You can probably stop pressing now, anyway.'

Jack looked at the wound site to make sure it had stopped spotting red. 'Well, we're making some progress, which is better than none. It would be good to catch up later today for a full briefing. You free after lunch, say two?'

'Sure, can do. What's the time frame on all of this now that Wells is on board? We haven't discussed that yet. Is that on the agenda?'

'Yeah, it would be good to get on top of specific goals this arvo.' He glanced at the clock on the wall. 'Okay, morning cameras are back on in ten. I'll head out and come back in.'

'I'll do the same. Just drop everything and head out. Belcher isn't likely to come dashing in here first thing, anyway.'

They walked back in, a minute past eight, just as Belcher and her entourage appeared, waiting for the Presidential car convoy.

'Meeting at two if you are free?' Jack asked Belcher hopefully.

'Obviously busy,' she replied, not looking up from her briefing folder. 'Just write up the minutes and give them to me. I'm sure you can manage that.'

'Right,' said Jack, looking at Pete with his eyebrows raised. They walked together towards the labs.

'We need to nut-out a compact goal board this arvo, just so that we are all on the same page Pete. Things get more complicated from here in terms of putting this together. We're also going to need to mock-up a prototype daily soon, too.'

'Agreed. Okay, see you for lunch or after.'

Jack made his way into lab eight. Tina was meeting him there to update him on her progress, and he was surprised when she walked in straight behind him.

'Tina. You're nice and early. We've planned a meeting at two, by the way, to discuss the timing with all of this. Now that Wells is on board, we need to get some better direction.' He could smell the perfume again, and it was playing with his head.

'Who's in the meeting?'

These images, her nakedness, triggered by her perfume, had to stop. It was probably some form of virtual sexual harassment, to keep thinking like this.

'Just the three of us.'

'No Belcher?'

'She's busy.'

'That makes me happy, as she's difficult. So, how was the trip?'

'I'll fill you in over lunch. It went really well. I wouldn't mind living on a private island.'

Tina laughed. 'Yeah, well, with the amount Belcher is paying you, maybe you could buy one?'

'I could come to think of it… now there's a thought. Well, in a few years anyway, if all of this goes to plan, and I wasn't moving to Mars. Talking of plans… let's get the equipment out. Lots to sort out today.'

They opened the storage cupboard and located the cube computers.

Jack reached over to grab the light leads, and then his mouth was close to Tina's. There was a pause and things could have gone either way. It was Tina who made the move. She kissed him, her mouth soft on his. At first, he pulled back from the surprise, but then he became urgent for the past, wanting to remember. He moved his hand behind her head, soft at her nape. The other made its way down her back. He pulled her in closer, feeling her warmth. He remembered, the memories cascading in, needing and wanting acknowledgment. He remembered all of it. How his body had responded to her touch, how soft her skin had felt, and how much she had nestled into his arms afterward.

She pulled back, suddenly.

'Oh my God, Jack. I'm so sorry. That was not intentional.'

Jack's heart was banging in his chest. 'No… it was…' What had it been? A memory that had ignited many others. 'We were good. I remember Tina.'

'Yeah, we were.' She smiled a small smile, nostalgic, reminiscent, and forgiving.

The moment was over.

'We need to get this equipment out. They'll wonder what we're doing in here.' Jack shook his head. 'Sorry to break this up, but we can't stay in here all day.' He leaned down and picked up one of the computers.

The moment was already lost in time.

Tina opened up her laptop and clicked on a file as if the kiss had never happened. It was as if someone had flicked a switch. Tina was suddenly scientist, more interested in information flow than recreating past encounters.

'I did some work on the integrity of the flow threads yesterday, ensuring that when the chip is inserted, the flow of information is uniform. Look, I can demonstrate it now.' She walked over to a tray on the far side of the lab and lifted a cover. 'I've got an actual sheep's brain here… it demonstrates using a light source, how we can release the information from the chip, uniformly. Important, because without this even flow, we're going to trigger stuff that we don't want to.'

'Cool brain set-up. You set all of this up yesterday?'

'Yeah. It's easier to see things with real tissue structures. Given we don't have any human brains lying around, a sheep was the next best thing.'

'I'm relieved we don't have human brains just lying around at this moment in time, otherwise we'd be asking Belcher for an explanation,' he smiled. 'I'm impressed. So, how's the uniformity?'

'Needs a bit of work. As you can see,' she said, flicking a switch, 'We're still pulsating somewhat, especially in the left hemisphere. This runs the risk of setting off random and unwanted neural-based reactions.'

'Solution?'

'Not sure yet. I was going to work on that today.'

'You go ahead. Good work with getting the brain in too. I'm heading off to lab four to do a bit of tweaking with the secondary hubs.'

'The hubs that are going to secrete the hyrantrocholine?'

'Yeah, I'm in two minds about where to place them. Kind of the same problem as you just demonstrated. It needs to flow steadily and not in too much of a spurt. Too much and it can destroy brain cells and not just information signals.'

'We will need to calibrate somehow, too.'

'We will. Not much that still needs to be done, hey? See you for lunch or at the meeting.'

'Jack…'

He looked at her, desperate for her to walk over and kiss him again. The feeling she gave him was more addictive than anything else he used. Maybe he should just walk over and place his lips back on hers? He felt himself stir in his pants at the thought.

'Nothing,' she said, as if changing her mind. 'See you at lunch.'

TODAY WAS a complicated problem on his plate, and he needed the kiss and the perfume out of his mind. Not an easy task, but one that was necessary given the complexity of the problem at hand. Creating hubs that could release even amounts of hyrantrocholine was not straightforward, especially as it had never been done before. However, to restrict free will, they needed to wipe over a stray thought and pair it with an algorithm. He pondered through the process, mapping out a basic flowchart on the whiteboard and summarizing what he knew in his mind.

A person has a chip implanted and then thinks of an idea that is going to take them off course. These rogue thoughts are highlighted already, having been computer-generated in all permutations as a preemptive measure… hopefully, anyway. This triggers the hyrantrocholine, which wipes out the thought before it can be acted upon. So, a course of flow was needed, a bit like finding the most straightforward route from one part of a city to another. In this case, the thought would originate in the cerebral cortex and attempt to make its way into the pre-frontal lobe. He tapped his pencil on the desk. Maybe a squirt of the hyrantrocholine should head towards the hippocampus as well, just for good measure. God, there was so much to do, and too many unknowns. How were they going to get a prototype done when they were effectively stuck?

The scientists worked through until lunch and then converged into the courtyard for a lunch break.

'How did you go this morning with the sheep's brain?' Jack asked Tina, picking up four thick slices of pizza from the cafe. 'I cannot believe someone has managed to make a pizza,' he added in disbelief.

'Slowly, but I'm headed in the right direction, at least. You?'

'Yeah, grappling with routes right now. I'm dying to eat this damned pizza. I'm starving.'

They sat outside at their usual table and waited for Pete to join them.

'So, what is Paxton Wells like in person?' asked Tina.

'Humble to be honest,' Jack said, his mouth full of stringy cheese. 'He's loaded, but he seemed genuine, down to earth. Played Belcher well. He's smart, that's for sure.'

'That would have been interesting to watch, I imagine… Belcher being taken on. Was it subtle?'

'Not really. They just served it out at each other. We're talking billions of dollars here in payments, in return for Wells letting people in on his plans.'

'No room for subtlety then.'

'None.'

Pete joined them with a steaming bowl of something, and a crusty bread roll.

'What ya got?' asked Tina peering over the bowl.

'It's chicken with pieces of… I believe corn? What's with the bread today?' He peered over at Jack's pizza. 'Someone must have found some flour looking at this.'

'Well, I'm just glad we can eat,' said Tina, inhaling her salmon sushi. 'We're lucky to have access to all of this. Most people have to make do with those disgusting protein bars.'

'Yeah, money talks around here. At least Belcher is spending some of the funds on keeping us happy and healthy. Can't complain about that, at least,' added Jack, his mouth full and the strings of cheese now stretching down his shirt front.

'So, the meeting… straight after lunch?' asked Pete, scraping down his bowl with the last piece of his roll.

'Yeah, we'll head straight there, I think,' said Jack, leaning back, belly full of pizza. 'God, I needed a decent feed of carbs. Hey, we had the luxury of fruit on the island, aside from the cake…'

'They fed you cake?' Tina asked. 'You do know that cake is carbs too?'

'The thing about that cake was that it had almost zero carbs. It was genetically modified on all accounts. It was quite tasty, which is unusual for anything that claims to be low carbs.'

'Sounds like an amazing island on all fronts. Wouldn't mind a zero-carb cake, come to think of it, or any cake for that matter.' She looked wistful, reminiscing about something that she had once enjoyed.

'Wells is an interesting guy, that's for sure. Clever bugger. I wish I were that bright.' Jack slurped his coffee.

'Charming.' Tina looked at him with a look of disgust.

He belched as a thank you.

'Says the guy who is leading a pioneering research project, never done before,' smiled Pete.

'There's bright, and then there's Wells bright. What's his IQ?' Jack asked.

'Hang on, I'll search for it.' Tina grabbed her phone out of her bag. 'Mixed results. This site says 155 but not official. Someone here says that he's no Einstein. Someone here estimates 177…'

'Bright but maybe not a genius?' Pete asked.

'Nah, he's a dark horse, I think. He wouldn't have Home Base up and running if he weren't super bright.' Jack looked upwards, trying to figure out where Mars was in the sky. 'Seriously weird to think of them up there now, isn't it? They're probably looking back at Earth. Shit, how weird would that be, actually being on Mars and seeing Earth in the sky? Hard to believe that will be us one day.' Jack shook his head.

'Isn't there like an original photo online, doing the rounds at the moment? It's the first picture of Earth from Mars. One of the rovers took it. I saw it once, and it made me stop in my tracks. We're just a small dot. No different from all the other dots in the sky. How's that for a mind-fuck?' Tina smiled at Jack, raising one eyebrow ever so slightly. He got the joke and reciprocated, a small enough gesture for Pete not to have noticed. 'I'll find it.' She showed them a grainy picture. 'This was the first-ever photo of earth from Mars. January 31st, 2014. See how inconsequential we are from a different perspective?'

Pete leaned over to take a look. 'Gees… tiny. Like, really tiny. Just a small dot,' he looked upwards. 'All of this and we end up as a small dot.'

'No wonder aliens never found us. Too small.' Jack smiled. 'We're an atom on a needle in a haystack. Too small to ever find. Probably a good thing. Can't imagine aliens would be kind to us. More likely, they would see our planet as something to take, and then get stuck into probing us all.'

'Yes, please' said Tina, keeping a straight face.

Pete laughed. 'Yeah, aliens find us and the first thing they want to do is probe us all? The rest of the universe is a perverted mess. Anyway, what if are it and there are no aliens? What if we are the first, full stop?'

'You talking the Fermi paradox?' Jack shook his head. 'When you think of where Earth is and then add the Kuiper Belt plus the Oort Cloud, there's no way we will ever be found. We're in the galaxy burbs guys.'

'Burbs?' asked Tina.

'Suburbs. We're hidden.'

'Okay, now we're branching into the too-deep for lunch conversation,' laughed Tina. 'Come to think of it though, is Wells going to be sending up the Underground Generation before us?'

'Probably,' said Pete. 'You wouldn't leave them down here with no sunlight. Anyway, with their resilience, they are going to make life easier for us.'

'True,' agreed Jack, getting up from his seat. 'Let's get this meeting started. Belcher wants minutes, so who's taking the minutes? Pete?'

'Yeah, I don't mind.' Pete shrugged his shoulders.

• • •

SEATED in front of the whiteboard, Jack began. 'Right, the most important piece of info from yesterday's meeting is the time frame. Wells said that we'd split the eight-hundred going, into two new craft, each having a capacity of 400.' He paused.

'What are you waiting for?' asked Pete.

'You have to type as I speak, remember.'

'I can touch type, Jack. It's okay, really. Anyway, I'm using the device that transcribes for me. You can talk normally.' Pete smiled.

'Really? You can type that fast?' Jack looked surprised.

'Yeah. That fast,' said Pete, nodding slowly at him. 'I'm also a dark-horse sometimes.'

'Fair enough, smart arse. Right, so the plan is to build new cargo craft first and then start taking out the infrastructure, and then there's the training for the eight hundred. Wells thinks we can be up there in five years.'

'Really?' responded Tina and Pete in unison.

'That soon?' asked Tina, sounding clearly surprised.

'Yeah, Wells explained that once society descends into panic, it'll be too violent to stay. His theory is that the human race will wipe itself out long before the planet warms.'

'Jesus,' said Pete, looking subdued. 'Really?'

'Yeah. It's terrifying, to be honest.' Jack paused for a moment. 'Human beings can get quite nasty when they think their existence is being threatened. The first group for instance turned on each other and killed each other so I heard. That's why he started the Underground Generation. Apparently mental health was shit up there. We're not nice when we're unhappy.'

The three of them looked at each other, the impact of the statement being strongly felt.

'Makes sense to do it sooner rather than later from the perspective of the world leaders,' Pete said. 'If they don't get voted in again, then what happens? Was Belcher going to take them as well?'

'Good point.' nodded Jack.

'So, if we're getting off that soon, then, is there a point to the chip?' Tina asked bluntly.

'Belcher and I discussed this on the island. There is. If we don't act and put people back into the professions, then things will break down faster than we can get off the planet. Plus, we need the workers to make the Mars infrastructure that we need.'

'I don't suppose anyone has asked the missing professionals if they want to go back to work? Just a thought,' added Tina, seeing the incredulous looks on Pete and Jack's faces at her suggestion.

'Yeah, the ones in Gaia Intentional Communities, eating mango for breakfast and sitting in wellness circles? We should ask them to go back to the shit that's going on outside this door?' Jack stopped. 'Look, this has been on my mind a bit, it's about the shit that's going on outside the door. I think we should move into this building to finish this off. It's unstable out there. There are too many riots and bashings for us to travel to and from the labs, after hours safely.'

'Sleep in the lab, perhaps?' asked Tina, 'with my dog?'

'No. There's a pretty neat living set-up in zone thirteen. I thought ahead when Belcher was planning all of this and got her to build apartments. They should be finished pretty soon. We can take a look later if you want. You can bring your stuff over, as well as your dog, although pooch won't be coming to Mars with us, you do know that?'

'Yeah, of course. I've got a friend who's going to take Evie for me, once the time comes.'

'What sort of pooch have you got?' asked Pete, sounding interested.

'King Charles. Ruby color.'

'Cute. I don't mind dogs. Grew up with an Irish Wolfhound. We named him Gatsby… as in The Great Gatsby. Massive thing. Ate kilos of food every day.' He stood up. 'Anyway, this is getting pretty real. It was like a theory up until now. Now that plans are in place, and things are moving forward. It's like I need time for my mind to catch up.'

'Yeah, me too,' said Tina, nodding. 'It's like the ball has started rolling, and we're being taken along with it now. Makes it far more real.' Tina sighed. 'I feel like we strapped ourselves onto a rollercoaster, and it just got to the top. Now, it's all about to gain its own momentum.'

'You like your analogies, don't you?' smiled Pete.

'Yeah. It seems I do.' Tina laughed. 'At least rollercoasters are kind of fun?'

'For some,' Pete added.

'IT'S NOT TERRIBLY ethical is it, at the end of the day?' said Tina, some hours later, looking at them both.

'No, not really,' said Pete, sighing.

'We're creating zombies essentially. Are we going to tell them that when they sign up?' Tina stared at Jack, waiting for a response.

'Hadn't even started on the marketing side of things, as of yet,' Jack said. 'I think though, that the chip is going to be released, emphasizing career choice, that's as much as Belcher has told me thus far. Can't see it taking off if we explain the rest of it.'

'So, we're not going to explain the full impact of what it does?' Pete stared at Jack. 'We're going to lie about the limiter?' he added, sounding frustrated.

'No, we're just not going to go into too much detail. So technically not lying. Just omitting.' Jack shook his head. 'Seriously, guys? Let's stay focused here. Our job was never to pass judgment on the ethics stuff.'

'I think ethics are redundant,' sighed Tina. 'It's not relevant anymore. We haven't even applied for an ethics evaluation for the chip, nor testing approval… why stop being irresponsible when it's time to sell it to people?'

'What the latest on the incentive money, Jack?' asked Pete.

'Belcher has agreed on $30k.'

'Yeah, that should get them in,' said Tina. 'That will be more money than most will ever have seen in one hit. Bees to honey. Shit to shoes.'

'Shit to shoes? I haven't heard that one before.' Pete waited for an explanation.

'Nah, I made that one up. True though. Where there is shit, one is always bound to step in it.'

'May even improve some of them,' added Jack.

'Having shit on their shoes?' Pete sounded confused.

'No. The chip might improve some minds. Remember where this sample is going to be coming from… I mean, I don't want to be like… rude… but it's not exactly the crème de la crème of society who will be stepping forward.' Jack folded his arms, ready for the moral outrage definitely about to be fired from…

'You just were,' said Tina, jumping on his comment.

'What?' asked Jack, knowing full well that he had lit Tina's moral fuse.

'Rude.' She shook her head at him.

'I'll take rude then, if being honest is rude.'

'Time frames. We need specific time frames,' added Pete, interrupting the tiff. 'Five years for lift off? When does our space training start?'

'Wells suggested around eighteen months. Longer than usual because you can't just kidnap all the world leaders, and take them away somewhere, for full-time training. We're all going to be staggered so that it doesn't look suspicious to people who politician spot.'

'So, if we work backwards… then we're looking at needing to finish the chip in about six months… then the roll-out… say nine months… that gives us only three months up our sleeve before training starts.' Pete shook his head. 'We're not ready.'

'No,' agreed Jack.

'One thing which is a tangent by the way,' said Tina, looking perplexed. 'Why are we still putting in a personality overlay at this late stage? Do we still need it? I'm grappling with its inclusion if we're due to fly away so soon.'

'Yes, we still need it,' Jack nodded.

Pete jumped in. 'Yeah, look, we need to keep the minds of this army, tribe, group… whatever we are calling them, in a consistent framework. Too many personality types and we could… actually, probably would run into problems. There will always be those who want to take charge, and we can't afford that. We just need simple to make this work effectively, although selectively. We'll do the controlling… well, some of it… better all around.'

'Fair enough,' said Tina. 'You only have to look at social media to see how many armchair experts there are out there. I suppose keeping it synchronized is better in some regards.'

'Nice to have the cameras in here, isn't it,' blurted Jack, his way of alerting them to shut up about the nuances of the personality overlay, in case anyone forgot about the swap and mentioned it. Belcher had eyes and ears everywhere.

'How about we go see the living quarters?' suggested Jack heading towards the door. The look on his face reminded Pete and Tina that eyes were watching and ears were listening.

'Yeah. I want to see where Evie is going to live in all of this,' said Tina, walking towards him.

18

———

NO DIGNITY
IN DEATH

Austin found Ellie tucked away in her breakfast nook.

'You're hard to find, hiding away in here.' He lowered his voice. 'I've been given a map for you. Keep it safe. It shows you how to get to the cave for the next meeting.' He passed her a tightly folded piece of paper and discreetly placed it into the palm of her hand.

'Thanks,' she said, transferring it into her pocket under the table. 'I'll keep my head down. There's enough gossip flying around without me needing to add to it.'

'Now, you still owe me an explanation on austerity measures. Coffee?'

'Sure. Thanks. I'm always up for a second cup. Pile in some faux sugar for me.'

'I haven't seen you down at the river during the past week,' he said, bringing back two steaming coffees.

'No, I've had to attend extra meetings this week, to discuss the mundane. Can't someone just make a decision and implement it without making us all jump through hoops?' She held up her hand and counted on her fingers. 'I've been a seedling, a triblet, a pebble, and a flut-fly… fruit-fly? Something like that this week. So many words being droned on and on… and the whole time, I've just wanted to be out there, in the river.'

'Well, I was hoping you weren't trying to avoid me, so I'm happy you were busy but not happy at all of your circle commitments. Come to think of it, my first few months were the same. Where's Dean, by the way? Do you guys ever do breakfast together?'

'No, we don't. He normally doesn't eat breakfast anyway, and given how much he parties every evening, there's little chance he'd be up for it, anyway. He emerges in time to go to work, but they never put us on any chores together, as they wouldn't want to risk us coupling up again, I imagine.'

'Same. Tyler and I have never worked together either. She plays tennis in her spare time. We separated…' he paused, thinking, 'probs in our third month here. She rarely wants to talk to me as it is.'

'Sad,' said Ellie, wishing that she had a better response.

'It is, and it isn't. I think that's the way to look at it,' said Austin. 'I can't do much about this situation, not really. I thought I loved her, and if you'd asked me a year ago, that was my truth. Now I just have a different truth, I guess. I've reconciled it all now. It wasn't easy. I'm just making it look easy because I've worked through it all. Now,' he said, abruptly changing the subject, 'I'd love to hear about the outside and everything to do with austerity.'

Ellie explained how tax rates had been on a rollercoaster, taken down as far as possible, then driven back up again. People had been pushed into despair. More houses had been abandoned after failing loan repayments, jobs had been lost, and people were hungry. Health insurances were dumped, Mums and Dads looted shops, and homes were regularly invaded.

Austin looked despondent. 'Hard to believe that's only in the past few months. That's harsh. They're forcing people into being helpless, and all politically driven. Makes me sick.'

'Yeah, there were rushes on all the shops that were still in business, not that there were many… people buying anything that was left to buy, and that led to the break-ins. People were finding it hard to find whatever foods were left. Some places were better stocked - you know, places that haven't been hit as hard. The prices, though? No-one could afford to buy any of it, except the rich. That's when they introduced the protein bars, which you would have known about. Those with money can still buy nice stuff and those without, can't.'

'Why add to the climate chaos? As if there wasn't enough already going on. How many have died, do you think?'

'In the latest storms or the riots?'

'Both,' he said.

'The last storms in my area wiped out about five thousand people, and there were close to two thousand killed in the riots. That was in the week before we left, anyway.'

'Not good,' he sighed. 'It makes me feel shitty.'

'Yeah.'

They sat in silence for a while, sipping on their coffees.

'Oh look,' he said, looking towards the door, 'here come the plastics.'

Ellie looked around and saw a trail of women arriving, their colorful nails and hair extensions making them look slightly alien, in amongst the drab of everyone else.

'I call them the acetone claws.' Ellie smiled.

Austin threw his head back, glad for a laugh, 'love it.'

'So, where are you working today?' asked Ellie.

'I'm in the toilets actually,' he sighed. 'Such a charming place of work.'

'Charming isn't the word I would use. It's diabolically bad. I had no idea how bad shit could smell.'

'Yeah, those drop toilets stink. I've been lucky that this is my first rotation in the toilets. Most get a round in the first three months. They must have forgotten about me.'

'Yeah, after this long being here? You'll probably have a second toilet rotation pretty soon after to make up. I've got another wellness circle later. Did I tell you that I got myself kicked out of a meeting? I tried to tell them that they couldn't gossip and ka-boom… I was sent out. That's how I ended up at your circle the first night.'

'Hey, be careful. You don't want to be identified as a troublemaker, or they'll tail you. Keep your mouth shut, no matter how much you want to say.'

'Really?'

'Yes, Ellie. Really. These circles and meetings aren't for our benefit. They are designed to weed out the un-settlers. Don't rock the boat here. The place works when everyone conforms, remember.'

'Yeah. You're right. Now I'm freaking out a bit. I've probably got myself labeled by now. This place infuriates me.'

'Me too.'

Ellie suddenly had an idea. An insane idea. However, it popped into her head at that very moment.

'I wish we were going to Mars.'

'Sorry?' Austin was taken aback. He stared at her. 'You serious?'

'Yeah, Mars. On that craft that they are making.'

'For real?'

'Yeah. Why not? I can't imagine staying in this crazy place forever.'

Austin thought for a bit. 'Well, maybe that should be our plan? Get out of here and fly off?'

They looked at each other. That look between two people, when you've had an idea, and it becomes real as the connection strengthens.

'Is it possible?' asked Ellie.

'Everything is possible if you are willing to do the work.'

'That's a cliché, you do know that,' smiled Ellie. 'Life never works that way.'

'Yeah I know,' he smiled back at her. 'But I'm about to go and shovel shit, and I'd rather be planning a life on Mars, so for now, it should be possible, if only in the confines of my own mind. It will give me something to aim for, when my boots become stuck in the squelch.'

ELLIE MADE her way to the library. She had swapped the toilets for books, a much nicer existence. She sighed though. If this were utopia, she would be happy to swap it for something else, like flying away to Mars. Had it been a realistic idea, she wondered?

Was it possible to get into a craft and fly away? There had to be something better than this place. Surely? She reflected on the notion of utopia, which only worked when people were blinkered into believing that they were in the best location, and it was evident that the probationary period was all about installing blinkers.

ELLIE CAREFULLY UNFOLDED THE MAP, behind red hut, to ensure that no one was watching her. The cave was going to be a challenge to find, as the last part required her to walk directly opposite the setting sun, through thick bushland. Ellie was hoping for the sky to remain cloudless, in-case she walked in the wrong direction and managed to get herself lost. Although she surmised that given Gaia had high boundary fences, at some point, she would undoubtedly crash into one of those and be able to find her way back, albeit with some explaining to do. She found the first section of the path and climbed up the wooded hill, smiling as she remembered her first meeting with Austin. She enjoyed his company and the fact that he didn't press her for answers that she wasn't ready to give, whether through insecurity or a lack of trust. He was allowing their friendship to unfold in its own time. She liked that. The path led her down the other side of the hill and towards the ridge of caves. At this point, she needed to face due east and then walk for five hundred steps. That required facing the setting sun, turning around, and remembering to count.

The act of counting out five hundred steps provoked anxiety within her. Who had measured out the steps? Did she need to do extra-long strides or smaller steps? She elected to keep her stride as normal as she could and look out for footprints or a bit of flattened earth that may indicate she was on the right path. She remembered to keep the peak of the mountain range in front of her, as instructed on the map, but all of this was done with her stomach forming a tight knot. What if she got lost out here and missed curfew? They would know if she hadn't tagged in for the night, and then *they* would come looking for her. She had to get this right. She stopped at a clearing and again looked at the map, her anxiety suggesting that she had miscounted and had walked in the wrong direction, perhaps slightly taking a curve to the left or right when she wasn't supposed to have done. The cave should be close according to her numbers. Where was it then? She walked towards a rocky ledge in front of her and then heard voices. She stopped to listen, making sure the sounds were familiar.

'Ellie. Over here.' It was Sims.

'Sims. Glad to find you. I made it.' She sighed with relief. 'I was convinced I'd walked in the wrong direction or taken the wrong number of steps.'

'You did good, Ellie. Welcome to our new cave,' he said, indicating for her to step inside. 'This is a perfect location for our meetings. Unlikely that anyone is going to stumble across us.'

Her eyes adjusted to the darkness, and she saw that Darinda had made a small fire in the center of a large cavernous cave. Ellie found a patch of soft earth and sat cross-legged, taking a deep breath of the musty, crisp air and looked around. The cave was beautiful with the golden light from the fire illuminating thousands of stalactites that dropped from the roof of the cave as if the pipes of an enormous cathedral organ. She could imagine people from long ago, seeking shelter in the cave, maybe sitting around a similar fire. Curiosity ignited within her, and she got up, and instinctively placed her hand onto a portion of the cave wall. Another hand might once have touched the same spot, perhaps ten thousand years ago. There was a cathedral acoustic in the cave, and she imagined faint remnants of sound. Lives lived, a baby crying, food being chewed, and the sounds of chatter.

Darinda called her over. 'We're about to make some tea, Ellie. Want some?'

'Sure. Are we doing any eye masks this week?' she asked, smiling.

'No. Nobody's birthday this week, unfortunately. Although, I wouldn't mind a celebration every week in amongst all of this misery.'

Darinda smiled warmly at her. A big grin emerged, in amongst her flushing complexion and the mass of greying curls that seemed to bounce around in a world of their own.

Ellie smiled back. 'This is a fabulous spot for the meetings.'

'I know. It's beautiful, isn't it? The best one we've had yet. Sims discovered it when he was walking a couple of weeks ago.'

Ellie looked around. Austin hadn't made it in yet. She wondered how he had fared doing shit duty all day. She drank the first round of tea and was helping to wash the cups in the bucket when Austin ran in, puffing as if he had run all the way from camp.

'Sorry, I had to shower again… was covered in shit. Sorry to be so graphic. I'm in the toilets… wow…' he stopped mid-sentence, having looked up. 'Stunning!' He sat down next to Ellie. 'What have I missed?' he asked.

'Nothing, we've just drunk tea. We're about to start, though. Late, but not too late.'

Darinda welcomed everyone and then asked for an update from Roger. 'I'm very interested to see if we have more information about Mars.'

'I do. What we know is going to take your breath away.'

'Well, this place has already taken my breath away, and Austin looks as if his breath has gone too, but let's see if there's any left.

Might prove that I'm still alive and kicking for another day. Let's hear it all,' said Darinda, leaning forward and bracing for the juicy information.

'Okay. Our source in Belcher's science labs, the one acting as a cleaner, has picked up all sorts of things. No-one notices a quiet cleaner lurking around, so it seems. Apparently, at night, the main CCTV is turned off, and the night CCTV loops every ten minutes. The scientists are taking advantage of this and are hiding a fair bit of info from President Belcher. This AI project is crazy shit. More than anything we ever saw in the CIA, in fact.'

'Wow,' said Darinda. 'So how much can we piece together?'

'At this stage, our source knows that Jack Cross is having his personality profile placed into some sort of chip as an overlay. It increases IQ and contains occupation files. It also contains a limitation aspect… stops free will, apparently. The reason for the personality overlap is still murky, but our source is going to try to find out more. Why has the chip been developed, and for what purpose? In terms of the political side of things, and I hope you all have good hearts for this bit of news… but it seems that our world political leaders intend to leave us and fly to Mars.'

'Bull fucking shit,' said Darinda, forgetting where she was. 'Sorry, folks. Language. I need a swear jar, it seems. But hell on a sausage stick. How reliable is your info, Roger?'

'Squeaky tight. What we don't know yet is what this chip is for, and how it relates to Mars. We don't know if there is a military aspect to this.'

'Wow. I'm blown away,' said Darinda, looking around the group flushed. 'Who else is speechless?' The group all raised their hands in the air.

'So, does anyone have any crazy ideas as to what Belcher would want with a chip that increases IQ, has limitations, occupation files, and includes Cross' personality profile?' Darinda shook her curls, which bounced up and down in agreement at the sensational aspect of the news.

'Oh… yes… one more bit… Cross is also a psychopath if anyone is interested.' Roger added.

'What? Shit on a donkey's arse… sorry, everyone. I need to say buttons or flowers or something. What? Is she building an army of psychopaths for something? Like, is she taking them to Mars as well?' Darinda stood up, pacing. 'What does this all mean?'

'Not sure,' said Roger, 'but it's an interesting thought exercise. Where is she getting all the finance to do this, for instance?'

'Yeah, the Southern States lost a lot of money after the President change, and to be honest,' said Sims, 'it hadn't even fully recovered from GFC2. They weren't exactly flush to start with. She's either printing her own money, or she's found another source.'

'Probs the other political leaders… remember I mentioned the summit? That's where all of this started,' said Ellie thoughtfully.

Darinda clapped her hands together. 'Excellent Ellie. Yes. I think you're on to something.'

'That would make sense,' agreed Sims.

Darinda stopped in her tracks. 'So when are our leaders intending on leaving us then?'

'Not sure yet,' replied Roger. 'Our source is working on that information too.'

'So, Roger, what's next?' Darinda was up again and pacing around the fire.

'Okay, so we will get some updates from our person on Wells' island as soon as he flies back. He's been on a work experience week and is due back in a few days. We have him electronically silenced in case anything is intercepted. Then we should get some idea as to how Wells is involved in all of this. I'm surprised he's working with Belcher on the AI though, given he's so close to finishing his own chip.'

'Excellent work, Roger. Thank you. I have to say that's more than I imagined it would all be.' Darinda sat back down. The circle quietly applauded Roger in appreciation.

'Right, fertilizer people, where are you? Louise and Edward?'

'Hi, yeah,' said Louise, sitting up.

'Hi, everyone.' Edward joined her.

'Okay,' said Louise, taking an obvious, deep breath. 'We had thought we might get our results in next week, but we have them for tonight's meeting. I can say right now, it's not good.'

'Right. Everyone prepare yourselves,' said Darinda. 'Do I need to stand up again?'

Everyone squirmed and re-arranged themselves in anticipation. 'According to our scientist, the news is that the Gaia fertilizer used specifically on the mangrove swamp is human cremation ashes.'

'Fuck me dead.' Darinda stared at them, before standing up. 'Sorry, everyone. Language.'

'What the hell?' exclaimed Sims. Everyone started to talk at once.

'Calm, please,' called out Edward. 'I know. It's beyond disgusting. From what we can gather, anyone that they want to relocate to a different community is euthanized. We don't know how yet, but then the ashes are used for the mangroves. The ashes contain the right minerals for them to grow better, apparently.'

The circle again erupted into outrage. 'They need to be stopped!' said Sims, angrily.

'Quiet!' ordered Darinda. 'We don't need to be heard from in here with this information. I suggest a cup of tea and some quiet time, and then we can discuss this further.'

They made tea, alternating between outrage and shock. The forced silence helped to calm down the collective reaction, still brewing and bubbling to the surface.

DARINDA OPENED up the next part of the meeting. 'Right, let's keep our shit together. With this information, we need to be even more careful than we have been. Otherwise, we'll be next.'

'I agree,' said Louise. 'I've counted fifty-three people who were moved this year alone. I'm sure if we tried to find them, that they won't be in a different Gaia community.'

'I feel sick,' said Ellie. 'Why would they do this?' She shook her head.

'You've all heard of sleepers?' asked Roger.

The circle looked at each other, shaking their heads.

'It's not uncommon for the military to euthanize badly injured people… no?' asked Roger.

Everyone looked horrified.

'Okay. What about the market price for human cremation and crops?'

'Roger…' Darinda stared at him. 'What the hell are you going on about?'

'Maybe this isn't the time?' Roger quickly shook his head at Darinda, willing the conversation to stop, given he seemed to be the only one who knew about it all. Now wasn't the time.

Darinda noted his discomfort. 'We can save that information for later. We already have two biggies on our plate tonight.' Darinda looked over at Sims. 'I'm also hesitant in asking for your update Sims, but we may as well get all of our information in. Any further with the sterilization issue in the alcohol?'

Sims shook his head. 'I'm sorry to add to all of this. I think we've already heard enough for one evening. However, I do have an update. It's confirmed as a drug called aelotrogynisis, and it destroys fertility in both men and women, over time.'

'Well, there's the fucking trifecta,' said Darinda. 'Sorry about my language, but this is a major flood of shit… it's just fucking coming out all over the place.' She waved her arms around as if batting off large amounts of shit attacking her from all sides, to emphasize her point.

'They are putting it in everything,' added Sims. 'The wines, mixers, spirits, and beer.'

'Unbelievable,' she added angrily.

'Apparently, it also creates heightened anxiety when anxiety is experienced.'

'The Fear. Yes… wow… now that makes so much sense,' said Darinda, nodding with conviction.

'So, when they tell people about The Fear, they get a double whammy of anxiety,' Austin added, thinking it through. 'They get a normal response and then a heightened response. So it feeds off itself, getting bigger.'

'Charming.' Darinda shook her head.

'They're sick, that's what they are,' decided Roger.

'Right,' said Darinda, coming to a point of understanding in her own mind. 'Essentially, we are living in a form of hell. Not utopia, as advertised. It is utterly paramount that we stay quiet. Undercover. We're going to have to shake things up to protect ourselves. How I'm not sure yet. Maybe not meet every week at the same venue? Ensure we're not being followed or missed. We might even roster ourselves in and out of meetings to make sure no-one sees any patterns of absence.'

'I agree,' said Austin. 'I'm going to leave early with Ellie and make it look like we've gone for a walk.'

'That's a start,' said Roger. 'Anything we can do to eliminate patterns. Most intelligence comes from observations of behavior, and when there is a deviation from a pattern, it's investigated. So we need to ensure we're not leaving a footprint at any time.'

'Actually,' blurted Darinda, jumping up and pacing quickly. 'Wait… just wait… I've changed my mind.' She stopped, looking at the group. It was apparent she was about to say something huge. Silence fell, and eyes watched her. Then she said it. 'We need to get the fuck out of here.'

The circle stared at her. There was a lengthy silence.

'What?' asked Roger, also now standing. 'Darinda. Sit down, please, and take a deep breath.'

'I said,' she started pacing again. 'We need to get the fuck out of here.'

'Seriously? Darinda. Are you suggesting that we try to leave?' asked Roger, lowering his voice.

Whispers erupted around the circle as they realized that Darinda was being genuine.

'I'm serious as hell,' she said. 'Yeah, we can huff and puff and try to take them on… but realistically? We don't stand a chance. The minute they find out, we know we'll be next.'

She hurried to the cave opening. 'Jesus,' she said. 'We're as vulnerable as a fly in a spider's web. Put the fire out. Quickly. We can't afford any smoke to escape.'

Ellie wriggled in the dirt uneasily. The mood had changed all of a sudden. This wasn't a group that now met to discuss what was wrong anymore. They now knew too much. They had crossed the line from being safe to putting themselves at risk.

'There's eight of us, though. Where would we go?' asked Roger, throwing the water from the billy onto the fire. It hissed as it died down, the wet wood reflecting back to the group their own feelings of subdued hope.

'Right now? Back to anyone's house.' Darinda looked around. 'Do any of you have a house that still might be in one piece and safe?'

'We gave the titles to Gaia, remember,' said Sims. 'I don't think we'd even be allowed squatter's rights.'

'I think mine is available, actually,' offered Roger.

'You still have a title?' asked Austin, sounding surprised.

'In my wife's name… I held on to it… just didn't mention it,' he explained.

'Where is it?' asked Darinda.

'Virginia.'

'Wow,' said Darinda. 'That's a damned eternity away. Anyone got a house closer?'

No-one spoke.

'How do you know that your house is viable, Roger?' asked Austin.

'I have security cameras. No-one can get in at this moment, according to my sources, who, if you are wondering, send my info to a small device I've managed to sneak into Gaia. So far, so good with detection.'

'You have a device?' Darinda looked at him. 'How did you manage to sneak it in? I remember getting patted down as if I was someone's pet when I arrived.'

Roger smiled. 'There are plenty of places to hide stuff, Darinda, on the human body.'

'Gross, Roger. I don't want to know after all.' She grimaced, her mind imaging body cavities filled with strange devices. 'Right who's in? Quick vote.' She looked around the circle.

'What are we voting for?' asked Austin, understanding that something huge had happened but that he wasn't sure of what he was being asked to vote for.

'Whether we should go and stay in Roger's house for the time being and get the hell out of here. I need hands.'

Eight hands were raised. Ellie wanted to leave now. Gaia was mad. Killing people off… the alcohol was full of sterilization shit, and the world leaders were plotting to abandon earth. Great. There was crazy, and then there was all of this. What is a word beyond absurd, she wondered? Insane perhaps?

'Okay,' said Darinda. 'I'm thinking we get out as soon as possible. I know that out there,' she said pointing, 'has several issues. I don't even know how safe it is right now on a scale of one to ten. We'll need transport by the way. Who can think of transportation?' Darinda's mind was moving fast.

'Gary,' said Edward quickly. 'The guy who drives the truck… the scientist who analyzed the alcohol. He could get us out the day after tomorrow when he's next here. He'll jump at the chance, I'm sure of that. Maybe we should take him to Virginia with us? He'd be into that. He hates them. Given we probably won't meet again until then, we should arrange a time now to meet. His truck arrives at five… morning. Meet near the rubbish room and be discreet. We can hopefully jump in. He'll cover for us.' Edward was thinking on the spot, and his sentences were jumbled, but it was a beginning. A plan for an escape.

'Okay, are you sure, Edward? I don't want all of us to turn up at the rubbish bins and then find a man shouting out to everyone that we're trying to leave.' Darinda looked serious.

'No. I can guarantee he's good. He's had lots of issues with them over stuff. He can't stand them. I am absolutely sure he'll hide us.'

Darinda seemed reassured. 'Right. Is everyone clear on that? Do not act differently, do not tell anyone, don't warn people. I think to get out of here alive is going to be an achievement with what we now know. Be especially careful this evening. Stay in pairs until curfew and talk about something you've just done. This isn't what I had planned, but I don't intend to take these fuckers on. There are too many of them, in too many places. We stand a chance out there to do better if we stick together and think on our feet. This was not how I expected tonight's meeting to go. I'm surprised at the outcome myself, but there's a line in the sand, and we just crossed it. I'm also sorry about my language tonight. Now go.'

ELLIE AND AUSTIN LEFT FIRST. Ellie's stomach was churning, and her mind was racing. The worst part was that she couldn't discuss any of it on the walk home. The information was too dangerous to leak out, as it would jeopardize the only opportunity they probably had to escape. Austin put his hand over hers, sensing her unease, and gently squeezed it. The warmth of his skin and the gesture made her smile. They looked like two people out on an evening date, rather than people returning from a clandestine meeting plotting to leave.

'Go to your bed and sleep,' said Austin quietly. 'It's safer there than anywhere else. Where are you working tomorrow?'

'In the library again.'

'Right then. All you have to do is put in a good day's work. Do you have any circles to attend?'

Ellie thought hard. 'Yes, I've got the same circle as the one I got forced out of last time.'

'Be really careful, Ellie. Keep your mouth shut and make sure your body language is relaxed if you get asked anything. They look for shit like that. The rhythm of your voice… slow it down, pitch it low and breathe deeply. Look everyone in the eye, smile, and compliment if the stare goes on for too long, like if they are searching for something.'

Ellie took in a deep breath. 'Okay. What about you?'

'Shit duty again, and I have a circle as well. I should be okay. My worst issue will be how I smell, I imagine.' He tried to lighten the mood.

'We can meet for breakfast?' asked Ellie hopefully.

'Yes, absolutely.' Austin looked at her and then turned her face with his hand. He gently placed a soft kiss on her cheek and then left. Ellie stood there, watching him go. That kiss, with all of its human tenderness, had given her hope. Maybe they could get out alive, and perhaps that kiss might signify the beginning of something new?

19

PIECE OF RUBBISH

I SMELL BAD TOO

Ellie took her place in the circle. She was mindful to slow her breathing, keep her hands loose on her lap, and maintain eye contact with others. Renay entered the room and sat directly opposite her, avoiding eye contact with her, until the meeting opened.

'Welcome my pebbles. In particular, we welcome Ellie back. I am sure that Ellie understands the need to be *with* the circle tonight and not *against* it.' She beamed a smile that was all wrong. Renay then looked directly at her and waited for a reply.

Ellie could hear Austin's voice reminding her to keep her expression loose, have a pleasant face, and to look at every person. 'I'm sorry, everyone. I was very negative in the last circle, and I apologize.' She gave a small smile, apologetic rather than cheerful. One that she hoped would be reciprocated.

The circle nodded at her with approving eyes. Faces smiled back at her, all except Millie, who wore a look of disgust that Ellie was back.

'Excellent,' said Renay, her fake smile now falling from her face. 'I believe we can move on from that. There is no room for people to be on the outside of any circle meeting. I'm sure that Ellie now recognizes that concept after her time of reflection.' It wasn't a question, being only rhetorical in nature, and Ellie shifted slightly, hearing the veiled threat attached to it.

Renay continued. 'I have some follow-up news that will be of interest to you all. After the information we discussed about Pam, we were able to catch her in the act of receiving illegal drugs, and have moved her to a different community.'

Ellie coughed, trying to catch her breath. Millie looked at her intently from her left.

'Everything alright there Ellie?' she asked, aggressively, still spoiling for a fight.

'Yes, thank you. I have a cold coming on, I think.'

Millie snorted and muttered something about people with weakened immune systems.

'Perhaps you should book yourself in for one of the new vitamin shots they are doing over in the medical center? I hear they boost the immune system in so many ways. A shot might ensure that your cold doesn't get any worse.' Renay said smoothly.

'Yes, thank you. I'll look into it.' She smiled back at Renay, aiming for an appreciative look.

Sweaty lady was already taking notes. Her underarm aroma was more pungent than ever. Ellie knew that she needed to act this through, remain calm and composed. In her mind, though, she was thinking how the circle had literally condemned Pam to death without realizing it. Or maybe they did know? She couldn't be sure.

'We are going to be changing Gaia's security measures at the gates after the Pam incident. All circles will be advised of this information over the next twenty-four hours. You guys get to hear it from me first, lucky you.' She smiled at her naughtiness in leaking the information out prematurely. 'This will mean extra guards and searches for all vans. We want to keep Gaia settlements free of external influences.'

Ellie held in her anxiety. She imagined Austin reaching for her face and kissing her. It worked, her heart slowing, and she felt herself calming again.

'When do I put the start date for that?' asked sweaty. 'The searches will be starting on Friday, first light.'

Ellie's whole body sagged with relief. Tomorrow was Thursday. They would make it out before the searches began. The meeting went on and more people were put forward for investigation, including Kayla, for bringing in Botox.

'She'll be removed, as well,' said Renay. 'We need to keep Gaia Thirteen, a place of uniformity. One where people don't make up the rules for themselves.'

Ellie again felt her anxiety rise. *Cool, calm and collected,* she told herself, over and over, like an internal mantra holding her together. Kayla had been condemned to death too.

'See, that wasn't hard, was it?' asked Renay, approaching her at the end of the meeting.

'No. Again, I'm sorry about that first time. I was really fired up and nervous.'

'Well, you have redeemed yourself today.' Renay stared straight into her eyes, searching her for something.

Ellie relaxed her face and smiled. She looked dead square into Renay's eyes. 'You have beautiful eyes if you don't mind me saying.' she said. 'They are violet? Didn't that famous actress have violet eyes? Taylor?'

'Why, thank you. Really, how kind of you… Elizabeth Taylor, in fact.' Renay appeared confused by her compliment. 'You're obviously feeling a lot better today, despite your cold?'

'Yeah, heaps. I feel a lot more settled. There's a lot to take in when you first arrive. Getting used to how things are done.'

'True.' said Renay. 'We see that you have become closer to Austin this week.'

Ellie looked startled.

'Oh, don't be surprised. We see everything you know. That's our responsibility as Board representatives.'

Ellie felt her blood drain to her feet.

'It doesn't matter that you're still married to that gorgeous Dean. Remember, we encourage people to share themselves.' Renay smiled at her. 'Remember to pop in and get one of those vitamin boosters. In fact, just as an extra favor, how about you meet me after breakfast and I'll take you there myself, to the medical center? It will do you good.' She smiled enthusiastically and then stepped away.

Ellie needed to run out of the room, but knew that was too obvious. Instead, she introduced herself to sweaty armpits who announced herself as Organza. Lonely and in need of a verbal purge, Ellie accommodated her while she told her all about her life before entering Gaia. For some, Gaia offered them more than they had had access to on the outside. People like Organza found a home, so long as they didn't say anything that turned them into fertilizer. All Ellie had to do was to make an occasional mutter and nod her head. This was as much that Organza wanted from her.

After she had extricated herself, she approached Renay again. 'Where would you like to meet me in the morning? I think the vitamin shot sounds like a great idea. I'm working in the library this week and would hate to pass this on to anyone else.' She inwardly congratulated herself on her tone.

Renay smiled at her. 'How about you find me outside the breakfast room at 8.30?'

'Sounds great. I'm pleased this has all worked out, Renay. It feels better to have so much positive energy around me.'

'Me too, Ellie. See you in the morning.'

'Thanks, Renay. Sleep well.'

Ellie walked as slowly as she could manage towards the door. Something in her made her want to run, but she had to maintain control. Left foot placed and now lift the right leg. Place it gently and smile. Keep the motion even and fluid. Look up and around and maintain eye contact, smile again, keeping everything rhythmic. Then she was at the door, and she slowly stepped over the small wooden step. Closing the door behind her, she took a deep breath. *Fuck,* that had been close. Had she fooled them? She doubted it, given the way Renay was acting, although maybe she was just paranoid? What was with them watching her too? She was worried for Austin. They either knew that they had been meeting in the circle, or perhaps it was just down at the river? Either way, getting out in the morning at five sounded like a fantastic plan to her at that moment.

Her cabin was again empty. Josie was mainly sleeping overnight at silver hut these days with her bible study group. Right now, she was glad for the space, if only to just calm her mind. It was racing with thoughts of the Board representatives barging in and executing her. She inhaled quickly, her pulse accelerating, feeling sick. She raced to the small washbasin in the corner and vomited, her stomach emptying itself as if in preparation for her to run fast. The medical center and vitamin shots. Shit, she thought, retching again. Was it in the vitamin shots? Is that how they were killing people off? No. Now she was being stupid. She needed to pull herself together. She sat down on the edge of the bed, wiping her mouth with a hand-towel dipped in cool water. Her instinct was to rush to Austin, but that would be stupid, especially if they had now put her on warning. She exhaled out deeply, struggling to get her body back under control. She could be wrong, she told herself. Perhaps Renay was just trying to help her feel better? What if she wasn't, though? There was one chance to get out in the morning. She hoped to God that Gary would arrive with the truck on time and that he would be receptive in taking them all. If he decided he wouldn't, then they were dead.

She wondered about going and seeing Dean again before she left. Probably best not to, and he was most likely sleeping next to someone else right now, anyway. She looked over at the small number of possessions she had brought with her. The necklace her mother had left her after the crash. She would take that with her, wear it even. That would be it. She would take nothing that Dean had given her. She looked at her wedding ring, still on her finger. She had never taken it off, not once. Now it needed to go. She twisted it and started to pull, only her fingers were swollen from the heat of the evening. She would need to wait until the cool of the morning to remove it.

There was an alarm clock somewhere in the hut. She'd seen in when she had first arrived. She searched the hut, finding it stuffed in the bottom of the shared wardrobe. She set it for 4 am, making sure that she gave herself plenty of time to rise and set off for the garbage hut. She lay down on her bed, staring at the ceiling, Gaia was deranged and evil, far from utopia in any sense of the word. Instead, it was a vitriolic, nasty place where people had forgotten their kindness, and had left it at the gates. What sort of people killed innocents off like that and then tore away their dignity, choosing to place them in a swamp? What sort of place imposes sterilization upon people without informing them? What would they do if someone didn't drink and then got pregnant? How did these people even operate from this premise?

Sleep evaded her the whole night. There was no way that her body would relax enough to allow her to drift into peace. She was on high alert the entire night, and the slightest noise from outside would set her heart thundering in her chest. Her mind raced with everything, from leaving the school, flashes of house, fence, and tree. Dean cheating on her. She imaged them, burning Pam in a fire and then spreading her on the swamp. Twice she had got up only to retch back into the basin. She imagined the acetone claws arriving into breakfast only to find Kayla gone and then getting stuck into their porridge topped with mango.

The muted beeping of the alarm, under her pillow, indicated that it was time to go. There were a few ways she could get to the garbage hut, ensuring that the surveillance cameras didn't see her. The route she devised in her mind wrapped around a little, but going the long way was the least of her problems. She just needed to make sure that she left enough time for the extra detours. Looking around her cabin for the last time, she didn't stop to reflect on happy memories, as there weren't any. The small hut had simply been a place where any hope she had arrived with, had gradually been eaten away. Then she remembered. Her wedding ring. She twisted it with her fingers and pulled it forcibly. Despite the pain, she kept pulling as she needed to be rid of Dean right now, to properly end something that was over, aside from the legality of their union. It came off, and she rubbed her now bruised knuckle.

She placed the ring on her pillow and glanced around. Life was about to change, again.

She opened the door to her hut and stood silently, her ears pricked for the slightest sound which might alert her to company. Hearing only her own heart, beating strongly with the adrenalin pouring into her veins, she searched around in the darkness. The sun would be coming up in forty minutes, which gave her an ample window of time to get to the garbage hut using the cloak of night as protection. She shivered in the early morning air, glad to have put on a warm tracksuit. She walked, stopping every few feet to make sure that no-one was following. She ensured that she couldn't be seen by the cameras, which quietly tilted their heads from left to right, scanning for anomalies. She waited until each camera was facing the other way before hurrying on her toes, making as little sound as possible, from one bush to another.

The eight silently assembled at the back of the garbage hut in the dark. They had all made it, with no-one arousing suspicion. Darinda indicated to everyone not to utter a word. No-one dared to. Silence. They waited, shivering in the dark morning air, waiting and hoping to hear the roar of the garbage truck, hoping that today was going to be the day. Austin could see Ellie trembling from the cold, so he quietly moved behind her and pressed his body against hers for warmth. She leaned back into him, feeling her body relaxing.

Out of the silence, only punctuated by the sound of early morning birds, calling for food, and frogs burping on the banks of the river, there was a distant rumbling. Everyone looked up, concentrating on the noise. Darinda punched the air silently. They heard a truck pull up and roll noisily through the gates, the beeping indicating that a vehicle had driven in. Roger stepped forward and indicated to Darinda that he would talk with Gary. The group could hear whispers, and then Roger appeared again with his finger on his mouth. He gave them a thumbs up and indicated for them to follow him. They did, in single file and as silently as possible.

Gary unlocked the back of the truck, and each of them climbed in as quickly as possible. The smell was overwhelming, and the floor littered with slimy vegetable leaves and mold. Ellie pressed herself up against Austin, and he instinctively wrapped his arms around her. She leaned back into him and felt him release a long sigh.

Darinda had warned them that the trip would take forty-three hours, one side of the country to the other and that they would need to change transport as soon as Gary had been deemed late, and they started searching for him. Roger said he had that side of things under control, so all Ellie had to do was get comfortable and hope. Gary then filled the back with garbage sacks and climbed back into the driver's compartment. They felt the truck moving down the exit road, and then it was stopped at the gates for the existing exit process. The eight held their breaths, and Austin tightened his grip around Ellie. They could hear voices, but then they felt the truck moving slowly forward as it made its way out of Gaia Intentional Community Thirteen.

'I think we're out everyone,' said Darinda, once the truck had picked up speed indicating that they were on the exit road and away from the community.

'Thank God for that,' replied Ellie, exhaling a vast breath of tension.

Austin kissed the top of her head. 'That was awful.'

'Yeah, mildly terrifying,' added Sims.

'Okay, Roger, explain to everyone what the plan is.' Darinda was back in control.

'We estimate that we have about two hours until they start searching for the truck, and then they'll do a headcount I imagine, either at breakfast or when work starts. We'll be changing transport at that point and organizing a toilet stop and refreshments. If you need to go to the toilet before then, we've got a bucket. It's not glamorous, but we can't stop for any reason. Gary is joining us by the way and he's happy to help with getting us all the way to Virginia. Any questions?'

Everyone was too tired to think of any and so the group huddled together in amongst the garbage and slept, body next to body, glad for the companionship and warmth. Ellie was jolted awake.

'HEY, SLEEPY. WAKE UP,' Austin said, tapping her on the shoulder.

The truck had come to a stop, and the back rolled open. Beams of sunlight flooded in, Ellie's eyes automatically squinting from their brilliance.

'Okay, everybody up. We're changing transport.' Darinda was already standing outside.

They slowly climbed out of the truck, tired and disorientated, and found themselves in a thickly wooded area.

'Where are we?' asked Ellie.

'Eldorado Forest. It gives us a chance to change transport without anyone seeing us,' replied Gary, looking around to see if he could see anyone lurking, who shouldn't be there. 'Hi, by the way. I'm Gary.'

Everyone introduced themselves, and thanked him.

'So, more than two hours?' asked Austin, noticing that the sun was higher in the sky than he'd anticipated.

'Yes. We recognize that they would have missed the truck after two, but we were on a back route into the woods by then. We figured we had a bit more time up our sleeves.'

Roger suddenly turned his head towards the west. 'I think our new transport is arriving.'

Darinda looked at Roger. 'Are you going to explain? You probably should.'

Roger smiled. 'Okay, listen up. There's a minibus coming to get us. For the next two days we act as Seventh Day Adventists, out spreading the word. Religious organizations have year-round driving permits, whereas garbage trucks only have localized permits. We can literally drive all the way across the country on the one permit if we are religious. Also, we've been given new identity passports as well.'

Ellie looked at Roger and smiled, assuming he was joking to lighten the mood.

'No, Ellie. For real,' said Darinda, smiling towards her.

'We need cover,' said Roger. 'This was a favor from one of my ex-CIA colleagues. Inside, you'll find suits for guys and dresses for women. Get changed. Just do it, no time for modesty, and start reading the material that's in the bus. Yeah, and remember your new names too, just in case we get stopped.'

'Are we likely to?' asked Sims.

'Not sure. If Gaia wishes to protect their archaic and evil practices, then yes. If they don't care and are glad to see the back of us, then we should be fine. At this point we are assuming that they found out about our meetings, so I'm anticipating they would want to silence us. Bad publicity for Gaia and makes the Illuminati look inherently evil, if we talk.'

'Best not to take any chances,' said Darinda.

'I'm hoping the minibus has brought food for us too,' added Roger. 'I'm sure everyone is hungry.'

A small white minibus pulled up, and Roger shook hands with the driver. The man then got into the garbage truck and then drove it away.

'He's going to drive it two hours north, if he can get through the dunes, and then dump it. Hopefully, they'll find it and assume that we went north and not east.'

They got changed, which was a relief, as their clothes had stunk from the garbage truck. Ellie had a flowery, light orange dress which she quite liked after the terrible assortment of clothes she had been allocated whilst in Gaia. Austin was in a black suit.

'You look kind of nice,' she smiled at him.

'Thanks. You look good too. Orange suits you, works with your hair.'

'Who are you now? I'm Ashley Higgins. I sound like a singer,' she said, looking at her new ID card.

'Pleased to meet you, Miss Higgins? Mrs Higgins? I'm Hamish McBride, eligible bachelor at your service.'

'It's Miss Higgins, thank you. Do you wear a kilt?' she laughed. 'Your name sounds very Scottish.'

'It does. Not sure about a kilt, though.'

'At least I smell better.' Her face then dropped. 'There's something I need to mention, Austin. Something happened last night.'

'What?'

'When I went back to that circle that I mentioned to you, remember, the one I got kicked out of?'

He nodded.

'Well, Renay, who was in charge again, approached me after the meeting and said that they were aware of us, as in you and me. Then she offered to take me for a vitamin injection at the medical center... today after breakfast... like take me there, herself.'

Austin looked perplexed. 'Not following,' he said.

'I'd mentioned that I had a cold, not that I do... but she saw me acting oddly and then said like they had seen us together and knew everything.'

Austin looked concerned. 'Okay. I don't like the sound of that.'

'Why? What do you think it means? I mean I have my own theories.'

'How much did she say she knew?'

'She was evasive. She mentioned Dean as well. Like they'd been talking about me recently. What's with your expression?'

'The injections. I'm thinking that they aren't just vitamin injections?' Austin looked serious. 'We need to get this info to Roger and Darinda immediately.'

They explained it all to them and Roger looked concerned. 'We need to get moving and fast,' he said. 'They may well have been onto us.'

'Wouldn't they have acted sooner?' asked Darinda.

'Not necessarily.' Roger was looking around. 'Everyone, we need to move it. Get into the bus.'

'Does anyone need the toilet before we leave?' shouted Darinda. Three people raised their hands.

'Okay, go pee, go shit, just make it fast. Find a tree. No-one is looking. Hurry.' She clapped her hands, hurrying them on.

Roger approached Ellie. 'The injections,' he said quietly.

'Yeah, I know,' she said angrily.

'Just put it behind you. Don't dwell on it,' said Roger, hurrying people into the bus.

'Wow. They had it in for me from day one,' said Ellie, as Austin approached. 'Everything I did or said was always jumped on. Then they want to kill me off? Fuckers.'

'It's just the way they are,' said Austin. 'You didn't do anything wrong. You were smart. You could see through them. Probably during the meeting where you stood up for Pam. They don't want people who can see through them. They want people who follow them.'

'They're a dictatorship.'

'Yeah, and we were vulnerable, all of us... and they used that to gain control of us.'

'What's with that Renay woman? She tries to appear so friendly, so nice... but underneath, she's a shallow, nasty, condescending bitch.'

'Strong words, but I agree. Yeah. You certainly didn't have to scratch far under the surface to see her true colors. She walks around with that fake smile plastered all over her face. I'm seriously glad we got out of there when we did. You had a close call there, Ellie.'

'I would never go back there. Utopia?'

'Yeah, it was more like hell,' agreed Austin.

'Hurry up and finish,' called out Darinda, standing at the bus door. 'The bus is leaving in thirty seconds. Wipe your arses and pull you damned pants up. Let's go.'

The three came running back and got onto the bus.

'Everyone belted in and ready?' called out Gary.

'Yes,' called out a chorus of voices.

'Okay then, let's get this show on the road,' said Gary, turning the ignition on.

Gary drove carefully through the forest, weaving around the massive fir trees and around tight, winding bends. The sunlight was streaming through the trees, creating sunbeams that led the way for them. There was a driver's mic onboard and to lift everyone's mood, after they had snoozed, Gary gave them a commentary about the Nevada Desert, which was kicking up a ferocious dust storm making it hard for him to drive. However, his stories, designed to ease the tension, were a welcome relief as the small bus was battered from the wind and grainy sand. From aliens to the weird characters who lived there. He managed to cut through the dust and provide them some relief.

'You got out, Ellie,' said Austin, reassuringly, once she had woken from a fitful snooze.

'I did… just,' she said, looking out of the window at the swirls of orange dust. 'That was close. I hated that place. I don't care where we go now, anything has to be better than that. You know, when we signed up, I had no idea that we became Gaia's property like that. They don't have that in the fine print, that once you hand over your cash and your assets, that you hand yourself over at the same time.'

'I agree. It felt like one of the tent cities, aside from the fact that they hadn't given us all a number. I don't know anymore. Is there anywhere left to go that is safe? Even the areas in the lucky zones, like yours was, are impossible to sustain now, with austerity measures as you outlined. We've all effectively been made homeless. Maybe Roger's house will be better, and we can all look after each other a bit. Have a fresh start?'

'We can hope,' she said. 'We probably need to read some of this stuff, by the way.' She picked up the wad of reading material from under her seat.

'Yeah, let's do it together. Might help the information stick a bit.'

Ellie rested her head on Austin' shoulder. She quietly thanked the universe for having granted their paths to cross that day at the river.

20

BLACK WIDOWS AND RAINBOWS
FAIRY TALES

Paxton Wells carefully drafted his email, thanking Morag for her time, intentions, and ambition, and then requested an immediate transfer of monies for the first installment. He smiled. A wad of money that large would be a welcome addition to his budget and more than enough to establish the momentum of converting ideas into practical applications. Not build anything like a transporter craft just yet, but it was a good infusion of much-needed cash for the drafting of a craft blueprint and the commencement of a logistics analysis. Wells was grateful that Belcher had arrived up on his doorstep when she had, although that morsel of knowledge should go no further than being noted on this page. Things hadn't quite gone to plan with his vision on Mars. Well, they had in the beginning when he was so full of playing the role of visionary. Money had been overspent at first through over-ambition and naivety, and keeping up with the business model and the construction of Martian infrastructure had been challenging. Having Morag as a silent partner would allow him to breathe much-needed new life into Home Base.

He skimmed his financial accounts and surmised that while things weren't dire, they could be better, as was always the case in business. That's where Belcher's money came in, and it could be spent wisely across the board if he were frugal with it. He'd been making good headway with his integration chip, designed to link computer with mind, and was maintaining the projected release date, albeit without ticking all the ethics boxes. His other investments were beginning to disappoint, and some of Belcher's money could get things back on track for him.

His grandfather had been the one to present to him the concept of building something like Home Base. He had been small, about six, and sitting on his knee, listening to fairy stories about lands far away. His grandfather had stopped in the middle of Rapunzel.

'Paxton, my boy. As I tell you these stories about brave men saving princesses, locked away in castles, I want you to close your eyes. Do it.'

Paxton had shut his eyes, eager to hear what his grandfather would say next. His voice had always been the calm, arriving after the storm of grenades hurled between his raging father and alcoholic mother.

'Imagine you are a prince, dressed in fine attire, on a horse of pure white, a magnificent stallion… with a long swishing tail and a mane of sweeping beauty… what shall we name him?'

Paxton had reflected for a bit, remembering something he had learned in school. A silly building that his teacher had shown him from somewhere he didn't know. 'Folly. We shall call him Folly, grandfather.'

'Appropriate, my dear boy. Now, imagine you are riding Folly, galloping… the wind blowing your hair… and he takes you into a world where you are a King. This is your world, Paxton… King Paxton, made by you and for you only. No shouting, no hurting, and no anger. You can create whatever you want in there. Imagine my boy, the endless possibilities.'

Paxton had smiled. At six, he could imagine this new place. A world where his parents could no longer contaminate his childhood innocence with their adult dysfunction. His eyes had become wide as his grandfather had spoken of magical doors, leading Paxton from this world into this new one. Of lollipop trees, chocolate rivers, and cotton candy clouds, which allowed him to travel anywhere and at any time. The notion that such a place was possible was tantalizing for his young mind.

'Never forget Folly, my dear boy,' his grandfather had said, some years later, on his deathbed. 'Always make sure you have somewhere to go. Even as an adult, you must always have somewhere you can call your own, that no-one else can contaminate for you.' An adult Paxton had tightened the grip on his grandfather's hand, the skin transparent with fragility, pleading with him not to leave, just yet.

'I will continue to ride Folly, and I will create many places. This is my promise, grandfather.'

His grandfather had become still and cold to touch, and Paxton had let his hand gently go, releasing both his grandfather and his childhood to rest. He walked to the door and then turned back to look at him one last time. 'However, I will share my world *with* the whole world and offer everybody a sanctuary and an opportunity for peace. Folly will take all of us there,' he had pledged.

The idea had sat patiently until Paxton had been financially able to start Home Base. It had been undertaken with an urgent sense that he was already late in starting it. It drove him passionately; planning, building, and then sharing. He pressed the live button one day, sending Home Base into cyberspace, allowing around-the-clock access to this world for a small subscription fee. On the first day, the site had crashed, overloaded with people clambering to get a glimpse of human beings on Mars, and he had earned his fortune from it within six months.

Another billion dollars was now coming his way. Until he had become rich, he hadn't known what a billion dollars looked like. A thousand wads of a million. He imagined that amount in a practical sense and failed. The human mind was incapable of imagining such vastness, just as he had tried imaging the plague of people on the planet at times. Sometimes he would see pictures of massive rallies or religious gatherings and catch a million people in one place. Sometimes he would look up and see stars in the sky and try to imagine the two hundred and fifty billion of them contained just within our Milky Way, each having been made with an intense amount of precision and longevity. He pictured millions of paper George Washingtons, merging into one giant patriarchal figure, and heard the metallic clashing of cold metal, the noise of a billion dollar coins. He owned billions of these, just as the creator of the universe owned all the stars in the sky.

The re-launching of Home Base was at the right time. He'd only taken it off-line because it was draining both his patience and bank balance. Too many death threats from people panicking, wanting to be the next to go up. With the sort of money he was planning on injecting, he could install the security needed to keep Home Base headquarters on the island safe. He poured himself a scotch and raised his glass at the photo of his father, which was kept on the shelf next to the window. Without his rages, the dream would never have been realized. 'Your anger turned out to save the human race, Father. Quite an achievement, for such a black soul,' he told the photo. He turned to the image of his grandfather, swirled the scotch in the glass, inhaled deeply, swilled and then swallowed the lot in one go.

21

BIDET

IT WASHES AWAY BULLSHIT

It was an all-male team that took shifts with the driving, simply because the long dresses got in the way of the pedals and had been deemed dangerous. They shared the driving into four-hourly shifts, making only short toilet stops along the way. Staying for any length of time only drew attention to themselves, which was dangerous at best. The first city they reached was Denver, with the bus having detoured away from Salt Lake City, too obvious as a resting spot for anyone trying to venture cross-country. Instead, they had traveled through back roads hoping to keep a low profile. Denver, the 'mile-high' city, was already buzzing as the dawn illuminated the mountains.

'What happened?' asked Ellie as they drove into the suburbs. 'It's just chaos out here.'

They passed numerous shopping cart villages along the way, with rows of mangy individuals lying on crumbling brick walls, some sleeping on dry and sandy verges and sometimes standing in the road, forcing the bus to grind to a halt. Fueled by drugs, they tapped on the windows, displaying empty mouths in states of decay, begging for food.

'Just keep driving,' called out Roger. 'Don't stop and don't open any windows. Try to avoid eye contact with these people,' he instructed everyone.

The front gardens of suburban houses were full of rubbish, sometimes as high as the eves. The stench of human excrement was, at times, sucked into the bus air conditioning vents, filling the bus with the aroma of rotten. People were roaming, dazed, staring vacantly into nothing. Ellie thought she saw bodies, left out to rot, but didn't say anything, as the horror unfolding in front of her was best left unconfirmed in her own mind. Sometimes, the corpses were so badly decomposed that she thought they might be stacks of rubbish, but the smell as the bus passed them was undeniable. Homes had been looted and lives obliterated, with belongings scattered and broken, as if found to have been too heavy to carry. Then there was the sound of human suffering, which made Ellie shudder. Snippets of stories, relaying the urgency and futility of the chaos. Gunfire rang out and then wailing, which would merge into screaming. Over and over, the dysfunction would occupy the bus, which quietly rolled on. A silent observer to the misery found in suburb after suburb.

'This is like the apocalypse,' said Ellie, disturbed by the view from the bus.

'Yeah, I mean you warned me that things had got worse. True anarchy in action and society breaking down,' replied Austin. 'The reason why we all sought refuge in Gaia in the first instance. I'm not sure what was worse though, looking at this.'

The center of the city was eerily empty, rubbish being hurried along the streets, rushing to nowhere, by a stiff billowing breeze. The bus quietly drove in between the skyscrapers, stopping at red signals that allowed ghosts, time to pass them at crossroads.

'Where is everyone?' asked Ellie, straining her neck from the bus to look at the tops of the buildings.

'I hear a lot of the city workers went into the Rockies, into the caves,' Sims replied, turning around from the seat in front. 'Safer than staying in the suburbs.'

'What about food? How do they eat out there?' she asked.

'I think they hunt deer… it's not allowed, but I don't think a ranger is going to stop them at this point. They would probably eat them too, if they had the chance.'

Ellie wondered if he was trying to crack a joke, but his face seemed serious. 'How many do you think are up there?' she asked, peering out of the window at the mountain range. It was snowy-white on top, sprinkled with humans eating deer, and maybe a ranger or two for breakfast.

'Thousands, I imagine.'

'Poor deer,' sighed Ellie. 'What happens when they run out of deer?'

'I suppose that's when they start eating each other.' Sims looked at her and shook his head. 'What did cavemen do when they ran out of food?' he asked her rhetorically.

Ellie stared at him. 'Are you saying…' she stopped, not wanting to articulate the thought.

He answered her question. 'Cavemen ate each other, more out of opportunistic cannibalism though. Humans aren't that nutritious, as it turns out. However, up there… in those mountains with so many people trying to find a food source? It won't be long.' He looked up at the mountains, imagining what might happen in the future. 'We are programed to survive at all costs, no matter what we do to each other. That's the problem,' he added.

They passed through Denver and then on to Colby, where the bus had arranged to stop for a more extended break to allow everyone to have lunch, walk and relax a bit. Ellie looked around her, extending her arms into the air. She took a deep breath, filling her lungs with the warm country air. 'They appear to like Spruce trees here,' she said, noting all the seedlings protected in plastic sheaths, that had been planted into every available grassy space.

'Yeah, maybe in this part of the world, they haven't heard of End Date?' added Austin, looking confused at all of the new plantings.

'What do you mean?' asked Ellie, standing on tiptoes, stretching her calves out.

'A Spruce isn't a great choice given End Date, as far as I know. They're slow-growing. These saplings won't be trees for another hundred years, well past 2088.'

'Strange choice,' said Ellie, slightly surprised. 'So, seriously, do these guys know about End Date? This seems a peculiar choice for greening up their town.'

'Maybe not,' suggested Sims, walking over. 'What's the population here, like five thousand? Maybe they think they're safe out here?'

'Do you think some communities think they are safe?' asked Ellie, 'Just because they're not in the thick of it? It's weird, this apparent calmness, when over in Denver and probably everywhere else, people are starving and trying to survive, moving into Gaia Settlements, into the mountains… shooting each other, and these guys are planting Spruce.'

They walked around stretching their legs, enjoying the feeling of blood getting back into muscles, stiff from so many hours on the bus.

Ellie watched some local kids playing in the playground. 'They are just getting on with living here, aren't they? Almost like they are oblivious to what is happening down the road. Complete denial, maybe?' she asked.

'Yeah, have you noticed all the grain silos, though?' asked Austin, pointing. 'Maybe they've filled them up, and they think that they can live off that for a while?'

'Maybe?' replied Ellie. 'They might think that End Date is the time where only food runs out? Maybe no-one has explained to them that the earth is going to burn. I imagine this town will fry out here.' She looked back at the children playing in the playground. 'They don't stand a chance if that's the case.'

'Actually,' said Sims, 'the prognosis isn't that grim out here for heat. That's not what's going to kill them. The tornados? That's a different story. They've had a succession of EF5 storms recently. More on the way, I've heard. Those silos must be cemented deep down for them to withstand that, as well as the houses. I'm surprised any of them are still standing to be honest. Anyway, Ellie, no-one stands a chance. End Date isn't selective. You, me, and all of these people? It'll be the gangs from places like Denver that start moving down from the mountains that will kill everyone. It'll just be a matter of time before they raid smaller towns like this, I imagine.'

'Gees, that's optimistic,' she replied, sounding deflated.

'I'm just surmising,' he replied. 'There won't be a happy ending anywhere, I'm afraid.'

'They're kids,' she said, observing how playful and relaxed they looked chasing each other around.

'… and we're big kids, Ellie,' sighed Austin. 'Kids who have lived a few more years. We didn't ask to be dumped into this mess. None of us did. We'll be heading towards old age before End Date even comes, but we probably won't make it that far. We have to live out our lives as best as we can, just like those kids.'

'I can't believe we're all going to die,' she said. 'It seems surreal... like a bad dream... how did we do this to ourselves?'

'Rhetorical, I'm guessing?' asked Austin.

'Yeah... I mean, I've gone over and over it in my head. It's just such a waste, and sometimes it just hits me between the eyes. We were so clever and yet so insanely dumb at the same time.'

'Greedy. We were greedy too,' Sims added, 'We had shitty politicians who were more interested in their own objectives than daring to limit the tendrils of big business.'

'Weren't we just?' she said. She shook her head, thinking privately for a moment. 'I'm heading back to the bus. Sometimes,' she said, sighing, 'I just want to shut my eyes and then wake up to something better.'

'Well, we have an opportunity right now for something a bit better. At least I am hoping it's a bit better.' Austin added.

'Me too. I hope so,' she said, settling back into her seat. 'We know nothing about Roger's house yet, where it is, how big it is. I'm just hoping it's in the countryside and not a city. I can't imagine trying to survive with the gangs we've seen in the cities.' Austin took Ellie's hand.

He smiled at her and squeezed it, reassuringly. 'Same. I've been wondering when we might get briefed on the next bit, but right now, I'm just very glad to be on the road and away from people who feed their mangroves, human beings.'

'Agreed. I'm exhausted, to be honest,' she said, yawning. 'I didn't sleep that well on the bus before. I'm hoping for a bit of shut-eye soon.'

'Well, my shoulder is still available. It sees the potential in branching out into a career as a pillow, in fact.' Austin smiled at her. 'I think the next bit is going to be better, Ellie.'

THE BUS CONTINUED through the day, stopping at Evansville near midnight. They drove through the outer suburbs, unable to get a good look at what framed the road because the streetlights were out. They saw fires though, lit in front gardens, and could hear loud music beats cutting through the air. People were dancing, silhouetted against the flames, drinking and screeching words that made little sense. They pulled into a fuel station, got out of the bus, and headed for the restrooms and cafe.

'Watch out for jaguars,' said a toothless woman, dressed in filthy clothes. She was begging near the doors of the fuel station cafe, a small wicker basket with one or two coins inside of it, in front of her. She smiled a toothless grin at Ellie, waiting for her to respond.

'Jaguars?' asked Ellie, turning to Austin. 'Does she mean jaguars, as in cats or cars?'

'Don't engage,' called out Roger. 'Keep moving straight into the cafe, Ellie.'

The cafe offered a small selection of protein bars, and Roger bought all of them.

'Have you seen any jags yet?' asked the attendant, serving Roger, who was paying for the small feast.

'No, sorry.' He didn't want to engage with the locals and sat with the others.

'What's with the jaguars?' Sims asked him, joining him at the table. 'Do they mean actual jaguars, as in animals?'

'It's fine, we're safe here,' said Roger to the group as they sat at the table. 'It's a bizarre story, but true. Years ago, they had these jags in the zoo here, and the male jag got cancer. Some animal liberationist thought he would break into the zoo, and release the pair into the wild, allowing the dying beast to taste freedom. Anyway, there was some eccentric who heard of this, and so he released his private collection of two more jags into the area… I think they released them somewhere near those angel mounds, just before the land went wild, and they did what all animals do… they bred like crazy. They think the cat with cancer lasted many years. Long enough to create quite a large family. No-one wants to shoot them either, something about local curses and bad luck. So they wander, breed, and hunt.'

'Okay, well, that's just so perfectly normal,' said Austin. 'A place full of roaming, hunting jaguars.'

'We live in a mad world,' said Roger. 'Nothing surprises me anymore.'

They boarded the bus again, the legs of the journey getting harder and harder to manage, as weariness and boredom set in.

'I suggest you all try to sleep for the next leg,' said Roger, as they settled into their seats. 'We're going to drive the next leg in one bit, we hope. It's up into the mountains and then down into Virginia. I suppose now would be a good time to give you a bit of information about where we are going. Take it away, Darinda.'

Darinda took the mic from Roger and spoke into it. 'As you know, Roger previously worked for the CIA and had a flat in Washington as well as a home out of town. When his wife died, he moved into the Washington flat, and the country house has remained empty since. However, I think you will find that there is ample room for everyone, and we'll have plenty of outdoor space to grow our own food. So, for now, please settle down. There will be short toilet stops, but we can only offer the bucket, I'm afraid, along the way. It's too dangerous for the bus to stop at designated rest stops, we believe, from this point onwards. We're heading back into larger centers and feel that the mood is too unstable. Are there any questions about anything?' She peered around the bus. No-one said anything, and no hands were raised.

'Great. Look, I'm glad we got out. I know it was impulsive to suggest all of this, but I still believe it was necessary. It's up to all of us now to make the best of whatever predicament we now find ourselves in. We've been given a second chance.'

Ellie shuddered. It was easy to forget that she had been next. How close had she been to death herself in all of this? However, Darinda was right. They had all been given a second chance, and it was necessary to look forward and not backward. If she stopped and faced backwards, she would end up mentally trapped, trying to process things that were way beyond her capacity. Looking forward, provided her with a clear and empty mental space, ready to fill with new experiences.

'Well, that sounds doable,' she said, turning to Austin.

'What, that there's a bucket available?' Austin was smiling.

'Very funny,' said Ellie. 'No. That the house sounds large enough for us all.'

'Yeah, and that we have room to grow food. We're lucky this is all available to us,' he added. 'Gratitude. I'm feeling very grateful right now.'

THE BUS DROVE ON, passing through the chaos and what was left of ordered civilization. The weather was erratic, throwing dust storms and dry lightning at the bus, and several times, they'd had to pull over while it all passed. Ellie, her face pressed up against the glass of the bus, tried to assimilate what she was seeing and ascribing meaning to it all. The larger the city it seemed, the more that had gone wrong. Anarchy had etched away at what had been normal. People seemed lost, not knowing what there was left to live for. Western society had promised meaning, albeit through a pre-determined order and structure. So, once the money ran out and there was no possibility of future success, meaning had become lost too. It had the effect of quickly stripping away gentrification, reducing people to basic sketches of human beings. Perhaps we'd been the same hundreds or thousands of years ago when survival was the only thing on our minds, she wondered. There was a lot to digest and assimilate into this new reality. Almost as if she had to start again with what she thought she knew.

THE BUS ARRIVED at a set of gates with the sun shining brightly in the sky. Ellie had been too tired to keep processing what she saw from the bus, and in the end, had just snuggled into Austin. He had wrapped his arms around her, both of them enjoying the mutual comfort.

'Where are we?' asked Ellie, stirring, and looking around.

'I think we've arrived,' yawned Austin, seeing the gates.

'Okay, everyone. We're here. Welcome to Virginia, and more importantly, welcome to my home.' Roger was smiling, obviously glad to see his house again and relieved to have finished the cross-country journey.

Ellie rubbed her eyes, 'Seriously?' she said, surprised at what she was looking at. The house was more of an estate. A vast building, three floors high with a formal topiary garden in front. 'This was not what I was expecting. At all.'

'No,' said Austin, sounding just as surprised. 'This is massive for a start. Wow…'

Roger guided them through the formal front garden, and into the house. It was huge. Room after room of chandeliers, striped cream wallpapers, white and blue curtains, brass fixtures, and teak wooden flooring.

'Let me explain,' he said to the bemused bus occupants. 'My wife received a large inheritance - quite substantial, from her parents, and her dream was to build this. She was very content here, and we raised three very happy children. I'm glad in a way that it's going to be appreciated again. It's what she would have wanted.' He stopped as if a painful memory had entered his mind. 'She died of cancer several years ago and was incredibly brave right to the end.' He paused for a moment and then regained his composure. 'The bedrooms are on the second and third floors, and all have their own bathrooms, so you should find yourselves very comfortable. We had an extensive bunker built in the garden, as my wife liked to *be prepared*, so to speak.' He smiled at his own memories. 'So for now, if everything is untouched, as it looks like it is, then we should have enough food for a while yet… mostly preserved, but it's better than nothing. In the meantime, Darinda and I will go and look at the veggie garden out the back, that is, if the birds haven't got into it. Hopefully, the pump still works too, as it's watered from a deep well we had built on the property.'

Ellie made her way up to the third floor to find a room. She wanted to be in a corner, up high and away from everyone else, something with a degree of solitude. She found the perfect space, down the end of the third-floor corridor in a room that wrapped itself around the corner of the building with views to the east and south. Her bathroom was nothing short of opulent, with a deep bath in the center, a rain shower and faucets of shiny brass. There was a separate washroom with something else that she wasn't sure what the purpose was. She was looking at the bath, wondering if it was too soon to run one, when Austin walked into the room, looking for her.

'Knock, knock, Rapunzel,' he said, smiling. 'I see you've snapped up the prime tower room.'

'Very funny. Seriously though, how cool is this place?'

'It is. I've managed to get the room next door. That is, if you don't mind?'

She smiled. 'That could prove convenient,' she said smiling. 'By the way,' she added, 'what is that?' She pointed to the device on the floor.

'A bidet. Have you never seen one before?'

'No. What's it for?'

Austin threw his head back and laughed loudly. 'Really? You don't know what a bidet is for?'

'No.'

'They're to wash the bullshit out of rich people's arses,' he said.

'Gross. Are you serious? Does it wash your butt? Why only rich people? Do they think their shit doesn't stink?'

Austin laughed again. 'Let me tell you a secret. Everyone's bullshit stinks.'

'Yeah, if you're into that sort of thing. I don't go around sniffing it, unlike you apparently.' She picked up a washcloth and threw it at him playfully.

'Oh, like that, is it?' he laughed and turned on the cold water and splashed her.

They laughed, mostly out of relief, to stand there joking about the inconsequential again, instead of wondering if their lives were about to be cut short.

'So,' said Austin, drying them both with a towel. His change of tone indicated that something was on his mind.

'What's up?' asked Ellie.

'Okay, just hear me out a sec.' He got up and closed the door to her bedroom. Then he looked around to make sure there was no CCTV. 'Why would Roger stay in a Gaia settlement across the country when he had all of this, including a bunker?'

Ellie pursed his lips together. 'That's actually a really good point.' They sat in silence for a bit.

'I don't know,' she said finally. 'It would have made more sense for him to have just come here.'

'Maybe he didn't want to be alone?' asked Austin. 'Although, what about his three children? Where are they?'

'I heard something about a falling out?'

'Over what, I wonder? He seems nice enough. Look, I don't want to ruin the moment. This looks great… unbelievable, in fact. But yeah, why move across the country? Do you think it would be worth just asking him?'

'As in, do we trust him enough?'

'Yeah,' Austin wrinkled his brow. 'It's hard to trust people now… especially after Gaia.'

'Look, I don't see why not,' said Ellie. 'He seems genuine? I can't see an ulterior motive. Think of the worst-case scenario. He's part of Gaia, and he has driven us all across the entire country to set us up in his mansion. Why? He would have just had us all made into fertilizer back there. Maybe he was lonely? Perhaps he just wanted to feel a part of something? I mean, they pitched Gaia utopia differently to the reality that we found. My guess is that his wife died here, he had a falling out with his kids, and he didn't want to be sitting here alone, surrounded by too many memories.'

'Yeah, you're probably right. Sometimes I feel like my trust has been shattered a bit after all of that, though.'

'I know. Me too. Look, let's put all of that on ice for now and explore the rest of this insane house.'

'Agreed. Right now, I need my mind to settle.' He took a deep breath and shook his head. 'Sometimes, my anxiety just kicks in. Time to relax a bit, I think.'

22

ROLL UP

STAND IN LINE

Jack met for a final meeting with Paul and Tina, to establish that everything was ready for the launch date. They had sat in countless meetings in recent months, perfecting every aspect of the chip. 'This is it. Once I give the green light, there can't be any further changes to the launch chip. Then the people will stand in line, and we will need to deliver.' Jack's face resembled haggard, from the lack of sleep and relentless stress.

'Well, my implant team is ready,' said Pete assuredly. 'Ian and Sam are trained in procedures at South Street Hospital, and Bianca's team are ready to go for post-operative testing. In the meantime, we're training up new teams, ready for the second wave of the launch.'

'I'm ready, too,' said Tina. 'Coding is complete, press releases are ready, and I've got local Government and businesses prepared to employ.'

'Okay, well I've got the final nuances of the chip working, Bill is looking after the manufacturing side of things, I've got the plans for roll-outs done… so… we may just be ready to present our final version to Belcher? Everyone happy with that?' Jack raised his eyebrows, hoping that they hadn't forgotten anything.

Tina and Paul nodded.

'I'm completely rat-shit,' Tina said.

'Sorry?' asked Pete.

'Tired. Exhausted. I have never worked that intensively. I'm just relieved that we've fallen over the finish line.'

'I agree,' said Jack. 'The good news is that once it rolls out, other people take over. We get to have a bit of a break, sit back, and watch. We only need to monitor and correct faults as they appear.'

'Hey,' said Tina, remembering something. 'Did you guys hear that Belcher's demanded a percentage of wages, direct from source? So, if she offers a chipped human into a business, she's asking for a flat fifteen percent of wages.'

'Yeah,' said Pete. 'I heard. That's millions more in revenue.'

'Well, think about it,' said Jack, 'They have no-one, and their businesses are failing. They get a good worker, chipped, dedicated to them, someone who stays on track… that's got to be worth fifteen percent.'

'She's savvy. That's for sure,' said Pete. 'She'll make a small fortune. Makes our wages look like peanuts.'

'That she will,' said Jack, 'although remember, there's no currency on Mars, so she might be rich on paper, but that's it. Right then, time to tell Belcher we are ready. Yes?' He looked at them one last time.

They nodded, albeit looking slightly apprehensive. Jack knocked on Belcher's door.

'Come,' she said loudly. 'It's you,' she said, looking up from her desk. 'Yes?'

'We're done. Ready to launch,' said Jack positively, 'and on time.'

'Good,' she said. 'You can send out the press releases then. I'm busy being a politician today.'

Jack stood there, waiting for more. There wasn't any. Belcher looked up at him, looking perplexed as to why he was still there.

'Anything else?' she asked.

'No.'

There was a pause. A pause which went from a small period of time, into an uncomfortable chasm of tension, promoting only self-doubt in Jack. He looked at Belcher, now busy sending an email, and turned to go. Silence was an extraordinary tool of power, even if unplugged, and in Belcher's case, she could make someone doubt themselves without having to say a word. He headed back to Tina and Paul.

'That went well,' he said.

'Sarcasm detected there,' said Tina.

'She's just so difficult sometimes… wooden.'

'She is a psychopath, like you… you technically shouldn't care.' Pete smiled.

'True words, my man,' said Jack. 'Okay. Are we absolutely sure that we are ready?'

'Yes,' they reassured him.

ANGUS SAT IN THE RECLINER, now shaped like him, from excessive sitting shifts. Coffee stained, with stale chip bits around the base of the faux-velvet seat-cushion and sweat marks from his thighs, the recliner looked like something that had been stolen from the side of a road. It gave off a subtle aroma of hopelessness and apathy that resulted in the lounge room feeling more like death row than a place of relaxation. The past few months had been hell though, with threats of eviction from their Government funded home, and nowhere to move to, aside from one of the refugee camps.

Angus had worked in the refinery since walking, jaded, out of school at sixteen. He'd started as a yard boy, doing whatever no-one else wanted to do like moving pipes, checking oil temps, and making coffee for everyone older. Angus had moved up a couple of rungs since then, but he liked being told what to do. Thinking wasn't his strong point and never would be. That's why he'd married Riley. She told him exactly what he needed to do, in a not-for-refusal kind of tone in her voice. He'd never refused her for anything for the record. Not extra money when she used to get her hair or nails done, and never when she'd asked for sex, which wasn't much anymore. They'd raised four boys, the oldest now twenty-three and the youngest eighteen. Riley had popped out babies as quickly as he'd popped out the rings from his beers.

They had chugged along happily knowing where their place was in the scheme of things, managing to save for a yearly holiday at the coast and paying the required rent in their Government subsidized home. Then the work had stopped, abruptly too, and the weather went crazy. Then life began to get complicated. Really complicated. Old rules were swapped for new rules which felt tighter and tighter, squeezing them out of everything comfortable. Angus didn't understand it all that much, and they floundered around, not knowing what direction they should follow.

Riley had sat them all down one night and had explained, as best as she could, about End Date and the four boys had cried together, for the first time in their lives. Later that night, Riley and Angus had cried too, for bringing kids into a world that would now fling discomfort at them and eventual death. Then they had wiped the tears away and decided to make the best of whatever was left.

MACE SAT STARING INTO SPACE, as he did at the start, the middle, and the end of each day. Tara looked at him and shook her head with despair. This latest bout of depression was worse than the last, sucking his soul inwards and confining him catatonically to the same space every day. He'd been okay up until End Date had been announced, busy working in his coaching business and almost ready to publish his life-plan book, the one he'd been working on forever. After End Date had been announced, his clients had shaken his hand, one by one, and then run into the hills. They'd swapped a goal-orientated life for a bucket-list life instead. Mace hadn't written a book about bucket lists though, and so overnight, everything he'd worked for had evaporated into a sea of human misery and panic. No one needed coaching anymore, and certainly, no one needed to read a book that might help them achieve their goals in a world where goals were redundant. Tara tried to coax him into eating each day, but Mace wasn't hungry, not for food, not for interaction and not for Tara. They had been lucky in that they had paid off their mortgage using Mace's inheritance a few years before. They could stay inside their walls, relatively safe, albeit keeping an eye out for raiding gangs every night, the sort of people who were looking for easy cash and stuff to sell.

Tara hadn't wanted kids and nor had Mace. She just wanted peace and quiet after a difficult childhood and didn't feel that she had the mothering skills needed to raise children herself. She'd been happy to stay at home, budgeting, cleaning, and helping Mace grow his business. It was simple and Tara like simple. Thus, Tara was also struggling with End Date because this was as messy as it gets. The weather had become erratic, swinging wildly between dry dust storms and ferocious cyclones that dumped the ocean onto them. Food was becoming harder to find, and Tara was struggling to negotiate the black market as a single woman. Now that Mace was slowly dissolving away in front of her, Tara was getting anxious about being left alone to fend for herself. This wasn't a city for a woman on her own, as she had neither the skills nor the temperament to know how to fight. It encouraged raging anxiety in her, the sort that made her feel perpetually sick, and woke her for mandatory rumination at three every morning. There were millions of stories similar to theirs, though. An uncomfortable, tense existence, lived out in a solitary context. Only no-one wanted help, because everyone was weighed down with their own suffering.

RILEY WALKED to the supermarket to buy some non-perishable protein food, as well as what she could barter on the black market. She'd taken some fresh tomatoes that she had grown in her backyard greenhouse. These could be swapped for bread, that is, if someone had made some. Sometimes, someone traded some canned food, which was a luxury, as was anything made from dairy. Some people still kept a few sheep and goats, so sometimes, she could trade for some cheese or yogurt. Walking along, she kept her head down, tracking the lines on the concrete. She didn't want to risk eye contact with the loners that sat leaning towards her, hanging off the front boundary walls, begging for money. She had looked up to cross the road when something colorful amongst the bleakness had caught her eye. It was shiny new, bright too… glossy, like the posters had been before End Date had been announced. Riley had found herself trans- fixed by the colors, a bold red and bright yellow, something suggesting excitement perhaps.

She had stood there, trying to understand it. It didn't make much sense, though. Something about having to pay thirty thousand dollars if you wanted to have one. Then she got confused. She must have read it wrong. Why would someone be selling something that cost thirty grand? No, she was wrong. They would give you this money to have a chip put into your brain.

'MAKES YOU SMARTER,' she told Angus when she got back from the shopping.

'Smarter than who?' he had asked.

'Don't know,' she had replied.

Angus had looked at her. 'You joking love?'

'No. You get thirty thousand for getting one. I told you already.'

'So they put what, a chip into your brain, and you get smarter?'

'Apparently. Look, I took a picture.' She took out her phone, mostly used for taking photos, as they couldn't afford a decent phone plan anymore. 'Here,' she said, handing it to him.

He looked at the photo, enlarging it.

'That's a bit fancy - an intelligence chip,' he read out. 'Guaranteed to increase IQ. Choose your occupation. I could become a bloody doctor,' he snorted, laughing.

'You a doctor?' She peered at the photo. 'I thought I'd seen everything. What's the catch?'

'Don't know. There's a phone number. Should I phone? We haven't used up our phone credits this month, have we darl? We could make a time for us to attend one of the information sessions.'

'Do it. Let's be brave, Angus.'

• • •

THE HOTEL CONFERENCE room was ablaze with excitement. Belcher had spared no expense in the information sessions, filling the room with all the luxuries that people had been missing out on. Hors d'oeuvres and champagne on silver trays, carried by beautiful, young waiters dressed in science lab coats. Tables with brilliant white table-cloths, and brochures on desks, oozing with color and vibrancy. She wanted to remind people how life used to be before everything went wrong. She knew that the familiar would bring the punters in, and it did. Every information session was full to capacity with people clambering to sign up for a chip that would make them smarter, wealthier, and happier.

The champagne was sucked out of fancy glasses, strawberries rejoiced over, and exotic cheeses sniffed, tasted, and mulled. Jack stood in front of them all like a deer in the headlights, overwhelmed at the sudden enthusiasm in his chip. The media were snapping his anxiety, making the allure of the chip even more tantalizing. A mad professor, the President of the United Southern States, champagne, and blue cheese. It was an event like no other. The whole event was bursting with some new… something different.

Jack stood before them all, the eager desperates, happy from the alcohol and satisfied from the free food. Their eyes had worried him from where he had stood, following him around without blinking, maybe in fear that something this good might disappear if they didn't concentrate hard enough. He'd made a few feeble attempts at humor to lighten the mood, and people had laughed way too loudly and clapped like thunder clouds. The whole thing felt almost as if someone had laced the bubbly with LSD. Maybe Belcher had, just for the fun of it all?

There was a short welcome by someone important, followed by a dry introduction from Belcher, who had disappointed the crowd on every night, despite them being tipsy. Then he would appear, say a few words and play the information film that explained the surgery, down-time, adaptation period, and finally, the profession profiling. The applause and cheering at the end had been a thunderous roar, every single time. Afterward, near the sign up-desk, they'd brought security in order to control the enthusiasm. People were begging for the chips, especially the medical, legal, and business types.

Tara had brought Mace, after seeing the information session advertised online. Mace had sat in his seat, staring, and Tara wasn't even sure if he had heard a word of it. She'd asked the right questions to the man in the lab coat, Jack his name was, a man who used the word fuck, way too many times in a sentence, and he had reassured her, that Mace's depression would most likely be *fucking cured* by the chip. She had looked at Mace, sitting in the chair, staring straight ahead, and had signed him up as a lawyer. The process was lax enough for her to give consent as his wife without him having even to agree. There wasn't anything left to lose. She'd drunk three of the free champagnes and left feeling happier than she had done in a long time.

AT THE END of the information sessions, Jack had over three thousand names on the list.

'Right,' he told Paul and Tina, flipping through the briefing pages after the last session had finished. 'Our first batch and within our predicted numbers, so all good there. Quite a spread of people, more men than women, majority aged between twenty and forty years old, overall health is okay, yeah… I'd say we are ready for implantation.'

'Excellent. It went off without a hitch. Did you see the media for it? They made it look like the best thing to happen to the world in a long time.' Tina looked relieved.

'That's both good and bad. It means that Wells has also probably seen it all now and is going to be wondering why no-one told him about it.' Jack looked concerned. Wells might wonder what else they had been hiding.

Pete was remaining positive. 'We can start with the medical, teaching, legal, cleaning and business sectors with these numbers. Then add some more in the second wave.'

'And the hospitals, schools, and businesses are ready to re-open and employ again?' asked Jack.

'They are ready. Although this is so weird,' sighed Tina. 'They're going to employ chip surgeons to operate… people who have never touched any surgery, any training and just let them out there?'

'That's the whole point of the chip, Tina,' said Jack, staring quizzically at her. 'It *does* work, you know.'

She laughed. 'I know… but… it's weird. One minute they're driving a bus and then the next minute they're doing orthopedics.'

'We're about to implant these little suckers and then stand back and watch what happens.' Jack picked up one of the chips in a yellow case. He perused the finished product. 'They look good. Nice smooth cube with little chip tendrils hanging off. Would I get one of these put into my brain? Probably. We did good, everyone. Well done.'

'Well, I'm ready in my quarter,' said Pete. 'We have the five operating rooms ready, all relevant staff have been trained. We are anticipating each operation to take about two hours, and they've got a twenty-four-hour roster prepared. Recovery will be at the East Street rehabilitation facilities and yeah… they are ready to receive. As soon as people are switched on and have been given the all-clear, they will go straight into their employment postings.'

'Great,' said Tina. 'Jack, how's quality control looking?'

'Good. We have the three agencies ready to oversee the analysis side of things as soon as the chip workers commence employment postings. I'm calling them Chippies, by the way.'

'I like that. Yeah, I'll go with that. Chippies.' Tina smiled.

'So,' said Jack, 'I guess once the initial batch of Chippies are out there, and we have some positive feedback, we can start the State Release Program.'

'I don't see why not?' agreed Pete.

'I still doubt the need for the overlay personality,' said Tina.

'I'm sitting on the fence with that one,' said Pete.

'Why have it in the first place? I mean, I get that Belcher is a blatant psychopath who wants to think that she is creating a small army of people… who, what? Think like her?' Tina shrugged her shoulders.

'Sort of,' said Jack. 'I'm sure Belcher wanted an army just like her, but putting my brain overlay in ensures that it reduces the extremeness of Belcher.'

'Are families going to notice, do you think?' asked Pete.

'What, that their loved one suddenly doesn't need them as much anymore?' asked Jack.

'Yeah. Isn't that going to raise alarm bells?' asked Tina.

'Probably not. They'll put it down to career stress, I imagine. Most doctors are so run off their feet, they don't relax in their downtime, anyway.'

'Not all Jack, you can't generalize an entire career sector.'

'Okay then, most are exhausted all the time. They are hardly at home in the first instance, so I doubt families will be able to pinpoint where all the changes are coming from.'

'Well, let's just hope and pray that this goes well. That we can stabilize things out there, to buy us enough time to get out of here.' Tina looked serious. 'That's what all of this is about, remember.'

'Of course,' agreed Jack. 'I hear that Wells has already been building the new cargo ships and is working on the prototype for the two transporters. Although once he sees the media on this, I bet he'll be contacting Belcher, asking a lot of questions.'

'Yeah, agreed,' said Pete, 'So, we flood the market with Chippies, stabilize the government, get the hell out of here, and go live on Mars.'

'That's the plan, buddy. Belcher was saying that training could start within a year at the rate we're going,' Jack said with a hint of excitement in his voice.

'It's a lot of change to deal with,' said Tina. 'I've only just got settled into the apartment, but I suppose the alternative is bleak.'

'Yup,' said Jack. 'We're just aiming to survive at this point.'

'Yeah, traveling to a planet that we know so little about,' said Pete cautiously.

'Better than dead?' asked Tina.

'Some days, I'm not so sure,' said Jack.

23

THE EARTH SMELLED

LIKE TRUFFLES

Ellie inhaled deeply at the end of her daily meditation, feeling safe and content. The last few months had been without incident. The group had settled into Roger's house and had been busy transforming the land and home into a working farm. The small parcel of land at the back of the house had been plowed and new crops planted. Similar to the Gaia model, the intention was to eat fifty percent of the food and then preserve the rest. This required extra room for food storage, and so a large underground area had been dug out and was almost complete as a second, temperature controlled bunker. Roger had also insisted on daily briefings, a habit left over from his time in the CIA. He reiterated every day that emphasizing and articulating one's goals, meant that you stayed on the right path more easily. Today, Roger seemed distracted, though. Even worried, thought Ellie, as she took her place at the meeting table. He called the meeting to order.

'Good morning, everyone. I'm glad you are all here.' He meant that too, and often spoke about gratitude, ensuring that the group remembered to be thankful for each other on a daily basis. There had been a few small tiffs, mainly personality clashes, but Roger and Darinda were good at ironing them out, ensuring that the minor didn't escalate into anything significant.

'I'll update you all on the crop yields in a moment and on the updates for the new bunker. However, something else has been mentioned through my intelligence contacts.'

Ellie found the fact he still used CIA vernacular, an endearing quirk.

'This is quite concerning, to be honest.' The group sat up in their seats.

'I've had reports that a well-organized gang is raiding houses in the area, in a systematic fashion. For food, resources… anything that they can get their hands on. It's not good,' he added, looking serious.

The group glanced at each other, obviously worried.

'From what we know, the gang does surveillance of a given street and ascertains which houses are going in and out for resources. Those that aren't, but inhabited, are assumed to have food sources… and they raid them. It's a complete job. They shoot the occupants and then take. Sometimes they base themselves in those houses and do further strikes in that area. In fact, it's not just one gang either. Recently there has been evidence of copy-cat gangs that have created turf wars. A bit like the cartel in a way, only for food, some of which is then being sold on the black market. It's all highly organised.'

'Wow,' said Sims, looking uncomfortable. 'That's not completely unexpected, but I thought it would take more time to get to this point. Is protein food getting that scarce?'

'Not wholly. It's opportunistic at this stage. Fresh food has become a valuable commodity. People are doing it because they can. People are sick of the protein bars.'

'Shoot to kill… is there no negotiation?' asked Austin, also sounding concerned.

'Unfortunately, these people are callous. So, anyone who has prepped is a target.'

'We prepped,' said Ellie.

'Yes,' said Roger, allowing her words to sink in around the table.

'We prepped, which means we are a target,' said Darinda. 'It's time to protect what we have.'

'How?' asked Ellie.

'Well, we're going to need to act quickly,' said Roger. 'My intelligence suggests that this group is a couple of suburbs away. It gives us about a month to do what we have to do to protect all of this.'

'So,' said Darinda, leaving the table and then wheeling in a whiteboard covered in black text. 'This is the plan. We're going to need to erect better boundary protection around the house, probably in three parts. Firstly, electrified barbed wire. That's so you get zapped if you try to cut through and shredded if you then try to climb over. Second, we're going to need a laser zone and lighting to detect anyone who miraculously gets through the first barrier. Third, we need to design an automatic motion sensor boundary that shoots at anything that moves. We're all going to need weapons training as well, and we'll have an observation roster.'

'Wow,' said Ellie, feeling vulnerable and surprised that Darinda and Roger had already drawn so much up. 'I have a question.'

'Yes?' asked Roger.

'How do we stop them?'

'Like I just explained,' said Darinda, looking back at the diagrams, confused.

'No… I mean, if there are going to be gangs, as in multiple… isn't there just going to be one wave after another? How do we stop *all* of them?'

'That's actually a good point Ellie.' Roger walked over to the window. 'We're going to have to think strategically. Make sure that our food source is protected, no matter what happens. If they get in, which we hope they won't, we'll need additional layers of protection within the bunkers. This means accelerating the completion of the second bunker and placing tight security into both… and fast. We need to make sure that we think our way through this. Be clever. Stop people from getting in. No good if they manage to get through our defense, as it further complicates what happens next. We need to protect our boundaries.'

Darinda joined Roger at the window as if both had assumed watch positions like Meerkats might. 'This is about outsmarting these dickheads.' Darinda turned to them. 'Today and the rest of the week is about planning and buying what we need. Next week, we build around the clock if we have to. Get that first fence up as a matter of priority. We'll bring the boundary defense layers closer to the house, as we can't manage the entire perimeter in the time we have. We'll also start going out regularly with the vans, making it look like we need to refresh our resources. This will also help when we receive deliveries for the fencing, put people off as to what we might have ordered. We don't have a lot of time, but we've stuck together before and pulled off the impossible, so I'm sure we can do it again.'

'… and we become savvy,' added Roger. 'Don't discuss what we need the resources for with any delivery people. As far as people know, we're building a tennis court, which probably sounds a bit strange in itself. It's the best I can think of. We can fix the barbed wire onto the fencing ourselves and tell people we have issues with wildlife on the grounds, thus the need for it. Split the orders over as many places as possible, so it doesn't look like we are buying in bulk. We'll pay cash only so that we can't be financially tracked. We'll pick up as much as we can ourselves, to minimize the numbers of people coming in and out. Choose a selective few to see what we are doing, so that we can show them our wildlife issues… and where we want to build our tennis court. Five tennis courts, given the amount of fencing we need… only they will each think it's only one if we spread the orders around. No-one is to mention any food that we grow and certainly not the bunkers.'

The table murmured in agreement. He continued.

'In terms of the bunker completion, I'll be working with Austin, Anna, Louise, and Gary, starting as soon as we can to get what we need in terms of supplies. We need to secure what we have and also finish everything for the second bunker. The rest of you, Darinda, Ellie, Sims, and Edward, you'll be planning the fencing boundaries and obtaining the firearms. If we can get this done in a week, then even better, if you can't locate what you need, let me know, as I'll use my contacts. I'm getting more vans in by the way. That means if you need to go and pick something up, you can. Always travel with a partner, though, even if it's a convoy of vans, and from now on, *always* travel with a gun.'

'I've never shot a gun,' said Ellie, sounding concerned.

'Who else has never shot a gun?' asked Roger.

Anna and Sims raised their hands.

'Okay, we'll have a lesson at two this afternoon. Everyone can join in. We'll do an intensive and make sure that everyone can at least shoot straight.' Roger turned to Darinda.

'Can you ensure everyone has a gun by this afternoon?'

'With your contacts, I think anything is possible,' said Darinda. 'We live in dangerous times,' she said, looking around the room. 'It's survival now,' she nodded. 'It's that time where we need to ensure the safety of our family.'

Ellie went up to her room and sat on her bed. This was getting real. More real than it had felt when she and Dean had driven from their home and into the Gaia community. She had thought that they had been traveling towards somewhere safer. Ironic really. Now they were going to be surviving in a place where gangs wanted to shoot them all dead. She shivered, acid gnawing away at her stomach. She wondered about shooting gangs of people who were opportunistically invading and thought that pulling the trigger could be justified. Could she shoot someone who was just hungry, though? What about roaming families who just wanted food for their children? Could she shoot them? What if a child turned up asking for food… what then? Roger had further explained about distancing herself from compassion. Their food was not to be shared under any circumstances because trust went out the window when people were hungry, and especially when children were dying from starvation. Roger had said that anyone, no matter what age, would be shot, if trespassing on the land. She needed to hide from it all, so crawled into her bed and pulled the covers over her face. She had thirty minutes before the boundary meeting, and her vulnerability could be private, just for a moment. She closed her eyes and found her safe place, where everything felt better.

. . .

Y'ALL, this is where we had got to, and it ain't pretty. Ellie exit stage left, and I'm entering stage right. I've got shit to say and right now, my anger has been found. I'm shitting dynamite. Ellie has to grow up right now. The time for having feelings, having fucking morals, has gone. Yeah, that's where we headed next, into a place without empathy. We shot each other's fucking kids. We did. We shot them when their eyes were still full of trust and fucking hope. They were just hungry, and so we killed them. Then we killed their parents and went back into our homes. We justified it through our self-righteousness, the sort that had started on social media, when everyone knew fucking everything and where uneducated opinions reigned supreme. You know what? I call that a line in the sand, where it became okay to blow children's brains out, so deliberately, so obviously and without remorse. It was our time of reckoning. We'd done it before, though, plenty of times, on the quiet where it was easier to do. During wars, invasions, you know, times when every fucking war leader had approved trigger-happy.

This was different because there was no umbrella of war. This was a transformation from nice humans into animal humans, which is what we truly are, once you take off the clothes of social conformity. We're no better than a lion, a rhinoceros, or a charging elephant. Blinded by our basic desires to protect one of our own, or ourselves, we charged, we defended, we killed. Were we nicer, back way before End Date was announced, when we were protected through due process? We had designed a system in which to complain and defend ourselves through words and ink. Complaints about stuff could be discussed and thought through, because time was on our side.

We just pretended to be nice. We hid behind our anonymity on social media, and we trolled, shredding the vulnerable, and laughed at other's mistakes. Why? Because we could. People had this way of explaining it by saying that it was social media that turned us all against each other. Kind of true in the sense that all of a sudden there was a platform where everyone could be seen and heard. However, we were like that to begin with, and then we found a way to be like that again. Hiding in social media allowed us to hate again *collectively.* We lost ourselves in our point making and our sense of entitlement. We forgot that we have to earn our dignity by being whole, decent human beings, no matter who we think we are.

The kids, though. Holy shit. We bred an entire generation of depressed people. Depressed, not through their own fault, rather, because they had fed off the system. One based on the declaration of independence that had been named The American Dream. It was nothing more than a fairy story. Fucking fairyland. That's what it was. A place to lie and indoctrinate the children and make them believe that if they just followed the system, that the system would work for them. What was that phrase written on every nursery wall? Yeah… follow your dreams, you can be anyone you want to be.

Really? Over my fucking dead shit arse. The truth? The truth came down to money. Digital, paper, old, new… it didn't matter. If you had money, you had a future. If you didn't, then good luck. Graduates didn't know that though until they stuck their fingers up at their parents and walked out into their bright and sunny futures. Then they realized that the life they had been promised didn't exist. They could see who had the money... the contacts… the networks… and who didn't. They were working three jobs to pay their rent, watching the ones with old cash, new cash mess around all the time, not needing to work, their futures already promised by someone who had probably sucked their father off… figuratively or not.

Instead, they bred like rabbits, because they needed someone to love them, to fill the empty voids within them. The population was already strained, but they popped them out like a fucking automatic tennis server before End Date was announced. Our population just kept rising, as the mercury did. Then they looked at all of these babies and wondered how they could live with themselves. Breeding more babies that were staring straight down the barrel towards suffering and death. If they weren't already depressed, now they were cat-a-fucking-tonic. Parents are wired, after delivering a placenta, to kill to protect their own. And so they did. They murdered for bread and water. They killed over chocolate and fresh fruit. Governments panicked and created the suicide boxes, and the entire planet wobbled in its own mess of death-stink. Then the zombie depressed, tried to get more food, and people like Darinda and Roger organized to shoot them, including their kids.

Yeah, you know what? Human beings were always destined to die by their own hands. No crystal ball meant we never saw it coming in full. I'm not talking about End Date per se either, because the scientists had been crapping on about that since the 1940s. It was more how we descended into the nasty fucking animals that we are. No-one saw how low we were prepared to go - wired to try to survive, no matter what. I warned you in the beginning that everyone loses in this tale. Fuck this, I need to go and re-fill my glass.

ELLIE MADE her way downstairs to the safety meeting, in which they would discuss the fencing boundaries. Darinda had created a generic purchase order. They would keep the orders the same size, only allowing enough for a tennis court from each supplier. Darinda had even mapped out where a tennis court might go, just in case anyone asked. Then they would collect the barbed wire themselves in the vans. The boundaries would be three meters apart, ensuring that if anyone got over one, they would face another quickly before they had time to get their bearings. The second layer of the boundary was sensor activated, and bright lights would illuminate everything. The third layer was designed so that a laser would shine a small red dot over your heart and forehead, and then the guns would shoot you. That was before you could even tell anyone the purpose of your visit. It saved shooting people themselves, she hoped.

The shooting practice at two was daunting. Roger had placed several soft plastic targets in the backfield to shoot at. Ellie could easily imagine flesh being shredded like cheese, as her gun tore off the plastic, piece by piece. It was a game of shooting them before they shot her, and Darinda screamed at her repeatedly as she paused when aiming. There was no choice in the matter, no room for consideration, just a demanding urgency.

'Just fucking shoot the shit out of them!' Darinda had yelled at her over the gunfire.

'I'm trying!'

'Ellie, that split second is where you lose your life. No room for taking a breath. Shoot on empty lungs. Shoot!' Roger had yelled at her.

After an hour, Ellie had transformed into a killer, organizing to place the barbed wire on fencing, place lasers to find an illuminated human heart, before blowing their chest and brains out of their body. She could justify it only in terms of need - the need for her own survival.

Austin was working with Roger to help construct the second bunker and fortify the first. There would be sensors near the stairs that would release fatal energy surges, killing anyone trying to gain unlawful access and then jets of fire, designed to crispy-strip intruders. The water supply for the bunkers needed to be secured using a well which Roger and his late wife had dug themselves, which fed off a little-known artesian supply. Roger planned to bring up as much volume as possible before anyone deflected the source to take as their own. The water would be stored under both bunkers, in purpose-built concrete tanks. It all boiled down to choice at the end of the day, with only two possible outcomes. Life or death. Alive or dead.

24

I WORK
REAL HARD

Angus woke with a pickaxe banging in his brain. He tried to reach up but couldn't find his arm to lift. He coughed but was perplexed. How could an arm cough? Where was his arm anyway? Lights kept shining in his face, blinding him. It was better to go back to sleep, so he allowed the black to fall over him again. He was awake again now, with the same blinding headache, only now he was swimming in a pool of dead fish, and a strange smell filled his nose. Then his nose was running with giraffes, as tall as the mountain that they were running through. His arms were running in front of him, and if he could only stretch out, he could grab one. He heard voices, someone telling him it was done. He remembered the voice, but how could he stretch out if he had no arms? His head, though, it was hurting, and he kept seeing lists… of something… lists of the names of bones and diseases, as if his head had a book of anatomy in it. Now he was cutting and sewing skin? Faces popped in and out, blurring, and he was talking, explaining, and holding a dying person's hand.

Another voice was asking him to open his eyes, and he did so. A strong light blinded him, attached to an apology. Then another voice, a familiar voice, Riley… it was his wife. He opened his eyes, and the room came into focus.

'Finally, sleepyhead, it's over. The chip is in, and you're fine.' Her voice was reassuring, and her smile was close to his face as she leaned towards him. The chip. Yes, the chip. He'd gone in and had the chip implanted, and now he was a doctor. He could think like one. Medical stuff was filed in his head in a new library. There were noises though, and too many faces, some dying, and he could see himself lifting a sheet to cover death. He opened his eyes again, Riley was still there. He would focus on Riley.

'Do you have any pain?' asked a nurse with a thick Scottish accent.

He nodded. 'My head,' he said hoarsely.

'That's okay, dear, we'll get you something for that. It will all be fine. Give it a day or two, and you'll be thinking straight again. You head is bound to feel a bit like mush at the moment, and the strong pain killers are going to make you feel a wee bit woozy as well.'

He felt his bed being wheeled somewhere.

'They're taking you to the rehab unit now, Angus,' said Riley gently. 'It's a ride in an ambulance, and I'll see you there. A bit later, love. Okay?'

He closed his eyes again. He could smell death. He tried to shake his head, but any movement just hurt. He felt a sharp scratch as a needle went into his arm. Then he was asleep again.

TARA WAS STANDING over Mace and had just watched a man called Angus come around. They'd taken him off to rehab already, albeit with a lot of wires and tubes attached to him. Nice wife, she had thought, smiling over at the woman who had not left her husband's side since he'd returned from theatre.

'It's okay,' the kind nurse had said, 'some people take a little bit longer to come around than others.'

Tara had waited for an extra hour, watching for any signs of movement from Mace who lay as still as a rock, his vitals being the only indication that he was still alive. Then he had woken with a jolt, trying to take the leads off. The nurses had sedated him again, needing to measure his vitals for a while longer. Tara had wiped his brow, and he had come around again, pushing her hand away.

'Fuck off,' he had said angrily to her, surprising her with his outburst.

She had looked over at the nurse who had reassured her. 'Some people just react badly to the anesthetic. He'll be fine soon. Don't worry.'

Tara had worried. He'd been depressed as it was going into surgery, and she could only now guess at the state he was going to be in when he came out of it. Mace stirred again. Tara stood over him, just as the kind woman had done over the man named Angus. An arm shot up, hitting her in the face, and blood started to pour from her nose.

'I told you to fuck off,' he snarled at her. 'Just fucking do it.'

The nurse stepped in quickly. 'That will be quite enough, Mace. You've hurt your wife with your silliness. Calm down and keep your hands to yourself. Everything has gone well. The chip is in, and we'll be taking you to rehab soon.'

'Not her,' Mace snarled. 'Get her the fuck away from me.'

The nurse took Tara aside and helped her stem the flow of blood. 'You poor dear, you're lucky he hasn't broken it. Happens to all of us now and again. He'll calm down. In the meantime, keep your finger pressing here. Follow him to rehab, and I'll let them know over there what has happened. Do you want a cup of tea, perhaps?'

Tara drove from the hospital to the rehabilitation unit. Her nose was throbbing and red, the swelling making it hard to breathe. Mace had come out of the surgery as if he'd had a complete brain transplant and not a chip insert. Catatonic was one thing she could deal with, but not this new aggression. She prayed that it would wear off, and that, as he regained full consciousness, he would also regain his composure. She was disappointed once getting to the rehabilitation unit. Mace was worse. She could hear him shouting at the nurses as she walked up the corridor, and one of them ran out of his room, crying.

'Probably best not to go in there right now,' said the nurse in charge. 'He's very aggressive. Was he like this in the first place, before the operation?'

'No.' Tara shook her head. 'No, if anything, he was completely passive… depressed, actually. Why do you think he's so aggressive?'

'We're not yet sure. He's the first to come out like that, though. Everyone else has come out relatively unscathed. Look, there's a lady in the tea-room. Riley… her husband just got moved to rehab. Did you spot them? Why don't you have a quick chat with her? It might cheer you up a bit?'

Riley looked up from her cup of coffee at the woman who had entered the room. She recognized her from the hospital. She could see that something had hit her nose pretty hard, too.

'Hi,' she said warmly. 'How are you doing? I'm Riley. It's been quite a day, hasn't it?'

Tara sighed. 'I need a strong coffee. My husband has come out like a monster, thus my nose… I'm Tara, by the way.'

'Nice to meet you, Tara. Really? Did he hit you?'

'Yeah. I leaned over to speak to him and he slogged me.'

'Can I do anything?'

'No. Just perhaps sit and have a coffee?' she smiled. 'I wish I could breathe properly. It's swelling up quite badly.'

'Maybe ask for an ice-pack? His anger could be related to the surgery drugs, combined with the wiring for the chip. It can't be easy, suddenly having all of that information in your head. My husband, Angus, got the medical chip. What about your partner?'

'Mace? He got the legal chip. Now he's apparently a bastard.'

'Look, have a cup of something, and we'll sit and chill for a bit, love.'

Riley indicated for Tara to come and sit next to her.

'Life, hey,' Tara said to her, trying to sound more cheerful than she felt.

'Yeah,' said Riley, smiling. 'It's all gone a bit pear-shaped out there, hasn't it?'

ANGUS WOKE AGAIN, this time feeling calm and without bright lights being shone into his face. He looked around his room, empty except for him. So, the chip was in, and he was okay. This was good. He tested the chip by thinking about being a doctor, and memories flooded his mind. Presentations, patients, procedures. It was flooding his mind too quickly. He pressed the button for the nurse in a panic.

'Too much,' he said, gasping and shaking his head. 'I need it to stop.'

'That's okay. Just breathe and allow all of your thoughts to wash over you. It's perfectly normal, as we've just filled your brain with an enormous amount of information. Can you do that for me, Angus?'

He nodded. These experiences, though, were his, as if he had lived them, done them, and he felt them. He thought back to being a… what was he again? He'd been a… something. Before becoming a doctor, he'd been a… his mind was blank. He couldn't remember what he had been before. He could remember his boys, his home, and Riley… but had he studied to be a doctor? No, that was stupid. He had memories of studying, long nights and remembering copious amounts of lecture notes, though. Maybe he'd always been a doctor? Nah. It didn't make sense. He was wasting time though in the hospital, that he knew. He needed to be up and working, back to his patients who needed him. Yes, he remembered that people needed him. These nurses, normally, they did what he asked them to, and here they were, bossing him around - nicely, but the sooner he got back to work, the better.

Mace was propped up for a light meal. His anger hadn't subsided, and he'd thrown his dinner tray across the room, smashing it and splattering bright orange protein mash all over the sterile white walls. The nurses had consulted the doctor on duty, and he'd phoned Jack in despair.

'The man is just blatantly aggressive. He's our first legal implant, by the way. He wasn't this aggressive, according to his wife, until the chip was inserted. The others have come out okay so far… no signs of this aggression.'

'That's not right,' said Jack, immediately calling an emergency meeting between Tina, Pete, and himself.

. . .

'WE'VE HAD one chap called Mace. He's come out aggressive as fuck, apparently.'

'Could just be an anomaly,' suggested Pete.

'Yeah,' said Tina. 'I don't think we should worry, just yet.'

'They are having issues calming him down. He doesn't want his wife in the room, and he smashed her nose when she leaned over the bed, apparently.'

'Gees,' said Tina. 'That's a bit harsh.'

'I think we just wait,' said Pete. 'If there's a second case, then yeah, we may have a problem.'

MACE WAS SEGREGATED AWAY from the other Chippies. The doctors gave him a sedative to help calm the aggression, which they put down to the meds used in the anesthetic. The rest of the Chippies were given a few days to recover from the surgery and then rehab began in earnest on a rotational basis. The first medical Chippies were sent off together, and the legals soon followed.

The medical Chippies were divided into groups of eight, keeping the numbers small so that intensives could be done with attention to detail. The first week of rehabilitation focused on memory testing and recollection of facts, essential if the Chippie medics were to walk out and into immediate medical positions. Angus found it odd and reassuring to name every bone, ligament, and nerve in the human body. Yet, when he went to compare it to what he had done before, he couldn't remember. It was as if his mind went blank every time.

Jack had nodded at the preliminary results coming in. The limiter was doing its job, stopping the Chippie from wanting to compare another occupation. So far, the medical chip had been unfolding without a hitch, with all the medic Chippies displaying the right amount of arrogance and confidence that doctors needed to do what they had to do. It had made him chuckle in fact when he had visited them, most of them telling him that there wasn't a medical basis for them to even be in a rehabilitation unit. He honestly couldn't see a problem with them leaving that week, even before all the tests had been carried out. The legal chip was running into issues, though. They now had twelve men who had gone through the implant operation, showing higher levels of aggression. Mace was by far the worst, exhibiting extreme antisocial behaviors, and as a result, he was still heavily sedated. The others had shown high levels of arousal when provoked, something which had worried Jack.

MACE COULD JUST THINK STRAIGHT ENOUGH through the haze of sedation to know what he needed to do. Four days after the operation and they had him strapped to a bed, stuffed full of drugs. His depression, the one he'd come in with, had transformed into raging anger just below the surface of his skin, and the slightest provocation would make it erupt, firing it at whomever was being a nuance. He knew that he needed to devise a better strategy that would reduce the outrageous treatment they were serving out to him. How dare they strap him to a bed, reducing his dignity to shreds. He decided that instead of fighting them, he would be the perfect patient. A yes man, doing everything they needed him to do. Then, and only then, would they release him. Then he would seek revenge for the humiliation of being strapped down and separated from the rest of the Chippie cohort.

This anger though, that he felt between him and the world was all-encompassing. He felt like the hulk, an ever-growing rage that seemed to know no boundaries, and hate filled every pore in his body. He knew he could kill if he wanted to, and that he could do it with no remorse and certainly no guilt. That he knew. Then there were the memories. Strange and random snippets of information about the law. Cases, trials, and people being led away to cells. He could recollect study at a university that had rooms with leadlight windows, and professors who had looked earnest and serious when discussing cases.

He asked his wife to fuck off every day, and she had watered him with salty tears. Her showers had been tiresome, coating him in pleading words that only made his feelings towards her more intense. He just wanted her to stop and be silent. Tara, her name was, and he could no longer stand her. He had no idea why he'd been with her for so long in the first instance. Her voice grated through his mind, cutting him, battering him with pathetic and frantic. Her desire to see him, to be intimate with him as a wife, friend, or anything in fact, just ignited the fuel of his distaste. He wanted her to go and die… to get away from him and leave him be. In the end, he'd told her to get out of *their* home, and so she had, moving a suitcase to her cousin's house, where she had said she would *wait*. He'd appreciated the silence in the ward. He needed neither Tara nor reminders of that stupid home he'd lived in with its garish china sets, blood orange wallpaper, and furniture-all bought initially with hope. There had to be more to life than having to spend his time surrounded by people who blatantly irritated him.

BELCHER TAPPED her foot on the ground as if impatient, which made no sense, given they were waiting for her to open the meeting. She'd called it, wanting an update on the implantation process, and they had arrived, sitting in a row in front of her like school children hoping for a good report. She folded her arms and then ran her tongue around her lips, methodically, several times, the action making Jack physically turn away. The thought of that tongue running over anything, repulsed him.

'So,' she said, turning and looking at each of them in turn. They stared back.

'Why the aggression in the legal chips Jack?' she asked, pouncing on Jack's face.

'It's the personality overlay we believe.' Jack felt he was brave in answering anything to do with the overlay.

'So, you are telling me that my personality overlay is causing this aggression?' she said, aggressively.

'Not exactly.' There was so much irony in the air, he wanted to laugh.

Peter wanted to look at Jack, give him a hint of warning. These words were heading into dangerous territory.

'Explain why the medical Chippies are doing just fine with my personality overlay then.'

Jack took a deep breath.

'We're looking into it, running some tests. We think it's just a random combination of legal material… as in algorithms, mixing badly with the personality overlay.'

Tina looked at Jack and shook her head slightly. Really Jack?

'Poor,' stated Belcher, drilling her eyes into him. 'Drivel,' she added.

Jack knew it was inadequate. However, it wasn't even her personality in the overlay, and she would probably turn inside out in front of them if he divulged that small nugget of information.

'Fix it,' she said. 'I will not see myself in these chip recipients, reflected in such a way,' and walked out.

'Cameras,' mouthed Jack quietly, reminding Tina and Peter that everything they said was scrutinized.

Tina nodded.

'Right,' said Pete, 'Let's fix the problem then. We'll head over to the rehab unit. Interview this Mace character and try to work out what has gone wrong.'

'Do you think it's the overlay?' asked Tina from the backseat of the car that Belcher had loaned them.

'It makes little sense. Why would legal information blend with my overlay to create this level of aggression?' asked Jack.

'What do we know?' asked Pete. The most levelheaded and strategic out of the three of them, he knew to start at the beginning and see if there was something they had missed.

'Maybe we need to go back over the case files?' suggested Tina, hopefully. 'There may be something in their medical records that we missed?'

'That's not a bad idea,' agreed Jack. 'Given we don't know what else to do. It's worth talking to the rehab coordinator as well. See if she's noticed anything else that she can't explain.'

'ALL WE KNOW,' said Sandy robustly, smiling through her round and sunburned face, 'is that the aggression started with Mace, and then there were more… all male and all exhibiting the same antisocial signs… irritability, short fuse, rudeness, aggression, and not wanting to be around family, which is strange. It's as if they come to, with a social disconnect. We've counted twelve so far and all of them legal chip recipients.'

'Can we look at the medical records somewhere? Would that be okay… we promise not to get under your feet?' Pete smiled sweetly at Sandy.

'Of course. I'll even throw in a coffee and some biscuits if you like?' Sandy smiled at Pete, thinking him a real gentleman.

Tina admired the way she could smile and maintain a cheerful perspective for a woman under so much stress.

They waded through file after file, starting with Mace. Pete drew up a table on the whiteboard to tease out any emerging factors, and there were a couple that were becoming more and more obvious.

'All male and they all had depression to start with,' said Pete. 'Fascinating.'

'Doesn't make any sense,' said Jack.

'Explain?' Pete asked.

'What about the medical Chippies? You can't tell me that none of them were depressed before having their implants?'

'Wait,' said Tina, remembering something. She got her phone out. 'Give me a sec. I'm going to check something.'

'I knew it,' she said after a brief phone call. 'I remembered something during the intake, and the zone coordinator has just confirmed it. The medical Chippies were asked if they had suffered from depression, and if they had, they didn't get to have the medical chip implant. Remember, we discussed ensuring that those in medicine should be as clean as we could get them?'

Pete nodded. 'I remember now. Just never knew those controls had even been put into place. Who was supposed to have briefed me on that?'

'You should have received a phone call from South Street. That didn't happen? Disappointing,' said Tina, looking concerned. 'I'll follow that up after the meeting.'

'That might explain the concentration of aggression in the legal Chippies. Those that had depression were told to become a lawyer or whatever, instead. Means we might get a few more in teaching, cleaning and business in the next round? Worth looking out for that. Doesn't explain a tangible link between the chip and depression, though.' Jack stared at the files and then up at the whiteboard.

'It's pretty conclusive to me,' said Pete. 'Those with depression have become aggressive.'

'No, it's only tentative… it's not a solid relationship.' Jack was scratching his head, looking confused. 'Why would pre-existing depression cause aggression in the first instance?' He chewed the end of his pen.

'My mother always said, never to put a pen into your mouth because you never knew if it had been in someone else's mouth first,' said Tina.

Jack quickly pulled it out and looked at her. 'Thanks, Tina, for that lovely thought.'

'My pleasure,' she said, smiling.

'So, this is certified diagnosed depression right, and not just I feel sad, kind of stuff?' clarified Jack.

'I believe so,' said Tina.

'Let's work the problem through then,' he said hopefully.

• • •

MACE WAS ALLOWED up and into the rehabilitation program. The nursing staff were relieved to see that whatever had been firing him up was subsiding, and quickly. Mace joined the other Chippies, and there were no further issues. It was decided to separate the twelve who exhibited the aggression into a special session for meditation, believing that it might help with their irritability.

Jack watched them through the window. 'We arrive, and then the staff are saying that there's no issue. We've been sitting here for three hours, looking for a causal link, and then we get asked to come and see this.'

'It's weird, that's for sure,' said Pete, looking at the twelve, perfectly co-operating Chippies.

'So, are we going to pursue this or not?' asked Tina.

'Did Sandy not know that it had resolved itself when she spoke to us earlier?' asked Pete.

'Obviously not,' said Jack. 'I'll repeat. Do we have an issue?'

'I'm confused. Doesn't look like it, I mean, look at them.' Pete looked over at the Chippies, who were listening attentively to their instructor.

'Maybe the problem ironed itself out?' asked Tina. 'They look fine to me.'

'From here, they do. Bit of a coincidence, don't you think?' asked Pete.

Jack's phone rang. 'Yes, on the way.' He turned to them. 'Belcher needs us back at the lab.'

'Right then. Problem sorted. We can go back to Belcher and tell her it was the depression, but that it's fixed.' Pete sighed. 'Waste of a morning, don't you think?'

'Sort of. Are we sure this is wrapped up, though?' Tina stared through the window again. 'It seems a bit too convenient, don't you think?'

'Why? Do you have specific concerns?' asked Jack.

'Not really. It just seems a bit unusual. Maybe Sandy is just too busy to be updated properly by her colleagues? I mean, it's good if it's sorted, but the timing?'

'Look, as far as I'm concerned, and with what I'm seeing, it's sorted. If it flares again, then we'll do something. I will tell Sandy that we can go full-steam ahead with the rest of the legal implants. Right now, we need to get back to Belcher and find out what other crisis she would like us to fix.'

'We need superhero capes,' said Pete.

Tina laughed. 'Funny,' she said.

Mace waited until the break, after the instructor had released them from breathing deeply, and drew a couple of the other Chippies close to him.

'We play the game. We do as asked, remember. Once we're released, then we sort matters out.'

25

———

THE PUMPKINS
FLEW

Jack asked me to write this chapter, mainly so that y'all could read it from an impartial perspective. The original chapter was written by one of the group, hiding out in Virginia, in Roger's house. Jack said that the emotionality was too high in their account, leaving out logical pieces of information necessary to understand everything. My turn now to say this and say it with truth, the sort that comes from an earthy, divine place, where the truth, in the form of recounted facts, sends those goosebumps up your backbone.

So Darinda and Roger had been coordinating the building of the barricades and the safety measures to protect the group from the gangs. The ones that were systematically raiding houses for the fun of it. Blowing the brains out of pleading human beings was kind of fun for crazies like them. Darinda had managed to build a three-layered boundary line. The first line, set back about ten feet, met…

'I want Ellie's account in the story.'

'Jack, you just told me to replace it with mine.'

'I've changed my mind.'

'When in the name of hell do you ever change your mind, Jack?'

'Now. Before I fly to Mars.'

'You serious, man?'

'Yeah. It could be one of the last earthly decisions I make.'

'Right. So literally mid-sentence, you want me to replace my account with Ellie's again, like a fucking merry-go-round?'

'Yeah, I think the story needs to see it through her eyes, after all.'

'You just told me to replace it with *impartial facts.* Those were your words.'

'I know. Sorry. Anyway, you're doing the finale. Maybe you should go and prepare for that?'

'Jack. You infuriate me.'

'I know.'

'True. Lucky we're blood, Jack.'

'Yes.'

'I'll go prepare the finale then.'

ELLIE WOKE in the middle of the night but couldn't understand why. Her heart was racing, indicating that perhaps she had awakened in the middle of a nightmare but couldn't recall one. She got up and went into the kitchen, thinking she could hear someone in there, and that perhaps a chat could provide her with enough comfort to regain her composure. There was no-one in the blackness that she could see, and she could hear the howls of some animal from far away, the kind that precedes horror in movies. She stood in the doorway to the kitchen, disorientated, feeling like a character in her own nightmare.

Turning, she made her way back to the stairs and up to her bedroom. She stopped outside Austin's room and lifted her hand to knock on the door. She'd hardly seen him over the past few days, she building the fencing system and he, completing the security in both bunkers. Crawling into his bed and feeling his skin against hers was what she wanted… needed right now. Comfort for comfort's sake wasn't part of this new world regime, however, as if vulnerability and emotionality were now deemed frivolous. She lowered her hand. He might think her weak if she demanded intimacy now, and her not knowing how to articulate such a need in words. It was as if her inner child was seeking refuge somewhere she could feel safe.

She made her way back to her bedroom, trying to make sense of what had woken her. Was it fear, she wondered? Fear that a gang was going to make their way past the elaborate and sophisticated boundary security measures and blow her brains out? She peered out of the window and only saw stillness, interrupted by the occasional howl from whatever animal was calling out to her in the dark. There was no movement or threat out there, and the reassurance allowed her to unlock a band of tight muscles in her abdomen, allowing her to breathe more deeply. She remembered her stress management techniques, and how slow, regular, deep breathing could reduce anxiety. She breathed in slowly for five and held the air in her lungs, then she allowed it to leave, slowly, methodically, and with total control. She repeated the exercise, feeling her negative emotions releasing with each breath out. She needed to control whatever was inside of her, the feeling that was making its presence known, but without explanation. She sat with it for a while, inviting it back so that she could make sense of it, but the breathing had reduced its force, leaving only a strange imprint that she couldn't decipher.

The past few days had been exhausting, and Ellie remembered from her teaching days that long hours and a lack of quality sleep could raise her anxiety, spiraling her into negative thinking. This panic attack in the night's dark hadn't been the first, and it was a warning sign that Ellie needed to regain control.

They had built a three-tiered boundary fencing system, designed to prevent people from gaining access to the house. It had been difficult digging the holes into the dry earth, deep enough to cement in the fencing posts, and even more challenging to place the razor-sharp barbed wire around the top of the metal H-frames. Darinda had fitted barbed wire before, to keep wildlife out of her property, so knew how to unroll it and tension it so it didn't snap and tear someone's face apart.

'We'll do this three times to ensure that you can't just step over it.' She called out, one foot on top of a fencing post.

'Sure,' Ellie had called back up to her. Being a petite build made it difficult to hold up her end of the wire roll which weighed eighty pounds, two-thirds of her body weight. However, this was not the place to complain, as the job just needed to be done as quickly as possible. Roger had made the decision to electrify this first boundary, including the all-metal fencing posts. He'd sent through a voltage that would kill anyone who touched it.

'This is naturally as illegal as it gets, but we're doing what we have to do,' he'd explained during one of the daily briefings.

'So don't go touching it,' added Darinda. 'Otherwise, you'll fry.'

'Yes, in all seriousness, when you now drive out of the property, which we will keep to a minimum, we'll have a deactivation switch for the fence. Reactivate it once you are through the gates. That's critical. Don't take fluids near it, and guys… don't pee near it. It's a dangerous voltage which will cause cardiac arrest.' Roger looked around the room.

'Questions?'

Ellie noticed that Austin wasn't there. She'd wanted to catch up with him for a few minutes, but he was pouring cement for the bunker.

'Right, my team, we're off to set up some, *blow your brains off* type of stuff today. Should be fun,' Darinda looked excited by the thought.

Ellie shook her head. How did things get to this?

'So, we'll set up eight guns which pivot on these ball bearings.' Darinda was explaining the automatic laser detectors, which sensed movement. 'These tell the guns where to aim and fire. Anything standing in the arc of the laser light gets shot into tiny pieces. These are little beauties,' Darinda said, holding one up. She pointed it at Ellie. 'Never point one of these at anyone.'

Ellie fell flat to the floor as fast as she could.

'Ellie, it's okay, I was just demonstrating.' Darinda laughed, 'it's okay, you can get up.'

Ellie stood back up, somewhat sheepishly.

'So, we set them up and then secure them. The secure bit is imperative. They must be balanced and even, so that when they fire, they can compensate for the force of the bullet action.'

She handed each of them a machine gun. 'Where did we even get these?' asked Anna.

'Roger. He has access to everything. We could have tanks in here if we wanted to.' Darinda stopped as if happily imaging several tanks on the property. 'These will do just fine.'

They worked another day, again digging the holes for the gun posts. Each machine gun was secured to a post using a swivel ball.

'Make sure each gun has a wide horizontal and vertical swing. That way, we overlap the firing area.'

The lasers were set up in a crisscross pattern, each designed to sense movement from the ground to fifteen feet. They activated the firing sensors, which in turn activated the machine guns. Darinda used weathered pumpkins to demonstrate, calling Roger over to witness their achievement.

'I'm throwing the pumpkin,' she yelled out. An orange sphere flew through the air in a perfect parabolic shape.

'Nice throw!' yelled out Roger.

The pumpkin headed towards the ground, flying across several sensor areas, and all hell broke loose. Three of the machine guns took aim and fired. They obliterated the pumpkin.

'Way to go, Darinda and team! Very impressive annihilation of the small orange intruder!' Roger clapped, smiling.

Darinda leaned down and picked up a second pumpkin. She again threw and watched it being blown apart. 'Whoa, look at that thing blow!' she yelled in excitement.

Ellie shuddered. While it was fun to see the pumpkins get shot down, it wasn't hard to substitute a human body into the picture.

'So, we're done out front,' said Darinda. 'How's the bunkering going, Roger?'

'Almost done. We've finished the second and just need to complete the water transfers and security.'

'What have you got in mind?' asked Darinda.

'Flames actually. We've set up the internal staircase leading into each bunker in a flame-retardant material. Intruder gets in and gets vaporized from the jets that line the stairs. There's a door at the bottom that opens into the actual bunker which automatically seals if the jets activate.'

'Clever,' Darinda nodded her head. 'What about the main house?'

'Cameras, motion detectors. I think we'll be okay with the boundary fencing, though.'

'We should be. Even if it acts as a deterrent and the gangs think it's all a bit too hard.'

'I hope so,' said Roger, 'I hear that they are systematic in their raids, though.'

Darinda shook her head. 'Well, we can only do what we can do,' she said.

'True words, my dear.' Roger sighed. 'Fucking people,' he added.

'Roger… I've never heard you swear.'

'No,' he sighed. 'I don't often, but everywhere we turn, people are getting in our way.'

'I know,' agreed Darinda, sadly. 'But this at least gives us more hope for a bit.'

'I'm just sorry it wasn't for longer. It would have been nice to have found some peace in all of this.' He gazed around the property, taking it all in.

'Yes, I agree. Coffee?' asked Darinda.

'That sounds like a great idea. We probably need to change the subject. Otherwise, we'll infect everyone with our sadness.'

ROGER CALLED the daily briefing meeting to attention. Austin had finally resurfaced, his skin now olive-brown after several days working out in the sun. Ellie sat next to him, glad to have her friend back and glad to have finished all the hard labor.

'So, well-done team in getting all of that done. Essential work to ensure that we can stay as safe as possible. Our next task is preserving. We have quite a lot of food ready for picking, which we need to do as quickly as possible. This will help if people get a visual in terms of how much we are growing out there. If we make it less visible, then maybe we'll make breaking in look less appealing. So, I need to take two people with me into the city to get supplies for the bunkers, just in case we are forced into them, and Darinda is going to explain preserving methods.'

'Okay, gang. Preserving is more fun than rolling out barbed wire, I promise. We are going to be pickling, dehydrating, and freezing our food. First, however, we need to pick it. So let's do that first, and then we can get prepped.'

Roger drove in with Anna and Sims to buy generators, fuel, batteries, first aid, alcohol, rope, and other bits and pieces. His late wife had already done a lot of the prepping, but with the extra people, he needed more. Enough perhaps for an extra couple of weeks, just in case they all got forced down into the bunkers.

Ellie was picking fruits, carefully collecting each piece and placing it into her hip basket. Austin was in the row next to her, close enough for comfort, but too far for meaningful conversation. They worked, taking only a short break for lunch, each understanding the urgency in their work.

The sun on her skin and the work reminded her of Gaia, and how she had loved being out in the cornfields. It had been one of the few places where she had truly felt content there. She laughed at her irony.

· · ·

SHE AGAIN WOKE in the middle of the night, her clothes
drenched in sweat. This time she could remember the dream. She
was being forcibly held down by someone… she knew it was
Renay, but her face was blank in the dream and with no features.
There was a needle being shown to her and someone telling her she
would sleep. As the needle had pricked her skin, Ellie had woken,
her heart blasting out of her chest, fast enough so she couldn't
distinguish one beat from another. She gasped, sitting on the edge
of her bed, her feet dangling. She needed Austin, but not like this,
with sweat and wet clothes.

She stood under her shower instead, the heat of the water washing
the dream away. They had almost killed her, that she knew for sure.
She'd only just escaped with her life, and perhaps in an ordinary
world, this fact would have been emphasized as traumatic, and
counseling needed to de-brief and process its intensity. Only out
here, everyone had trauma. There were no counselors, and the
fragile got picked off, one by one. She just needed to suck it up. All
of it. It was then that her eyes watered with loneliness and fatigue,
and she sat on the base of the shower floor, water pouring all over
her, knowing that the tidal wave was forming. Then she released it
all. Working at an unforgiving school, losing her home and her
parents. Dean sleeping with everyone and not caring, her close
encounter with death at Gaia and now the fact that they had to
shoot to kill. Life as she had known it was over. She was now living
in a brutal new reality that had no escape other than death.

She was getting dressed into a fresh t-shirt and shorts when she
had heard animals in the distance howling again. This time, she
had knocked on Austin's door, wanting him more than her need for
sleep. Her clothes smelled like the sun, where they had warmed
themselves dry the day before, and her skin like lavender from the
shower soap. Austin had outstretched his arms, indicating for her
to come to him, and she had. She lay down next to him, and he had
wrapped his arms around her, and it had felt exactly as she had

imagined it would, no words having been necessary. She turned in the bed and then their faces were close. It was instinctive, that first touching of their lips. A gentle, honest connection that had promised so much more. She was about to tell Austin how she was feeling when she heard a noise, like a dull thud, beating against the window. Then Roger's voice yelling and then Darinda shouting something.

'What's going on?' Austin was up, his naked frame silhouetted in the window.

'What is that?' asked Ellie, fear pricking her skin.

'It's a fucking helicopter. We need to get out. Now!' He screamed his urgency towards her.

He grabbed a t-shirt and shorts and then grabbed at Ellie's hand.

'Quick, down the stairs. Run! We'll head out the kitchen door and straight down to the back of the property.'

'What about the fencing? It's electrified.'

'Shit!' Austin dragged Ellie onto the ground as a round of machine fire blasted through the bottom windows of the house.

'Crawl. Fast… just… hands and knees, Ellie… Quickly!'

They crawled out of the room, hearing glass shattering from downstairs.

'I can hear Darinda. Head towards her voice!' Ellie screamed out.

They crawled down one flight of stairs, the lights from the hovering helicopter shining into each window of the second story and then firing. The noise was deafening.

'We need to check on the others,' urged Ellie, tugging at Austin's shoulder.

'No! No time. We have to get out of here, Ellie. If you see the light, roll into a shadow, and keep your head tucked in. Move fast!'

They made their way down the second flight of stairs, small shards of glass embedding themselves into their knees, their hands groping into the black.

'Just get up and run for it!' Austin yelled at her once they were at the bottom.

'Austin. Is that you? How many are with you?' Roger was in front of them, standing at the bottom of the stairs, ready to coordinate everyone. 'Where are the others?' he yelled over the sound of breaking glass.

'I don't know. They're firing into all the rooms. We haven't seen anyone else.'

'Get out!' Roger yelled over the steady thud of the helicopter and the sound of screaming from upstairs. 'I've deactivated the fencing. Go out the back. Quick! Just go!'

'Where? Where will we meet?' panted Austin, trying to catch his breath.

'They've used a fucking helicopter!' shouted Darinda, approaching them breathlessly, at the bottom of the stairs. 'Where are the others? Hopped straight over the fencing they have. Bastards. We need to get out. You guys ge...'

There was a sudden beam of light from the helicopter that illuminated Darinda's face. Her eyes turned to it, knowing. Then time slowed. A small red dot appeared on Darinda's face. Ellie knew what the dot was and what it would mean in just another passing moment of time. She raised her arm to push Darinda away from the red dot. There was a sound, loud and direct, and then Darinda's face exploded in front of her. Her crumpled body fell into Roger's arms, and another light illuminated his face, shocked and contorted from what he had just witnessed. He screamed. The sort of scream that animals do when they have one last proper lung full of air. There was another bang, and then Austin grabbed Ellie's hair and pulled her backward, down onto the ground.

'Get the fuck out of here! Now!' he screamed at her. 'Now!'

She couldn't remember how to move, stunned into a statue-like snake form, but felt herself moving, like a worm being carried off in the mouth of something. Her ankle was being pulled by Austin, now trying to get her to safety. She looked back at Darinda and Roger now lying together, her mind trying to comprehend how you could go from a moment of life and then to a moment of death so quickly. She let out a primitive scream, full of anger and rage and indignation at the horror that had just been unleashed. Then Austin's face was in front of her.

'Ellie, you need to fucking concentrate, and you need to shut the fuck up. They'll hear us. We need to run from here to the back. Can you see the fence line? Yes? Ellie? Look at me! LOOK at me!'

'Yes!' she screamed at him, her eyes full of terror.

'The helicopter is at the front of the house. Take this. Use it!' He handed her a machine gun.

Then she was pushed out into the garden, Austin pushing her along.

'Fuck. We can't get to the back fence. They're shining the light into the back garden. Head into bunker one. Fast!' He pushed her along, hand on her shoulder.

'Wait!' he yelled suddenly. 'Wait for the light to start along the back boundary again. We'll run when it's dark.'

They ran towards bunker one in the darkness, throwing themselves inside, and Austin slammed the entry door shut.

'Quick, further in Ellie. I'll seal the internal door, and we can activate the jets. I know how this works. Thank God.'

He pushed Ellie in, and she fell to the floor, curling into a fetal position. She heard the door being sealed and then a whooshing sound as the jet fuel prepped up the security system.

'We'll be okay in here for a while. We're safe for now.' Austin then collapsed onto the floor next to her, panting to catch his breath and his composure. Then there was a strange silence in which they came to terms with the burning fact that they were the only two who had made it. Survival now rested on them alone.

26

———

RED DUST

POPES AND REINDEERS

'How long does it take to drive from a rehabilitation center back to the lab? Did you stop off for lunch? A spa treatment or maybe a mini-break?'

'Sorry,' mumbled Jack. Belcher sounded as irritable as someone who had been tortured for several hours.

'Wells will be here in just over an hour,' she said.

'What?' chimed the three of them together.

'Wells is coming here?' Pete was surprised, 'Like now?'

'No, I was just saying that the Pope is coming over on a reindeer.' Belcher looked at him with a mixture of sympathy and disdain.

Jack, Pete, and Tina went mute. They would let Belcher say what she needed to say and then get ready for Wells. She was in one of her moods.

'Why the silence?' Belcher asked, oblivious to how much scary she could emanate from her person.

Jack was worried. 'Wells will be here in an hour? What does he want?'

'Oh, my fucking lord. Do I look like an oracle, Jack? I don't know. I just hope everything is now sorted with the chip. Did you fix the aggression issue?'

'Yes,' said Tina confidently. 'It looked like it was a small issue to do with depression meds and anesthetics.'

'Good,' then we don't need to disclose that to Wells.

'I thought we weren't discussing the chip at all?' said Jack, looking confused.

'Of course, we aren't. However, given it's out there as public knowledge, I'm assuming he's found out and wants an explanation. For all we know, he's coming over to tell us the whole deal is off. Get changed, the lot of you. I want professional.'

An hour later, they were seated in the conference room, looking contained, relaxed and professional, but feeling as tense as was humanly possible. Wells arrived on the dot, and Belcher ushered him into the room.

'Nice to see you again, Jack.' Wells gave him a firm handshake. 'Paxton. Good to see you. Let me introduce my colleagues, Pete and Tina.'

He shook their hands warmly.

Belcher invited everyone to sit and then jumped straight into it. 'We can offer you coffee and biscuits. Not as glamorous as your home-made cakes.'

'I'm fine. I just ate, actually. Thank you.'

'So, an unexpected visit. What's so important?' Belcher was direct.

'I wanted to discuss this in person with you. It's too sensitive to be put into an email no matter how good the encryption is.'

'Okay,' said Belcher, crossing one leg over the other and clasping her hands on her lap. She licked her lips and then swallowed. 'I'm ready.'

Pete, Tina, and Jack looked at each other. Something was about to go down.

'Look, I've had my team doing some fairly significant research concerning Home Base and what our number capacity should be… can be, in fact. Unfortunately, we can't sustain another eight hundred up there long term.' He waited, allowing the statement to sink in.

'Please explain,' said Belcher, uncrossing her legs and planting them firmly on the ground, as if preparing for battle.

'Well, it's simple. We can't grow enough food. Recently, Mars has been experiencing a massive dust storm, and when I say massive, it far exceeds anything that we experience here on Earth. It seems that every three years or so, Mars throws up these entire planet storms, and they last for several months. As a result, we lose half of our crops as we can't sustain that much artificial light for that length of time. We've just come out of a five-month storm. Dust covered the entire planet, including our solar power system. Eight hundred more to feed during that sort of weather isn't feasible.'

'Can't we send up more greenhouses or hydroponic systems?' asked Tina.

'No,' said Wells. 'Even if you protect the plants in greenhouses, inside or outside, we can't sustain enough plant life to feed the sorts of numbers you need up there. Remember, our numbers are going to increased dramatically when the Underground Generation goes up. I have to account for them as well in all of this.'

'So how many more can we sustain?' Belcher asked.

'An extra handful.'

'A handful?' Belcher stared at him in disbelief. 'What's in a Paxton Wells handful?'

'Twenty to twenty-five.'

'Really?' asked Jack, sounding surprised.

'Yes. I've only just analyzed the numbers myself, based on this new data, so to be honest, I'm as shocked as you are. It changes the game plan quite a bit. Remember that I have at least four hundred extras going up earlier than planned from the Underground Generation.'

'Yes,' was all Belcher could utter. 'It certainly does change everything.'

'However, on the flip side, being more positive, it means there isn't as much of a delay if your handful wanted to get up there. You'd need training, of course, but it means we can bring it all forward quite considerably. I won't need to build two new commuter craft for a start. Just one new craft, as well as send up other resources. With End Date inching forward and things deteriorating in manufacturing as they are, I don't have much time to get the equipment built that's needed to sustain things for good up there. This whole situation is extremely fluid, and things are deteriorating faster than I anticipated. I'm planning on sending up most of my Underground Generation much earlier too.'

'Yes, we understand that,' said Jack. 'We've noticed some pretty dire decreases in our ability to get our materials manufactured, despite our plan with the chip recipients helping to fill in the gaps.'

'So, what else brings you here?' asked Belcher. Everyone looked at her, surprised at her question.

Wells looked at her and smiled. 'You're a woman that doesn't miss much, Morag. That's why I like working with you.'

'You know about the chip now, obviously.' She looked at him, her eyebrows raised.

'I always did,' he said. 'It's nice though to speak to you face-to- face about it. The first thing I do when considering business partnerships is to create detailed profiles on people. I knew about your chip when we met on the island, and to be honest, I liked the fact that you held onto the idea. I may well have stolen it otherwise. It's an excellent piece of research and all credit to you, Jack. Also, you do know that I partly own South Street Hospital? I'm one of the silent owners.'

Jack looked at Belcher. Did she know he was a part owner of the hospital? So now Wells knew everything. Clever man to have played dumb and to have chosen to sit back and just watch them play this all out. He liked him even more.

'Well, our chip is safely out there, and with things deteriorating at the rate they are, who cares if you copy it now or not. The deed is done, so to speak.' said Jack, with a hint of defiance in his voice.

'Exactly,' said Wells. 'I have bigger fish to fry than create another IQ chip to place inside a human being right now.'

'Like getting us off Earth and onto Mars?' said Pete, hopefully, trying to steer the conversation back to the notion of who would be included in the lucky twenty-five handful.

'Peter wants to know if he's still going to Mars,' said Tina.

'Of course, you are going to Mars,' smiled Wells.

Belcher looked around the room and then stood up, obviously agitated.

'Your income stream for the project comes from our leaders, who all think that they are being saved. To continue providing you with the money you need, I'm going to essentially be… obtaining it fraudulently. That's what you are asking me to do. This could prove dangerous for me if anyone finds out.'

'I'm certainly not advocating that you go and lie to our world leaders, Morag.'

'No, but for me to generate the capital that you need, it means continuing to ask the leaders for the upfront payments and pretending that they are still going.'

'Yes,' said Wells.

'I'm presuming you want the same capital, despite the reduced numbers?' asked Belcher.

'Yes. It seems silly to waste such a financial gift.'

'It was never a gift, Paxton. I expect you to send up more resources for this Wells handful. More food, more materials.'

'Of course, that will be part of our new plan, Morag. The money will also help to send up the Underground Generation. Their resilience and skills will help you once you are there.'

'Fine, then that is how it will be.'

'Fine?' Pete spluttered. 'What if everyone finds out that they aren't now going? You'll create a war.'

Tina jumped in before Belcher de-balled Pete. 'It's every person for themselves, Pete, and we're the lucky ones. We get the escape route. By the time we have finished our training, and have taken off, they will still be wondering when their training starts.'

'So, when is our training?' Jack asked.

'When would you like to start?'

'Tomorrow?' he asked facetiously.

'Fine. I'll email you all the details. It won't be tomorrow, but we can get the ball rolling. Oh… one more thing.'

Belcher looked at him.

'I want a mix of implants in my handful. I'm presuming that given it will be the four of you, the rest can be chip recipients to make up a full compliment. No empty seats and no family… sorry Tina, you just flickered with hope. So send a list of possible names. I may even choose them myself. I like the idea of your chip and feel we can work together to modify it to do other things in the future. We can use the Underground Generation to implant once up there. So I want the information for the chip now as well. Better to plan the Home Base experience assuming we'll need to work on the chip.'

'That's not entirely ethical, planning to experiment on people with the chip on Mars,' said Tina.

'No,' agreed Wells, 'but nor was any of this to start with. I mean it's not ethical to have babies born who will never see direct sunlight, is it?'

Belcher walked towards the door. 'I'll take you to the rehabilitation center myself Paxton, if you would like to see what's going on.'

He smiled. 'You know me too well, Morag.'

Jack, Pete, and Tina sat in a collective silent protest for a bit before Jack indicated that they should go for lunch outside of the building. It was tiresome, never being able to discuss things openly in the workplace.

'Well, that's just the most fucked thing I've heard in ages,' said Tina. 'What about our extended families?'

'I don't think he wants extended families up there,' said Jack. 'Not with those numbers.'

'How the hell do I wave goodbye to my parents knowing I'll never see them again?' asked Tina, sounding frustrated.

'There's technology to contact them once we're there,' Pete said, sounding hopeful.

'It's not the same,' retorted Tina.

'No. I understand that.'

'How many are you, Pete? Cause I'm only one,' Jack asked.

'Just one. My wife and son weren't coming anyway,' he paused. 'She wants to stay with her parents apparently and has my son convinced to stay with her.'

'I'm sorry, Pete.' Tina looked over at him, seeing how difficult the situation was for him. She was surprised he hadn't divulged any of it before.

'I've just concluded that life is a stinker right now,' he replied.

'Wells didn't say he was coming with us. Did you notice?' asked Tina.

'Well, if he isn't coming with us, he's probably got his own craft sorted. Although when he wants to leave is anyone's guess.' Pete replied. 'I think he'll stay for a bit longer myself, wrap things up before heading up. He didn't mention his craft, though?'

'My God, you wouldn't want to be scared of change right now, would you?' said Jack.

'It's like everything we knew is out the window, and we're in this new crazy place,' added Tina.

'… and, it's all only going to get crazier,' said Pete. 'Imagine being on Mars.'

• • •

BELCHER TOOK Wells up to the rehabilitation center, complete with Presidential flair. A full entourage should put him back into place, she thought. Nothing like a stream of bodyguards, personal advisors, and god knows who else, to reinforce who held power on her turf.

'Please, call me Paxton again, Morag.'

'Fine, Paxton. This change of plan is difficult. However, if it gets me off this sad and lonely planet, then fine.'

'It will. I promise. I think you are in for a huge surprise too. Remember, I've kept the details for Home Base from the public for many years. As we leave, I'm going to open it all up again. Let people see what they are missing out on.'

'Cruel.'

'I didn't intend it to be a cruel action… more out of interest. It's changed a lot since everyone last saw it and especially now that I'm sending up individuals with fewer mental health problems. I don't think the public enjoyed watching people sitting around depressed most of the time in the lava tubes, nor killing each other off. That's why I switched it off to be honest. The new individuals though? They are already used to a lack of sunlight and freedom.'

'So, allow several billion people to tune in to the ones that got away? Nice.'

Belcher extended her hand to Sandy, who had enthusiastically approached the Presidential party.

'Madam President. Wonderful to see you here. I hear you would like to watch the Chippies in action? I have a medical group who are doing very well. They dissected cadavers this morning without a hitch.'

Wells extended his hand. 'Nice to meet you, I'm Paxton Wells.'

'Yes,' said Sandy, her face becoming slightly flushed. 'I know. You were on the cover of Time last year, and you probably won't remember, but we were on the board for the hospital a few years ago.'

He smiled. 'Sorry, memory like a sieve. Did you read the article in Time?'

'I did,' smiled Sandy, ignoring the fact that he hadn't remembered her. 'I thought the interface concept for your chip was excellent. Similar to the fundamentals of all of this when you think about it. Funny how sometimes people have the same ideas... or rather, concepts at the same time.'

'Kind of you to say, Sandy.'

'My pleasure,' she said, her face still busting with pink.

WELLS WATCHED in fascination and awe as the medical Chippies were tested on anatomy and case presentation treatment. They didn't miss a beat, demonstrating that the implanted files were doing their job.

'I've heard rumors about a limitation device.'

'Yes,' said Belcher, smiling. 'A world-first, actually. It allows us to control impulses in a recipient. Stops them from acting on distracting thoughts.'

'I'd be interested in how it all works,' smiled Wells.

'Certainly,' said Belcher. 'As soon as my seatbelt is on and I'm counting down to Mars, figuratively speaking, of course, I'll give you the full, scientific blueprint.'

He laughed. 'Fair enough. Your secrets can stay with you for a while longer. However, what you have done is impressive, Morag. That sort of technology could be incredibly useful.'

'Thank you, Paxton.'

'You're in for some fun with the training, by the way.'

'I can't wait,' said Belcher dryly.

'I hope you like carrots too. That's what seems to grow well up there… as well as small amounts of rye, cress, and tomato.'

'We're taking food up with us though, aren't we?'

'That's actually what I also wanted to discuss with you. I was thinking of moving the funds for the second commuter ship over to cargo ships. We can fill them with non-perishables. I've found a supplier who stocks the supermarkets in the climate fortunate areas. We can have what we want, for a price, naturally. However, we have the funds, so we should take advantage of what's on offer. You can choose your favorite wines, anything dehydrated… cans… that sort of thing.'

'So, you definitely can't send up enough food for eight hundred extra people?'

'No. Firstly, that amount of produce would be too difficult to find, and secondly, it's not sustainable, as I explained. It's so fickle up there, we risk losing too many people if things go wrong.'

'So, the original funds will be redirected into sending extra resources up for a smaller group, plus your Underground Generation? I don't have a problem with that. It's better for all of us.'

'Then, we have ourselves a deal.' He held out his hand for her to shake. Instead, she diverted her hand and wiped her nose with it. Then she smiled and moistened her lips with the very tip of her tongue. He retracted his hand quickly, leaving it frozen mid-way between his position to shake and his pocket. She noticed his action and promptly held her hand out to shake it. Her eyes met his, and the power play was complete. Wells shook the moist and glistening hand of Belcher without so much as a blink.

27

STEAKS

AND GLASS

Angus had plunged into his aged recliner, coffee in one hand and the tv remote in the other. Life felt good, despite the recliner having seen better days. There were stains on the faux material from sweaty thighs, smeared burger sauce, and there was an imprint of Angus' back where he'd spent way too much time watching the television. Angus had joked that if they could make it look more like Jesus, that they could have sold it for millions.

He called out to Riley, who was working hard in the kitchen. 'I think we need to replace these chairs. They've seen better days. Are there stores still selling new furniture?'

'I think there are a couple of warehouses still in business. We might find something nice now that the money is sitting in our bank account,' she called back, beaming with hope.

'It's good to be home, love,' he added, sounding more cheerful than he had in a while.

'Well, it's nice to have you back. Despite having the boys, it's been awfully quiet without you.' She stood in the doorway, leaning on the doorpost, still having appreciation for the man she married so many years ago. 'What would you like for dinner, Angus?'

'Something that involves a nice juicy steak. A real one, as a treat darl'. We deserve that.'

'Steak? Have you gone all fancy on me now that you're a doctor? I suppose we can afford it now. However, don't you go getting all high and mighty with me, just because we can afford steak.'

He laughed. 'I aced the anatomy testing, you know. I can name every single bone in the human body.'

'Save it for a trivia competition. I'll go and get your steak.'

She grabbed her bag and headed out the door. 'This means I can go inside that fancy butcher next to the mall. I've never been there before. You have to phone before they will even open the doors. Full security in there, I've heard as well. I suppose there's a first for everything.' She smiled, excited at the thought of being able to afford real steak. It was priced well out of most people's reach, and she anticipated a few hundred dollars wouldn't be unreasonable to spend on a large piece of rump.

'I'd love a beer too, Riley,' he called after her.

'A beer as well? Are you allowed to drink?' she stuck her head back around the door.

'They didn't say we couldn't? Riley, be careful out there. I'll send one of the boys out with you.'

'Fine, I'll treat you and the boys to a fancy meal and some beer.' Riley loved to look after her men, not out of a sense of duty, but because family meant everything to her. These men were her tribe. Four of them created in her own body, of her own flesh. She would have done anything for them. There had always been an assumed agreement between Angus and herself, that it would be best for her to stay at home and look after them all. This had made her happy, and now that Angus was a doctor, she was even happier. There was a spring to her step as she headed out to the mall to find the meat.

Angus reclined in the chair. He enjoyed a bit of solitude. Thinking time, as he now called it. Silence was now something he relished, rather than feared. The chip had enhanced his mind in so many ways. Not just in a medical sense, but almost as if his whole thinking had been reformed and reborn. He was thinking faster and more clearly, and when the news had come on, he could remember more facts and link things together. He was a man with opinions now, and he cared about more than he had done before. Tomorrow was his first day at his new job, a position as a general doctor, treating people with minor medical troubles. If that all went well, he was informed that there was plenty of room for promotion in the day surgery.

The money was unbelievable too, so much more than he had ever earned, despite the hiked-up income taxes. He understood that his base salary would be reduced by fifteen percent, as Belcher would be taking that as commission. He didn't mind. The chip had been far more successful than he had ever envisaged, and the money, including the thirty thousand he'd already received, was more than enough.

MACE, on the other hand, was a man seething under his skin. He loathed his new mind, one in which he was compelled to think, to act, and to engage. He didn't want to. Mace had spent the past eight months chair-sitting, brooding about the past and all the wasted time he had spent crafting his book, one that would never see the light of day. All of those carefully chosen words, thoughts, his research, effort, reflection… and now… none of it mattered.

There had been a time for him to shine - the moment he had anticipated for so much of his adult life. He'd anticipated *that* moment for the book launch. When he would become 'someone' and not just Mace. Then it was gone. All that work had been pointless. Now, after the operation, things had changed again in his mind. He was gone too, like someone had puffed him out like a candle flame. His head was now full of other information and for some reason, every time he tried to think about his coaching business, he couldn't form his thoughts properly.

He'd bided his time, waiting for his fifteen seconds of fame, carefully building up his coaching practice before assuming he could become guru status. Publish too soon, and he may not have the audience base for book sales to gain momentum. He'd never considered a too late, the notion seeming preposterous when it had finally dawned on him that *too late* had already arrived and that his book was well over the setting horizon. The game was over, as he knew it, and now he was a lawyer. It had been Tara's idea, not his. She probably wanted him out of her hair and into something with respectable plastered all over it. He had forced her out of his hair, as it all had turned out, washing away any residual love in the process. He couldn't stand her, nor her choice of furnishings, and if there was one positive about going out to work now, it was the fact that he could get further away from everything that reminded him of her.

There was also revenge to seek for the indignation of having been strapped to a bed, a place where his mind had spiraled into a dark place, one so black, it had appeared unfamiliar to him. He had been told that his anger was *unjustified and unacceptable,* so they had said, using a tone that could only have been interpreted as patronizing. One that you would use towards a naughty child in a classroom. Their uniforms had outranked him in this setting, strangers who had humiliated him. He'd had a sovereign choice to turn Tara away, a woman who made his skin crawl and his fists want to lash out. Now he was a lawyer, defending what, he wondered? Why did anyone care if people shat on each other anymore? The world was over. The game had ended. That fact alone, meant that revenge for all he had gone through, was more applicable than concentrating his mind on legal jargon. He wanted his thirst quenched by blood, and he needed a vent for his anger. There was a rage that felt like a million bugs, clawing under his skin to get out.

AUSTIN AND ELLIE lay for a while on the floor of the bunker. It was eerily quiet, Ellie's pounding heart now quietening, and her breath slowing.

'Okay, we need to get clean.' Austin heaved himself up off the floor and looked down at his hands. They were covered in blood. Was it his own, he wondered? He glanced over at Ellie and was careful to keep his expression neutral. Thankfully, there were no mirrors around as Ellie had copped the brunt of most of Darinda's face. There was blood too, trickling from cuts on her feet and knees where she had run and crawled over shards of glass in order to escape.

He fetched the first aid kit from the bathroom cupboard. Everything was here, as needed, as Roger's wife had spared no expense in setting the bunker up and Roger had double-checked everything and had added more. They would be comfortable and safe for the time being, but he wasn't sure if the helicopter had seen them entering. He knew that the gang would eventually find both bunkers and try to gain entry, but they were fitted with security as tight as it got. Then again, three lines of boundary security hadn't worked when their helicopter had dropped out of the sky.

He turned on the water heater and then helped Ellie into the shower, noting that she had sat when her legs had failed to hold her up.

'What next?' Ellie asked him afterwards, subdued from trauma.

'First, I'm going to clean up your feet and knees. Get the pieces of glass out and disinfect the cuts. I don't want you to get infected. Then we'll take a breather.'

'Yeah, my feet are killing me.' She reached down and could feel sharp pieces of glass embedded in her feet.

'I'll give you some brandy for pain relief.'

'Okay,' she said, staring more into space than towards him.

'We need to eat too, and pack some bags just in case we need to leave in a hurry, and we also need to think through what our options are.'

'Are we safe in here?'

'I think so. Jesus, I hope so.'

'I thought the barbed wire, fencing, sensors, and machine guns were enough.'

'I don't think any of us were expecting the helicopter, Ellie.'

'No.'

'I'll find us something to eat. I know you're probably not hungry, but we need to keep our strength up in case we have to run. Maybe you could manage to sip on some soup, perhaps?'

'Austin…'

'Yeah?'

'Are they all dead?'

'I think so. I'm so sorry, Ellie.'

'This world is fucked, Austin.'

'Yes. It is.'

ANGUS SAT OPPOSITE THE PATIENT, slightly reclining in his luxury leather chair.

'How can I help you today, Mr. Hertwright?'

'I've got a pain in my chest Dr Morley. Here.' Duke Hertwright, a rugged eighty-three-year-old, indicated to his chest where it hurt.

Angus smiled. Dr Morley suited him better than hey fucker, or garbage mouth, which he'd been called down at the refinery in previous years of employment. Riley had warned him that people were going to be much nicer to him in this new job. Show some respect, even.

'Take you shirt off and I'll have a listen.' He pulled the shiny new stethoscope from around his neck, which he now wore as a badge of honor, and told his patient to breathe in and out, slowly and deeply.

He was amazed just how everyone did exactly as he asked them to. No-one had said go do that yourself, for the whole week. Instead, they'd hung off his every word.

'I think we'll do a chest x-ray just to be safe,' he said, adding, 'you've had a nasty cold and I want to rule out any pneumonia.'

'Yes, doctor. Thank you.'

He filled in the x-ray form as well as a prescription for antibiotics, amazed at how he knew how to even spell the drug, let alone get the dosage right. He signed it and then handed it to his patient.

'Thank you, doc. I don't know what I would have done today if you hadn't started here this week. They were going to shut down. I couldn't get an appointment when I was sick last week, and then you came along, as well as a few others… and now I can get seen to. I feel like the luckiest man alive.'

Angus smiled. 'Well, let's get you sorted out so that you can feel a bit better. Let's get your x-ray and we'll take a look at it. Ensure you take the whole course of drugs and let me know immediately, if you feel any worse.'

MACE HAD STARTED at a legal firm that had seen better days. Empty offices, a lack of stationary, broken cable leads and clumped instant coffee greeted him on his first day. He was handed a wad of second-hand case files and told to start at the beginning - whichever way that was. He'd had a choice of offices and had chosen the best of what was still functional. Spacious, with views over the city, he'd cleared away the remnants of the previous occupant and then positioned himself in the leather chair, ready to wade through whining and litigious crap. He pulled the top file from off the misery-mound and opened it. A woman from the fortunate climate sector was demanding legal action over disparaging comments made about her by two sales assistants whilst she was in some shop fitting room, trying on a dress.

Mace snorted, laughing. This was pure wank. How much would he be paid to call this woman on the phone? Forty dollars? Then he'd teleconference her for an hour, that's another two hundred bucks. Maybe write a letter to the fashion store? That had to be worth four hundred dollars? Then this woman would thank him for *sorting out all of her crap.* He laughed again. All she wanted was to let the sales assistants know that she had the money to put them back into their places. Yeah, he could be a lawyer. He picked up the phone and punched in her number.

BELCHER MET with the team in the meeting room.

'Jack, Tina, and Pete. Our training schedule has come in from Wells.'

'Wow, so soon?' Tina was surprised at the speed at which things were progressing. They had only done the preliminary release with the chips and hadn't had time to decipher the evaluation data yet.

'Yes,' said Belcher. 'Remember that things have changed. My priority now is to collect the funds and allow Wells to get as many resources as he can to Mars. We also have to start training and according to the information, start eating a certain diet, so that we can easily adapt to the Mars diet if need be.'

'Are the leaders going to hand over the funds given the current climate out there?' asked Pete.

'You mean the riots in Europe and shit?' asked Jack.

'… and shit?' replied Tina. 'They just lost over a million people in Latvia during a big freeze. Yeah. They are going to be begging to leave the planet.'

'The climate out there at the moment is precisely the reason why they will hand over the funds. These events now are bigger than most Governments can handle internally. I am presuming that most leaders would prefer a quick exit, rather than having to deal with all of this.' Belcher handed them out a booklet. 'This tells you everything that you will need to know. I suggest that no-one else knows about the timing changes, especially not family. We don't need a leak.'

'Of course,' said Pete.

'I suggest that we start planning our national roll-out. That way, it can coincide with my request for funds. If they think everything is rolling out as planned, I'm sure I'll get the funds quickly.'

'So, are we actually rolling this out nationally or just looking like we are?' Pete sounded confused.

'I suggest you send out all the necessary paperwork to get the ball rolling, and we'll go from there.' Belcher nodded at her own directions, reassuring herself that this was the right direction to take. 'The more we are seen to be expanding, the better things look.'

'How much is Wells still asking for?' asked Jack.

'A hundred billion and then another thirty in two months.'

'Gees,' said Pete. 'That's a lot of canned food going up to Mars.'

'So, does he tell us what he's specifically spending it on?' asked Tina.

'Yes, there's a condensed summary on page five. Remember that the Underground people are also going up early. Any further questions?'

'Yeah, when are we expecting to be up on Mars?' Jack threw a stress ball into the air and caught it.

'Six months.'

'Six?' said Jack, sounding alarmed. 'That's a lot sooner than we were anticipating. Why the rush?'

'Wells has indicated that even if we stabilize the workforce and thus add ballast to our Governments, that people are becoming more unstable and erratic. Wells's people predict that things will destabilize quickly from this point onwards. We leave, or we get caught up in it all. They are calling it anarchist flares.'

'I doubt if we will be rolling much out in reality if he's talking six months.' Tina looked at Jack and Pete for confirmation. They nodded in agreement.

'Then accelerate it all, starting now. I'll leave you with it.' Belcher left.

They read the booklet, page by page, trying to digest this new reality. The rising tension triggered the need for a drink in Jack. Were things getting so unstable that everything had been brought forward by this much?

'Is anyone else feeling like the chip was fucking pointless?' he asked.

'Not really… well, sort of, I suppose. Wells wants us to include the Chippies in the cohort that's leaving, so it wasn't *all* in vain. He also wants to use the technology on Mars with the Underground people.' Pete was trying to sound positive.

'It's pointless if the intention was to stabilize things,' Tina added. 'However, in terms of manufacturing? Yeah? I think we got a bit of extra time from it.'

'I don't agree,' said Jack, looking annoyed. 'We just got the chips implanted, and now we're being told to leave the planet. A waste of it all. Just a total waste. I had so much more I want to do with it all.'

'It's not our fault though if things are destabilizing faster than anticipated out there.' Pete shook his head.

'What about the plan, though, that the Chippies would help to fill in the gaps and stabilize the workforce? Wasn't that the whole plan? How do we know it wouldn't have worked if we'd stayed for longer?' Jack sound annoyed.

'I think we need to concentrate on the fact that in six months, we're heading to Mars.' Pete looked upwards as if he might catch a glance of Mars above them. 'If things are going to destabilize as much as they are predicting, then who the hell wants to be caught in the middle of all of that?'

'Yeah, I agree,' said Tina. 'People aren't very nice when they get angry. Personally, I'd rather take my chances up there. Six months though,' she sighed. 'Then I'm supposed to say goodbye to my parents. Shit, this is hard. There's no easy way is there?'

Jack wandered over to one of the security cameras and shrugged his shoulders deliberately into it.

'And what point are you making there, Jack?' asked Peter.

'I don't know. How about a fed-up sort of point?'

'Fair enough. God, this changes everything, doesn't it,' said Tina. 'It becomes hellishly real now. We're going to be living on Mars.'

'Well, I suppose we need to look at Wells's checklist,' said Pete, re-opening the booklet. 'Okay, first, we need to have full medicals at some medical place and change our diet to… let me see… carrots, rye, cress, and tomatoes. That's going to feel restrictive.'

'What about all that canned and dehydrated food he said that he was sending up?' asked Tina, looking confused.

'Yeah, I guess this booklet was published before he organized that? Or maybe that's the bottom line up there? Although none of that makes sense because the booklets are for us. I hope his attention to detail is better in the execution of all of this. Maybe it's in the summary page?'

'So long as he has a billion dollar's worth of booze up there, I'm happy,' smiled Jack. 'In fact, I'm going to email him myself and make sure he sends it up. I can see it now,' he said dramatically. 'Cocktails at six, looking back at Earth. I can see myself partaking in that.'

'How do you drink if you're wearing a space helmet?' asked Tina.

'There are always way to drink,' said Jack. 'I'll put in a feeding tube if I have to.'

'The space training part looks interesting. Two-week training sessions at some space training facility in Texas,' said Pete, glancing down the page.

'When do we do that?' Tina was flicking through the pages, trying to find out.

'Soon? I can't find the exact dates.' Pete searched the page.

'Hey…' said Jack excitedly. 'Look at what we have to do! Mac six. Spinning, vertical lift offs and underwater stuff!'

'Underwater? To go live on Mars?' Tina laughed.

'It's for when we melt all the ice on Mars because we'll inevitably heat the place up,' joked Pete.

'Well, don't joke about it. We stuffed this planet up. Why wouldn't we go and mess up another one?' added Jack. 'I suppose I don't need to go over the secrecy with all of this, do I?'

Tina and Peter stopped what they were doing.

'I mean, we tell anyone, then we're probably dead,' he said, looking worried.

'Yeah, I know,' said Tina.

'I'm not going to go blabbing,' Pete added. 'We have one shot at getting out of here, so I'm going to take it.'

'Are we sure we have to leave so soon, though?' asked Tina.

'Wells says so. He seems to know what's going on out there,' said Pete.

'You have doubts?' asked Jack.

'End Date isn't for ages, that's all. It seems like we're jumping the gun a bit.' Tina shrugged her shoulders.

'End Date was never just going to be the problem,' said Pete. 'People were always going to be the problem.'

'There are reports of gangs doing systematic looting already on the East Coast, so even if you had bunkered down, you're not safe,' Jack said, looking concerned.

'Christ,' said Tina. 'Really? Are they looting over there, even before the food has run out? That surprises me. It really does. They were supposed to be in one of the fortunate areas.'

'Once the gangs multiply, it'll be like one of those apocalyptic movies about the end of the world. I'd rather be on Mars,' said Pete.

'It's not just here. It's worldwide. Europe is chaos as people are just ignoring border control now. They can't shoot everyone who is running from one country to another. Asia has gone under in places already. Bangladesh is gone… India, South China, Australia, The Philippines… it's everywhere. There's nowhere to hide.' Jack sat back and stared at the ceiling. 'The only other option would be to blow our brains out instead. End it all.'

'Seriously, Jack. Shut up.' Tina rolled her eyes at him.

'I am being serious. Look at the fucking choice we have. Here, or in a Mars bunker, so that we can drive each other completely nuts, until age snuffs us out.'

'I could not live in a bunker *all* the time. Imagine being stuck with people underground twenty-four seven.' Pete grimaced. 'I was bad enough during lockdowns for the pandemic, years ago.'

'Lava caves on Mars for extended periods. No fresh air. Both realities are prison sentences. I can see why he decided to start an Underground Generation.' Jack raised his eyebrows questioningly at Pete.

'I guess the reality is setting in,' said Pete.

'Yup,' replied Jack, standing. 'I'm now going to go home and drink. If ever there was a day to numb the pain. It's today. Pete, you are in charge as I won't be good for anyone in about forty-five minutes.'

MACE LAY IN HIS BED, unable to sleep or relax. He had moved away from Tara and into a hotel, allowing her back into their home. It was a nice hotel too, the sort that she had always begged to stay in over the years, and he'd always refused because three stars was effective and five stars a waste of money. Now that he was lying in the softness of the king bed that allowed him to stretch out, he'd thought perhaps five stars was quite nice. She'd been phoning him too, pleading with him to come home. He'd told her to *fuck off*. She had cried and wailed, and he'd thought her weak. If he had suggested she walk on hot coals to prove her love for him, he thought she would. She was desperate and pathetic, trying to remind him of some happy past that they had shared. He figured that if he treated her badly enough, that she would give up in a few more weeks, a place that he was looking forward to.

He had spent the day going through files, and so far, the work had been straightforward. Help shut whining people up and be paid for it. Be on their side, no matter how stupid whatever it was that they were complaining about. The system worked. Smile a fake smile, say false words, and then collect the money. However, revenge still needed to be sorted for the rehabilitation center, and he was meeting with some other Chippies after work tomorrow to have a drink and a chat. They were as keen as he was to right their own wrongs. He knew that on his file, all the nonsense had been included… and he would always be remembered as a man who had to be strapped to a bed - a naughty boy in need of punishment. The rage simmered underneath his skin, and he knew that his revenge could take a day, a month or a year to plan, but that the end result would be just as enjoyable.

AUSTIN HAD OPENED some canned food that they had eaten with bread rolls, left when they'd been working on the bunker the day before. Austin had held the packet of fresh bread, feeling momentarily overwhelmed as it was Roger who had brought it in, smiling and offering everyone a piece. The bread had been a rare find at the shops. Home-made by the shop-owner's wife that morning, in fact, and Roger had been chuffed to have been in the right place at the right time to buy it. Roger had been one of the good guys, he hadn't deserved to be shot. People were just animals, Austin thought. He tried to keep the mood stable though, and not be too angry, as he could see that Ellie was struggling. Her feet were now at least glass- free, although he couldn't say the same about his own. That was the next job, otherwise, they wouldn't get very far if they had to run.

'So, if we run Austin, where are we running to?'

He'd been wondering when she might ask such a question.

'We could head north to Canada… or perhaps back across country?'

'Canada might be cold.'

'Not a lot of the time anymore, but it still can get cold in mid-winter, depending on how far north you go. Still some fish to be caught up there I've heard, and enough space to avoid most people.'

Ellie thought about heading all the way back across the country. To what, though? To be closer to the Gaia people who had wanted to feed her to the mangroves? It would be better to head north and up into Canada.

'So how are we going to know when to safely get out of here? Aren't they out there? We'd stick our heads up and just get caught, wouldn't we?'

'Yes, but Roger had some cameras installed, so as soon as I get them working, we should have a good view of the outside. Right now though, we are safe, we have food, and we can sleep. Out there is a different matter.'

She ate her bread and quietly sighed. 'I miss Darinda and Roger… and the others.'

'Yeah, me too.'

'Her face… it just…'

'Yeah, I know. Best not to go over it too much, Ellie, for your own sake.'

'What about the others? What do you think happened?'

'I don't know for sure, but they fired a lot of rounds into the house.'

'Right. So, there's no chance they are alive?' asked Ellie quietly.

'No, I don't think so.'

'It would have been quick?'

'Yes, Ellie. Very.'

She sat eating, numb, watching Austin cut the pieces of glass out of the soles of his feet.

28

NAUGHTY
LITTLE BOY

J ack stared at the choice of bottles in front of him, speculating that there was enough liquor to kill several individuals in that one cupboard. He removed every bottle that he owned out from the cabinet, and then lined them up from biggest to smallest. Part of him was motivated to go and get his gun and shoot them for fun, but that would mean no alcohol for him to enjoy and one big mess to clean up. He got a glass instead and poured bourbon. He sculled the glass, the pain reminding him that he was still alive in this mad and fucked up world. He poured a glass of vodka next and gulped that too. His throat was burning, and his stomach wincing from the poison, but it soon delivered the comfort he was after. He needed to be numb so that he could think through the aggression problem in the lawyers.

There was a simmering thought that he hadn't mentioned to anyone about the personality overlay issues - no need to add fuel to the fire that was now burning. The behaviors from the legal Chippies he'd been told about, had worried him, reminding him of his past behaviors. He'd treated so many women as if disposable over the years, just like Mace's attitude towards Tara. The alcohol was inviting him to shed layers of carefully built defences to avoid the stuff that he never liked to think about, namely his own crappy behavior.

He thought back to previous relationships in which he'd offered affection and interest towards a string of women so that he could get them into his bed. Empty promises of stability only to discard them when they'd become annoying or needy. Except for one woman, Tina. She'd been an exception in the early stages of their relationship, where love had run through his veins as it should have done. Then something had changed. He'd wanted another woman instead of Tina, and a pattern of invitation and rejection had been generated within him. He hated neediness because it required something from him that he didn't have to give.

Was it emotional attachment, he wondered? An inability to connect to anything other than a purely physical level? He liked to fuck women, that was about it. Rarely, he also liked their company. Mostly, though, he just wanted out as soon as he knew he was in. The chase… the conquest… that was it. Once he knew he wanted out, he would then destroy. He would belittle, abuse, and banish women who thought they had found something more with him. He wanted a no-strings moment, and yet every time he found a woman, they started designing the future, with him as a central character. He had married by mistake, and he had often wondered if it was the universe's way of taking the piss out of him, to give him children that he could never love, and a wife that he'd hated to the core.

He drank from the bottle of gin. This was more like it. The alcohol was coaxing out his dark side, the one that he endeavored to hide from everyone else. He put on some music and danced with his glass. Alcohol as a dancing partner was way more fun than a woman because, at the end of the evening, he could just put the bottle in the garbage and the evidence of shared activity was gone. Sex now, was a porn movie, or his Amy Doll, promising what he needed and only what he wanted. A chapter of fun with a neat and tidy end. He downed a blue drink, a liquor, so the label advised him, and then another, which took him to his happy place.

Happiness meant celebration, something out of the ordinary. He laughed out aloud and danced his way, clumsy, to his bedroom. It was an exaggerated notion given he'd only a mattress on the floor with a solitary blanket. Opening the second drawer down in his only piece of bedroom furniture, he picked up his Ruger LCP11. He felt cold metal on his warm hand, heat which could be traded with a close dance. He moved in slow motion around the lounge room, the gun tucked up to his chest, Mad World played through his speaker creating a scene worthy of the lyrics. He swayed from left to right, the gun out front, doing a hypnotic repetitive movement. He kissed the weapon after the song finished, singing the final lyrics *bad world*, and then placed the end into his mouth. He could do it and not go to Mars to live with the lava people. He ran his tongue around the hole, wondering if he did it for long enough, whether the gun might explode with excitement - what a fucking way to go, he concluded.

AUSTIN COMPLETED the link for the surveillance cameras. 'Okay…' he spoke slowly, inspecting the visual.

'What's out there?' Ellie asked, needing reassurance.

'It's okay… no-one. I can see the chopper, that's all.'

'So, are they in the house?'

'I think so, I can't see them outside?'

'So, how do we run if you think they are outside?'

'We don't… for now. Right now, we're safe.'

'How long are we going to be living in here?'

'How long is a piece of string Ellie?'

'Right.'

Ellie looked around her. There were four rooms to the bunker, which was luxury compared to other bunkers - a bedroom with a king bed, bathroom, kitchen, and lounge room. There was plenty to do, as the bunker had been supplied with everything from board games, a PS7, movie library, scrapbooking, cross-stitch, and gym equipment. She felt vulnerable, though. This gang had managed to score a chopper, and no-one had seen that coming, not even Roger. They had made a complete mockery of Darinda's boundary system as well as her face.

Austin's mind was racing. It was around three hundred feet to the boundary, and that was if the fence remained off. It would take the gang a while to figure out how to turn it back on again, that is, if they stayed. They might though, because the house was set up for long-term survival. Austin and Ellie would need about twenty-five seconds to get from the bunker and out through the back fencing. Austin's mind was spinning. How much food would they need to carry with them if trying to get to Canada? It was no use if they didn't have transport. They would need the van. That meant getting out through the front gate. Even if they did get on the road, they would face more gangs, and now there were only two of them.

'Where's the air vent for the bunker?' asked Ellie.

'It's camouflaged up near the septic system. It's a double system though, so we've got a backup just incase. It's been designed to look like part of the sewerage system.'

'I suppose that's good.'

'Yeah.'

Neither of them wanted to verbalize that if the gang blocked off the air vents that they would suffocate and die. For all the prepping that had been done, including the security at the entry point and the impenetrable bunker shell, the air ventilation system was the one vulnerability that plagued every bunker.

'Let's just do a quick inventory, Ellie. It'll make us feel more secure. We've got plenty of food down here, that's for sure. Roger's wife set this up for a five-year stint, and she was pretty clued up with her food choices too. I think a lot of this she's preserved herself too. Look, plums in brandy, Indonesian style chili eggs, fried noodles, and frozen bread that we can defrost and toast. It's not too bad.'

'I agree, and we've got the activities to do as well. I'm just sick of feeling vulnerable, Austin.'

'Yeah, me too. Don't worry, we'll find a better place, but we need to bide our time and make sure that when we do leave, we give ourselves the best possible chance to survive.'

'Is there any hope out there?'

'Some, if you can find the right place to go.'

'On this planet or up there?' she pointed to the roof.

'Well, I suppose if you're one of Wells' chosen few, you can leave the planet altogether.'

'Maybe we should do that?'

It had been meant as a glib remark, but its weight suspended everything for a moment. There was a silence between them as the statement hung in the air, demanding more attention.

'What, seriously leave Earth and go to Mars?' asked Austin. 'I mean I know we talked about it at Gaia, but…'

'Why not? Might be better than Canada,' she said, shrugging her shoulders. 'Although we'd have a hard time adapting.'

'Well, remember there was talk of a craft with that woman, the new President of the United Southern States.'

'Belcher.'

'Yeah, Morag Belcher. Wasn't she supposed to be speaking with Wells or something?'

'Yeah, but she's based in the south, and Wells is on an island off in the Pacific somewhere.'

'How would we get on a craft going to Mars?' Austin looked at Ellie, seeking a solution.

'We probably can't,' she sighed. 'We don't have the skills to be needed.'

'Don't we?'

Ellie stared at him. 'No. I mean, I'm a teacher, one of thousands, nothing special about that. That isn't going to ignite anyone's opinion about me, let alone make them jump at the opportunity to include me on that craft.'

'Ouch!' said Austin. 'Hard words Ellie. Don't underestimate yourself. I've got an undergraduate degree in plant biology, a Master's in microbiology, and my legal stuff. Why wouldn't that be useful for Wells?'

'Maybe? He probably already has people with three PhDs working for him. I mean, Austin, are you serious?'

'I think I was for a moment, but it would mean going cross- country again, with the van and heading back into Gaia territory.'

'I'm not sure about living on Mars anyway,' said Ellie. 'Never feeling the sun on your face again and having to wear breathing apparatus… and those dust storms can last for months. I'd rather be fishing in Canada, I think.'

Austin smiled. 'You still wouldn't ever get to feel the sun on your face.' They laughed.

Ellie's face went still. 'I can't get that image out of my head.'

'I know. It was awful,' said Austin.

'They blew her face off, Austin.' She looked over at him, shaking her head, her eyes still disbelieving.

'Yeah. I know.'

'How do I get that out of my head?'

'Time,' said Austin.

'This is hard.'

'Yeah, I know. We have each other though, and I think that's what we should concentrate on right now.'

'True.'

Austin walked over and put both of his arms around Ellie and held her tightly. He wanted more from her at that moment, but this wasn't the time. The woman was shot to pieces, he thought, without realizing how inappropriate his choice of thoughts were. She just needed him to hold her up for a bit, then, he could love her as he needed to. Silent tears rolled down Ellie's face, as she grieved for everything that she had once known as her truth. Darinda and Roger, Sims and Anna, Gary, Edward and Louise, and from the fear of knowing that she would need to leave the bunker and head back out into the unknown.

• • •

MACE WAS SITTING in his office, looking out over what was left of the city. It wasn't that it had been dismantled, it was just looking tired and barren. At least the garbage that had been piling up had now been removed by a specialist group of Chippies that had sprung onto the scene. God, he'd never seen people so happy to pick up shit before. He turned and looked at the folder pile on the desk, a third of what it had been the week before. He hadn't realized how efficient he could be as a lawyer, or that he knew how to play the game so well. After he'd made his way through the pile, he was going to be given court cases, and get stuck into some real stuff, he'd been advised by someone above him.

He still wanted blood, though, whether figurative or real. He was planning a small act of revenge in his mind and thought he had one pretty well worked out, reinforced by his meeting with other Chippies. It was that bitch Sandy, Head of the rehab unit who had been instrumental in strapping him down. It had seemed appropriate that she should get a taste of her own medicine. He smiled at the thought of her helpless, exposed, and vulnerable, just as he had been, with nurses spoon-feeding the food into his mouth, as if he were a child. He could make her plead and beg too if he wanted, and he felt himself go warm at the thought.

JACK WOKE with a gun next to his head and a headache that felt like it had gone off in his mouth. He'd drunk enough to kill several men, but the relief from being plastered had done its job. For a few hours, he had laid on his floor, off his face, and not a care in the world. He hadn't cared if he was going to Mars or Jupiter, preferring to swim around in a place where the edges were blurred, and his mind was floating in a vacuum. His phone beeped at him with a text message from Pete.

Where are you? We're going to Texas for training ahead of time.

He shook his head, inhaling the filth on his carpet, trying to comprehend the text.

What? he texted back.

His phone rang. It was Pete. 'Say again?' he asked Pete.

'Pack a bag for two weeks. Belcher wants to start training now. She's sent the National Release info out and has secured the funding.'

'Wait… since yesterday?'

'Yeah.'

Jack looked at the time on his phone. 'That's like eighteen hours ago.'

'Yeah… I know… she's like super-woman or something.'

'Shit.'

'What?'

'I'm pissed, she'll see me pissed.'

'No, she's going independently, apparently. We're to find our own way there.'

'That's a lucky break.'

'In terms of the money though, people are desperate. They'll send the money express email if they can. Lick her tits if she asked them to do that.'

'Pete.'

'What?'

'That's just fucking gross.'

'It was meant to be.'

'You do realize you've put that image in my mind. I feel contaminated.'

Pete laughed.

'Okay… when and where?' Jack pulled himself up into a sitting position.

'When are you licking her tits?' Pete chuckled.

'For fuck's sake. Change the subject before I vomit.'

'You know she would say the same about you?'

'What is the relevance of that, Pete?'

'Just saying, for equality and all that.'

'Anyway, where do I need to be and when?'

'Okay,' Pete was in serious mode again. 'We've booked some flights. Meet us at the lab for eleven.'

'Sure. Oh, one more thing.'

'Yes?'

'So, what does one pack for space training?'

'Clothes where you can wash vomit out of them easily, I hear.'

'Lovely.'

'Haven't you heard of the Vomit Comet?'

'No.'

'Fun times ahead, Jack. See you at eleven.'

. . .

WELLS SAT opposite Belcher in a room, looking out over the ocean. He offered her a *lavenstraw* muffin, flavored from island lavender and strawberry.

'I thought it was time to give you a tour of Home Base HQ,' he said.

'Good. I've been waiting,' she said back, not showing the slightest hint of excitement, as she caught the crumbs falling from her mouth.

Home Base HQ was on an isolated part of the island, at the highest point, away from the possibility of tidal surges and contained within an expansive white dome, obscured by a dense selection of foliage. Belcher thought it looked banal, given what it controlled.

'Just to refresh you. After End Date was announced, everyone's initial reaction was to want to escape the planet, and I became incredibly popular, as you can imagine. People were willing to sell their mothers to get to Home Base.'

'Yes, I can imagine,' said Belcher, wondering how much her own mother might have been sold for. Not much, she deduced. She wouldn't have made it to the moon.

'They've been down in the lava tubes for the past few months due to the storm, but are beginning to surface now. They haven't coped terribly well… that's why I'm only sending people up whop are now primed for the experience. If you like, we could speak to some of them?'

'How? Isn't there a time delay in communication?'

'Yes, normally, there is. It extends from four to twenty-four minutes, depending on where the planets are in alignment. However, I developed a photonic form of communication, which is much faster and more consistent.'

'I wasn't aware of that,' said Belcher. 'Photonic?'

'There's probably a lot you aren't aware of. When I shut everything off from the public many years ago, I also kept most of my new technologies secret. I've been working away quietly at it all since then. We can have almost near real-time communication thanks to this new technology.'

'Sounds like there is a lot for me to see,' said Belcher.

'There is,' he said, scanning his eye into a security pad outside the entrance door.

'Is the Underground Generation here as well?'

Paxton paused. 'Perhaps, only no-one sees them. It has to be that way. They need to live in an authentic context, away from other people.'

'I'm glad I'm not one of them,' said Morag, beginning to realise that living underground might not be as savoury as she had imagined.

'You need to go through a few sterilization procedures, I'm afraid, nothing too dramatic. It's to make sure we don't bring sand, dirt or dust into the building with all the computer equipment.'

'No problem,' said Belcher, walking through into the cleansing chambers.

They then entered a large circular room that was filled with computers, holograms, and model terrain maps of Mars.

'It looks like a movie set, according to some people,' laughed Wells.

Belcher raised her eyebrows at him, not appreciating his sense of humor. 'So, show me how it all works,' she said. 'I've invested many billions of dollars into this, and I want to see what I'm getting for my money, and where I'm going to be living.'

'Money can buy the most amazing and the most wonderful Morag, both of which I believe I have captured with Home Base.'

He introduced Belcher to his team of scientists and then left her with them for the Base tour.

'I'll be back in about an hour. I have an urgent appointment, I'm afraid. We'll also set up a chat with someone on Mars if you are interested, after your tour?'

'Of course. I have many questions.'

'Right, done deal. See you in an hour and enjoy your tour.'

Belcher stood in the middle of the room, aware that she had felt something. A feeling, perhaps? It was unusual to have her body filled with an unknown mass, and so she studied it. She couldn't tell if it was excitement or fear, but observed it with an objective analysis until it subsided.

'Madam President.' A voice startled her. It belonged to an unimpressive middle-aged woman, slightly over-weight, with a muffin top spewing forth from the top of her one-size too small, denim jeans. Belcher looked her up and down, which was noticed by the woman. She paused on her face, noting the premature wrinkles from sun exposure and crow's feet. Belcher didn't have crow's feet, as those were reserved for people that had laughed during their life-time. The sorts of laughs that aren't polite or forced, but real *from the heart* laughs that crinkle the sides of the eyes. She finished her appraisal of the woman and sighed with disappointment.

If the woman, named *Mouse* by her colleagues due to her quiet nature, had noticed the sigh, she didn't react. Instead, she warmly welcomed the President to Home Base HQ and showed her the terrain maps, programs for further developments, and the accommodation on the planet. Belcher didn't say much in response, but Mouse had already identified her as an arrogant bitch, the sort of woman that uses stealth tactics to undermine the confidence of another. A condescending look here, and a demeaning sigh there.

'Mr Wells has arranged for several bulk orders of sample food to be delivered, if you would like to see that.' She didn't glance at Belcher for confirmation, but walked towards the back of the dome. 'Along this passage, which is underground for better temperature control, we have several storage areas.' She stopped at a door and unlocked it, exposing a large warehouse sized room full of boxes. 'These are the samples of various foods that he has ordered, which include the sustenance travel pouches. The actual food supplies are being delivered to the launch site though, ready for boarding into the cargo craft.'

'Explain what you mean by pouches?' Belcher asked.

'The travel food comes in preserving pouches with a fold-up straw. It's liquified though, like hot chocolate, tea, and coffee. Then we have solid foods like tacos, Japanese shrimp, yogurts, chocolate-covered nuts… just nothing that crumbles like chips or carbonated drinks because you can't wet-burp up there on the spacecraft. We also have some canned food, but the pouches are lighter and easier to pack.'

'How much food will be going up before our departure?' Belcher asked.

'You mean how much in terms of longevity of supply?'

'Yes.'

'Forty years' worth which includes food for the Underground Generation. After that, you'll need to be feeding yourselves.'

'So, you don't intend to go there?'

'No, never. I'd much rather live a full life here on Earth than try to live up there.' Mouse smiled and shrugged her shoulders. 'Would you like to try a hot chocolate?'

'No.'

'We're ready for communication,' called out a voice.

Belcher was led back into the dome and towards a small area with a curtained booth at one end.

'If you would like to sit here, we'll connect you with Gus. He's one of the scientists living at Home Base.' Mouse then walked away, rolling her eyes at the ceiling, glad to be away from the most wooden and lackluster human being she had ever come across.

Belcher was fitted with a headset. Gus would appear soon, and then she could speak with him. She had a million questions swirling around in her mind.

'We've only just managed to get communication up and running again. The dust storm was fierce up there, played havoc with our photonic signals,' advised Neil, the man who owned the voice.

Belcher watched as the screen lit up. She could see the vague outline of a person, but there was so much grainy static, it was hard to see exactly what was on the screen. The screen crackled and hissed.

'Excuse me,' said Neil, leaning over her, 'I'll just try to get a better connection.' He took a headset and put it on.

'This is Home Base HQ to Home Base Mars. Do you read?' Crackle and hiss. It sounded like someone was trying to speak, but the interference was too significant to make out what they were saying.

'Sorry about this,' said Neil. 'Having said that, this is better than what we've been getting to date.'

Belcher waited as Neil tried several more times. 'I don't think this is going to happen,' she said, getting up out of her seat.

'No, appears not. Sorry about that. It's the storm. We can try again later if you would like?'

'Yes. Next time,' said Belcher. She had seen enough. Wells was obviously getting on with the preparations, that's all she had needed to see… that he was being responsible with her money.

They met up again in his office, and Wells unrolled a blueprint. 'This is the craft that will be taking you to Mars,' he said. 'We've been able to update it considerably, incorporating the changes you sent through. It should be a much more comfortable ride as a result. We've been able to add some areas for personal space, which always helps on long-haul flights.'

'I wanted my own space,' Belcher said, looking closely at the blueprint. 'I don't see it. Did you not get my second amendment?'

'As in?' Wells asked.

'A separate place for me to undertake the entire journey.'

'Right,' Wells sounded surprised. 'As in, you want to be completely separate from everyone else for the *entire* flight?'

'Yes. I'll need verbal communication between myself and the crew, but I want to be on my own.'

'Fine. You can have it any way you want, Morag. I suggest you draw up a list of exactly how you want it, and I can get it included in the design. Anything is still possible now, as we're only commencing the interior assembly next week.'

'I already did that. You need to find the email Paxton.'

'Sure,' he said, scanning the email inbox again. 'Anything else you need to see?'

'I don't think so. We just need to go through the rotational aspect of the training. Two-week blocks, three groups rotating. That way, the rollout can continue. What about the Chippie selection? When do you want to do that?'

'Yes, by the way, I like the term Chippies. It suits them. Look, I think I can let your team choose who, just no legals, given their history. Do that when you get back and send me some names when you have chosen.'

'Departure date at this stage?'

'Not entirely sure, but with training underway and the craft being built. It'll be within six months.'

'And you are sure that there is such a degree of urgency?'

'Absolutely. Look, I'll be following soon after, on one of the cargo ships. I've got a few more things to tie up before I can leave, make sure that whomever I leave in charge is competent to run things from this end. We can't keep propping the chaos up. It's going under and fast.'

'Okay then, I'm glad I've seen all of this Paxton. I feel that my money is being spent wisely. Keep it that way.'

'Of course, Morag. I want this to work as much as you do.'

She looked at him, 'I would expect that as a bare minimum Paxton.'

29

I FEEL YOU

SPIN ME AROUND

Jack, Tina, and Pete were ushered into a room, where a solidly built man was eagerly waiting for them. 'Welcome to Mars training. I'm Jeff Jackson, call me JJ,' he smiled, demonstrating two rows of perfectly whitened teeth. 'I'm a representative from the Home Base Space Academy and a former member of The Consolidated Military. While you are here, you'll be undertaking an intensive two-week program, completing four rotations that will help you adapt to living on Mars. We'll prepare you for G force acceleration, isolation, and confinement, and body weight changes you will experience on the Martian surface. During the next two weeks, we're going to cover a lot, but I'm going to accentuate that there is so much more that you're going to need to do before the lift-off date, which we don't know the exact timing of just yet before you ask.' He grinned, before taking a deep breath and started to speak again.

'Most of what you will cover will be here, at the Home Base training facility, but we'll also be heading over to Hawaii later, to learn how to walk on a surface similar to what you'll get on Mars.

We'll be looking at survival techniques and technical operations on our simulator equipment. There will also be a training course in Martian farming and basic medicine and individual sessions with our psychologist. It's going to be intense and challenging, while being rewarding.' He paused to take another breath. 'It takes time to adjust to the notion that you will be leaving Earth for good. No questions? Great, let's get started.' He moved them outside, before they had even sat down, and towards a minibus.

'The A310, also called The Vomit Comet, will let you see what one third and zero gravity feels like,' he continued as the bus took them to the airport. 'Essentially, it's a commuter plane stripped bare. It flies in parabolic patterns. If I tell you to lie down, you do it.'

'Lie on the floor!' JJ yelled at them through a megaphone, as the plane climbed steeply. Just as it leveled off, he shouted at them, 'Rise!' The effect lost them two-thirds of their body weight, similar to how it would feel on Mars. Jack started to do one-handed pushups, and Pete did a somersault but didn't get high enough and crashed into the side of the plane.

'Backs to the floor! And don't be smart next time!' he yelled at them.

They quickly lay on the floor as the plane tipped downwards, ready to climb again. The engines whined, straining to pull the aircraft into a steep ascent. This time, as it leveled off, they experienced zero gravity and lifted towards the roof. Tina made the mistake to push off from the ceiling, not realizing that in zero gravity, she wouldn't slow or stop. She crashed into the floor and then bounced up again towards the ceiling.

'Just do as I say. We don't want anyone getting hurt!' JJ advised them.

The plane repeated the same ascent and descent over and over. 'Lie flat!' he yelled.

'I think I'm going to throw!' called out Pete.

'Into the bucket,' JJ quickly passed him a yellow bucket with *vomit* written in red on the outside. It had a suction opening so that the vomit was trapped within the bucket and didn't release into the plane. Pete heaved his breakfast into it.

'Oh God, I've never been good around vomit,' said Jack, trying to get away from the smell. He grabbed Pete's bucket instead and also heaved into it.

'Guys, seriously?' Tina moved to the other end of the plane, as JJ called out again into the megaphone.

'Jack, you have your own bucket. Do not use Pete's!'

'Can he stop yelling?' said Tina under her breath.

Pete groaned. 'I feel so sick.'

'Your vomit smelt worse than anything I've ever smelled. Seriously, dude. What sorts of bacteria are lurking in there?' asked Jack, still feeling queasy.

'You having a go at my gut bacteria now?'

'Fuck yeah,' said Jack. 'They deserve it.'

'Please take your seats in preparation for landing!' called out JJ, again through the megaphone.

They were driven back to the Home Base training facility in preparation for the simulated zero-gravity walking exercise.

'Eat first. You have twenty-five minutes before we leave for the pool.'

None of them eat much, still feeling queasy from the plane.

'Hope you are all comfortable being forty feet down in 6.2 million gallons of water,' said JJ on the minibus. 'You'll be completing this next exercise over in the Home Base Neutral Buoyancy Lab. This one will teach you how to maneuver in zero gravity, while in one of the most bulky spacesuits you're ever gonna have to wear.'

Once there, it took them forty-five minutes to suit up into large white spacesuits. Heavy weights were clipped onto their ankles and wrists to ensure that they sank to the bottom when they entered the water.

'Hi, I'm Sam,' a young woman in a scuba suit told them. 'I'm going to be training you today to complete reduced gravity maneuvers in spacesuits, just as you will have to do, perhaps on your craft during transfer, and on the Martian surface. At the bottom of this pool, we have a complete mockup of some of the equipment on Home Base that you will encounter, as well as the transfer craft. Once we lower you down, the other divers will help you under the water, and you'll be attached to an umbilical, so don't worry too much.'

Tina's heart was pounding out of her chest. She hated being underwater at the best of times, let alone being weighed down deliberately, so that she would sink to the bottom.

She was led to the side of the pool and helped in. Immediately she started to sink.

'Try to breathe more deeply,' Sam encouraged her through the earpiece. 'Remember the hand signal for up? Yes?'

Tina held up three fingers.

'Good,' said Sam. 'Now, try to walk along the bottom, bouncing in small steps.'

Tina bounced along the bottom, seeing that Jack and Pete were already on their backs, twirling and mucking around.

'Now, we will give you something to attach to the external structure,' said Sam, dropping down a piece of white metal. 'Try to see if you can place that where it needs to go and screw it in. You'll need to undo the casing first.'

Tina dropped the screws eight times. The gloves were clumsy and trying to do anything which required fine motor skills was near impossible.

'That's why we send you up with a crew,' smiled Sam. 'This sort of training takes a long time to master, but it's nice to get a feel as to what zero gravity might feel like.'

The rest of the time allowed Tina to walk in the transfer craft, becoming acquainted with the holding straps, and get herself moving from one end of the craft to the other.

Three hours later, they were back on the surface.

'Time for a late lunch, and then this afternoon, we intend to lock you away for three days in the isolation chamber.' JJ led them to the cafeteria. 'I'll see you up at the main building in an hour. We'll be flying out to Hawaii late this afternoon.'

'God, it's fast-paced, that's for sure. That pool was amazing. Better than the plane,' said Jack, as enthusiastically as a child.

'What's our anticipated flight time to Mars? Anyone know yet?' asked Pete.

'Yeah, it depends on when we leave. If we leave in six months, our journey will take around two hundred and three days.' Tina said.

'You've been doing your homework,' said Pete, sounding impressed.

'Yeah, well, given the sudden rush with it all, I thought I'd better get with the program, so to speak. I've been starting to cut back on sugar too.'

'Why? Isn't he sending up any sugar?' Jack asked.

'Don't know. It just said in the guidelines to reduce sugar and protein consumption so that you can adapt to the tomato, rye, and what was it?'

'Cress and carrot, wasn't it?' offered Pete.

'I wonder what foods he's going to send up? Imagine knowing, though, that whatever you have is the last of it forever. I'd be too scared to eat it.' Tina thought back to the protein bar she had been given for lunch and hoped that nothing like that was going to be sent to Mars. It tasted disgusting, like dense putty, flavoured with bad coco.

'So, when are the Chippies going to do their training?' Pete asked.

'I'm not sure,' said Tina.

'What about Belcher?' Jack asked.

'No sign of her. I'm presuming she's going to do the training on her own?' Tina surmised. 'I'm guessing it's just the three of us for the next two weeks.'

THEY FLEW TO HAWAII, the surface as close as they could get to one similar to Mars. For three days, they were placed in solitary confinement in a small complex with only one communal room, a bathroom, and three small bedrooms. JJ had explained that it would allow them to appreciate what close confinement with each might feel like. To go outside, to escape one another, they were required to fully suit up in a spacesuit that weighed in at a hundred pounds. JJ had explained to them that the real weight of the Martian spacesuits were three times that, and incorporated full life-support systems, but if they had worn one of those while still experiencing Earth's gravity, they would have fallen over from the weight.

By the second day, Jack was already irritable and squabbling. He had tried taking time out and had lumbered up and down the pebbly paths, but it had proven to be hot and exhausting. Pete had shut down and had slept, while Tina had stuck air pods in, with the understanding that she was going to listen to music during her waking hours.

'The flight over is going to be hell if you guys don't sort all of that out,' JJ had commented after watching snippets of the video footage. 'That's after only three days together? Guys, you've got over two hundred coming up together. Be *nice* to one another, and remember that if you use up your energy batteries, you need to re-power them with something… so don't use them so much.'

JJ had shaken his head while debriefing with them at the end of the two weeks. 'I'm going to say that we need a lot of improvement across the board. For your own sakes, because you are the ones leaving the planet and going to live up there.' He indicated up with his hand. 'You need to learn to live better next to each other, and Tina, you need to go to your local swimming pool and sit on the bottom for a bit. Pete, find a rollercoaster and sit on it for a day so that your stomach can toughen up to motion. Although, I don't believe there are any still working out there, so ignore that. Jack, either make sure you drink more alcohol or just become a bit nicer… find some tolerance, and no, not to the alcohol. Can you do that for me?' He didn't wait for confirmation. 'Now, your next training is in a month, and we'll be going up in the jets to experience some G-forces, and you'll get a ride in the infamous centrifuge. Challenging, but not impossible. Any questions?'

Tina had a hundred questions, which she had saved up since arriving. JJ was patient in answering them, including explaining whether the amount of training they were doing was going to be enough.

'Good question. It used to take a lot longer. We would have astronauts in training for years for space missions. Now? We just train you for the bits you need. Fewer emergency scenarios and no need for craft piloting programs. Also, you guys don't need to do all of your own maintenance. The pilots are in charge of that. All you have to do is sit and be nice to each other on the way over, and perhaps help out if a major emergency takes place, which it won't.'

BELCHER CALLED them into her private conference room as soon as they returned.

'Must be serious to be going so formal. We've never used the Presidential conference room for a meeting,' whispered Tina as they sat waiting at a large oval table.

Belcher walked in quickly and sat down. 'I had the pleasure of meeting with Wells on his island while you were at training. I got a full tour of Home Base HQ as well as almost speaking with someone currently living on Home Base.'

'You actually got to speak with people living on Mars?' Jack was surprised. He had thought that Belcher was space training somewhere as well, not meeting with Wells on the island.

'No, not quite. They have recently suffered from a severe dust storm, and we did try to link up, but unfortunately, the link didn't work. I saw them, just didn't actually get to speak to them.'

'What's the communication delay like?' asked Jack.

'Apparently, they have developed a new technology using photons, so Wells says. This means that you can communicate in almost real-time.'

Jack shook his head at Pete and Tina and shrugged his shoulders.

'Photon technology? Never heard of it.' Pete said, confused.

'Photonic, to be exact,' added Belcher. 'There are a lot of things we haven't heard of. Wells has kept everything to himself for the past several years. However, Home Base is more impressive than I imagined. In the years since he went silent, he's been developing it. The building infrastructure is more extensive, especially underground in the lava tunnels. It's actually quite comfortable. He's also provided me with a breakdown of the investment monies.'

'Is he planning to make it online and live again?' Jack asked.

'Yes, and charge a new subscription fee.'

Peter raised his hand. 'I've got a question about the Chippie selection. Where are we at with that?'

'Yes, that was one of the reasons I called you in. Wells has asked that you make the selections.'

'So, not people with families, I'm assuming?' Tina asked.

'No. Single and prepared to leave. Oh, and no legals he has said. However, don't just barge in and ask them. You'll need to be more discreet and then segregate them. Make sure they can't tell other people. Draft up a confidentiality agreement at the very least. Let me know when you are ready and I'll get legal to sign off on it.'

'So, this roll-out. What do you want us to do?' Jack asked.

'Keep going as usual,' said Belcher. 'I need the leaders to know that everything is going ahead as usual.'

'Well, we've done all the test groups, and everything seems fairly sorted. The doctors, lawyers, teachers, business, and basic services Chippies are now comfortably positioned in the workforce. The aggression issues have ceased, so we're ready to do a real roll-out.' Pete said.

'Right then, go ahead and start recruiting nationwide. That should take you to the next training block. After that, we can look at another batch of chip insertions. Then I suggest we market worldwide to ensure that the leaders can see that we are making progress.'

'Fine,' said Jack, sounding a bit pissed off. 'I'm presuming the suggestion of a worldwide rollout is for show only?'

'Do you have a problem?' asked Belcher.

'No.' He did, but he wasn't going to share it with her.

'So, what is your problem?' asked Tina as they sat having coffee in the cafe.

'So obvious that I have a problem?' laughed Jack. 'Just the fact that all the work in the chip is now being limited in this way. I mean, we came up with some pretty clever technology there, and it had a lot of potential… plus all the extra stuff I had developed over in my lab.'

'Yeah, but you need to re-think the notion of potential,' said Tina. Jack looked at her quizzically.

'The world we live in doesn't do potential anymore. You can't think like that anymore,' she said, sipping her coffee.

'It's innate, though,' said Pete, thinking. 'Humans have depended on potential to survive, otherwise, there's nothing to look forward to.'

'You mean hope? That's what potential is, isn't it?' Jack asked.

'Yeah, we've lost hope. It was the glue that kept everything together.' Pete shrugged his shoulders.

'It's not only that,' added Jack. 'This training seems illogical… rushed and bitty. I don't know, it's like Belcher has panicked and suddenly wants us to leave too soon.'

'I don't think it was Belcher who made that decision. It was Wells remember,' said Tina.

'His predictions showed that things were falling apart more quickly than anticipated,' agreed Pete.

'Fucked. All of this. Just fucked,' said Jack. 'Including this watery coffee. I'm ordering a drink.'

30

ARMS WRAPPED

LEGS FAST

Austin buried his face into Ellie's auburn hair. It smelled like almond massage oil and sex, both now regular treats since they had fallen into the bunker. He traced his fingers along the side of her face, and she stirred, nuzzling into him. He kissed her cheek, taking a moment to have gratitude for such a small pleasurable moment. Ellie was his everything and would remain his everything, as long as he continued to take a breath. He smiled at his own vulnerability. Weeks ago, he would have ridiculed himself for being so emotional, so full of feelings, but now, things were different. It was as if the confinement had crystallized what was important, and it wasn't what he had ever imagined for himself.

Years earlier, he would have been described as driven, having been focused on his career, his marriage to Tyler, and getting to the top of his career. His feelings had always been well down his list of important, probably why it had been so easy to let Tyler go at the Gaia settlement. Now that succeeding was pointless, all he had to do was survive, and survival came in batches of twenty-four hours that started with the rise of the sun and ended with the blackness of night. Ellie had taken the edge off this new reality for him, softening the daily sense of futility that was easy to feel when things were quiet. She had helped him to become still, instead of frenetic, substituting moments of now, instead of future goals and ambitions, and rumination about the past.

He was monitoring the gang who, as he had predicted, had stayed to camp out at the house. Given they now had security, a food source, and what was left of the house after rounds of their manic and obliterating machine gun fire, they were in no hurry to leave. Austin kept a notebook next to the video footage, noting that there were five gang members, three men, and two women. He figured the pilot was ex- military by looking at him, and it made sense… although where the hell they had gotten a chopper from? He pondered whether the attack had been specifically targeted, with Roger's CIA network of contacts, among the immediate suspects. Austin wasn't sure if the chopper was the gang's preferred method of travel, and if so, why hadn't Roger heard of this?

He had shielded Ellie when seven bodies had been removed from the house and had been burned in the back field. As the smoke of his friends had stained the grey of the sky, the anger he had felt had been enough for him to have taken himself into the bathroom and quietly weep from the sheer angst of helplessness he had felt. Then he had returned to Ellie, and they had made love for the first time. Gently, tenderly, and with honesty. It was all he could do, turn his anger into love for the only person in the world that he had left.

As the weeks had passed, they had stopped fighting with their predicament and had accepted it. Days were filled with discussions about what they might eat and what activities to do. They made love in the afternoons and fell into long sleepy naps, and in the evenings, they drank, watched movies, and made love again. Their interaction became the focus of each day and a more mindful way of existing unfolded.

Austin had observed as to how the gang spent their days. At first, they hadn't left the house, spending their time clearing out the shards of furniture they had blown to smithereens. Wooden boards were brought in from the shed to replace the shattered windows, and the walls and door frames that had been blasted into fragments were shoveled out and stacked into the bonfire to use as kindling. As the weeks had worn on, the gang had started raiding again and would leave in the vans, or the chopper and then return with their spoils. Austin noted that they always left one gang member on guard when they left.

AUSTIN HAS LOST HIS EDGE. I'm telling y'all. Too damned soft to tell this properly. I'm taking over because people who are trapped in prepping bunkers lose their sense of stability, rationality, sensibility, and objectivity. I'm supposed to be prepping myself for the finale, but this takes precedent right now. Readers, I'm guessing you don't want to be learning about how he brushed the hair off Ellie's soft and supple skin, or how many times they behaved like bonking rabbits with Ellie gazing longingly at his manhood. Keep it inside your pants, Austin, it's not a romance novel as Jack already told you, and this time, I agree with him.

So prepping bunkers… Jesus Christ. They are designed to keep you alive when nothing else will, aside from a full-on life support system at a hospital that doesn't have a shortage of beds and ventilators like in the twenties Pandemic. Bunkers are fancy boxes dug into the ground, as big as your pockets allow and crammed with shriveled up exhibits in jars, cans, and sealed bags. Some people dedicate their entire fucking lives to prepping. There are prepping people who pickle eggs, reaching high into chickens' arses to collect them, so desperate are they to pickle everything they can find that moves or doesn't. Jack told me that's not true. Really, Jack? So people don't put their entire fucking hands up the arses of chickens? Well, I'll be darned.

There's one vulnerability that mocks the shit out of these elaborate prepping bunkers, though, and that's the fact that human beings are the nasty fuckers that we are. So, let's just say you've gone and had a big, beautiful bunker built for when the shit-hits-the-fan as it has done now for Ellie and Austin. They were lucky in that Martha, Roger's wife, not that anyone has given the poor woman a name yet in this story, built one with intelligence and money. Two ventilation systems in case one broke, built in a faraday cage to protect from EMF attacks. It was made from solid steel, had a decent septic system, and was heavy enough not to float to the surface. Inside she put exercise equipment, food, stuff to do, and hopefully got those who built it to sign a confidentiality agreement. Otherwise, the people that built them? Can come back and raid them.

A simple, forty-dollar metal detector can find a prepping bunker, though, and the ventilation shaft can always be found by someone looking for one. You can transmit Covid-19 down a shaft if you sneeze in the right direction, too. So, while they are safe from most things, prepping bunkers aren't safe from human beings, being the cunning predators that we are. The other point is that you're also stuck in a bunker with whomever you've chosen to join you, and while that might be fun for a couple of days, it can become a living hell. For Austin and Ellie, they created a love-nest as a way to cope, but were they trying to escape properly? Hell no. Making love and stroking each other's cheeks was more comfortable than trying to run to a van and drive to Canada.

Then there is the aspect of why you're in the damned bunker and what is left for you to escape back into. Ever been camping in the wilderness? A place where there is no running water and no toilet?

It's fun for a few days, and then the novelty wears off. You just crave a shower, a soft bed, and a bathroom to shit into, without having your arse swarmed by flies. When the shit hits the fan, people aren't going to be standing there, arms extended, happy to see you. You're going to be seen as a threat to their existence, or a person of interest, especially if you have stuff they want. You'd better be in a pack because the ones out there roaming in ones or twos ain't gonna to make it. You'd better make sure that you know how to shoot to kill as well, because you are going to need to shoot every fucking thing that moves. That is, if you want to survive.

Austin and Ellie? Safe in their bunker, only because the gang was too stupid to think that a second bunker might be on the property. They'd found the other one, newly built and not hidden yet, freshly stocked with food, and so they had delighted in finding it and felt so much luck for finding this particular property. None of them imagined for a moment that it had a second bunker, so no one went looking. Austin and Ellie played out a romance novel, probably due to both of them suffering from adrenal overload. Escaping from Gaia and then dealing with everyone they knew being shot and then cooked into diced crispy strips, was enough for them to need some time-out. I don't blame them, and y'all shouldn't either. However, objectivity was thrown out the window and replaced with sentimental claptrap.

So, after weeks of fucking, sorry… love making… Austin decided that they needed to run and get to Canada, which had been built into a place of salvation in their minds. Winter was here, and they needed to leave before any more snow blocked the roads. He wrote lists in his spare time, of what they might need. The problem was that they weren't going to be able to dash with the amount of stuff they needed. It was going to be a sensible pack in the back of a van to ensure that they could survive the journey. This meant killing someone, namely the gang member, who was always left on guard when the others went out.

Okay, so just say you're in a bunker like the two of them… hear me out on this one. The only way out is to kill someone, like *actually* do it. How do you do that without being shot yourself first? That's the dilemma that Ellie and Austin had. The only proper shooting training they'd both had was a one-hour tutorial in the back garden, where they'd shot plastic targets and not a beating heart out of a human being. So, Austin sat Ellie down, and they drew a picture of a human being because that's what you do when you have too much time on your hands. They spent days deliberating over where to aim, and whether a well-executed shot was better than a spray of bullets.

They played darts to see who the better shot was. It wasn't like they could fire off rounds of ammunition in a prepping bunker to see who came out on top. Can you see where I'm going with all of this? They had totally lost their objectivity and had descended into games. Games that, if not played out well, would kill them once they released the hatch. However, in the end, a plan was finally put into place, and they rounded up the food they needed, packed several layers of warm clothes, lined up containers of fuel, and made sure to include a backup pair of boots each. Looking at their list, in the end, it was fair. Enough to get them to Canada and survive while they were finding their feet.

ESCAPE DAY CAME, and the four members of the gang went out in one of the vans. This left three vans on the property. One was parked facing the exit, which Austin liked, as it meant they wouldn't need to waste time in turning it around. He picked up the gun, after Ellie decided that watching someone else's face possibly explode all over her yet again, wasn't going to be an option. Austin would raise the hatch, go find the gang member and shoot them dead. Then they would pack the van as quickly as possible and then get the hell out of there. It was a plan that could work if the universe smiled down on them with its lovely, warm, fuzzy metaphysical grin. They deserved a smile from Karma after everything they had already been through.

Austin had called Ellie over to him, needing to play out one of those movie scenes, dripped in sentimentality. He had told her everything that a loved human being needed to hear. She had looked deeply into his eyes and said the same words back to him, and the two of them had felt shit scared but deeply connected. That connection gave them the strength and bravery to do what needed to be done to survive. Austin had watched the white van leaving the property and had noted the remaining gang member was a woman. Then he had stopped seeing her as a woman and instead saw her as an enemy. The target, and one that had to be obliterated, no matter what, just as Darinda and Roger had said he should.

They turned off the burning jets of fuel at the bunker's entrance, and Austin had slowly opened the hatch. Machine gun in hand, he had crawled over the dry ground to the nearest cover. Ellie watched from inside, the blood in her veins going cold as the only man she loved became a moving target. Austin, on his haunches, gun ready to fire, moved slowly towards the house. The woman was in there, making breakfast, an activity that had now turned from benign into a death sentence. If she had time to prepare, she would have thought the punishment extreme, just as Darinda would have thought, before her brain was blown out of its thinking shell.

Austin felt sorry for the woman in a way. She didn't know that eternal nothingness was waiting in the wings, biding its time until she could be seen to take aim. Death is a fickle entity, though, and human beings have long known that it takes what it wants, how it wants. Our God, if he exists, has long been called an unjust God. One that watches babies suffer, and evil people thrive. As Austin crept along the side wall, hoping to get the shot in from the back balcony, with its extensive glass windows, death pondered over the two human beings and which one should come with him.

Ellie watched the video screen, waiting for Austin to give her the signal to start bringing the bags up. He suddenly froze, and there was a show of movement in the back of the house. He raised his gun, ready, and Ellie could see the concentration etched into his face. He fired, the bullet hitting something. He ducked, seeking refuge behind a post, and was as still as the statue of David, posing as a fountain next to him. Ellie saw what happened next, and she was mouthing words and screaming from a well deep inside of her. It was as if time slowed to a motion where no matter how she tried to climb the stairs, it was never going to be fast enough. Some would say it was lucky that she wasn't still watching the screen when the woman quietly walked up behind Austin, who was facing west, and blew his head off from the east. He wouldn't have suffered.

Ellie heard the second gunshot, and she used her fingernails to grip and claw her way up the metal stairs of the bunker, grabbing back time itself, in order to warn Austin. She saw sunlight which temporarily blinded her, and some would say that this was kind and that the universe was protecting her. As she stood, like a duck at a fairground perhaps, the woman reacted to the movement, took aim, and shot her. It wasn't a clean shot, and Ellie fell to the warm soil that she had once plowed and would soon return to herself. She saw Austin in the distance, which meant that her last vision of life was of the man she loved. Most of him, anyway.

She looked now towards the soil, stained with the life force of her own blood, remembering the corn she had planted at Gaia. She wondered how tall it would be and what had happened to the worm that she had saved that day. Then she smiled with relief. Death was welcome now, preferred over the constant battle to survive and see those that she loved, taken from her. Her breathing slowed, lightness over heavy, blood draining into gravel and weeds. She understood the finality of her last, brave step towards death, understanding that there was also an urgency. Otherwise, the woman would push her into eternity, using the gun. She glanced upwards and took one last look at her world, pain fading from gratitude, calmness replacing fear. She gasped a final, shallow breath, smelling the soil's earthy aroma, and whispered a last thank you for her life. She closed her eyes and saw the blackness coming for her. She allowed herself to be consumed hoping that somewhere in that darkness, that she would find Austin. That gave her hope, and at the very end of Ellie's life, after all the suffering that had robbed her of her potential, the universe gave hope back to her as a final gesture. Ellie Monterey then died, holding hope in a still heart, her mind now quiet and at peace.

The woman who had shot them couldn't believe that two people had walked onto the property like that. Later when the gang got back, and had found the second bunker, they laughed as they went through all the great shit they had found. The woman found Ellie's almond oil and had conditioned her hair with it, and that night as they burned Austin and Ellie on the bonfire, the woman's lover commented on how good her hair now smelled.

Y'all, that's what human beings do to each other, and that's why we are the number one predator on this fucking planet.

31

MACE

CAN HURT YOUR EYES

Mace walked from the courtroom, having shredded the dignity of a woman who deserved no less. His client had paid him a shit ton of money to crucify her, and so he had. In his new world, he was paid to offend, to reduce, and to hurt, and it felt like he had come home. There wasn't anywhere else he would rather be than practicing law, and his mind refused to entertain the idea of doing anything else. Now that court had finished, the next part of his day could begin.

Tara had finally got the message, however slow, as apt for such someone of her calibre. How long had she whined and cried, pleading for him to please, just turn back into the man she loved. He had no use for her now, though. He had needed her once, but not in this new world where he finally had some power. He had allowed her to have the house, one which held no value for him, and all he felt was a relief to have extricated himself out of the union. His life had moved on into a new paradigm, and he was looking forward to seeing where it led him without the shackles of pathetic, binding him to the superficial and trivial.

. . .

SANDY DIDN'T KNOW that this day would be different from others, and she had arrived at work, feeling optimistic about the immediate future. The chips were being implanted, and regular groups of patients were going through rehab, reliably, as planned. They were meeting their quotas, and the chips were allowing people fresh starts. The lawyers' aggression issues were still causing problems at times, but they had organized daily sedation while in the program. The sedation calmed them during the program, making them look like the other Chippie cohorts. She didn't need to tell anyone outside of the rehabilitation unit about their ongoing issues, as she may have looked incompetent. Sedation seemed an easy solution for a problem that might jeopardize everything else. The salary she was being offered to Head this part of the chip implant process was worth staying mute for, and the nation-wide roll out was about to start, which would increase their numbers substantially.

Mace had waited in his car, excited now, to act out his revenge. Biding his time had been part of the plan, as the planning for this revenge had been entirely enjoyable. He had gone through many scenarios in his mind, each changing how his punishment was going to manifest. He knew three things, however. Sandy had made him feel humiliated, had reduced him to begging, and had then recorded it all into the fabric of time in her notes. Therefore, Sandy would need to suffer the same. He would humiliate her, make her beg, and then make sure that no-one would ever forget.

There was nothing in the paperwork that he had signed before getting the chip that had suggested he would tolerate humiliation. They had broken the bonds of trust between patient and procedure. Now the price would be paid for doing that. It would be a tit for tat, an eye for an eye, an even punishment. He chuckled… tit for tat… appropriate, apt, and well deserved. This revenge was going to be satisfying, and he felt his excitement brewing.

Sandy had finished work, feeling satisfied too, and her mind had been full of what she was going to organize for dinner when a man had approached her. She had vaguely recognized him, but couldn't place him in the dark. Then he had ushered her toward a car, saying that someone had been hurt. Her nurse instinct had kicked in, and she had eagerly rushed to where he had been indicating, to commence any necessary first aid. As she had leaned over to look for the victim, he had hit her on the back of the head and then had bundled her into his car. Easier than he had expected, as no-one had been there to witness anything.

He drove her out of town and to an isolated field and undressed her. He then placed a hospital gown over her and cuffed her to a fence post on one side, and a small branch of a tree on the other. Sitting in a folding chair from his boot, he sat down in front of her, waiting for her to come around. He sat, one leg over the other, hands on his knees, wondering what sort of smile he should greet her with. He tried a few, taking selfies on his phone and decided on the smirk, an expression that would let her know that he found her situation funny, rather than serious.

He had chosen his tone of voice, which would be the same condescending tone that had been used with him, the words still resonating in his mind. *Mace, your behavior is unacceptable, and we need you to co- operate.* They had called him unacceptable, just as his mother had done when he was six. No-one would ever shame him again, that he was certain about.

Sandy had come around and realizing her predicament, had gone through several typical phases of response. At first, she had been confused, then scared. After that, she had pleaded with the man, and then she had got angry. Mace had just sat, silently watching her, his phone filming it all, which had unnerved her even more. For an hour, he had refused to speak. Eventually she ran out of words, which was his cue to start.

'Your behavior Sandy is completely unacceptable. What do you think is going to happen next?'

He had then crossed his legs, folded his hands on his lap, and watched again.

He knew that the human mind could punish itself, just as his own had done, for the days they had forced him to be handcuffed to his bed. Instead, he said very little to Sandy, allowing her own mind to invent the punishment that was headed her way. He watched, and he smirked, laughing when his smirk made her cry.

'Oh enough,' he had said to her as if telling her off. He got up, folding the chair and drove off, leaving her there, in the dark, and it was some way before her screams stopped invading his sense of peace. He would go back for her because he didn't intend to kill her. He just wanted her to be alone, restrained, and not have her own sense of power. That's what she had done to him, and Karmic justice allowed for an equal punishment to be dealt back.

He had then gone for dinner and had enjoyed a hearty meal of steak and wine, at an exclusive restaurant that served legal professionals only, savored even more because of Sandy's predicament. He returned sometime later, and Sandy was pleading for her life, shaking now from the cold. He slapped her across the face to shut her whining up. He didn't need another Tara in front of him.

'Shut the fuck up,' he ordered.

She had nodded, acknowledging in her own mind that this man in front of her was dangerous. She had worked out who he was and realized that this was being done for revenge. She knew that he could kill her, his mood, and need for revenge as fickle as the wind, wrapping itself around her. She had prayed to God during her time of aloneness and had settled matters with him, despite never having spoken to him before. She had been disappointed when this almighty God had remained silent at such an urgent time of need.

'How does it feel,' he had said at her, 'to feel so fucking vulnerable? This is what you did to me, you bitch.'

She had trained in psychology to know that this was a rage attack and that Mace had been seething for all of this time, wanting to exact out the same humiliation his fragile ego had felt. He was speaking dangerous words though, which made him potentially lethal. Terminology aside, she surmised that she might need to change her reactions if she wanted to live. She had to re-think tactics.

'Mace, I had no idea who you were. I'm sorry. We shouldn't have restrained you.'

He had liked the word sorry and also the illusion that he was someone who shouldn't have been messed with.

He ranted then at her and the world for over an hour. A rage being unleashed that had caused Sandy to shiver more than from the plummeting temperature. If she didn't get clothes soon though, she *would* freeze to death. Then he had suddenly stopped, untied her, placed her in his boot, and had driven her back to her workplace.

'Now, go and walk in there, just with your hospital gown on, and allow everyone to see your vulnerability. That's something they won't forget in a hurry.'

She had, and her colleagues had sprung into action. Sandy was savvy enough to say that she hadn't got a clear picture of Mace because she knew that he would return and kill her if she did.

Mace had then driven to his invitation-only meeting. The schedule hadn't been finalized, but they all had the same feeling that they were being drawn together for the same reason. There was also going to be a guest speaker at some point, someone famous. Mace smiled to himself. This new life was going to be one hell of a ride.

32

—————

UP

UP AND AWAY

Yeah, my time again, the beginning of the end as I refer to it all. I need to explain how time passes quickly when you need it to slow, which is a particular quirk of the universe.

Some would argue that time actually doesn't exist in the first instance. Rather, it's just a human construct that allows us to organize millions of *now moments* into three categories. *Then, now and next.* Before End Date, the world had promised a future with hope. In the now of the moment, chaos reigned. The future didn't exist anymore, not for the human species and nor the millions of other species that were trapped on this burning lump of rock.

People used to miss the subtle nuances of it all, believing that the world was going to end, when, in fact, the world wasn't going to end at all. The world was simply kicking us out because we hadn't known when to stop pillaging it. We had become parasites, feeding off our host until our host had screamed enough! Look at Venus and Mercury… planets as dead as a doornail, and Earth wasn't stupid. She could see her future if she had allowed us to keep going, and so she had served notice and had given us a departure date, 2088 AD. Her pandemic warning in the twenties hadn't changed anything either, despite forcing us into our homes and providing an opportunity for quiet contemplation over matters. Instead we whined about our temporary imprisonments like spoiled children. Earth would go on to re-invent herself, possibly taking a break from having life on her surface to share her days with. At some point in her future, she might decide to start it all up again and throw a form of life into the infinite of possibilities. After that, billions of years from now, our sun would take the earth and burn her for being too close, and nothing about us or our planet would remain. That's the ultimate definition of futility. So futile that it fries your everything.

I USED to catch a bus that rode through a suburb that had that post-code number, 2088. My parents had moved us from New Orleans with the promise of a fresh start for my father, who was now paid to be a subservient to some city CEO. At first, in my youth, it was just a bus, taking me where I needed to go. Some days I would go to the local beach and soak up the sun, feeling that I owned a little part of it with my regularity of attendance. I walked around it, becoming familiar with its trees, potholes, and the small things that only regulars would notice. It was my home, my place of belonging, and it was fucking beautiful. I was thankful too, that I didn't need to walk up that damned hill every day after work, and the bus would whine as much as my heart and lungs would have done as it gripped its rubber to the road, inching towards the top. Then, as I moved out of home, I would catch another bus from there, and head back to my small bare flat, one that I called my castle.

As I got older, I started losing my blinkers of youth and became aware of hidden messages that emerged during the bus ride, only apparent to those wearing years of wisdom. I began to notice the houses, all perched with views, understanding that I could never afford one. I would watch the people who didn't know how lucky they were and noted that their clothes were different from my own. I'd be taken to the edge of the water by this bus, where the lapping would somehow calm my anger at this unfamiliar smell, called affluenza. I would catch a boat to take me to the hive where I worked hard, realizing that the amount I got paid per hour was play-money to those people in the perching houses. One day, the stench of it all assumed the name of oppression. I was never going to be one of those people because I had the wrong parents… the wrong lineage… the wrong mind-set. I understood the line that distinguished them from me. I started to feel anger and resentment and then hatred. I moved just about as far away as I could. I moved fucking countries in fact, and then I met Jack, the perfect antidote to someone as jaded as I was. That's the reality of those that have and those that don't. I hated that place after that, so when End Date was announced as 2088, I just shrugged my shoulders, because it was the fucking affluenza that fucking caused it all in the first fucking instance.

THE TRAINING WAS OVER, and Jack felt that it hadn't been enough. An understatement, given what they were heading into.

'We're not nearly ready for any of this,' he said to Pete as they sat debriefing back at the lab.

'I think we'll be okay. Trust Wells… he's been sending people up there for years. He knows what he's doing.' Pete sounded calm with it all.

'That is true,' said Tina. 'I've heard that the craft takes off more gently than they used to, if that's any consolation for what we're heading into.'

'I will continue to argue that leaving now seems premature.' Jack sounded frustrated.

'I don't agree,' said Pete. 'Even though the start of the national rollout was well received, at least what we've managed so far, news from Asia, Australia, and Europe is pretty dire. Their weather is catastrophic right now, and millions more are dying. Everything is destabilizing. We don't do crises well. Remember the lockdowns and the pandemic?'

'Well it wasn't just rebellion. People lost their mental health too,' said Tina, remembering it all, somewhat vaguely, through the eyes of a younger person.

'Yeah, I know,' agreed Pete. 'The pandemic really showed us all where our weaknesses were.'

'So we have ten days before lift-off. How messed up is that?' Jack interjected.

'Are you okay?' Pete had asked him, sensing that Jack was starting to fray around the edges.

'Yeah, I'm just angry. It's not like we're going on a holiday. We're leaving the damned planet.'

'Better than staying,' said Tina, matter-of-factly. 'That's how I cope with it all. I don't want to be shot or starve to death… or watch my parents die. This gives us a chance, albeit on a new planet. I'm excited too.'

'The Chippies are going to be joining us later today, don't forget,' said Pete. 'They've just completed their training.'

'What about Belcher?' Tina asked.

'Missing in action, that's what she is,' said Jack, sounding frustrated. 'She's been hiding on Wells' island the past five weeks, although I hear she's finished her training.'

'Well, she doesn't need to keep the pretense of Project IQ alive anymore, does she… I mean, she's received what was it again?' Pete looked at Tina.

'Three hundred and fifty-three billion,' she said. 'I took a peek the other day at the finance files.'

'Holy shit.' Jack shook his head. 'That's a lot. How much of that did she give to Wells again?'

'All of it, except for the money each Chippie got. You can't exactly use money on Mars.' Tina sighed.

'… and the leaders still think they are leaving?' Jack shook his head with incredulity.

'Yup,' said Pete. 'Five years, she told them.'

'Well, she's pulled off the con of the century,' Jack snorted.

'Yeah, I can't believe we got away with it all.' Tina shook her head in disbelief.

'So, when is Wells going to be joining us on Mars?' Pete asked.

'He said a few weeks on one of the cargo ships. He wants to send up more supplies before he leaves. With that sort of money, he can send up what he wants.' Tina said.

'Yeah, hopefully his manufacturing issues will resolve now that we've sent him all the Chippies.' Pete looked hopeful.

'Well, we're all going to be one big happy family up there, aren't we?' said Jack, sarcasm dripping from his lips.

Pete and Tina looked at each other with concern. Jack was unraveling.

The Mars Chippies arrived and were excited to be going. Chosen from a vast group, Wells had changed his mind and made it his decision to evaluate the shortlist that Jack had made. He wanted only the best up on Mars, and Jack had agreed. It was essential that they chose carefully, especially given his personality overlay was still playing itself out in numerous, subtle ways. Some of them were drinking too much, others had a deep-seated hatred of women. There were stories of rudeness and isolating behaviors. Jack was lucky that Belcher was such a screwball herself, as she never doubted that the personality overlap wasn't her own.

Y'ALL. Jack invited me onto the ship, and I said no. He said there was room for one more. I didn't want to leave Earth to go live on a big, dusty red planet. I wanted to see the end out for as long as was possible. You need a new drinking buddy, I told him. I reassured him that there would be some other dumb ass up there that there would drink with him, and he told me that I was stupid. Maybe I am.

Cutting to the chase of all of this, leave-day arrived, and goodbyes were said. It's hard to articulate the pain of saying goodbye to everything you have ever known, and the group was emotionally drained by the time they were to depart for the launching site. More tears were shed than in the last cyclone that had wrecked Georgia. Packing had been limited, with only one small bag allowed. Medicals had been undertaken, and then there was nothing left to do, other than get on the craft. Wells had been particular not to disclose anything about the launch location, in case the information got into the wrong hands. They were flown to Dallas and then traveled by bus, with the mood swinging from excitement to fear. Tina had spent the morning crying after having said goodbye to her parents and Evie, and Jack was already drinking. Pete was mute, staring out of the window. The only people who weren't a mess were the Chippies, who sat calmly, staring out towards the sea, on the horizon. Belcher had worn huge sunglasses and was listening to something through her air pods and refused to interact with anyone else on board. There was no standard way to react to what they were about to do, and no manual available.

The craft was waiting patiently, held up by metal anchors on either side. A massive silver rocket that could seat twenty-five human beings. It shone against the backdrop of smoky grey air and the emerald blue of the sea behind. There was a hive of activity surrounding it, with cargo being packed, engineering checks, and a sense of business. Then the bus dropped them off without heraldry, which seemed to be inappropriate given what they were about to do. Wells was waiting for them.

'Welcome,' he said, beaming.

'Fuck this,' replied Jack, drinking from a bottle of vodka.

'Jack, you'll need to sober up for launch,' Wells told him.

'Fuck off,' replied Jack.

'Loving the choice of name for the craft,' said Tina.

'What, Folly?' Wells smiled.

'Folly as in insanity, craziness, lunacy, extravagance, or plain old stupidity?' Tina asked, wanting to know which one applied.

Wells roared with laughter. 'All the above, definitely. A little of each, I think, given what we are all doing.'

He shook hands with Belcher. 'Well, we got here in the end, Morag,' he said to her positively.

'We did Paxton,' she agreed.

'A new beginning Morag, an adventure without an end, perhaps? You are venturing out there,' he pointed into the sky.

She looked up briefly and then squinted against the sun.

'Into an endless blackness, away from the safety of Earth.'

'Shut up, Paxton,' she said, 'you are a businessman, not a poet.'

'Fine,' he said smiling, 'point taken.'

There was a lot to prepare for before the launch at six, and they were kept busy, with tours of the craft, explanations about the technical aspects of the flight, and were introduced to their flight Captains, who reinforced some information they had learned during training.

Five o'clock came too fast, and then it was time.

'Right then. I suppose it's time to say goodbye to Earth.' Jack looked around, trying to gauge what was appropriate for such a moment.

The moment was intense as the astronauts were taken out to face the setting sun for the last time. Tina looked around, photographing in her mind what warmth felt like. She inhaled deeply, smelling the sea, hearing the waves and watching the gulls fly into the wind. This was Earth, so beautiful, so magnificent and yet dying. She stood directly with her face into the sun and whispered something that only she and the earth were privy to.

Each of the astronauts engaged in a small ritual as a last goodbye, and they linked arms to demonstrate solidarity. Jack fell to his knees and placed his face onto the warm ground. He inhaled and then sat up onto his knees.

'Goodbye, my planet and God willing that you recover from all of us.'

Then, as the last of the light hid itself behind pink-tinged clouds, it was time to suit up.

'Hard to believe this is it,' said Tina solemnly, stepping into the enormous white spacesuit.

'Yeah,' said Pete. 'I don't know what words are appropriate for a moment like this.'

'Fuck the lot of them?' offered Jack.

'Oh my God, Jack, sober up!' Tina sounded frustrated.

'Fine,' he snapped at her. 'Two hundred and four days, in this contraption?'

'It's pretty spacious, though, you have to agree,' said Tina.

'Hey, did you see that Belcher has her own area in it?' Pete said.

'Yeah… at least we won't need to see her for two hundred and four days. It would have been worse if she were going to be sitting with us.' Tina was smiling with relief.

'IT'S TIME,' announced Wells. 'Lift-off is in one hour. Can you please now all enter the craft and secure yourselves for take-off? Anyone wanting a sedative should take it now so that it takes effect before lift-off. I'll be with you via satellite link as soon as you are out of earth's orbit.'

THEY BRACED as the engines began to hiss, and as they slowly awakened, a slow whine turned into a roar. Then there was a rumble from beneath them and a vibration that coursed through their bodies. Gigantic billows of fire and steam rose from beneath the craft, shrouding their last views. The metal brackets fell away, and then there was thrust that forced them down, down, down into their seats, their bodies thickening, heavy and weighted.

'Well, fuck this,' said Jack as he watched the ground fall away, and a few of the other astronauts called out in fear. It was a fast ascent, not like being in a plane that coasts horizontally, before reaching its relatively low altitude. They fired upwards towards the heavens, and the dark blue of the early evening, became darker and darker until they were in black.

The engines released and fell one by one, and then they were weightless, and an eerie calm took over the craft as the craft turned away from the Earth and towards Mars.

'I am so glad that bit is over,' said Tina, 'Although I was under the belief that the craft was going to do a more subtle take-off, like in training and do a couple of rotations around the Earth before we left?'

'Welcome to Folly,' said Wells' voice. Tina looked up and saw Wells on the live-link screen.

'I have approximately eleven minutes to speak with you using this service. Then, we'll obviously be linking it to our photonic technology. How was that take off? Looked amazing from here.' He paused as everyone nodded in agreement. 'Photonic technology? Really, Morag?'

Belcher had been quietly dealing with the take-off and the fact that the planet was seeming to be swallowed up by the blackness of space, and disappearing behind her. She wasn't in the mood for Wells' wisecracks at that moment.

'What?' she asked his image, which she could see on her own screen.

'What? is an excellent question, Morag. An excellent question in fact. A good place for us to start.'

The astronauts were busy getting comfortable in their seats, some taking photos of the disappearing Earth from their windows, others getting reading material out of zipped up seat pockets.

'Tina… Tina, please look at me when I'm speaking to you.'

Tina looked up, surprised by Wells' tone, which sounded impatient. 'Better,' he said. 'Good girl in doing what is asked of you. Now, the word *Folly*. You were astute to ask me what that meant, however in the most descriptive list you gave me, you failed to provide the true nature of what folly actually means… in this case, if I'm being most exact, I can tell you now. Are you sitting comfortably? A folly is indeed a madness… an extravagant madness at that.'

The astronauts looked at each other. Wells wasn't making much sense.

'What's he going on about?' asked Jack.

'I don't know. He's talking about the name of the craft or something.' Pete was confused. 'He seems a bit stressed, to be honest.'

'Is everything okay with the flight?' Tina asked, sounding concerned.

'I'm presuming so…' Jack looked around. 'Everything has gone off without a hitch so far.'

'So,' Wells continued, 'Let's assume that the craft is a folly and that as the designer of said craft, that perhaps my own sanity could be questioned because of the design? Although insulting, I will wear the label proudly.'

Belcher sat upright. Her skin was crawling with something. She rubbed her arm as if to get it off. 'Wells, can you just explain yourself? We've just taken off, and we're trying to adjust to all of this. It's difficult enough as it is.'

'What did he say?' asked Tina, feeling a bit lost as to what his point had been.

'Something about the craft being a design of madness or something.' Pete looked around at the craft, which seemed well within normal to him. 'Did you ask him about the name of it or something?'

The satellite screen then divided into four quadrants. One was empty, one had Wells in it, and the other two had Belcher and the other astronauts.

'I'm confused,' said Tina.

'I'll go and have a quiet word with the Captains. I'll be back in a min,' said Jack, unbuckling his seatbelt. 'I'm going to have to deal with the zero-gravity though, could take me a bit to get used to this.' He laughed as he floated upwards.

'Now, I'm going to need calm when I explain the next bit.' Wells chuckled. He was so amused with himself that it took him a while to gain his composure again. They watched as he tried several times to start a sentence, but couldn't because he was laughing so much.

'The next bit?' muttered Pete. 'Yeah, we get to spend a crazy amount of time together.'

'Yes, correct!' said Wells, sounding excited. 'Full marks to Pete. He's a bright boy that one.'

'Is he on something?' asked Tina. She was looking around to see if everyone else was finding this behavior bizarre.

'Yes!' shouted Wells. 'I'm high on suddenly discovering I'm the wealthiest man on the planet, thanks to Morag.' He clapped his hands towards the screen.

Belcher was getting annoyed. 'Wells, what the fuck is going on?' She had heard several keywords that had made her feel stressed. Wells wasn't making sense.

'Okay, from the beginning, my dearest Morag. Are you all sitting comfortably… oh, of course, you have to be strapped in otherwise, you'd be floating around. Jack, sit down. Hurry because the story is about to begin.'

Jack, who was floating halfway to the cockpit, turned and shook his head. 'No, I want to ask the Captains something.'

'Sit first and then ask afterward. Please, Jack.' He waited. Jack did as he was asked.

'Right, should I start this with once upon a time? No. Too juvenile for such a massive amount of brainpower. Okay, how about… when I was a little boy, my grandfather told me, as I was sitting on his knee, that my mind was powerful, able to create anything I wanted, including a place where human beings could find salvation and safety and run away from all the bad stuff. The seed was planted, and it was a very good seed, extremely good in fact, because I *needed* somewhere to go. I really did. All that shouting and screaming… Mummy crying and Daddy drunk. Hardly conducive to a happy childhood. Later, as I graduated from university, I had an idea. A very good idea, in fact. That I would create a whole new world. One that provided an escape, control, and hope, just as grandfather had told me to.'

'Yeah, you built Home Base.' Jack was irritated by Wells and the excessive number of words coming from his mouth.at that moment.

'I did,' laughed Wells. 'Here, let me show you something that might help me explain all of this.' The image switched to Home Base on Wells' island.

'Hang on. Why are we streaming from there?' Pete asked. 'They're the guys we spoke to on Mars Home Base, aren't they?' He looked at the people dressed in the Martian spacesuits. The Martians waved at them. 'Are we live linked to Mars?'

'Let me introduce you to Home Base,' said Wells dramatically. The image showed the central dome area from the island and then panned around to a blank wall.

'Wait for it,' Wells said.

A wall started to move aside, revealing a considerable warehouse complex covered in red dirt and small mounds. 'This is where we do our Mars experiments,' Wells explained.

Small buggies were traveling around in a dome-shaped building. 'What's he doing?' asked Pete. 'I don't get this.'

'Right Time for the reveal. Exciting isn't it when you just know that everything is about to change. Okay, the beginning.' He clapped his hands like a small child, clearly excited about what he was about to say. 'At first, Home Base was something that I had built here on my island. Mounds of red dirt, some cellophane over a light for the sun, and I got away with that for years. People would log into the site, and I would set up small amounts of live-action, like people building things, a greenhouse where they grew food. This fan here,' he said, pointing to a massive industrial fan, 'whipped up the dirt to make it look more real.' He flicked a switch on it, and as the blades got faster, so the dirt was whipped around, looking like a dust storm. 'Then they, the people, of course, wanted more. So I grew the set, and I had to keep adding more and more scenes, and it consumed every minute of my day. Tiresome!' he called out, bobbing his head with silliness. 'So, to cut a long story short, I closed it down. In 2028, to be precise. There. The End. Ta-dah!' He stood there beaming, waiting for applause. 'People had seen it, and so in their minds, they thought it was still there.'

Belcher demanded more from him. 'Wells, what do you mean? You built Home Base first as a set? Where are the Underground Generation based? There?'

He laughed, clapping his hands together again, as if pleased with himself. 'No, I didn't build Home Base firstly as a set. I only built Home Base as a set. There is no-one in the Underground Generation either. I just said there was. Sledgehammer difference using only one word. I tried to warn you, didn't I? I did, I did, that I did. You can't deny that when you came to the island, I said… and I repeat absolutely verbatim, *some say it looks like a movie set.*' He waited for Belcher to react.

'A movie set? You mean what we saw on the island is a movie set?' Even Belcher was struggling to keep up.

'Are you saying that you built a replica of Home Base on the island?' asked Jack. 'That seems a bit extreme? Or is that where the Underground Generation live? Why do that just so that people could think they were looking at the real thing? Was the link to Mars too difficult to secure?'

'No, silly Jack, simple Jack… oh sorry, that's simple Simon. No, no, no. I built Home Base *on* the island.' He waited as the information started to sink in. 'There is no other Home Base. Mars is as desolate as the rest of our universe.'

'What the fuck?' exclaimed Jack, thinking he'd heard him wrong.

'What about the boxes of food?' asked Tina, not keeping up. 'They were real. I saw a whole warehouse of food. They weren't a set… were they? You sent those up?'

'Did you open any of them? Any of you? No. You. Did. Not,' he said slowly and pedantically. 'They were empty boxes, aside from ones we had specially packed for you.' He stopped to allow for a dramatic pause. 'My biggest expenses have been rockets, although I own enough land so that no-one can get too close to my launches. Everyone always watched them online and never looked for detail. I had to build the folly, however, in the form of the beautiful craft you are in, and that did use up a few billion out of the money you sent my way. That was the fun bit, having a craft purpose-built for my needs. As for all the training? Even civilians can enrol in those for the right price. Money talks and I happen to have a lot of it. It was easy to set up training for you.' He stopped. 'I need to take a deep breath here. So much to say. I've been trying to keep it all in, all this time too. So hard. It's the equivalent of being acutely verbally constipated. Painful in fact.' He wiped his brow.

'Morag, my darling, I've just patented your chip and the limiter. It's going to give me enormous power, and given End Date isn't for another forty or so years, I'll be able to live my life out happily, prosperous, secure, and having some fun along the way. You, on the other hand, are going on a little adventure… which again, I did mention, when I said that you would be going out into the *endless blackness*. You can't blame me for not dropping extremely large hints, none of which you were apparently smart enough to assimilate. Now, are you getting it?'

The Chippies were starting to get agitated. 'What does he mean?' asked one of them.

'You fucking bastard,' said Jack, raising out of his chair. He understood precisely what Wells had shared. 'You crazy, stupid little fucker. You son of a bastard. Where are we going, Wells?' Jack was floating, trying to grab onto something. He was panicking now. Grabbing and reaching, his thoughts fragmenting. 'Where are we going, Wells?' he screamed.

Pete tried to restrain him, to calm him, but Jack was grabbing the hooks on the walls and trying to get to the cockpit. 'I need the Captains!' he roared. He banged on the doors to the cockpit and then kicked the door in. Three empty seats greeted him. 'Where are the fucking pilots?' he screamed. 'Wells! Where are the fucking pilots?'

A few of the other astronauts got out of their seats but were floating and bumping into things. One vomited, and the mess swirled around in the air.

Tina started to scream and clawed her way to the exit door. 'Get me out of here!' she screamed, scraping her fingernails at the lock, the ends of her fingers, bleeding. 'Open the door… *please!*'

Pete stared around him. He was frozen in his seat. He turned and looked out of the window, looking into blackness, aside from the glow of the sun. Even that was fading incrementally as the ship fled from the earth as if a fugitive escaping from something.

'Oh, seriously? Calm down, you silly bunch of chickens. Let me answer your questions one by one, with some order please. Now, the Captains, Jack? The ones you met before take-off? They missed their flight. Oops!' Wells bent over, laughing at his own punchline. 'Wave at the Captains, everyone. Technology is astounding these days. You actually took off using the autopilot by itself.'

The Captains stood next to Wells, waving and smiling. Then Wells dramatically saluted, and they marched off, patting each other on their backs.

Jack sat in the Captain's chair. 'Turn the ship around Wells. Turn the fucking ship around!' He looked for a steering stick, wheel, or something that made sense. Instead, the flight deck was full of unknown dials, switches and levers, none of which he knew how to operate. 'Wells, turn it around, you bastard!' Jack took a deep breath. If he could work this out, he could turn the craft around and get them back to earth somehow.

'I can't. If, and I repeat if you manage to figure it out, then you can turn it around. Land on Mars if you want to? I can tell you where you are heading if anyone is interested? No?' He looked around. 'That's a shame because literally, you won't bump into anything by my predictions. Just an endless and smooth journey into the black. There's so much more,' beamed Wells.

'Did we even take off?' asked Pete. 'Maybe it's like in that movie… what was it called? They told all the people they were going to some planet. Only the ship had never taken off.'

'Oh… no,' said Wells. 'Sorry. No, I would never be so obvious. No, you did, in fact, take-off - watched it myself. Amazing how much fuel a launch can use.'

Pete felt the sweat bead on his forehead. He felt sick. He reached forward and found a vomit bag and then heaved into it.

'Oh, Morag, by the way,' said Wells, starting up a new conversation. 'I was able to hack into that legal chip of yours before they inserted it at South Street. I did a bit of re-coding to ensure that they all had higher levels of aggression and would be compliant with my input demands. I deleted the existing personality overlay for mine… well, a modified version of mine, anyway. My army, as I have called them, is nearly ready, I'm just organizing for another few thousand legals to be implanted. I have a nice army of willing individuals at my disposal, who are going to run things the way I want them to be run. The Military is loving the idea. An entire, compliant, global army to play with, which should get things back under control. By force Morag. Force. Not economic reform.'

Belcher looked up, shocked. 'You hacked our chip?'

'It was easy. I own the hospital remember, which made it easy to access the files. It was brilliant technology, but not hard to hack. Well done, Jack, Tina, and Pete. Brilliant work, aside from the firewall for the programing. That was substandard.'

'So, the legal chip issues weren't due to our personality overlay?' Pete shook his head.

Wells roared again with laughter. 'Did you really think that Jack's personality overlay would have any discernible effect? None. It was my coding, directing them. Mace was my test, and able to exact revenge for me on Sandy from rehab as a result. That was my test, to resolve compliancy, and it went off without a hitch.'

'What did you do to Sandy?' asked Jack, sounding alarmed.

'Revenge,' smiled Wells, as if the answer was obvious. 'She humiliated me in a meeting a few years ago, and I took the opportunity to get my revenge. All the legals will do exactly what I ask them to do. They will think they thought of the idea, but I'm like a puppet master, inside their heads.'

Wells stood there like a child waiting for praise from his parents. 'Well?' he asked.

'Why?' asked Morag. 'Why send us up here? It's expensive.'

'… um… because I could afford to,' laughed Wells. 'More fun than just killing you off.'

The astronauts sat back down, just staring at him. None of them knew what to say.

'Seriously? No praise? No clever boy? Disappointing. All of you.' He pulled a silly frown.

Jack tried to reason with him, changing his tone. 'Wells, you don't have to do this. We could have worked with you. Imagine how much we could have achieved together, further developing the chip.'

'No, your mind is limited, Jack. You can only see everything superficially. You drink, you work, you drink, and you work. Like a silly pendulum that only aims to balance every now and again. It's not enough. You are not enough.'

Tina started to cry.

'It will be okay, Tina. We'll sort something out.' Pete sounded wooden, though, and in shock. His mind not properly comprehending this new, unexpected reality.

'Why, oh, why was this so easy? You should be thoroughly ashamed of yourselves. All this time, with me dropping all of those hints and NONE of you got there. Not even a little bit. Morag, why would I make cake on my island? The soil can't grow anything edible. You were so trusting! Did you see crops anywhere? No.'

'Wells. Where the fuck are we going?' screamed Jack, banging his fist into the headrest of the Captain's seat.

'I told you... into the blackness. Who knows what you are going to see? What an adventure awaits you all. I mean, you've got five hundred days-worth of food, and if you then started eating each other, you could well stay alive for a couple of years out there. Who has the most fat on them?'

Tina heard screaming and realized it was the sound of her own voice. Her mind was numbing, not able to comprehend what Wells was telling them. Wells had sent them up in a craft... only there never was a Home Base on Mars and no Underground Generation? It made no sense.

'So, where's the settlement on Mars?' asked Pete, his mind now shut down.

'So slow. So extremely slow,' said Wells with a sigh.

'Why?' shouted Jack. 'Why the fuck do this to us?'

'Because I could,' said Wells, matter-of-factly. 'It's as simple as that. I wanted the chip for myself. You know I've been working on a chip of my own for years… well, not me per se, but all the people I pay to work for me. Your chip was well advanced in terms of anything I could ever design. I don't like to be shown up, Jack.'

'So, you just took it?' Jack shook his head.

'Yes. In the end, I just accelerated your departure too, and none of you actually looked outside, to see what was in front of your eyes. It was fun building a real craft. More fun than snuffing the lot of you out.'

Jack lowered his head. He *had* questioned the accelerated departure date.

'The other leaders are going to worship me… I'm about to provide them with a new military task force. A compliant, intelligent army that will do exactly as they are told. I'm about to become a savior. Perhaps even a God… who knows? I think God would suit me, in fact.'

Belcher sat back in her chair and started to laugh like a young child. At first, it was a small laugh, more like a giggle, 'You fucking little bastard Paxton,' she said. Then the laughter wouldn't stop. It just kept going and going, getting louder and more uncontrollable. Then it morphed into screaming. Belcher looked out of the window, and her *rouge allure velvet number 46* opened as wide as it could. 'No!' she screamed at Chanel in the reflection. For the first time in her life, she had been outsmarted and could see her own demise on the horizon.

'See, I knew you would love it,' said Wells, smiling at them all. 'Especially you, Morag. Now I must go. I genuinely wish you all the best out there. Think of yourselves as pioneers… doing something that no other humans have ever done before. If you do learn how to fly the ship and manage to get back, then please drop in and see me. Now go, before I get all sentimental.'

There was silence as the screen went dead. A painful silence, one in which terms and conditions of this new reality were assimilated. They were hurtling out into the darkness and may never be able to turn back, let alone land anywhere. They were trapped in a moving coffin, entombed in darkness.

33

___

RED ALLURE VELVET 46

PARTING LIPS, PARTING WAYS

Paxton Wells arrived at the meeting a little late after his flight from Dallas. He was welcomed by the roar of several thousand lawyers, all of whom had been fitted with the adapted chip.

'Thank you for joining me in this, our new Chapter!' he shouted at the faces looking up at him. Their enthusiasm excited him.

The crowd roared and Mace raised his arm into the air, his hand in a fist. He punched the air to show solidarity towards his new leader. Wells noticed Mace in the crowd and nodded. He'd done well with the revenge. Perfectly executed.

'Must there be a new war?' he asked to the now silent and expectant crowd. 'Asks yourselves, as there is no victory in being a pacifist. There is no victory when we do not stand together. Today marks a new dawn in a world we will shape. One in which our collective strength will ensure economic reform. One that will allow us to gain control and ensure that what is left of the future is ours!

Let our work begin!' Wells shouted to them, his eyes wide with the promise of global control. 'We are the new army. We are the new power and we will dominate and succeed! Anything is now possible!' He looked up at the sky. 'Safe travels to them and let our new chapter begin!'

The thousands in front of him roared, punching the air with their fists.

I TOLD Y'ALL this story was a piece of fucking futile shit. That's it. The end. You see, human beings find places of hope to hide, and then other human beings arrive and fuck it up. You can't run and you can't hide. You can't leave the planet and you can't stay. Remember that, for when End Date gets closer. There is no escape. I often wonder what happened to Jack in the end. Did he manage to turn the ship around, but only find that he then got lost in all that darkness? I used to look up, and imagine him strapped into that seat, in the black, until two years had passed and then I put his memory away, because I didn't want to imagine who they ate first. I wondered about Tina and Pete and the Chippies who had been recruited. I used to have nightmares, thinking I was up there with them, because I almost was, remember?

This wasn't supposed to be the end of this story, as in the beginning, this was supposed to be a story that told a different ending. One about Mars and Home Base and how the human species survived and went on to populate Mars and beyond. They didn't though. Humans went extinct. Yeah, humans went extinct despite our clever, stupid brains. Jack would never have believed this ending in the beginning, but I've done the right thing in finishing it, the way he would have liked.

Wells went on to create his armies and they tried to stabilize The Chaos by shooting everyone that didn't comply. It was always about control and power after that. The two things that human beings have always been driven to obtain. I wrote this end bit, just to let y'all know how bad it got. It was the end, well before End Date, no hope anywhere. Those that prepped and chose to live underground were locked into self-imposed prisons until the armies went around and found them and confiscated the food. They were shot where they were found. The earth heated up, and more and more died from lack of water, or starved. Whole countries went down, and we suffered as if we had already been thrown into hell. Gaia, our planet punished us for what we had done, and her final act was to burn everything, including Wells, who died screaming about the injustice of his death.

Now that my job is done, which I feel I did to the best of my limited ability, I'm exiting this place. I'm going to do what Jack should have done that night and pull the trigger. I'm not scared of death no more. It was just a matter of timing, as I couldn't leave this story incomplete. I didn't want to leave y'all wondering what happened. I suppose an apology is necessary too. If you were looking for hope, then I'm sorry. Really fucking sorry. There are no happy endings in a world like this one. If there is an afterlife and y'all end up where I end up, then we'll meet again and perhaps we'll discuss it all over a bourbon or two… with Jack, who would offer you a glass of everything. I suppose this is it then. My last words to you. I ain't got any more to say because there isn't anything left to say. Maybe I'll just wish y'all the best. Will that do? Will that end things properly for you?

BELCHER LIFTED the gun to her lips. Chanel was quivering. Then she put the gun down and reached into her handbag. She got out a small mirror and studied her face. Her hair was set in place, into her tight and precise bun. Her eyes, though, were watering, and she blinked. This was not the time for sentimental thoughts or expressions of emotion, just as it had always been. She reached into the bag again and placed the red around the quivering. Not as neat as she had always done, but they would do for this next and final act. Then she pursed them together, needing to feel Chanel just one more time. Putting her bag down, she picked up the gun and placed Chanel around the barrel. Morag Belcher would fall on her sword, as was appropriate.

She pulled the trigger. No-one heard the bang, as Belcher was locked away in her private space on the craft. The bullet shot through the bone and tissue and then exited, diving into the specially reinforced cabin casing, transposing from killer to artifact. No-one heard the bullet shatter her skull into a thousand pieces which released themselves around her corpse, still strapped to her seat. Small droplets of blood and bits of her brain were splattered against the windows and then ricocheted off, busily meandering throughout the weightless cabin. Her mind, now in pieces, searched for meaning in this strange afterlife, artificially lit by several small bulbs, not at all what it had been expecting. Belcher was entombed for eternity, seeking a state of permanence as might be fitting for a person of notable repute. The small craft felt its way through the eternal blackness, ever so quietly, with all the astronauts strapped inside, and a corpse who had once been named Morag Belcher.

Chanel, slightly pointy at one end, still wearing the aroma of stale coffee, floated gently, occasionally bumping into something, leaving a macabre stain. Some might have said that Chanel was trying to tell the story from her perspective. A story of allure, of red, of velvet. Others would have said that it is never appropriate to project attributes onto something that isn't alive.

. . .

JACK STARED out of his window, having sought solitude in the flight deck. He gazed into the deep black, noting the sprinkles of distant stars, too far to ever reach, feel, or acquaint with. He drank from a bottle of vodka, gulping it down. Every minute was one less to anticipate and one more to experience, until he, too, would become one less. One less of the hundred billion human beings who had experienced life. The species that remembered who they were in the end. The number one predator designed as the perfect killing machine, whether through physicality or mind. Paxton Wells had turned out to be the alpha predator on planet Earth, and no-one had noticed or guessed that he would be the one.

Jack typed as quickly as he could into the communications log, still active in the flight cockpit. He had a few hours left to send the recount of Wells' madness back to Earth, hoping that the correct version of events would make it to his friend. He was relying on the truth being written down and included into the finale chapter of the story. A friend he would never see or hear from again. He picked up his glass and saluted him.

'To the truth my friend.'

Jack felt somewhat honored at that moment, seeing his smallness in all the vastness, as it was clear that his planet was indeed, just a tiny part of something so much bigger. We were an anomaly, he thought, given exquisite breath on a small, lonely blue planet that had decided to reacquaint itself with solitude. We had been greedy, not wholly through evil intent, but mainly because we outgrew ourselves. Maybe next time, she would get it right? Our tiny, clever blue planet, alone in its place in the infinite, would make plans for the next species, one that perhaps contained a limiter, to stop it from taking too much. Then earth too, would be swallowed up by something bigger than she could ever be, and time would record her own End Date.

'Just fuck,' he said into the blackness, as the warm burn of the vodka took effect.

THE END.

AFTERWORD

We just keep getting in the way of ourselves.

ABOUT THE AUTHOR

Juliette A H Cavendish is a British born writer, now living in Australia. She is the author of Ziforah, The Psychopath Who Nearly Lost His Arm, The Third Thought and Consequences, all due for release in late 2020/early 2021.

She is published by London Red Publishing.

Juliette lives in Ballarat, Victoria, Australia.

Visit www.juliettecavendish.com.au

for more information.

http://www.ziforah.com